This Book Belongs to

....

AUTUMN
PUBLISHING

Published in 2021
First published in the UK by Autumn Publishing
An imprint of Igloo Books Ltd
Cottage Farm, NN6 0BJ, UK
Owned by Bonnier Books
Sveavägen 56, Stockholm, Sweden
www.igloobooks.com

0621 002
2 4 6 8 10 9 7 5 3
ISBN 978-1-83903-067-3

Printed and manufactured in China

Disney

365 STORIES

AUTUMN
PUBLISHING

Disney

101 DALMATIANS

New Year's Day

It was the first day of the new year, and Pongo and Perdita were out for a walk with their humans, Roger and Anita.

Perdita sighed happily. "Oh, Pongo. What a wonderful year we've just had. We found each other, and now we have fifteen puppies to be thankful for!"

"Yes, darling, and think of all we have to look forward to this year," Pongo said.

"Can you believe the puppies stayed up until midnight last night to ring in the new year?" Perdita asked. "And they were still awake when we left! I do hope they don't tire out poor Nanny."

"Yes, that was quite a party we had last night," Pongo agreed. "Lucky would have spent the whole night watching television if we had allowed him to. I have never met a dog who liked to watch so much television!"

"Perhaps we should be getting home now," said Perdita.

"I suppose we should," said Pongo. "But I'm sure Nanny has been taking good care of them."

Pongo and Perdita gently pulled on their leads to let Roger and Anita know it was time to go home.

"Nanny! Puppies! We're home!" called Roger as he and Anita took off their boots and

Pongo and Perdita brushed off their paws on the mat in the hall. But no one answered.

"Pongo!" exclaimed Perdita, her panic rising. "Where are the puppies?"

Pongo raced up the stairs and began searching the rooms one by one. Perdita went to check the kitchen.

Pongo hurried into the sitting room to rejoin Perdita, who was on the brink of tears. "Oh, Pongo!" she cried. "Where can—"

"Hush, darling," said Pongo, his ears pricked intently. The two dogs fell silent.

Then they both heard it: a tiny snore coming from the direction of the couch. There, nestled among the cushions, were the puppies, sound asleep!

"I found Nanny!" Roger called. "She fell asleep in her chair!"

Perdita was busy counting the sleeping puppies. "… twelve, thirteen, fourteen… Oh, Pongo! One of the puppies isn't here!"

But Pongo had trotted into the next room. "Here he is, darling!" he called. "It's Lucky, of course. He's watching the New Year's Day celebration on television."

The Sleepover

"Comfortable, Piglet?" Pooh asked. The two friends were having a sleepover at Pooh's house.

"Oh, yes," Piglet replied. "Goodnight, Pooh Bear."

Piglet lay in the darkness of Pooh's room. The darkness at Pooh's house was much, much darker than it was at Piglet's house. Pooh's bedroom was also much quieter than his own room at night.

"Pooh Bear?" Piglet whispered. There was no answer.

Piglet heard a soft, low rumbling. The sound grew louder and then softer, over and over again! *Is that the sound of a heffalump?* Piglet wondered.

"Oh dear!" Piglet shouted, running to Pooh's bed. "Wake up! P-p-please, P-P-Pooh!"

"Hmm?" Pooh said drowsily, sitting up. Piglet was hiding under the covers in Pooh's bed.

"Why, Piglet," said Pooh. "What's the matter?"

"It's that horrible n-n-noise, Pooh," Piglet stammered. He listened for the noise, then realised he couldn't hear it. "That's funny," said Piglet. "The noise stopped as soon as you woke up, Pooh."

"Hmm," said Pooh. He shrugged. Then he yawned. "I guess that means we can go back to sleep."

"Pooh Bear," said Piglet timidly, "could we, well, have the rest of our sleepover another night? I'm just used to sleeping in my own house."

Pooh put his arm around Piglet. "I understand, Piglet," he said. He helped Piglet gather his things and then, hand in hand, they walked to Piglet's house.

Piglet was happy to be at home. "Thank you so much for understanding," he said. "I suppose you'll need to get home to bed now?"

"That does sound like the thing to do," Pooh replied. "But first I might sit down for a little rest."

While Piglet put away his things, Pooh sat down in a chair. By the time Piglet came back, Pooh was making a soft, low rumbling sound. But in the comfort of his own house, it didn't strike Piglet as anything other than the sound of one sleeping bear snoring.

"Sweet dreams, Pooh Bear," he whispered. Piglet climbed into his own bed and drifted off to sleep. It seemed that he and Pooh were having their best-friend sleepover after all.

Off-Road Adventure

"Lost toys! Lost toys!" announced Mike the microphone. "Help needed!"

"What's wrong?" asked Woody.

"It's the Green Army Men!" Hamm the piggy bank cried from the windowsill. "Andy left them outside and it's raining. Now they're stuck in the mud!"

Buzz and Woody hurried to the window and peeked through the rain-splattered glass.

"How are we going to help them?" Woody cried.

"What about RC Car?" Hamm suggested.

Buzz and Woody climbed inside RC, and the race car took off. RC zoomed out of Andy's bedroom and down the hall. At the top of the stairs, Buzz and Woody held their breath. "Here we goooo!" Buzz cried as they bounced down the stairs.

"Ouch! Oof! Oww!" yelped Buzz.

RC raced to the kitchen and through the swinging dog door.

"There they are!" cried Woody.

"Situation critical!" shouted the Green Army Men. "Assistance needed immediately!"

RC Car veered into the dirt and parked near the Green Army Men. Woody swung his lasso and looped the rope around the soldiers. Then he tied the other end of the lasso around RC's bumper. As he reversed, RC pulled the Green Army Men to safety. When they were all free from the mud, RC Car drove up the pathway and through the dog door. But when he got to the stairs inside, everyone groaned.

"How can we drive back up the stairs?" asked Woody.

"Don't worry!" Hamm yelled from the top of the steps. "We're on it."

The toys had put together a train track leading right up the stairs. RC Car gunned his engine and up he went, just as Andy's mother pulled into the driveway. The toys quickly pulled the tracks back into Andy's room and put them back where they belonged.

"That was close!" said Woody. "But I think we got away with it. Andy's mum will never suspect a thing."

Downstairs, Andy's mother scratched her head. "I wonder where all this mud came from," she said.

Monkey See, Monkey Do

"Come on, Abu!" Aladdin called across the busy Agrabah marketplace.

From his perch atop the basket seller's cart, Abu barely heard the call. He was captivated by the monkey he had just spotted peeking out at him from behind the fruit seller's cart. Abu jumped off the basket cart and darted over to say hello.

But the other monkey scurried away and hid behind a wheel. From his new hiding place, he peeked out at Abu.

Abu looked around, trying to think of a way to draw the monkey out.

The fruit seller was distracted, so Abu hopped up onto the cart and picked up an apple. He balanced it on top of his head. Then he scurried over to the edge of the cart and peered down, hoping to attract the other monkey's attention.

Abu heard monkey chatter behind him. He turned round to find the monkey standing at the other end of the fruit cart, balancing an apple on his head, just like Abu.

Abu picked up a pear and an orange. He began juggling them in the air, hoping to amuse the other monkey.

Not to be outdone, the monkey also picked up a pear and an orange and began to juggle them, just like Abu.

Abu grabbed hold of the cart awning, then flipped over and swung from the awning by his tail.

The other monkey did the same.

Abu thought this game was fun, but now he wanted to find a stunt that the other monkey couldn't copy. Abu looked around and saw Aladdin coming his way.

Abu had an idea. He jumped off the fruit cart, darted over to Aladdin and scrambled up the length of his friend's body until he was lounging comfortably on top of Aladdin's head.

The other monkey stared at Abu in amazement. The closest human was the fruit seller.

Throwing caution to the wind, the other monkey scurried over to him. But he'd only climbed as high as the fruit seller's shoulder before the man chased him away.

Hiding behind the basket cart, the other monkey crossed his arms, pouted and watched that sneaky Abu laugh and wave goodbye as he rode away on top of Aladdin's head.

Donald Takes Flight

"Daisy, I have a surprise for you," said Donald Duck one clear spring day. "I've been taking flying lessons."

"That is a surprise," said Daisy Duck.

Donald took Daisy to a nearby airport. On the runway sat an old-fashioned plane with open-air seats. Together they climbed into the small plane. Then Donald started the engine.

"Can you do any tricks?" shouted Daisy.

"Sure!" called Donald. He steered the plane into a loop the loop.

"You're a very good pilot, Donald!" Daisy cried, clapping her hands.

Donald was so proud of himself he decided to fly out to sea. Before long, however, the plane's engine began to cough and choke.

"Uh-oh," Donald said as the plane began to drift towards the water.

"Is something wrong?" asked Daisy.

Donald knew they were running out of fuel, but he didn't want Daisy to find out. "Everything is fine, Daisy," Donald said nervously.

He looked down and saw something floating below them. It looked like an airport runway! But what would a runway be doing in the middle of the ocean?

As the plane drifted closer to the water, Donald realised he had no choice. He'd have to land his plane on the floating runway.

Suddenly Donald noticed it wasn't a runway at all. It was the top deck of a huge ocean liner!

"Duck!" yelled one of the passengers.

Donald zoomed over their heads and carefully landed the plane on the long, wide deck.

"Hey, it really is a duck!" cried one of the passengers.

Just then an announcement came over the ship's speakers. "Good evening, ladies and gentlemen. Dinner is served!"

Donald helped Daisy out of the plane. He was sure she would be upset, but she wasn't.

"Dinner on a cruise ship!" she cried. "Donald, you're just full of surprises, aren't you?"

"Yes, indeed," said Donald with a huge sigh of relief.

"Oh, Donald, you're the best," said Daisy.

No, I'm not, thought Donald. What I really am is one lucky duck.

A Day without Pumbaa

"Mmm!" said Timon. "Breakfast time!" Timon was showing Simba how to catch some very sneaky bugs in the jungle. "Too bad Pumbaa has to miss out. I haven't seen him. Have you? Ooh! There's a good one!" Timon crouched behind a log and was about to pounce, when—

"AAAHHH!" Pumbaa swooped out of the trees, swinging wildly on a vine. He crashed straight into Timon.

"Oops! Sorry, Timon," Pumbaa said.

"Sorry?" shouted Timon.

"It wasn't on purpose," Pumbaa said.

"You never do anything on purpose," Timon replied. "You're a disaster! You couldn't catch a bug if it flew into your mouth."

"That's not true!" Pumbaa protested. "I'll prove it." The clumsy warthog lunged for a grub, only to fall head first into a puddle. Mud splattered Simba and Timon from head to toe.

"That's it!" cried Timon. "I've had it!"

Pumbaa hung his head. "It would be better if I just left," he said. And with that, he plodded back into the jungle.

Just then, Simba saw lightning. He looked up at the threatening clouds. "Timon, we can't let him go!"

But Timon was too mad at his friend to worry about him. He went back to bug hunting.

The storm came and went. And then so did lunchtime – but still, no Pumbaa.

"You shouldn't have been so hard on him," Simba said. "I wonder if he's okay."

"He's fine," snapped Timon. "Besides, he walked out on us, remember?"

Just then, the friends heard a rustling sound coming from the riverbank. Wham! Pumbaa tumbled out of the jungle, knocking into Timon and Simba. All three of them crashed into a large tree trunk. Pumbaa had brought bugs for his friends, but they went flying into the air.

"I'm back!" Pumbaa said.

"So we see," mumbled Timon, trapped under the warthog.

Embarrassed, Pumbaa stood up. "I came back to say I missed you," he said. "But now look what I've done! I'm the worst friend ever."

"Now, wait one minute!" cried Timon. "That's just not true!"

"You're a wonderful friend, and we missed you, too!" Simba said. "Welcome back."

"We even missed your disasters," Timon added. Pumbaa smiled.

Disney

ATLANTIS
THE LOST EMPIRE

Out for a Spin

One day, Princess Kida was showing Milo and the rest of the explorers the wonders of Atlantis. The explorers wanted to search for treasure, but Milo preferred to go exploring with Kida.

The princess led him up the staircase of a huge pyramid. When they reached the top, they found a shark-shaped vehicle.

"It's an Aktirak," Kida told him.

"Can we take it for a spin?" Milo asked.

"If you wish," Kida said.

Kida used a crystal that hung around her neck to start the engine. Then she and Milo climbed on.

Milo pushed a button and the Aktirak blasted into the sky! He and Kida dived low over the water, skimming the waves. Suddenly, a school of flying fish burst out of the water and surrounded the flier. One flapped in Milo's face and he nearly lost control.

"We've got to get back to land!" he exclaimed.

The Aktirak shot up into the sky.

"Beware of the cliffs ahead!" Kida warned.

Milo tried to manoeuvre the vehicle, but the Aktirak could not fly high enough. They were about to crash!

"The cave!" Kida cried, pointing to a hole in the side of the mountain.

Milo steered the Aktirak through the entrance. Twisting the flier, he dodged stalactites hanging from the cavern roof. Then he saw the head of a huge stone fish in the cave wall. Its mouth was open, and daylight streamed through it. He twisted the controls, and the Aktirak flew right through the fish's gaping mouth.

Just then, the flier's tail scraped the stone fish and the Aktirak flew out of control.

"Hang on!" Milo cried.

The flier hit the side of the pyramid and bounced. It landed at the exact spot where Kida and Milo first found it.

The others heard the crash and rushed over. They found Milo and Kida standing next to the wrecked flier.

"What happened?" Audrey cried.

"We went out for a spin," Milo said.

"Are you saying you actually flew this wreck?" Audrey demanded.

"I did!" said Milo. "But it's pretty obvious I need to sign up for Atlantean driving lessons!"

Just Desserts

Belle walked to the village, thinking about the wonderful book she had just finished reading. It was full of fire-breathing dragons, magical wizards and brave princesses.

All of a sudden, Belle's thoughts were interrupted by a great crashing noise. Even before he spoke a word, Belle knew who was walking behind her. She would recognise that stomp anywhere.

"Gaston," Belle muttered.

"Belle, is it true?" Gaston said. "Have you come out from behind a book?"

"Bonjour, Gaston," Belle said. She was tempted to open her book again on the spot.

"Off to market, eh? I shall accompany you," Gaston announced.

Gaston followed Belle into shop after shop, keeping up a steady stream of chatter about himself and his exploits.

"My, Gaston, you certainly do boast well," Belle said in a flattering tone.

"Yes! Thank you!" Gaston said, before realising that Belle was not complimenting him. His smile disappeared briefly as he opened the door to the bakery.

Belle stepped inside and quickly asked for an apple tart before Gaston could begin speaking again. When the tart was in her basket, she waved to Gaston and the shopkeeper. "Goodbye!" she called, walking quickly towards the forest path.

"Belle, wait." Gaston caught her arm.

"I really have no time to linger, Gaston," Belle replied. "I must get home to make dinner."

"I can walk you home," Gaston said, puffing out his massive chest. "I insist upon it. You need protection."

Belle laughed. "Protection from what? These woods are my backyard!"

"From predators. Monsters. Thieves," Gaston said dramatically.

Belle sighed and shook her head.

Just then, they heard something coming down the path ahead. Something large!

Quickly, Gaston pushed Belle out of harm's way. Belle tumbled to the ground. Her basket went flying.

"Look out!" Belle yelled. But it was too late.

The 'predator' emerged. It was her father's horse, Philippe! For the first time that she could remember, Belle smiled at the sight of Gaston. The apple tart had landed right on top of his head!

Peter Pan

Captain Hook's Shadow

It was late evening in the Darling household, and Michael was playing a game with his brother John in their nursery. Michael was Peter Pan and John was Captain Hook.

"All right you two, time for bed," Wendy said, walking into the room.

"Five more minutes?" John pleaded. But Wendy couldn't be convinced, so they grumbled and crawled into bed. Soon, John and Wendy were fast asleep, but Michael couldn't stop picturing Captain Hook and Peter Pan. Suddenly, a crash startled Michael. The nursery windows were open, and a shadow was on the far wall. A shadow that looked frighteningly like Captain Hook. Michael wanted to cower under his sheets. The shadow grew larger against the bedroom wall as it crept. It was heading right for Wendy!

Despite his fear, Michael knew he had to protect his sister. He grabbed his wooden sword and lunged for the shadow, just as it leaned over Wendy's bed. The shadow moved back, and Michael swiped his sword again, but the shadow came at him with his hook. Michael dived under his bed and suppressed a cry as the shadow jumped onto the bed, reaching for him. Michael's heart pounded, but he knew he couldn't stay under his bed

forever. Suddenly, he heard someone call out.

"Cock-a-doodle-doo!"

"Peter Pan!" called Michael as his hero flew in. "I'm so glad you're here… Captain Hook is…"

"It's just his shadow!" Peter Pan said. "You have to help me catch it, Michael."

Peter dived for the shadow, but it dodged. Michael suddenly wasn't scared now he knew it was only a shadow. He grabbed his sword and helped Peter corner the shadow. A few minutes later, the shadow was tucked safely into a sack.

"I stole the shadow for a prank," Peter explained. "But he got away and started causing trouble in London."

"That's awful," Michael said. "I'm glad we caught it."

Peter moved to the window ledge. "Thank you, Michael. Tell John and Wendy I said hello."

Peter said goodbye, then flew out into the night.

"I will," Michael promised. He got back into bed smiling. He was glad to have one more adventure with Peter.

Imagine That!

The carnival was in town and Pinocchio couldn't wait to see it. He grabbed his friend Jiminy Cricket, and off they went!

Pinocchio was awed by the marvellous sights. "That elephant is amazing!" he cried.

"I suppose," said Jiminy politely.

Next they came to a lion's cage. The big cat opened his mouth and roared.

"Look at those teeth!" Pinocchio marvelled.

Jiminy Cricket nodded. "They're pretty big, it's true."

Then they saw a giraffe.

"What a long neck!" Pinocchio exclaimed.

"Giraffes are all right, I guess," said Jiminy with a shrug.

Pinocchio was confused. "If you don't like elephants, lions or giraffes, what kind of carnival animals do you like?" Pinocchio asked.

"Fleas," said Jiminy.

"Fleas?" Pinocchio said, even more confused.

"Come on! I'll show you," said Jiminy.

Jiminy led Pinocchio to a tent with a sign that read Flea Circus. Inside, Pinocchio saw a tiny merry-go-round and little swings. There were small animal cages and a little trapeze. There was even a tiny big top with three miniature rings. But no matter how hard he looked, Pinocchio could not see any fleas.

"That's because there aren't any fleas," Jiminy explained.

"What's the point, then?" Pinocchio asked.

"The point is imagination," said Jiminy. "Why, you can do anything with your imagination. You can even see the fleas at the flea circus."

Pinocchio laughed and joined in the game. "That flea is going to jump through a ring of fire," he said. "I hope he makes it!"

"Now the fleas are doing acrobatics," Jiminy declared.

"Look! They've made a flea pyramid," said Pinocchio. "And the flea on top is standing on his hands!"

After they had watched the flea circus for a long while, it was time to go home.

"What did you think of the flea circus?" asked Jiminy Cricket.

"It was the most amazing circus I've ever seen, and I didn't really see it at all!" Pinocchio replied.

"Yes, indeed. You imagined it," said Jiminy Cricket. "Imagine that!"

Mulan

Soup's On

Mulan stood in the kitchen, moodily stirring a pot of soup for supper. Grandmother Fa sat at the table, sorting through grains of rice. Neither one of them spoke.

They were both lost in thought at the recent news they had received: Mulan's father, Fa Zhou, had been ordered to join the Chinese army in order to help protect the Emperor from the invading Huns. Mulan was distraught, for she knew that if her father joined the army and went into battle, he would surely die.

"Why must my father fight?" Mulan asked her grandmother suddenly. "He is but one man, and the Emperor would never know the difference if he didn't join. Yet what a difference to our family it would be if he were to die!" She sighed heavily.

Her grandmother also sighed and continued to sort the rice silently for a few moments. Then she stopped and turned to Mulan. "You are partly correct. One grain of rice, such as this one that I have in my hand, is small and insignificant." Then she held out her hand and tipped the grain into the large bowl of rice she had been sorting. "Yet together, you know, all the grains of rice in this bowl could feed many people. The Emperor needs an army of many, many people in order to defeat the invaders."

Mulan shook her head miserably, afraid that if she spoke she would cry. Grandmother Fa was just as unhappy as Mulan, but the older woman realised that it was useless to protest against some things. She stood up and walked silently out of the kitchen.

Mulan continued to stir the soup, even though it didn't need stirring. Next to the pot sat a small bowl, which contained a peppery red spice. She picked up the small bowl and looked at it thoughtfully. "One grain of rice is small and insignificant," she said to herself. "And yet, a tiny pinch of the spice from this little bowl could change the flavour of this whole pot of soup. Perhaps one person can make a difference, if she follows her heart."

Mulan dumped the whole bowl of spice into the pot and smiled.

"Soup's on!" she cried.

Finding Ne-who?

"The coral reef is falling down, falling down, falling down…"

Nemo was home, brushing up against the anemone, when the most awful singing he'd ever heard in his life made him cringe.

Nemo poked his head out of the golden tentacles to see who was making the awful racket. It was Dory! Nemo should have known.

Nemo swam as fast as he could towards the regal blue tang fish. "Dory! Where have you been?" It seemed like a whale's age since Nemo had seen the fish who helped his dad to rescue him from the dentist's fish tank.

When Nemo got closer, Dory stopped singing. That was good, but when she looked at him, her face was blank.

"Did you say something?" she asked.

"Dory, it's me. Nemo," he replied.

"Ne-who?" She looked at Nemo blankly. "Sorry, kid, don't know you. I was just swimming by, minding my own business, singing a song. Hey, why was I singing? Am I famous? Maybe that's how you know me."

"Dory! We're friends, remember?"

"Friends? I just made friends with a hermit crab… I think." Dory swam in a circle looking for the crab, but got distracted and started chasing her tail.

"Please try to remember, Dory," Nemo said. "You helped save me. You helped me find my dad. You know my dad. Big orange guy? Three white stripes? Looks kind of like me?"

"My dad? Looks like you? Sorry, kid, you don't look anything like my dad." Dory looked at Nemo like he was crazy and began to swim away.

Nemo swam after her. "Just think about it for a second," he pleaded. She had to remember something. "I'm Nemo!"

Dory did not turn round, but she slowed down. Swimming in a wide circle, she came back. She looked at Nemo sideways, then started laughing so hard, bubbles came out of her nose.

"Had you going, huh?" Dory gave Nemo a big hug and smiled at him slyly. "That was just my little joke. You know I could never forget you!"

Nemo giggled as he swam circles around his friend. "Good one, Dory!" He grinned.

Dory smiled back. "Good one, who?"

Nemo groaned. "Oh, Dory."

Bows and Arrows

"Thanks, Mr Hood!" Skippy Bunny hopped around holding the bow and arrow Robin Hood had just given him. "This is the best birthday present in the world!"

"Want me to show you how to use it?" Robin asked.

"Yes!" cried Skippy.

"See, you put this here." Robin lined the arrow up with the bow. "Then pull here and let it fly."

The arrow soared through the air and landed in the centre of a tree trunk across the yard.

"Wow!" Skippy cheered.

"That's nothing!" Robin said. He handed an apple to Skippy. "Here. Put this on the head of that scarecrow."

"Sure thing, Robin!" Skippy said and hurried off.

As soon as the apple was in place, Robin let another arrow fly. It zipped through the air and hit the apple, neatly slicing it in two.

"Can I try?" Skippy asked.

"All right," Robin said, placing a new apple on top of the scarecrow's head.

Skippy pulled back the bow, but when he let go, the arrow landed only a few inches in front of him.

"That's okay," Robin said. "It happens to the best of us!"

"Even you?" Skippy asked.

"Well, not me. I never miss!" Robin boasted as he pulled back his bow.

Just as he did, Maid Marian's carriage rolled by. Robin's head turned, and his hand slipped off the bow. The arrow fell to the ground a few inches in front of him. Skippy giggled.

"What's so funny?" Robin asked crossly.

"Nothing!" Skippy said, hiding a smile.

"Ahem. As you can see," Robin said, "even the most experienced archers lose their focus occasionally. But it helps if you think of a goal and keep your goal in mind while you draw the string back, aim and let go. I like to think about setting the sheriff's trousers on fire!"

Skippy decided to give it a try. He pulled the string back and then he let it go with a twang.

The arrow sailed through the air and split the apple in two. Robin's trick had worked!

Abracadabra

Manny was not at his best. Gypsy could tell. Already that day, he had lost two magic wands and stepped on his turban. And with the matinee show at P. T. Flea's World's Greatest Circus about to begin, Gypsy knew she had to be on her toes.

"Ladies and gentlemen," Manny announced, "prepare to be stunned and amazed by the Levitating, Flaming and Disappearing Water Torture Chamber of Death! You will watch as my lovely and talented assistant, Gypsy, climbs inside this chamber," Manny motioned towards the empty takeaway box at his side, "where I will bind her hands and feet. Then I will fill the chamber with water, seal it, levitate it five inches off the ground and set it ablaze. And finally, you will watch in awe as the chamber disappears before your very eyes!"

Manny and Gypsy had rehearsed the act thoroughly. Everything was planned down to the last detail. But if one little thing went wrong with the trick, Gypsy could be in big trouble.

As it turned out, one little thing didn't go wrong – three big things went wrong!

First Manny tied Gypsy's hands and feet together too tightly. Then he filled the chamber too high with water. Finally, he locked the trapdoor. Together, he and Gypsy had rigged an escape hatch in the back side of the takeaway box. Once Manny sealed her inside, Gypsy wriggled out of her bonds, opened the trapdoor, and, unseen by the audience, escaped from the chamber before Manny levitated it, set it on fire and made it disappear.

Luckily, Gypsy hadn't left anything to chance: she had stowed a sharp shard of glass inside the box. She had learned to hold her breath for ten minutes. And she had put a release latch on the inside of the trapdoor, just in case Manny forgot to leave it unlocked.

She was safely out of the chamber in one minute flat.

At the end of the trick, Manny called Gypsy in front of the audience. "How did you do it, my dear?" he asked dramatically.

"It was magic!" she replied, with a smile and a sigh of relief.

A Mouse in the House

Alice was a daydreamer. Once, she dreamed of a silly place called Wonderland.

When Alice awakened, her sister suggested they have some tea.

Alice began to tell her sister all about Wonderland. "I know I was only dreaming," said Alice, "but it all seemed so real! I attended the strangest tea party, at which the Mad Hatter and the March Hare – they were the hosts of the party – kept offering me tea, but refused to serve me any." Alice picked up the teapot to refill her own cup. "And you won't believe it, but inside the teapot lived a little…"

Just then, the lid of the pot Alice was holding flew open and a little whiskered face popped out.

"Eek!" Alice yelled, slamming down the lid. Her mind raced. How could the Dormouse from her dream have crossed over into her real life?

Alice finished her tea and cookies as quickly as possible. When her sister went to pour more tea, Alice grabbed the pot away and insisted, "I'm sorry, but there isn't any more!"

"My goodness!" Alice's sister declared. "Now you're acting like the Mad Hatter and the March Hare!"

Alice slipped away with the teapot as soon as she could. "Maybe if I doze off again I can dream this little fellow back where he belongs," she said.

But Alice couldn't fall asleep. Finally, she lifted the lid of the pot. "I'm sorry," she told the Dormouse. "I'm not sure what else to do." But the Dormouse knew. He jumped out of the teapot – and was chased by Alice's kitten, Dinah! The Dormouse ran into the stump that led to the rabbit hole of Alice's dream, but the kitten stayed behind. The inside of the stump looked too dark and scary to the little cat.

Alice waited, but the Dormouse did not come out again.

That night, as she slept, Alice dreamed of Wonderland again. She was back at the unbirthday party, waiting to be served a cup of tea. The Dormouse threw open the teapot and gave Alice a sleepy grin. "Thank you, miss!" he said. "And whatever you do, please don't dream about your cat!"

Basil Saves the Day

It was young Olivia Flaversham's birthday, and she was celebrating with her father.

Suddenly, there was a knock on the door. Mr Flaversham told Olivia to stay in the cabinet while he investigated.

Olivia hid, but then she heard a commotion. She peeked her head out to see what was happening and saw a big, scary bat grab her father.

Olivia needed help. So she set off to find Basil, the great mouse detective.

Basil knew who the bat was. His name was Fidget, and he worked for Basil's archenemy, Professor Ratigan!

Later that evening, as Basil paced back and forth, Olivia screamed! Fidget had appeared in the window. Basil, Olivia and Basil's friend Dawson raced outside and followed the bat to a toy shop. Inside, Basil noticed that mechanical parts were missing from many of the toys. Suddenly, Fidget jumped out of a toy cradle. The bat stuffed Olivia into a bag and flew away!

Now Basil and Dawson had to save Olivia and her father!

Dawson showed Basil a piece of paper that Fidget had left behind. It had come from the riverfront. The two tracked down Fidget and followed the bat to Ratigan's secret lair.

But Basil had walked right into a trap! Ratigan tied Basil and Dawson to a mousetrap and then left.

Basil thought hard. He calculated the timing of the trap and came up with a brilliant idea that would save them.

"Ready… steady… now!" Basil yelled to Dawson. They were free!

Basil and Dawson found Olivia and raced to Buckingham Palace. There they discovered what Ratigan was up to: he had forced Olivia's father to build a robot replica of the queen. Then Ratigan had replaced Queen Moustoria with the robot.

A huge crowd was listening to the robot queen. It was announcing that Professor Ratigan was her new royal consort!

Offstage, Basil and Dawson finally took control of the robot queen.

Ratigan's plan was foiled!

Basil rushed onstage and yelled, "Arrest that fiend!"

Ratigan was defeated. But even better, Olivia and her father were reunited at last.

Across the Sea

Anna and Elsa were on a royal tour. In the kingdom of Zaria, they were treated to a grand festival.

"We've heard so much about your special talents," the queen said to Elsa. "Won't you show us some of your magic?"

Suddenly, Elsa felt very shy. "Would you like to join the dancing, Your Majesties?" she asked, changing the subject. "That looks like fun."

The next stop on Anna and Elsa's tour was a kingdom called Chatho.

Queen Colisa led Anna and Elsa into an art gallery.

"Would you like to add a sculpture to our collection?" she asked Elsa.

Suddenly, Elsa noticed a block of ice under a spotlight. Once again, she felt a wave of shyness.

Anna jumped in. "Ice sculptures are my specialty!"

Later, as they pulled into the last city on their tour, Anna asked Elsa why she didn't show her powers.

"I guess I just got nervous," Elsa admitted.

Suddenly the sisters spied a familiar face. It was the Duke of Weselton. "What is he doing here?" Anna asked.

The Duke smoothed his coat as Anna and Elsa got off the ship. "I am visiting my mother's cousin's wife's nephew if you must know. If I were you, I would turn your ship around right now. Vakretta is having an unbearably hot summer. Not that you would care."

"Take us to the kingdom," Elsa said firmly.

As the Duke led the sisters into the village, they saw Vakrettans sprawled out, sweaty and tired.

This time, Elsa didn't feel one bit shy. She knew she had to cool these folks down. After conjuring some snow clouds, Elsa saw the townsfolk start to come to life.

Soon, Vakretta turned into a frozen wonderland. The citizens slid down the snowy piles on wooden planks.

A few hours later, it was time for Anna and Elsa to return to Arendelle.

"Did you have a good trip?" Anna asked her sister.

"I did," Elsa replied. "I'd say that was the best royal tour ever... until next time, that is!"

Eeyore's New Old House

One blustery January day in the Hundred-Acre Wood, the wind blew so strongly that it knocked Eeyore's house right over! So Eeyore went to Pooh's house.

"Well, Pooh," Eeyore said, "it seems that January just doesn't like me. Or my house. So I'm afraid I will have to stay here with you. If you don't mind, that is."

Pooh assured Eeyore that he didn't mind and offered him some honey.

"I'd prefer thistles, if you have any, which of course you probably don't," Eeyore said. "Oh well. Perhaps Rabbit has some."

Rabbit did have some thistles, so Eeyore settled down to stay with Rabbit. But Rabbit's house was so full of vegetables and gardening tools that there was scarcely room in the burrow for Eeyore.

"I suppose Piglet may have more room, though I doubt it," said Eeyore.

Piglet told Eeyore he was welcome to stay with him, and even made Eeyore a little bed next to the pantry, which was full of haycorns. But Eeyore was allergic to haycorns, and soon his sneezing almost knocked Piglet's house down.

"One house knocked down today is more than – achoo! – enough," said Eeyore. "I'll just have to try Kanga and Roo."

But Kanga and Roo's house wasn't quite right, either. Eeyore was just about to try Owl's house when his friends showed up.

"Eeyore, we've found you the perfect house to live in!" Piglet cried.

"I doubt that," Eeyore said as they led him through the Wood. "The perfect house would have thistles, and enough room, and no haycorns. But where am I going to find a house like that?"

Soon they arrived at a snug little house made of sticks with a pile of thistles in it. "Here it is, Eeyore," said Piglet.

"That's my house," said Eeyore, hardly able to believe his eyes. "But my house got knocked down."

"Piglet and I put it back together again," Pooh said.

Eeyore looked at his house and then at his friends. "It looks like January doesn't dislike me so much after all," he said.

Fish-in-the-Box

"Ariel?" Flounder called out timidly, poking his head inside Ariel's secret grotto. Ariel had told Flounder to meet her there, but she hadn't arrived yet. "I guess I'll wait for her inside," he said to himself.

He swam round slowly, gazing at Ariel's collection of things from the human world. The rock ledges were filled with various objects the princess had found in sunken ships and up at the surface. It was Ariel's favourite place. But without Ariel there, Flounder found the place lonely... and quiet... and creepy.

Flounder swam past one object that he had never noticed before – a square metal box with a handle on one side.

"I wonder what that thing does," said Flounder, staring at the handle. After a few moments' hesitation, Flounder summoned his courage. By flapping his tail fin and pushing the handle with his nose, he managed to turn it around once... twice... three times. Nothing happened. Flounder was halfway into the fourth turn when... boing! The latch to the top of the jack-in-the-box released and the spring-loaded jester inside popped out and lunged at Flounder.

"Ahhhhhhhhhhhh!" Flounder screamed as he raced backwards away from the jack-in-the-box and collided with the lid of an open treasure chest. The force of the collision caused the lid of the chest to slam shut, trapping Flounder inside.

Moments later, Ariel swam into the secret grotto.

"Flounder?" she called. "Are you here yet?"

From inside the chest, Flounder yelled to Ariel. "Mm-nn-eer!" came the muffled cry.

Ariel followed the sound of his voice and swam over to the chest. Lifting the lid, she found her friend inside. "What are you doing in there?" Ariel asked with a giggle.

Thinking quickly, Flounder replied, "I'm about to do my imitation of that thing." He pointed at the jack-in-the-box. Then Flounder sprang suddenly out of the chest, raced out the door and kept on swimming. He'd had enough of Ariel's secret grotto for one day!

Tough Audience

The sticker on the door read 'Enter at Your Own Risk', but Mike wasn't scared. He had never met a kid he couldn't crack up. Tossing his microphone from one hand to the other, Mike sauntered through the wardrobe door to face his audience.

"Hey, how ya doin' tonight?" Mike greeted the kid. The boy in the race car pyjamas just glared. "Did you hear the one about the monster who made it in show business? He really clawed his way to the top." Mike paused for a laugh, but the kid was silent.

"All right. I can see you're a tough audience. Enough of the B material." Mike pulled out all the stops. He told his best jokes. He worked the room. But the kid didn't even crack a smile. Mike prepared to let the one about the seven-legged sea monster fly when he heard tapping on the wardrobe door.

Mike pulled the door open a crack. "I'm working here," he whispered.

Sulley poked his head in. "Mikey, you're dying. You've been on for twenty minutes and you're getting nothing. There are plenty of other kids to make laugh tonight. You can come back to this one later."

"No way," Mike hissed. "He loves me. When he laughs he's going to laugh big. I can

feel it."

Just then, a rubber ducky sailed through the air and hit Mike in the eye. "See? He's throwing me presents."

"Cut your losses, Mikey. Let this one go." Sulley put a large hairy paw on Mike's head and urged him back through the door.

"I'm telling you, I've almost got him," Mike said through clenched teeth.

"And I'm telling you to give… it… up." Sulley pulled harder on Mike. Mike grabbed the doorframe and braced himself. Suddenly Sulley lost his grip, and Mike flew backwards, skidding on the rubber ducky and crashing to the ground.

"Why, I oughta…" Mike leapt to his feet, ready to charge at Sulley, but was interrupted by the sound of laughing. In fact, the kid was laughing so hard, tears streamed down his face.

Mike high-fived Sulley. "You know, some kids just go for the physical comedy," he said with a shrug.

Money Matters

"Greetings, slotted pig," said Buzz.

"Hello, Buzz," said Hamm the piggy bank. "How are you getting used to life here in Andy's room?"

"Life on this planet is interesting," Buzz said. "I look forward to giving a full report to my commander upon my return to base."

Hamm rolled his eyes. Buzz had no idea he was not an actual space ranger. It would be funny if it weren't so… annoying.

"So, pig," Buzz continued. "Today I noticed Andy placing several round silvery discs into the slot on your back."

"Yes," began Hamm, "that was—"

"And now these silver discs reside in your stomach cavity?" Buzz interrupted.

"Well, yes," began Hamm, patting his full belly. "But—"

"Aha!" Buzz cried. "I have determined your power source! What an interesting life-form you are! This will definitely make it into my report."

Hamm shook his head as Woody and the rest of the toys walked up to join them.

"What's going on?" Woody asked.

"Greetings, cowboy," said Buzz. "I was just enquiring about the pig's power source."

"He's talking about the coins in my belly," Hamm explained.

"No, Buzz," said Bo Peep. "Those aren't power sources. They're money."

"What's money?" Buzz asked.

"It's what people use to get the things they need – like food or toys or comic books," said Woody.

Buzz thought for a moment. "Perhaps I need to procure some of this power source… um, I mean money… for myself," he suggested thoughtfully.

The rest of the toys started chattering excitedly. They had never thought about what they would do if they actually had some money! Woody started daydreaming about what he would buy. Then he looked round and laughed out loud. "We're toys!" he said. "Toys can't just go to the shop and walk up to the counter to buy things!"

"Speak for yourself, cowboy," said Buzz. "Perhaps you've forgotten – I am not a toy!"

Hamm shook his head at the crazy, mixed-up space ranger. "I give up!" he said.

A Tiny New Friend

It had been a week since Cinderella's stepmother had forced her to move out of her bedroom and into the attic of the old house, but Cinderella was still not used to her new sleeping quarters. The only other soul around to keep Cinderella company was a skittish little mouse who she had seen scurrying in and out of a hole in the corner.

One day, at suppertime, Cinderella slipped a piece of cheese into her apron pocket. That evening, when her work was finished, Cinderella hurried up to her room and pulled out her sewing basket. She used some scraps of fabric to make a mouse-size suit of clothing: a red shirt and cap, a tiny orange coat and two brown slippers.

Cinderella carried the clothes over to the mouse hole and knelt before it. She pulled the cheese out of her pocket and placed it, with the clothes, in the palm of her hand. Then she laid her open hand just in front of the mouse hole.

"Hello in there!" she called.

The mouse cautiously poked his head out of the hole and sniffed the air. Seeing the cheese, he inched out of the hole and over to Cinderella's hand. He paused and looked up at her.

"Go ahead," she said kindly. "They're a gift just for you."

The mouse scampered onto her palm, picked up the cheese and the clothes, and hurried back into the mouse hole.

Cinderella waited patiently for a few minutes, still kneeling in front of the hole.

"Well," she called after a short while, "let me see how they look on you!"

Timidly, the mouse came out in his new outfit. Cinderella clapped her hands.

"Perfect!" she said. "Do you like them?"

The mouse nodded. Then he jumped, as if an idea had just occurred to him, and scurried back into the mouse hole. Cinderella frowned. Had she frightened him?

But her worries vanished when the mouse reappeared – along with several other mice, who followed timidly behind him.

"More friends!" Cinderella cried. She hurried to get her sewing basket, delighted to have found the warmth of friendship in the cold attic room.

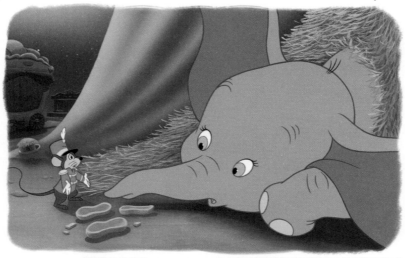

Hide-and-Seek

Dumbo had been the newest baby in the circus for quite a while. Then, one day, the stork arrived with a brand-new delivery – a baby giraffe.

"You know, Dumbo," said his friend Timothy Q. Mouse, "I think we should ask that new baby to play with us."

Dumbo nodded. He loved making new friends!

"Hello, Mrs Giraffe," Timothy said. "Can your lovely new baby come out to play?"

Mrs Giraffe agreed and the three new friends set off.

"Okay, kids," said Timothy, "what do you feel like playing? How about hide-and-seek?"

Dumbo and the giraffe nodded happily as Timothy closed his eyes and counted.

"Ready or not," he said finally, opening his eyes. "Here I... hang on! Don't you guys know you're supposed to hide?"

No, actually, they did not.

Timothy sighed. "Okay, let's take it from the top. When I close my eyes, you guys hide. You find a place where you can't see me and I can't see you. Like this." Timothy ducked behind a popcorn tub. "Get it?"

Dumbo and the giraffe nodded slowly.

"Okay then, let's try this again. One, two, three..." Timothy counted to twenty, then

opened his eyes.

"No, no!" he groaned. "You can't hide behind the popcorn tub. You're too big. Let's try this one more time."

Again, he closed his eyes and counted. Then, very slowly, he opened them and looked around.

"Much better!" he said, surprised. Of course, it didn't take him long to find Dumbo's nose sticking out of a pile of hay or the giraffe sticking out from behind the clowns' trunk.

"This time, guys, try to find a place for your whole body to hide," Timothy said.

Dumbo and the giraffe waited for Timothy to close his eyes once more. Then they quietly hid again, but this time they picked places that covered their whole bodies.

And do you know what? They hid so well, Timothy Q. Mouse may still be looking for them to this very day!

The Sweetest Song of All

"Why is Quasimodo so sad?" asked Hugo.

"Judge Frollo has commanded that he never leave Notre Dame Cathedral," answered Victor. "He's lonely because he has no friends."

Just then Quasimodo appeared.

"Good morning, Quasi!" Hugo cried. "Nice day for ringing bells."

"I guess so," Quasimodo replied, staring at the people far below.

"Cheer up! What do they have down there that we don't have?" Hugo asked.

Quasimodo frowned. "I don't know because I've never been there. But I hear people laughing and singing."

Then Victor spoke. "The sweetest songs of all can be heard in this tower, if you do what I tell you to."

"I will!" Quasimodo cried.

"Then fetch a piece of firewood and a knife from the kitchen," Victor commanded.

Quasimodo quickly returned with both.

"I want you to carve statues of lots of different birds," said Victor.

Quasimodo nodded. For two days, he worked. On the third day, he showed Hugo his first carving.

"Wow, that really looks like a dove," said Hugo.

"I'm going to carve a finch next," Quasimodo vowed.

Over the next few weeks, Quasimodo carved hundreds of birds out of wood – larks and thrushes and robins and sparrows. Each statue was better than the last. He worked so hard that he nearly forgot he was lonely.

Finally, he showed Victor and Hugo a carving of a beautiful nightingale.

"It is your best work of all," Victor told his friend.

Quasimodo was so proud that he set his bird on the highest tower so they could all admire it.

The next morning, he was surprised to see two real birds perched next to his statue. More birds soon arrived. Some even built nests. Soon, hundreds and hundreds of birds lived in Notre Dame. They woke Quasimodo with their songs in the morning and they sang him to sleep at night.

Victor had told Quasimodo the sweetest songs of all could be heard at Notre Dame, and he was right. Since that day, birds have always lived in Notre Dame Cathedral.

An Excellent Cook

Tiana and her father, James, loved to cook. One night, Tiana decided that she wanted to make dinner all by herself.

"What are you going to make for us, sweetheart?" asked her mother, Eudora.

"Gumbo!" replied Tiana. That was her father's specialty. He even had an enormous pot that he kept especially for his gumbo!

Little Tiana sat perched on a stool, stirring, seasoning and tasting. "I think it's done," she announced finally.

"Okay," said James as he tasted a spoonful. "This is the best gumbo I've ever tasted!"

"Eudora, our little girl's got a gift," James continued. "A gift this special's just gotta be shared."

And so the family decided to invite their neighbours to enjoy the gumbo on the back porch. Soon the night air was filled with the sounds of clinking spoons, conversation and laughter.

"You know, the thing about good food," said Tiana's father, "it brings folks together from all walks of life. It warms them right up and puts smiles on their faces."

When bedtime arrived, Tiana's mother and father came to tuck her in. Tiana leaned out her window and made a wish on the evening star.

"But remember," added James, "you've got to help it along with some hard work of your own." Then, thinking of the night filled with good food, family and friends, he said, "Just never lose sight of what's really important."

Tiana looked at the picture that her father had once given her of the restaurant he wanted to open. It was her father's dream to open a restaurant in the old sugar mill, and now it was Tiana's dream, too. She was ready to work hard to achieve it – with the help of the evening star, of course.

Tiana's father gave her a kiss goodnight, and then left her room. As he shut the door, Tiana looked out at the evening star. "Please, please, please!" she whispered.

I will make our dream come true, Tiana promised herself as she went to sleep that night. And with that, she fell asleep peacefully, knowing she would have the courage to succeed.

Friday Night Fun

Mater looked out at all the sleeping tractors in the field. Then, as Lightning watched, he quietly drove up to one and honked. Beep! The startled tractor woke up, tipped over and moaned as its wheels spun helplessly in the air.

Suddenly, headlights shone in the two friends' faces. It was Sheriff.

"You should know better," he said. "I'll see you both in traffic court tomorrow."

The next morning at court, Lightning and Mater were sentenced to community service.

"Why don't you help Ramone clean his shop?" Sheriff suggested.

"You bet," answered Lightning.

But as they cleaned, Mater accidentally knocked over a can of pink paint. The lid flew off and the paint splattered Lightning.

"You sure do look pretty in pink," said Mater.

"Let's see how you look in it!" shouted Lightning. He threw an open can of paint at Mater. After a few minutes, they were covered in paint!

When Ramone peeked in, he got splattered, too. "Look at my shop!" he cried. "Get out!"

The friends left the shop and drove to Doc's garage. "Boys, boys..." Doc sighed when he heard what they'd done. He gave them one last chance. "Go find Bessie and surprise Flo with a new paving job."

The friends started paving, but then they decided to race. They had so much fun that they forgot all about the paving job at Flo's. By the time they remembered, it was dark.

The next morning, Mater and Lightning drove over to Flo's. Just about everyone in Radiator Springs was hard at work, trying to finish the paving job. No one had been able to drive in for their breakfast fill-up!

Mater and Lightning knew they had made a mistake. It was up to them to fix the road.

A few hours later, they were done. The V8 Café looked fantastic, and everything finally went back to normal – until Friday night rolled around again...

"Hey, buddy," whispered Mater to Lightning. "How 'bout a little tractor-tipping fun ternight?"

Disney
Sleeping Beauty

Sleepless Beauty

"Oh, there, there, little Aurora. There, there," cooed Flora, trying to calm the crying, fussy baby princess. Flora and her fellow fairies, Fauna and Merryweather, stood huddled over the cradle of tiny Aurora and looked down anxiously and helplessly at their royal charge.

The three good fairies had taken the princess from the castle after the evil fairy Maleficent had put a curse on her. Perhaps if Maleficent couldn't find the girl, the curse would not work. But the baby had not stopped crying since Flora, Fauna and Merryweather had arrived with her at the secluded cottage in the woods.

"Oh, goodness!" cried Fauna. "What have we got ourselves into? We don't know the first thing about taking care of human babies!"

Flora gave Fauna a comforting pat on the back. "Now, now, don't panic, Fauna," Flora said. "It may be harder than we expected. But this is the only way to keep the princess safe from Maleficent."

Merryweather and Fauna knew Flora was right. So, one after another, they tried different things to try to get the baby to stop crying and go to sleep.

"Well," said Flora, "fairy babies are soothed by a sprig of dandelion root placed in their cradle. Let's try that!" Flora hurried out of the cottage and returned minutes later with the sprig. She laid it at the baby's feet. But the princess cried on.

"Perhaps she needs to be entertained!" suggested Fauna. Flora, Fauna and Merryweather locked arms and danced a little jig. But baby Aurora took no notice – and kept on crying.

As the fairies fought over how to calm the baby, Flora accidentally nudged Aurora's cradle, causing it to rock gently back and forth. Soothed by the rocking, the baby's cries slowly grew softer and softer.

"Fauna!" cried Flora. "You've done it!"

"Look how much she likes the rocking!" added Merryweather.

The three fairies continued to rock the cradle gently back and forth, and soon Aurora drifted off to sleep.

"Well," Fauna whispered to the others, once the baby was sleeping soundly, "that wasn't so hard, now, was it?"

It Takes Two

Mowgli shouted and cheered. He'd just escaped from King Louie and the apes with his friends, Bagheera and Baloo.

"That was a swinging good time!" Baloo called. Bagheera was less enthusiastic.

"Next time, stick to the plan. We're lucky to be alive! Now… let's find somewhere safe for the night."

"Relax," Baloo replied. "If anyone comes, I'll give them some of this." He paused to flex his muscles.

"Oh Baloo, we can't always rely on brawn. Sometimes we need brains!"

Mowgli sighed as his friends argued. He didn't need protecting. He had the brawns of a bear and the brains of a panther, if only they'd give him a chance! Just then, Mowgli heard a rustling above him. A flying squirrel glided and landed on a branch.

"I want to try that!" Mowgli cried. So, whilst his friends argued, he practised swinging from vines with his new squirrel friend. Soon enough, he was swinging effortlessly. The sound of rushing water met Mowgli's ears, and the trees parted to reveal a thundering river. It was a large gap, but the squirrel didn't falter.

"Okay, let's swing," Mowgli said.

But when he was halfway over the water, he slipped and fell into the river… only to be caught by Kaa the snake!

"Trusssssst in me," Kaa hissed. "Slide into my coils." Mowgli couldn't swim, so he didn't have a choice. He grabbed onto Kaa and allowed himself to be pulled into a tree.

"Oh, a sssssssssquirrel," Kaa said. One look into the snake's eyes, and the squirrel was under his spell. Using his brain, Mowgli didn't look into Kaa's eyes. And using his brawn, he wrapped Kaa's tail around a rock and dropped it. Kaa fell from the tree and his new friend was free! The squirrel squeaked in thanks and took off into the trees.

Later that night, as he was falling asleep, Mowgli heard Baloo and Bagheera were still arguing.

"He used his brains to help that squirrel," Bagheera said.

"It was brawn! He used that rock to stop Kaa!" Baloo countered.

Mowgli smiled with the knowledge that he'd used his brain and brawn to save his new friend today.

Travelling at the Speed of Stitch

Stitch was bored. Everyone seemed to have somewhere to go and something to do during the day but him. Lilo went to school. Nani went to work. And Jumba and Pleakley headed off to serve beachgoers at their new snack stand, the Galactic Burger.

Stitch decided he needed a job. He and Lilo looked through the newspaper, searching for a job just right for a small blue alien with a huge love of adventure. "Listen," said Lilo, pointing to an ad. "'Wanted: tour guide. Must have an outgoing personality and lots of energy'. That's you!"

The next morning, Stitch arrived at the tour agency wearing his best Hawaiian shirt and a big smile. Since no one else had applied, Stitch got the job!

"Aloha!" Stitch exclaimed when the holidaymakers arrived. He loaded them on a tour bus and pressed down on the accelerator as far as it would go. "Palm trees!" he yelled as the scenery passed by in a blur. "Pineapples!" he shouted as they drove through a fruit stand.

Finally, the bus screeched to a stop at the beach. "Surfing!" Stitch announced, hurling his group onto surfboards and pushing them out to sea. After being battered by the waves, the tourists were eventually tossed back onto the beach.

Stitch herded them over to a barbecue pit. "Luau!" he exclaimed.

But instead of food, Stitch produced several flaming torches. Nani's friend, David, had taught Stitch how to juggle fire. The little alien was sure the holidaymakers would want to learn, too. Thank goodness Stitch just happened to bring along a fire extinguisher!

The last stop on Stitch's tour was the twenty-four-hour hula marathon. He gave his guests grass skirts and insisted they dance until they dropped as he played the ukulele. When they returned to the tour agency that night, the holidaymakers emerged from the bus exhausted, battered, bruised and confused. The first thing they saw was the sign on the front of the tour agency: Hawaii: The Most Relaxing Place on Earth. Unless, of course, your tour guide happens to be from the planet Turo!

A Lady's Touch

Late one night, Lady's ears perked up and her eyes flew open with a start. The baby was crying! Lady climbed out of her basket, pushed open the swinging door with her nose, and tiptoed up the front stairs.

Inside the nursery, Jim Dear and Darling were trying to calm the baby.

"Oh, Jim, I just don't know what's the matter with him!" said Darling.

Jim Dear sat groggily at the edge of the bed, looking at his wife helplessly. "Well, we know he isn't hungry," he said, "since we've just given him a bottle." He massaged his temples as though they hurt. Then he noticed Lady, who had walked tentatively into the bedroom. "Hello, Lady," he said to her.

Lady took a few steps closer to the cradle, where Darling was laying the baby down. His little fists were closed tight and his shrieks had turned into loud sobs.

"We just don't know what's wrong with the little guy," Jim Dear told Lady. "We've fed him and changed him, and I've sung him every lullaby I know. Maybe you can figure out what's bothering him!"

That was all the invitation Lady needed. She jumped up onto the bed and peered into the cradle.

The baby opened his eyes and looked at Lady. His cries dropped to a whimper and he reached out to touch her soft fur. His tiny hand grabbed hold of her ear and tugged. Lady winced, but held still. With her chin, she began to rock the cradle, and with her furry tail, she beat a rhythmic thump, thump, thump on the bed.

"Ga!" said the baby as he broke into a gummy smile. Still holding Lady's ear, the baby giggled.

"Oh, look, Jim Dear!" cried Darling delightedly. "Lady has got him to stop crying!"

"I just don't know what we'd do without you, Lady!" Jim Dear said gratefully.

Rock, rock, rock went the cradle. Thump, thump, thump went Lady's tail.

Soon the baby's eyelids grew heavy, and then his eyes closed. Tears still streaking his little round cheeks, he relaxed his grip on Lady's ear, smiled and fell asleep.

Disney
Bambi

The Winter Trail

One winter morning, Bambi was dozing in the wood when Thumper came over to play.

Bambi followed Thumper through the forest. The sky was blue and the ground was covered in a blanket of fresh snow.

"Look at these tracks!" Thumper said excitedly. He pointed to a line of footprints in the snow. "Who do you suppose they belong to?" Bambi didn't know, so they decided to follow the trail. They soon came to a tree.

"Wake up, Friend Owl!" called Thumper.

"Have you been out walking?" Bambi asked.

"Now why would I do that?" Friend Owl replied. "My wings take me where I need to go."

Bambi and Thumper continued on. Next, they spotted a raccoon sitting next to a tree, his mouth full of red berries. "Hello, Mr Raccoon," Bambi said shyly. "Did you happen to see who made these tracks in the snow?"

The raccoon shook his head and began tapping the tree.

"I know!" Thumper cried. "He thinks we should ask the woodpeckers."

Soon, Bambi and Thumper found the woodpecker family. "Did you make the tracks in the snow?" Thumper called up to the birds.

"No, we've been here all day," the mother bird answered.

"Who can these tracks belong to?" Bambi asked.

"I don't know," Thumper replied.

They soon reached the end of the trail and the tracks led all the way to a snowy bush where a family of quail was resting.

"Did you make these tracks?" Thumper asked.

"Why, yes," Mrs Quail answered. "Friend Owl told me about this wonderful bush. So this morning, my babies and I walked all the way over here."

Satisfied that they had solved the mystery, Thumper and Bambi turned to go home. Behind them, they found a surprise – their mothers!

"How'd ya find us?" Thumper asked.

Thumper's mother looked down at the tracks in the snow.

"You followed our trail!" Bambi cried. His mother nodded.

"Now, let's follow it back home," Bambi's mother said. So that's just what they did.

Grumpy Rajah

I t wasn't always easy being the daughter of a sultan. Sometimes Jasmine thought she would be the loneliest girl in Agrabah if not for Rajah, her pet tiger and best friend.

But apparently, it wasn't always easy being a tiger, either. Rajah was having a bad day.

"What's got into you?" Jasmine asked him.

But Rajah just looked at her and growled again.

"Hmm," Jasmine said thoughtfully. She hated it when Rajah was down, but what could she do to cheer him up?

As a princess, Jasmine wasn't allowed to do much. But one thing she could do was be a good friend to Rajah, and she was determined to do just that.

"You know what you need?" Jasmine asked.

Rajah paced back and forth.

"You need to try to relax!" Jasmine told him.

Rajah just looked at her.

"You know," Jasmine explained, "loosen up, have a good time."

Rajah began to growl again.

"All right, all right!" Jasmine held up her hands in surrender. "I'll stop."

But she just couldn't let it go. She really wanted Rajah to be happy!

Jasmine patted her tiger on the back. "You know, Rajah, I wouldn't be saying this if I didn't care about you. You have to enjoy life, not growl at it! Look at me – I spend all my time talking to the brainless, unpleasant princes my father brings round. But I still try to have fun whenever I can!"

Rajah lay down and put his paws over his ears.

Finally Jasmine understood. "You're jealous of all those princes!" she said.

Rajah looked up. Jasmine was right. He was sick and tired of all those princes coming to the palace.

Jasmine lovingly scratched Rajah behind the ear. "Jealousy isn't very becoming," she teased him, "even in tigers. I know I haven't been spending much time with you lately, Rajah. But it's not like I have a choice. The law says I have to find a prince to marry."

Princes, Rajah thought. *Yuck!*

"But you know," Jasmine continued, hugging her tiger around his big furry neck, "I like you better than any prince."

Rajah began to purr. Jasmine smiled.

"Princes!" Jasmine said. "Yuck!"

Groundhog Day

Winnie the Pooh pounded on Piglet's front door. "Wake up! Wake up!" he called to his friend. "Today is Groundhog Day!"

Piglet dressed quickly and moments later the two friends were hurrying to the homes of their other friends who lived in the Hundred-Acre Wood.

"Today is Groundhog Day!" shouted Pooh and Piglet together as they woke Tigger, Rabbit, Owl, Eeyore, Kanga, Roo and Christopher Robin.

Soon the group of friends arrived at the Thoughtful Spot and everyone sat down to wait.

"Um, exactly what is it that we are waiting for?" asked Piglet.

"Why, groundhogs, of course!" said Pooh.

"But what is it that is supposed to happen on Groundhog Day?" Piglet persisted.

Being a bear of little brain, Pooh was unsure how to answer. He looked expectantly at Christopher Robin.

"There is an old tradition," the boy began, "that says the second day in February is the day that the groundhog comes out of his hole after a long winter sleep. If he sees his shadow, he decides that there will be six more weeks of winter. If he doesn't see it, he decides that spring will soon be here."

A few more moments went by and then Rabbit cleared his throat. "Pooh," he said. "Do you expect that the groundhog will take much longer to appear?"

"Oh!" Pooh replied, looking at his friends. "I haven't the faintest idea how long it will take to see a groundhog, as I don't know any groundhogs personally."

Suddenly, Gopher's head popped up from the ground in front of them.

"Aha!" shouted Pooh, triumphantly.

"It's only Gopher," said Rabbit.

"I believe Gopher will do quite nicely today," said Christopher Robin. "Gopher, do you or do you not see your shadow?"

Gopher blinked in the sunshine, then looked down at the ground. "I ssssay," he said. "I ssssuppose I do sssseee my sssshadow."

"Well, that's that, then," said Christopher Robin. "Six more weeks of winter. Thank you very much, Gopher."

"You're welcome," replied Gopher. And with that, he went back into his hole.

Childhood Times

It was a beautiful day in the little kingdom of Arendelle. King Agnarr and Queen Iduna proudly stood in the castle courtyard greeting their guests. If all went well, Arendelle would have three new partners in trade by the end of the visit.

Upstairs, Anna pleaded with her sister. "Elsa, can we play with the magic?"

"We're supposed to stay in our rooms and not disturb the guests," Elsa said.

"Elsa, pleeeeease?" Anna begged. "We can hide. They'll never see us!"

"Okay!" Elsa said. "But we have to be very quiet. Come on. We'll go to the kitchen."

Inside the kitchen, Elsa cut loose! She made huge amounts of snow and ice.

"See that pan?" Elsa shouted. She hit it with a flying snowball. "Woo-hoooo!"

The two girls were having so much fun that they barely saw the king and queen arriving with their royal visitors! Quickly, Anna and Elsa slipped upstairs.

When the king and queen entered the kitchen, they were surprised to see all of the ice. But the royal visitors thought the snowballs were wonderful.

"Oh, my. This is just what we need on a warm summer's day!" exclaimed the baron, spooning the snow into a cup.

In the ballroom, Elsa filled the room with snow. Suddenly, the girls heard the guests coming. They raced back to their room.

Down in the ballroom, the baroness slipped and landed in a pile of snow.

"Oh, dear," the queen said. She and the king rushed to help the baroness.

"Snow angels!" the baroness cried out. "I love snow angels. What a delightful surprise!"

"I say," the baron chuckled. "The kingdom of Arendelle stops at nothing to please its visitors!"

After the visitors had gone to their guest rooms for the evening, the king and queen went to check on their daughters. Both girls appeared to be sleeping soundly, but as soon as they were alone, the girls' eyes popped open.

"Elsa, do you want to play?" Anna asked.

"Anna, we can't! We're already going to be in a tonne of trouble tomorrow," Elsa said.

Anna leant back onto her pillow and sighed. "Still…"

"It was SO worth it!" both girls said together.

Disney
101
DALMATIANS

Pongo Carries a Tune

"I don't know what we're going to do," Roger Radcliffe told his wife, Anita. "We have all these puppies to feed and I don't have one song to sell!"

"Don't worry," Anita told him. "I'm sure you'll be inspired soon."

"I'm glad you're sure!" said Roger. "Because all I've got is a bunch of used paper." He pointed to the overflowing bin.

"Don't give up," said Anita. "I know that you can do it."

After Anita left, Pongo watched Roger pace in front of his piano. "Pongo, old boy, I must have written ten songs in ten days. But they're all terrible," he said. "What am I going to do?"

That night, Pongo talked to Perdy about Roger's dilemma. They sat in the middle of the living room, surrounded by puppies.

"Roger has already written ten songs," explained Pongo. "He just doesn't think they're good enough to sell. But I know they are – I've heard him play them, and you don't live with a songwriter without developing a good ear for hit songs."

Perdy knew what he was thinking. "Do you know the way to the music publisher?" she asked.

Pongo nodded. "I've been for walks there dozens of times."

After Roger and Anita had gone to sleep, Pongo padded into the music room and gathered up the sheet music from the bin. Then he sneaked out of the house, carrying the music to the publisher's office. Pongo pushed all the pages under the door, then trotted back home.

The next day, the phone rang. Roger answered.

"You what?" Roger said. "You did? You are? But how did you…? Oh, I see… Well, thank you. Thank you very much!"

Anita rushed over. "Who was that?"

"My music publisher," said Roger. "He's buying ten of my songs."

"Ten songs!" cried Anita. "I thought you didn't even have one to sell."

Roger scratched his head in confusion. "I didn't think I did."

"So what happened?" asked Anita.

Perdy looked at Pongo and barked. Her husband sure could carry a tune – all the way across town to Roger's publisher!

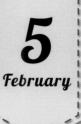

Hide, Dude!

"Come on, Squirt!" Nemo cried happily. "Race you to the coral shelf!"

Nemo took off, pumping his mismatched fins as hard as he could. His young sea turtle friend laughed and swam after him. Squirt was visiting Nemo at his home on the reef.

"This way, dude!" Squirt yelled, flinging himself through the water. "I'm catching some rad current over here!"

Nemo hesitated for just a second, watching as his friend tumbled along past some stinging coral. Squirt was so brave! Even after all that Nemo had been through – being captured by a scuba diver, then escaping from a tank to find his way home again – he still got scared sometimes.

With a deep breath, he threw himself into the current. He tumbled after Squirt, fins flying as the water carried him along. Finally, he came out the other end of the current, landing in the still ocean beside Squirt.

He giggled. "Hey, that was fun!" he cried. "Let's do it again! Squirt? Squirt, what's wrong?"

The sea turtle was staring into the distance, his eyes wide. "Hide, dude!" Squirt cried. Before Nemo could respond, Squirt's head and legs popped into his shell and he landed on the seafloor with a flop.

Nemo started trembling. What had scared Squirt so much? He looked round, expecting to see a shark. But all he could see nearby were a few pieces of coral with a lone Spanish dancer floating along above them.

"Hey," he said. "What is it? There's nothing scary out here."

Suddenly Nemo realised something. "Haven't you ever seen a Spanish dancer before?" he asked.

"A… a Spanish wha-huh?" Squirt asked, still muffled.

"It's a kind of sea slug," Nemo explained. "Don't worry, Spanish dancers are nice."

Finally, Squirt's head popped out again. He smiled sheepishly at Nemo. "Sorry, dude," he said. "I never saw one of those before. It totally freaked me out."

"It's okay." Nemo smiled back. He already knew that new things could be scary – and now he realised he wasn't the only one who thought so. "Come on, let's go play," he said.

Snake Eyes

"I'm ssstarved," hissed Kaa the python as he slithered across the jungle treetops. "I need a sssnack."

Suddenly, Kaa noticed a small figure relaxing on a tree limb. It was Mowgli. Kaa slithered over to him.

"Are you feeling sssleeepy?" hissed Kaa. "You look sssleeepy; jussst look into my eyesss…"

Mowgli tried not to look into the snake's eyes, but it wasn't easy. When he turned one way, Kaa was there. When he turned another, Kaa was there, too!

"Ssslip into sssilent ssslumber," Kaa hissed. "And sssleep… sssleep… sssleep…"

Mowgli's body went completely limp. Kaa had hypnotised him!

Kaa's fangs watered as he coiled his long body around Mowgli. The python opened his giant mouth above Mowgli's head and—

Hey! Someone had jammed a stick into his jaws!

"Hello there, Kaa," said Baloo, leaning one big paw against the tree.

The python's powerful jaws snapped the stick. "You ssshould not insssert yourssself between a sssnake and his sssnack," he hissed.

"Oh! Sorry!" said Baloo. "I was just admiring how very talented you are."

"Talented?" Kaa said.

"Sure!" said Baloo. "I'm very impressed with how you hypnotised Mowgli there. I bet you could hypnotise almost anything in the jungle."

"What do you mean almosssst?" said Kaa.

Baloo coolly polished his claws on his fur. "Well, let's see," he said. "I bet you can't hypnotise… a fish." Baloo pointed to the pond.

"Jussst you watch me," Kaa told Baloo as he slithered towards the pond. Hanging his head over the water, Kaa hissed, "Jussst look into my eyesss. You feel sssleeepy… sssleeepy… sssleeepy…"

Suddenly, Kaa stopped hissing and moving. He just stared into the water.

Bagheera stepped up to Baloo and whispered, "What's the matter with him?"

Baloo just laughed. "Kaa was so determined to prove me wrong, he didn't even notice the water was reflecting back his image. That crazy snake hypnotised himself!"

Hamm's Heavy Burden

Hamm's head hung low. He had barely moved in days.

"Hamm just hasn't been himself lately," Woody said. "He doesn't play with us anymore. And Andy has been paying more attention to him than ever."

Woody stood up and walked over to Hamm.

"Oh. Hey, Woody," the piggy bank said sadly.

"What do you say me and you take a walk down to the toy box and say hi to the Green Army Men?" Woody asked.

Hamm's eyes lit up, but when he looked across the room, his face drooped again. "No thanks," he said with a sigh.

Woody put his arm around his friend. Something was really wrong.

"Talk to me, Hammy. What's going on? You're not yourself."

Hamm looked at his hooves shyly. "It's just, well… uh… do I look fat?"

Woody put his hand over his mouth to keep from laughing. "Hamm, you're a pi—" Woody stopped himself when he saw Hamm's hopeful look. "A perfectly proportioned pig," he finished.

"I just feel so heavy lately," Hamm said. "And you know, I should feel great. Andy has been dropping coins in my slot almost every night! I can't remember when he paid this much attention to me. I mean, I'm not you," he concluded.

Woody nodded. He knew Andy paid a lot more attention to him than to most of the toys in the room. But he wasn't sure what to say to Hamm to make him feel better.

The next morning Woody was still worrying about Hamm when Andy raced into the room. He pulled Hamm off the shelf, took the cork out of his belly and shook him over the bed. Coins rained out of Hamm's stomach.

"Thanks," Andy said, patting the piggy bank. He gathered up his loot and dashed out of the room.

"Wow, do I feel better." Hamm danced a little jig. "But now maybe I'm a little too empty."

Woody and Bo Peep beamed. "Looking lean there!" Bo Peep said, poking Hamm in the side with her staff.

"Heads up!" cried Woody, tossing Hamm a new coin.

Ariel and the Whale Song

One day, Sebastian was planning a concert for the whales and Ariel was singing a solo. "The whales are migrating through Coral Cove today," Sebastian told Ariel. "I promised your father this concert would be timed exactly to their passing over us."

Ariel desperately wanted to meet a whale. But how would she do that if she was singing in the concert? Then, she had an idea. "Are you up for a quick trip to Coral Cove?" she asked Flounder. "They never visit us at the palace, this is my only chance."

Soon they reached Coral Cove, but she couldn't see any whales. Then she heard something from above. They swam to the surface, but still couldn't see any whales.

Suddenly, Ariel found herself next to a huge tail that surrounded the friends with bubbles. When the bubbles cleared, Ariel was amazed at what she saw. It was a mama whale and her baby. And they were singing!

"Whale song," Ariel whispered.

"It's beautiful," said Flounder, amazed and also relieved it wasn't a shark.

Ariel listened to the melody and sang back to them. Then, the two whales headed towards the ocean's surface and flew into the air. They created a beautiful arc over the water, then belly-flopped onto the smooth surface of the sea.

The huge waves sent Ariel and Flounder soaring into the air. When they landed back in the water, they burst out laughing. It had been an amazing afternoon, but now they needed to get home.

Later at the concert, it was time for Ariel's solo. She decided to make a slight change and sing the beautiful whale song she had learnt earlier. As she sang, Ariel could feel the water's currents change and she knew the whales were passing by. She smiled and sang even louder to honour her new friends.

A Royal Pain

"Sir Hiss, wake up! Wake up!" Prince John shouted into the face of his royal adviser.

Sir Hiss awoke with a start and sat bolt upright in his tiny cradle at the foot of Prince John's bed. "Wha–what is it, Your Highness?" Hiss replied. He shook his head and tried to shake off his sleepiness. "Is everything alright?"

"No, everything is not alright!" Prince John snapped. "I don't know how you can sleep while I lie here wide-awake, tossing and turning!"

Sir Hiss realised that he would not be allowed to sleep until Prince John fell asleep. So he sprang into action, trying everything he could think of to send the prince off to dreamland.

First he brought the prince a drink from the castle kitchen.

"Twecchh!" Prince John spat out his first mouthful. "This milk is warm!"

"Well, yes, Your Majesty," replied Hiss. "Warm milk will help you get to sleep."

"Take it away!" the prince ordered.

Next Sir Hiss tried singing a lullaby. He crooned, "Go to sssssleep, little princccccce…"

But Prince John scrunched up his face, wiped it with the back of his hand and yelled, "Say it, don't spray it!"

Sir Hiss was annoyed, but he had one more idea.

"Why don't you try counting sheep?" he suggested.

Prince John did as he was told, but before he had got to ten, he lost his patience.

"Oh, I don't care how many sheep there are!" he thundered.

Sir Hiss was at the end of his tether. And he was completely out of ideas. Then he spotted the prince's money bags, piled high in one corner of the bedroom. Suddenly, he knew just what to do.

"Okay, Sire," said Sir Hiss. "Then how about counting your money?"

Sir Hiss opened one of the money bags and pulled out a handful of gold coins. As he dropped a coin back into the bag, it made a soft clinking sound. He dropped another, and then another… Prince John closed his eyes and began to count each clink.

"One… two… three…"

Before he got to ten, Prince John was fast asleep wearing a huge grin.

Of Mice and Rice

"Cinderella! Help!" shrieked Drizella. Cinderella dropped the broom she was holding and rushed down the hallway. "What is it, stepsisters?" she called.

"We're stuck!" yelled Anastasia.

Cinderella hurried to the parlour. She barely managed to suppress a giggle at what she saw. Her two stepsisters were stuck in the doorway, so hasty had they both been to leave the room first. With a bit of tugging and pulling, Cinderella managed to get the sisters unwedged.

Smiling to herself, she headed back towards the kitchen.

"Meeeeeowww!" came a cry.

"What on earth…?" said Cinderella. She hurried into the kitchen. Lucifer the cat was howling at the top of his lungs.

"What's the matter, Lucifer?" she said, running over to the fat feline. "Oh, you silly thing. You've got yourself stuck, too!" Cinderella laughed and tugged him out of the mouse hole he had wedged his paw into. With a haughty look at Cinderella, the cat strode away.

Cinderella peeked into the tiny mouse hole. The mice crept cautiously forwards.

"You little dears," Cinderella said softly.

"Why, you're all shaken up! Well, do you know what I do when I feel sad or afraid? I find happiness in my dreams." She picked up her broom. "You see this broom? I like to pretend it's a handsome prince and the two of us are dancing together!"

Suddenly the mice dashed for their hole – someone was coming! It was Cinderella's stepsisters.

"What on earth are you doing, Cinderella?" asked Drizella.

"I was just, uh, sweeping," Cinderella replied quietly, blushing.

"Well, you looked as though you were having too much fun doing it!" snapped Anastasia.

Then a nasty smile appeared on her face. Picking up a bowl of rice from the table, she dumped it onto the floor.

"Perhaps you need something else to sweep!" she said, and with a mean laugh the two sisters left.

Cinderella's mouse friends rushed out and began to pick up the grains of rice. Cinderella smiled. "You know," she said, "I think we'll be just fine if we all look out for one another."

Chaos in the Kitchen

"Now, now, dearie," said Flora to little Aurora, "it's time for your nap." Flora had just given the baby her bottle and settled her in her cradle.

"Time to make supper!" Flora said to Fauna and Merryweather, turning away from the snoozing baby princess and clapping her hands together purposefully.

The three fairies gave each other uneasy grins. It was the first meal they had to prepare in the little cottage in the woods, where they would live until Aurora's sixteenth birthday.

In order to keep Aurora well hidden, the three fairies had vowed to give up their magic wands and live as ordinary humans. But none of them had ever cooked, cleaned or cared for a baby before. This was going to be quite an adventure!

"I shall cook a stew," said Merryweather. The others thought that was a wonderful idea. Stew sounded hearty and delicious. What a cosy meal for their first night in the cottage!

"I'll bake some blueberry biscuits and mash the potatoes!" said Flora.

"Are you sure you know how?" asked Fauna.

"How hard could it be?" said Flora. "Fauna, why don't you make a salad to go with Merryweather's stew?"

"I'll try!" said Fauna brightly.

Soon Merryweather was chopping meat and vegetables, Flora was mixing flour and water, and Fauna was slicing and dicing the salad vegetables.

An hour later, dinner still wasn't ready. Merryweather's stew smelled like old boots. Flora opened the oven and pulled out her biscuits, which were as flat as pancakes. The mashed potatoes were terribly lumpy. And somehow most of the salad greens had ended up on the floor.

The three fairies looked at one another in dismay. "Back to the drawing board, girls," said Flora. "But let's not be too hard on ourselves – after all, we've got sixteen years to learn how to cook without magic!"

"And that's how long it's going to take!" replied Fauna.

Merryweather laughed. Fauna was obviously joking – wasn't she?

Basil's Blunder

Dawson was just settling down in front of the fire at 221½B Baker Street when he heard a sharp rap on the door.

Basil put down his microscope and marched to the door. "Yes, yes. What is it?" he asked.

On the doorstep stood a very young, very wet and very bedraggled-looking mouse. He had no hat or umbrella to shelter him from the London rain. He wore a book bag over one shoulder and in his hands was a damp package.

"I'm looking for—"

"No. No. Don't tell me," Basil said. "Let me guess."

He started pacing about the room, as he usually did when he was deep in thought. Basil hated interruptions, but he loved mysteries.

"Come in, dear boy," Dawson said, ushering the boy into the room and taking his worn coat, package and book bag. "Have a seat by the fire."

"That is Dr Dawson!" Basil said. "And you," he said, "are a university student!"

"Y-yes," the boy stammered.

"I'd say you are a struggling student by the looks of things. You appear to be tired from too much studying. But what are you looking for?"

"I was looking for a—"

Basil put his hand up. "You've lost a parent?" he said. "No! An instructor? Perhaps. But wait. You arrived on my doorstep with something in your hand." Basil whirled and pointed at the damp package. "Aha!"

"Yes, sir. It's for—"

"Please don't tell me!" Basil cried, examining the box. "Why, the address has washed completely away!"

Dawson leaned towards the shivering student and whispered something in his ear. Basil was so busy pacing he did not even notice when the dear lad whispered back his reply.

"I have solved the mystery, Basil," Dawson said. "The package is for you!"

Basil looked at Dawson. "How do you know?" he gasped.

"It's elementary, dear Basil," Dawson replied. "This student has taken on a job as a delivery boy to pay his school bills. And... I asked."

Pixie Play

"What do you say, Tink? Can you get it?" asked Peter Pan.

Peter and Tinker Bell were floating high above the streets of London, right outside a large open window. Inside, three children were sleeping soundly.

Tinker Bell nodded and darted through the window.

The last time Peter had visited this house, the children's St. Bernard, Nana, had spied him outside the nursery window. She'd tried to grab him, but all she got was his shadow. Tonight Peter had come to get his shadow back.

Peter watched from the windowsill as Tinker Bell flew around the nursery. First she flew over the eldest child, Wendy Darling, and then over the girl's two younger brothers, John and Michael. None of them woke up.

But when Tinker Bell flew over Nana, the dog awoke with a sneeze! Tinker Bell's pixie dust had tickled Nana's nose.

"Woof! Woof!" barked Nana, trying to grab the fairy. But the poor dog's feet couldn't find the floor! The pixie dust had lifted her off the ground.

Now Nana was floating around the room! Peter started to laugh. The dog obviously didn't know how to fly. Suddenly, the pixie dust wore off and Nana's paws hit the floor again. With an angry growl, she charged at Peter Pan!

"Yikes!" Peter cried, darting back through the window with Tinker Bell right behind him.

"Back to Never Land, Tink!" he said. "We'll get my shadow back tomorrow night."

And with that, Peter and Tinker Bell soared into the sky and vanished.

Back inside the nursery, Wendy suddenly woke up. "What's this?" she cried, touching the window. Her hand sparkled with pixie dust. "Peter Pan must have come back looking for his shadow. I'm sorry I missed him," Wendy told Nana with a frown of disappointment.

"Woof! Woof!" barked Nana.

"Yes, I know," Wendy replied. "Time for me to go back to bed."

As Nana licked Wendy's cheek goodnight, Wendy promised herself that she would be ready to meet the remarkable Peter Pan the next time he paid her a visit!

Happy Valentine's Day

"Whatcha doin', Doc?" Happy asked.

Doc was hard at work carving a heart out of a piece of wood. "I'm making a present for Snow White," he replied.

"A present for Snow White?" Happy exclaimed. "Oh, dear! Did I miss her birthday?"

"No, silly," Doc said. "It's Valentine's Day."

"Valentine's Day?" Happy turned to Dopey. "Have you ever heard of Valentine's Day?"

Dopey shook his head.

Doc cleared his throat. "Valentine's Day," he began, "is a very special day that gives people the opportunity to let loved ones know how important they are."

"I'm giving Snow White these handkerchiefs," Sneezy said as he sneezed into one of them. "Well, maybe not this one."

"That's very thoughtful," Doc answered. "I'm sure she'll be able to use them."

"If he has any left," Grumpy said.

Then Bashful shyly held out a pink and purple paper flower he had made.

"Wonderful! And you?" Doc asked Dopey.

Dopey held up a paper airplane he'd just made for Snow White.

"You know what I'm going to do? I'm going to juggle for Snow White for Valentine's Day," Happy said, gathering several apples.

"She'll love that!" Doc said.

Sleepy yawned as he held up a pretty card he'd made.

"And you?" Doc asked Grumpy.

"Well, all right," Grumpy confessed. "I wrote Snow White a poem."

Just then, there was a knock on the door to the cottage. Snow White had arrived!

"Happy Valentine's Day!" the Seven Dwarfs sang, each holding up his gift for Snow White to see.

"What a wonderful surprise!" Snow White exclaimed, giving the Dwarfs the valentines gifts she had brought for them and placing a kiss on each of their cheeks.

The Dwarfs looked at their valentines. They thought they were the most beautiful valentines presents they had ever seen. And for once, even Grumpy was pleased.

Power Outage

It was night time in the arcade. The toys were all gathering in Game Central Station when, suddenly, the power went out!

"I think we're stuck," Wreck-It Ralph told his friend Vanellope. He was right. With no power, no one could leave Game Central Station.

"Never fear," Fix-It Felix, Jr. called out. "My trusty hammer and I will have this fixed in no time."

Ralph and Vanellope started to make their way towards Felix to help, but it was hard to see in the dark. Crash! Vanellope ran right into someone. It was Gene, the Nicelander mayor from the Fix-It Felix, Jr. game. He seemed scared.

Gene explained that he had never spent the night away from home before.

Vanellope and Ralph knew they had to find a way to distract Gene until Felix could fix the power. Vanellope had an idea. "Party!" she shouted. "Come on, everyone!"

The video game characters wasted no time following Vanellope's lead. Soon they were all happily playing party games.

"Come on, Gene," Ralph said, pushing his friend towards a limbo line. "You should give it a try."

Gene took a deep breath and limboed under the pole. He could really bend!

Vanellope could see that Gene was starting to feel better. And she knew just how to keep him feeling that way. She grabbed Gene and dragged him towards the starting line for a three-legged race. Before Gene could object, Sour Bill waved the starting flag. The racers were off!

"Vanellope!" Gene cried as he tried to keep up with her. "Slow down!"

"You slow down, you lose!" Vanellope said. "Come on, Gene. You can do it!"

Suddenly, one of the racers tripped. Everyone went flying – except Vanellope and Gene. They crossed the finish line in first place.

"I did it! I won!" Gene shouted happily.

"Well, we won. But you were great!" Vanellope said.

"And look, you made it through the night!" Ralph said.

Just then, with a bang, Game Central Station lit up. Felix had fixed the power.

"You know," said Gene, "maybe being away from home isn't so scary after all."

Disney
Lady and the TRAMP

Tony and the Tramp

Tramp licked the last of the tomato sauce from his chin. "So, what do you think, Pidge?" he asked Lady.

"That was the most wonderful meal I've ever had," Lady gushed.

"What did I tell ya?" Tramp boasted. "There's no one in the world who can cook up a meal like Tony!"

"I couldn't agree with you more," Lady said. "Can I ask you a question?"

"Sure thing," Tramp said. "Ask away!"

"I was just wondering," Lady began, "how you and Tony met."

"How I met Tony?" Tramp laughed. "Now that's a story!"

"I'll bet!" Lady said.

"Well, see, it goes like this," Tramp began. "It was a cold and snowy night. I don't think it had ever been that cold before, and I know it hasn't been since. I had been walking uphill for miles. Icicles were hanging from the tip of my nose."

"Wait a minute!" Lady interrupted. "You were walking for miles uphill? In this town?"

"That's right!" Tramp said. "You've never seen the likes of it."

"Exactly!" Lady told him. "You know why?"

Tramp shook his head.

"Because it isn't possible! There are no big hills around here!" Lady said.

"Okay, you're right," he confessed.

"So, then, what's the truth?" Lady asked.

"The truth is," Tramp began, "I wasn't always the slick and handsome devil you see before you."

"Is that right?" Lady was amused.

"And this one afternoon I was being harassed by a group of mangy mutts who outnumbered me ten to one. So I took off as fast as my paws could carry me. And as they were chasing me, along came the dogcatcher. Before he could get me, Tony came running out with a bowl of steaming hot pasta," Tramp explained. "He told the dogcatcher I was his dog. The dogcatcher didn't believe him. But when Tony put the bowl of pasta down in front of me, he had no choice. Let me tell you, I thought I'd died and gone to heaven."

"I can relate to that," Lady said, recalling the meal.

"And the rest," Tramp said, "as they say, is history!"

Homework Helper

Stitch didn't care for weekdays much now that Lilo was back in school. To Stitch they were the longest and most boring days of the week. So you can imagine Stitch's excitement when three o'clock finally rolled around and Lilo's school bus dropped her off.

"Lilo!" Stitch would shriek, racing down to meet her. "Playtime! Playtime!"

Usually, Lilo would toss her backpack onto the porch and they would hop on her bike.

But one day, Lilo didn't drop her backpack. And she didn't run after Stitch.

"Sorry, Stitch," she said. "My teacher says if I don't start doing my homework, she's going to have to have a talk with Nani!"

Stitch didn't understand. "Homework?" he said, peeking into Lilo's backpack.

"Homework," said Lilo, "is maths problems and a book report and a week's worth of spelling words that I have one day to learn! Now please, Stitch, be a good alien and shoo."

But Stitch wasn't about to give up so soon. He was back in less than a minute with a basketful of Lilo's favourite action figures.

"You've got to be kidding," said Lilo. "I am not playing superheroes. Can't you see I'm busy?"

This was mighty frustrating! But Stitch loved a challenge. Off he ran again, and this time he came back wearing a catcher's mask and vest and carrying a baseball, a bat and Lilo's glove.

"Play ball!" Stitch shouted.

Lilo almost got up, but then she shook her head. "No, Stitch." She sighed. "If I don't start these spelling words now, I'll never finish them tonight."

Stitch thought for a second, then dashed off once again. Lilo could hear all sorts of banging and slamming coming from her room. It sounded like Stitch was turning it upside down! *Oh, great,* she thought to herself. *But at least he's leaving me alone…*

Then, to Lilo's surprise, Stitch came back again carrying a book of crossword puzzles under his arm.

"Lilo play and spell words!" Stitch cheerfully told her.

"Why didn't I think of that?" said Lilo. "Stitch, you can help me with my homework any time!"

This Spells Trouble

"Woody! Bo!" Hamm whispered. "Have you guys noticed anything a little… off about Mr Spell lately?"

"What do you mean?" asked Bo Peep.

"His spelling hasn't been so sharp the last few days," Hamm explained.

Woody looked at Hamm in disbelief. "That can't be right," he said. "Mr Spell was made to spell. He never gets anything wrong."

Hamm shrugged. "See for yourself," he said.

Woody, Bo Peep and Hamm walked over to Mr Spell and asked him to spell rutabaga.

"Rutabaga. That's r… r… r…"

Woody and Bo Peep exchanged nervous glances.

"Great, thanks," Hamm said to Mr Spell, trying to act natural.

"Hey, how about the word 'platypus'?" said Woody.

"Platypus," Mr Spell repeated. "That's spelt p… p… p… p…"

Woody and Bo Peep stared anxiously at Mr Spell. Could he be losing his spelling edge? It was hard to believe, but how else could they explain what they were hearing?

"Okay," Hamm said. "One more question. How do you spell 'knick-knack'?"

"Knick-knack," Mr Spell began, "is spelt k… k… k… k…"

This was serious. Mr Spell was a really, really bad speller!

"Spell?" said Woody, laying a sympathetic hand on Mr Spell's back. "Are you feeling all right? You don't seem yourself."

"Oh, sure, Woody," Mr Spell replied. "I feel fine… fine… fine…"

As Mr Spell continued to repeat the word, Woody suddenly understood the problem.

"Hey! Hamm!" Woody exclaimed. "He's not spelling incorrectly. He just keeps getting stuck. Don't you, Spell?"

But Mr Spell couldn't respond. He just kept repeating, "Fine… fine… fine… fine…"

Woody gave Mr Spell a firm slap on the back. It didn't help, so he wound up and gave him a good whack. Mr Spell fell over on his side. The cover to his battery compartment came loose. Two corroded-looking batteries fell onto the floor.

"Heh, heh, heh," Hamm chuckled. "I guess Mr Spell just needs some new batteries!"

The Mysterious Backson

One morning, Winnie the Pooh woke up to his tummy rumbling. He was certain a visit to Christopher Robin would turn up some honey. But when Pooh reached Christopher Robin's house, he found a note taped to the door. Pooh couldn't read it, so he brought it to Owl.

"It says, 'gone out, busy Backson.'" Owl looked horrified. "Christopher Robin has been captured by a creature called the Backson!"

Luckily, Rabbit came up with a clever plan to capture the Backson. Pooh and Piglet got straight to work digging a pit. But Pooh's tummy still craved honey and he wandered off in a daydream. Tigger wandered off, too, to track the Backson on his own.

Pooh's friends were looking for Pooh everywhere when they heard a loud thud!

"The plan worked!" Rabbit cried. "We caught the Backson!"

The friends cautiously peered into the pit, only to discover that it was Pooh who had fallen in, not the Backson. They tried to throw in a rope so Pooh could climb up, but instead they all fell in – everyone except Piglet. Now Piglet had to save all of his friends!

As tiny Piglet searched for help, an enormous shadow fell over him. "B-B-B-BACKSON!" he shouted and ran off. But the shadow was only Tigger dressed as a Backson!

Back in the pit, everyone was relieved to see Piglet and Tigger. Soon the friends were able to climb out of the Backson trap.

Back above ground, Christopher Robin had appeared. Pooh handed him the note. Christopher Robin explained that he had written that he would be 'back soon' – not 'Backson'!

Relieved, the friends went on their way. There was just one problem. Pooh was still hungry for honey. He got to Owl's front door and pulled the bell rope... and realised that it was Eeyore's tail! Pooh decided that returning Eeyore's tail was more important than satisfying his tummy, and he brought his friend the tail right away. Eeyore was so relieved to see his tail that he gave Pooh a big pot of honey. All his honey dreams had come true after all!

A New Job

Bernard was a simple mouse. He liked his nice, quiet job as a handymouse, he liked to eat a nice hunk of cheese for dinner, and he liked to fall asleep reading a nice book each night. He didn't like the number thirteen, black cats (or cats at all, actually) or the colour green.

Another thing that Bernard didn't like was danger of any kind. He liked to play things safe. Bernard steered clear of all animals bigger than he was, any cheese he had not purchased himself and anything vaguely resembling a mousetrap.

So when the office he worked in announced it was moving its location from the basement of 1515 Hudson Street to 1313 Hudson Street, he knew it was time to find a new place of employment. One thirteen in the address would have been bad enough, but two? Well, it just would not do!

That afternoon, he bought a copy of the Rodent Report. Munching on his Limburger sandwich, he read the Help Wanted section.

"'Cheese tester,'" he read. That looked promising! But then he took a closer look at the advert and saw the words experimental and hazardous.

Bernard shook his head.

He was never going to find a new job! He put the paper down next to him, but suddenly another advert caught his eye. Desperately seeking handymouse, it read. Experience required. Apply at United Nations building, subbasement. Rescue Aid Society.

"That's it!" he cried.

Since Bernard had more experience than any of the other applicants, the job was his!

"Congratulations!" said the French delegate.

That night, Bernard's friends took him out to celebrate his new job.

"The Rescue Aid Society," his pal said. "Wow. Could be exciting, don'tcha think?"

"Oh, no," replied Bernard. "I'm going to be the handyman. No danger. No intrigue. I'll be mopping floors. Fixing leaks. No adventure at all, you can count on that."

His friend raised his glass for a toast. "To your new job," he said.

"To my new job," said Bernard. "May it be safe, quiet and non-adventurous. Just the way I like it!"

A Manner of Speaking

Bambi and his mother were out for a summer's walk. As always, they stopped by the rabbit den where Thumper lived.

"And how are you today, Thumper?" asked Bambi's mother.

"I'd be better if my mum didn't just give me a dumb old bath," he said.

"Thumper! Mind your manners!" his mother scolded him.

Bambi and Thumper were given permission to play hide-and-seek, and so they headed off into the woods.

Bambi turned his back to Thumper, closed his eyes and started to count. "One… two…"

"Save me! Help! Bambi, save me!" Thumper cried suddenly. Bambi whirled round to see Thumper hopping towards him with a terrified look on his face. A moment later, a mother bear emerged from a nearby cave with three small cubs toddling behind her.

Though he was terrified, Thumper still managed to make a rude comment. "That's the meanest-looking creature I ever saw!"

"I beg your pardon?" the mother bear said angrily. "First you come into my home and disturb my children, and then you call me mean? I think you owe me a big apology!"

"Do it!" whispered Bambi. "Apologise."

"I'm s-s-sorry you're mean," Thumper stammered.

"Thumper!" Bambi cried. "That isn't funny."

Thumper looked confused. "I wasn't trying to be funny," he said.

"Try again!" the mother bear boomed.

"Um…" Thumper tried again. "I'm, um, sorry I disturbed your cubs… and, um, you look just like a mama bear should look… which is big. And nice."

Before the mother bear let Thumper and Bambi go, she said, "Like I always tell my children: manners are important! You remember that."

Bambi and Thumper ran home as quickly as they could. When they arrived at Thumper's, his mother said, "Just in time for a nice lunch of greens."

Thumper was about to tell his mum how awful he thought the greens tasted, but he changed his mind. "Thank you, Mama. That sounds wonderful," he said.

Thumper's mother beamed. "What lovely manners! I guess you have been listening to me, after all!" she said, as pleased as could be.

Disney

Beauty and the Beast

Belle's Flight

One day, Belle and her father, Maurice, were on their way to Paris to visit the French National Library. On the way they stopped at an inn to rest. Over dinner, Belle met a young woman called Sophie who was travelling to England in a hot-air balloon! "I built it all by myself," explained Sophie. "Why don't you join me for a short flight?"

Belle and Maurice were thrilled. They scrambled inside the hot-air balloon and took off – the world seemed so small from high up!

But moments later there was a rumble of thunder and large raindrops started falling. "We better land!" Belle shouted over the wind. Sophie turned down the fire to start the descent.

However, as they came down, the balloon hit a tree. RIP! They plummeted to the ground and the hot-air balloon was ruined. Sophie was devastated. "Don't worry, together we can fix it," Belle reassured her new friend.

The next day, Belle, Maurice and Sophie got to work. They sewed, weaved and hammered. Soon, the balloon was as good as new!

"You saved the day," said Sophie. As thanks, she gave Belle and Maurice a special gift: the blueprints of her invention.

"When we go home, we can build a balloon together," Belle told her father.

"But first, let me take you to Paris!" Sophie exclaimed.

Soon, Maurice and Philippe were back on the road, but this time with special flying guides! "We're nearly there!" called Belle from the balloon.

When they finally entered the library, Belle couldn't believe her eyes. There were books on every subject. She couldn't wait to start reading, but first on her list… maps of the world!

Float Like a Butterfly

One day, Dumbo's best friend, Timothy Q. Mouse, found Dumbo looking sad.

"What's the matter, little guy?" the mouse asked the elephant. "Have people been teasing you about your ears again?"

Dumbo nodded. The little elephant looked totally miserable.

Timothy was trying to think of a way to cheer up his dear friend when he saw something. "Look, Dumbo!" he cried, racing over to a nearby fence post. "It's a butterfly cocoon!" Timothy said excitedly.

Dumbo came over to examine it.

"And look – it's about to hatch into a butterfly," said Timothy. He looked thoughtful for a moment and then he turned to Dumbo. "You know what? You're a lot like the little caterpillar that made this cocoon."

Dumbo looked at Timothy, confused.

"Yep, it's true. You see, a caterpillar is something nobody really wants around much. They think it's kind of plain-looking, and it can't really do anything very interesting. But then one day, the caterpillar turns into a beautiful butterfly, and everyone loves it. And you know what? I think you're going to be that way, too. When you get older, everyone is going to admire you rather than tease you!"

Dumbo smiled gratefully at his friend and wiped away a tear with one of his long ears.

Suddenly, it started to rain.

"Oh, no!" cried Timothy. "The butterfly is going to get its new wings all wet. It won't be able to fly if it gets rained on. What'll we do? We need an umbrella!"

As Timothy looked this way and that for an umbrella, Dumbo smiled and unfurled his long ears. He draped them over the fence post so that they made a lovely roof for the insect, protecting it from the falling droplets of rain.

"Great idea!" said Timothy admiringly. The two friends stood there during the downpour, which didn't last very long. While they waited, they watched the beautiful new butterfly emerge from its cocoon and unfurl its colourful wings. When the rain stopped, the butterfly spread its wings (which were quite dry, thanks to Dumbo) and flew away.

And They're Off!

"What are you doing, eh?" Kenai looked up to see Rutt and Tuke standing and staring in disbelief. The two goofy moose were trying to determine just what Koda, the young bear cub who was travelling with Kenai, was doing.

"Koda is watching those centipedes," Kenai replied.

Koda looked up. "They're racing," he said.

Rutt looked surprised. "Gee, I didn't think centipedes knew how to race."

"Everybody knows how to race," Tuke told Rutt. "Even a hoof-for-brains like you."

Koda's eyes sparkled. "That's a great idea!" he said. "You guys should have a race! Ready, set, go!"

Both moose stood still, staring at him.

"Where are we going?" Rutt asked.

"You're just supposed to go!" Koda cried. "You're racing, remember?"

Tuke stepped forwards. "Come on, Rutt. Keep up."

"No! You're not supposed to tell him to keep up!" Koda cried. "You're supposed to run away from him!"

So Tuke took off at a gallop, but Rutt just stood there watching him.

"Well?" Kenai said. "Aren't you going to run after him?"

"Run after him? Why would I do that, eh?" The moose looked confused.

Koda growled with frustration. "Because that's what you do in a race!"

Rutt nodded. Then he ambled off after Tuke.

The two bears glanced at each other. "Even the centipedes could beat those two," Koda whispered to Kenai.

Kenai laughed. "Let's follow them."

First the bears came upon Tuke, who had stopped to eat twigs. Then they found Rutt rolling in the mud. When Tuke caught up to Rutt, the two started gossiping about some squirrels they knew.

"Maybe some animals just aren't meant to race," Koda said sadly.

Kenai could tell the little bear was disappointed. "You may be right," he said. "But I have an idea."

"What?" Koda asked.

Kenai grinned. "Race you to the river!" he cried. And he took off with Koda chasing him happily, laughing all the way.

The Cosiest Carriage

O'Malley, Duchess and the kittens were visiting Scat Cat, one of O'Malley's oldest and dearest friends.

Scat Cat lived in a broken-down carriage that had once been very grand indeed. But the wheels had fallen apart long ago, the cushions were shredded, and there was a huge hole right in the middle of the worn, tattered roof. Still, as far as Scat Cat was concerned, his home was perfect.

"I feel free here," he told the kittens. "I can come and go as I please. And when I stretch out on the cushions at night, I look up and there are the stars a-twinklin' and a-winkin' back at me!"

A few days later, there was a knock at Madame's door. It was Scat Cat.

"You'll never believe it," he said. "I went into town to stretch my legs, and when I got back... poof! The carriage was gone!"

"Naturally, you will have to stay with us!" said Duchess. "I'm sure Madame would be delighted to have you as our guest."

But after only one night, Scat Cat began to feel sad. Everything at Madame Bonfamille's happened according to a strict schedule. Scat Cat missed doing as he pleased.

"You know what I miss most?" Scat Cat

told O'Malley and the kittens. "My old carriage. What I wouldn't give to be able to look up at the sky and count the twinklin' stars..."

The kittens decided to help Scat Cat. Madame had been complaining about her old carriage. So Berlioz climbed into it and began clawing at the old cushions. Marie joined him. Soon, the cushions looked just like the ones in Scat Cat's old carriage!

Finally, Toulouse crashed through the carriage roof, making a huge hole.

"Oh, my!" exclaimed a voice. It was Madame. She surveyed the damage... and smiled! "At last I have an excuse to buy a new carriage," she said. "Let's take this one out to the junkyard at once."

"I don't believe it!" cried Scat Cat when the kittens led him to his new home. "It's purr-fect! How can I ever thank you?"

"It was our pleasure," said Berlioz. He flexed his claws. "It's not every day we're thanked for clawing something to pieces!"

Disney
Tangled

Rapunzel's Challenge

Rapunzel and Flynn stood in the forest. She had bet him she could do anything better than he could. Now she had to prove it.

Flynn pointed to a tall tree. "Do you think you can beat me to the top?"

Rapunzel squared her shoulders. In a flash, she threw her hair onto a branch and swung gracefully up into the tree.

Flynn pulled out two arrows and used them to climb right past Rapunzel.

Suddenly, from up above, Flynn heard a voice call down. "Yoo-hoo! Flynn Rider! What took you so long?"

Flynn looked up and gasped. Rapunzel was sitting at the top of the tree. "How did you get up there so fast?" he cried.

Rapunzel pointed to her golden hair.

"That's cheating," Flynn argued. "You can't use your hair to help you. I demand another contest. And this time, no hair."

The two decided to have a race next.

"First one to the river wins," Flynn declared.

Rapunzel and Flynn sprang forward. But as Flynn raced along, he accidentally tripped over Rapunzel's hair!

Rapunzel didn't realise what had happened. She kept running and sprinted to the river's edge. She had won!

"That wasn't fair," Flynn panted. "You used your hair again."

Flynn insisted they have one more contest. Rapunzel sighed. She had beaten Flynn twice. Surely she could do it again.

Flynn pointed to the river. "Let's see who can cross this first," he said.

Rapunzel was nervous. She had never learnt to swim! As Flynn dived into the water, Rapunzel looked around. How could she get across? Suddenly, she had an idea.

Flynn panted as he climbed out of the river. "I did it," he said. "I won!" Then he looked up. Rapunzel was standing on the shore, completely dry.

"I don't understand," Flynn said. "You got here first? And you're not even wet?"

"That's because I didn't swim across," Rapunzel said. "I swung across."

"Oh, I see," Flynn said. He shook the water from his hair and grinned slyly. "Then I win! Remember? No hair!"

"I didn't use my hair," Rapunzel said. She held up a long, thick vine.

Flynn sighed. He hated to admit it, but Rapunzel had beaten him fair and square!

Mater's Jukebox

"Yeee-ha! Ready or not, Radiator Springs, my jukebox is ready!" Mater called. He had made a fantastic jukebox and he couldn't wait to show all of his friends.

Mater hooked the jukebox up to his towline and off he went. The first car he saw was Ramone, but Ramone didn't have time to listen to the jukebox. Little tractors were messing up his body paint shop! "I've got to clean up this place!" Ramone cried.

Next Mater passed by his best friend, Lightning.

"Sorry, Mater!" Lightning called. "I've got to round up these little tractors." Lightning zoomed after another little tractor as it darted away.

At Casa Della Tires, Luigi had no time to hear Mater's junkyard jukebox, either. "No-no-no-no!" Luigi cried. "Look at Luigi's Leaning Tower of Tires! Now she is just Luigi's Pile of Tires!"

Mater knew he had to help, but how? He rounded the corner and found Sheriff. "Hey, Sheriff, you'll never guess what I made…"

"Mater! I've got no time today for lollygagging. I need to round up these little rascals." Sheriff turned on his siren and drove away after the tractors.

For such cute little fellas, those tractors sure are causing a load of trouble! Mater thought. *I gotta put away my jukebox so I can help my friends.*

As Mater headed back to his scrapyard, he cranked up his jukebox and began to sing along with the music.

A tractor followed him shyly. Soon the other tractors started trailing after Mater and his jukebox! To his surprise, Mater noticed the music was attracting all the little tractors. He turned up the sound and started a little tractor roundup.

"Well, lookee here!" Mater shouted. "These little fellas like my music!"

The whole town cheered. "Hip, hip, hooray for Mater!"

"That's music to my ears!" Sheriff sighed.

Everyone was happy. The tractors were out of trouble, and the music was great!

Crack the Whip

Mickey woke up and looked outside. It had snowed overnight! "It's a perfect day for ice-skating!" he cried. "I'll invite all my friends."

When Mickey and his friends got to the pond, everyone laced up their skates and made their way onto the ice.

"Hey, I have an idea!" shouted Mickey. "Let's play Crack the Whip!"

Nobody else knew how to play, so Mickey explained the game. "I'll start as the leader," he said. "We all join hands and form a line. Then we all skate round and round in a big circle. Once we get going, the skater at the end of the line lets go!"

"That sounds like fun!" said Goofy.

They all joined hands and began skating in a circle.

"Okay, Donald, let go!" Mickey said.

Donald let go and went sailing away. Round and round and round the rest of the gang went.

"Now, you go, Daisy!" cried Mickey. Daisy let go and went flying away across the ice.

Next went Huey, then Dewey, and finally Louie. Goofy followed them.

Now just Mickey and Minnie were left. Round and round they skated. Then Mickey shouted, "Let go, Minnie!"

Minnie let go and zoomed off with a squeal.

Mickey continued to skate. When he finally came to a stop, it took quite some time for his head to stop spinning.

"Wasn't that fun, guys?" he said. "Want to do it again? Guys? Where is everyone?"

Mickey looked around. Where had everyone gone?

And then he saw them: seven pairs of ice skates at the ends of seven pairs of legs were sticking out of seven different snowbanks, kicking away!

"Uh-oh," said Mickey. He dashed over to the side of the pond and, one by one, he pulled all of his friends out of the snow.

Goofy shook his head, and snow flew everywhere. "That was fun!" he said cheerfully. "But I sure could use a cup of—"

"Yoo-hoo!" came a cheerful cry. It was Grandma Duck, standing at the edge of the pond. She was carrying a thermos filled with hot chocolate!

"Hooray!" cried all the friends. It was the perfect way to warm up.

The Chosen One

The Little Green Aliens looked up as something moved overhead. "Ooh," they cried. Was it the Claw? The Claw was their master. It descended from the sky and decided who would go and who would stay. But this time it was not the Claw. Instead, the small door on the side of their home opened. Dozens of three-eyed aliens just like them poured in.

"Welcome," one of the original aliens said to the newcomers. "This is the Choosing Place."

Another alien gasped. "Look!" he cried. "One of the new ones is not like us. He is… different."

The others cried out in surprise and confusion. One of the new aliens had only two eyes on his round green head!

"What is the matter with your face, stranger?" one of the Little Green Aliens asked. "You don't look like us."

"I… I don't know," the two-eyed one said hesitantly. "I have always been this way. A Voice from above once said that… that…" His voice trailed off.

A three-eyed newcomer spoke up. "I heard the Voice," he said. "It said that it was a Manufacturing Defect."

Suddenly there was a great whirring sound from above.

"The Claw!" someone cried. "It moves! It descends!"

The aliens waited, gazing upwards hopefully as the Claw came closer and closer. Finally, its talons closed over one round green head.

"The Claw has chosen!" they cried.

A child's muffled voice came from somewhere outside. "Cool! I got the best one!"

The aliens watched as the Claw raised the Chosen One above the others. They gasped as they recognised the strange two-eyed newcomer.

"The different one has been chosen!" one of the Little Green Aliens exclaimed. "The Claw has chosen him despite his Manufacturing Defect!"

"The Claw knew that the different one was special," someone else added.

The others nodded solemnly. "We will learn from the Claw," one of them said softly.

"Yes," another finished. "From now on, we will welcome all newcomers, no matter how different."

The others nodded. The Claw had shown them the way.

A Whale of a Tale

"Hop aboard, explorers!" called Nemo's teacher, Mr Ray.

Nemo, Tad and the rest of the class jumped on the back of the big manta ray. It was Special Guest Week and they were going to the Drop-off. When they reached the reef's edge, a blue tang fish swam up to meet them.

"Hello, everyone," said the blue tang. "I'm Dory… um… am I? Yes! Just kidding! I'm Dory, and I'm very happy to be here!"

"Dory, can you teach us something about whales today?" asked Mr Ray.

"Well, let's see… whales are very big, but they eat little creatures called krill. And I should know. One whale I met almost ate me!"

"Sandy Plankton said Nemo made up that story about how you and Nemo's dad got eaten by a whale!" said Tad.

"I did not make it up!" cried Nemo.

"Well," said Dory, "technically, Sandy Plankton is right. We weren't actually eaten by the whale…" Tad smirked, until Dory added, "We were just in the whale's mouth for a mighty long time!

"You see, the whale was just giving us a ride to Sydney. I find if you talk to a whale beforehand, it clears up most ingestion issues," Dory explained.

"Excellent lesson!" said Mr Ray. "Now teach us a few words in Whale."

"Oh, okay," said Dory. "Here's a phrase you can use if you're ever in trouble. Now repeat after me: 'Caaaaannnn yooooouuuu heeeeelllllp mmmeeee?'"

"Caaaaannnn yooooouuuu heeeeelllllp mmmeeee?" the class repeated.

"This is stupid," said Tad. "You didn't…"

Tad stopped talking. Everyone just stared at Dory in horror.

Slowly, Dory turned round. A blue whale was right behind her!

"Weeeee weerrrrre juuuuusssst praaaactiiiiissssssinnnng!" Dory told the whale. "Nnnnnnooooo heeeeelllllp nnnnneeeedeeeed. Thaaaaanksssss aaaannnnnyyyyywwwaaaaayyyyy!"

With a loud bellow, the whale wished her a nice day, then swam off.

"So, Tad, do you believe Dory now?" asked Nemo.

"Wow, that was so cool!" cried Tad. "I can't wait to tell Sandy Plankton how I was almost eaten by a whale!"

Nemo and Dory just sighed.

Detective Lucky

It was a blustery night, and the Dalmatian puppies were listening to a bedtime story. Lucky loved bedtime stories. Especially ones about detectives! Oh, how he wished he could be a detective. Long after the story had finished and the puppies were tucked up in bed, Lucky was still awake, thinking about solving mysteries. Suddenly, his ear flicked.

Creak, squeak, BANG!

What was that? Lucky shot upright. A mystery! He sneaked past his sleeping parents to the doggy door. It led him outside, and soon he was into the garden, ready to investigate. All around him, Lucky could see shadowy shapes. He thought about going back inside, but he stuck out his nose and sniffed. An unfamiliar smell made his nose twitch. A clue!

He followed the scent into the woods, not realising how far he was from home. The smell led to a wooden log and he poked his head inside. Two eyes appeared, wide and frightening. Lucky yelped and ran. He didn't know where he was in the dark forest, and scary sounds were coming from all around.

Suddenly, something furry bumped into Lucky and he fell, tangled in the stranger's limbs. Then a familiar voice said, "Lucky? Is that you?"

It was Sergeant Tibs, the cat who'd helped them escaped Cruella De Vil!

"Sergeant Tibs!" Lucky cried in relief. "I was trying to be a detective, but now I'm lost and scared and…"

"Don't worry," Sergeant Tibs said. "I know what to do."

He took Lucky to an old barn, where the Colonel was waiting. Sergeant Tibs explained the situation and the Colonel raced out of the barn to start a midnight bark.

Bark! Bark! Bark!

Soon, the night was alive with yapping dogs.

"Follow the calls," the Colonel said. "They'll lead you home."

Lucky thanked the Colonel and Sergeant Tibs, then followed the barks. Now he was less scared, he realised the sounds he'd been hearing were an owl, a raccoon and a squeaky gate! When he finally sneaked back into the Dalmatian Plantation and into his bed, Lucky slept with the knowledge that he'd solved his first mystery. He was a real detective after all!

The Den of Doom

"Where are we going, Baloo?" Mowgli asked. He and Baloo had been travelling through the jungle for a while now.

"Have you ever heard of the Den of Doom, Man-cub?" replied Baloo in a hushed voice.

Mowgli gasped. "The Den of Doom? They say that the Den of Doom is a giant cave filled with bears who will eat anything – or anyone! They say that even Shere Khan is afraid of them!" he exclaimed.

"Mmm-hmm," said Baloo. "They do say that. They also say that all of the bears in the Den of Doom are over eight feet tall, that their teeth are green and razor-sharp, and that their battle cry is so loud that the whales in the ocean hear it and shake with fright."

"And we're going there?" Mowgli squeaked. "We can't!"

"Too late, Man-cub," Baloo said with a grin. "We're already here!" He picked Mowgli up and strode right into a thicket. The boy looked around in surprise.

Mowgli had expected to see lots of fierce, angry bears. Instead, he saw hundreds of relaxed, happy bears having a really good time. Bears were swimming in a small pond, splashing and laughing. Bears were resting in the cool shadows of the cave. Bears were playing tig out in the clearing and chomping on piles of ripe, delicious fruit. It was, in short, a bear party.

"I don't understand," Mowgli said to Baloo. "This is the Den of Doom?"

"Yep," Baloo said happily, grabbing a palm frond and fanning himself with it. "It used to be called the Den of Delights, but we had to change the name. See, everyone in the jungle knew that the Den of Delights was the most fun place around. We bears never turned anyone away from our party. But then it got so crowded that it just wasn't fun anymore. So we spread a few rumours, changed the name, and presto – it's the Den of Doom! Now no one bothers us bears anymore."

"But what about me?" Mowgli said anxiously. "I'm not a bear."

"You're an honorary bear, Mowgli," Baloo replied with a smile. "You sure have enough fun to be one."

Babysitting the Troll Tots

Anna, Kristoff and Sven were visiting Troll Valley to babysit the troll tots. Bulda took Anna and Kristoff to the tots. "If they get hungry, you can feed them smashed berries. And they may need a leaf change. But it's just about their bedtime, so they should be sleeping soon."

As the adult trolls headed off, Anna waved. "Have a great time! Everything is going to be... a disaster!"

Anna, Kristoff and Sven had turned to see that the toddler trolls had escaped from their pen. They were running, climbing and swinging all over the place.

"Oh... no, no," Anna said, rushing to help a few trolls who were climbing up the boulders. "That's dangerous."

The more Kristoff, Anna and Sven tried to calm the little trolls, the wilder they became. They weren't hungry and they weren't dirty. They just wanted to play!

Suddenly, a cheery voice interrupted them. "Hello, troll babies!"

It was their friend Olaf! As Anna turned to greet him, she tripped and fell into a pile of berries.

Anna lifted her head, her face covered in dripping purple goop. The little trolls burst into loud giggles. They stampeded towards her,

lapping up the berry juice on her cheeks.

Anna laughed. "Well, I guess that's one way to feed them."

After the trolls were done, they sat in a heap, happy and full. Suddenly, a strange smell floated in the air. The trolls looked down at their leaves.

"Uh-oh," Kristoff said knowingly.

Anna and Kristoff set about changing the trolls. Soon everyone was clean and sweet-smelling once more.

Anna noticed that the trolls were swaying. Some of them were having trouble keeping their eyes open.

"Maybe Kristoff and Sven would like to sing a lullaby," she suggested.

"Rock-a-bye troll-ys, in your small pen," Kristoff sang.

"Time to go sleepy for Uncle Sven," Kristoff crooned, switching to Sven's voice.

By the time the adult trolls returned, the wee ones were sound asleep.

"Wow, great job," Bulda whispered.

"It was easy," Anna replied, elbowing Kristoff.

"Piece of mud pie," Kristoff added.

Disney

Winnie the Pooh

Tigger's Moving Day

Tigger loved to bounce. But he kept bouncing into things in his house.

"Tigger, you don't have enough bouncing room in this little house," said Rabbit. "We've got to find you a bigger house. That's all there is to it!"

Soon Tigger and Rabbit found a wonderful new house. "It is a bouncy house," said Tigger. "The kind of house tiggers like best!" He bounced and he didn't bump into anything. "But," he said, sighing, "I won't live next door to little Roo anymore."

"I know you'll miss being so close to Kanga and Roo," said Christopher Robin, "but now you'll live much closer to me. Just think of the fun we can have being neighbours."

Kanga told Tigger she would bring Roo to visit. Tigger felt better and invited everyone to stay awhile. But Rabbit put his paws on his hips. "We aren't finished yet. We need to move all your things from your old house to this house," he explained. Rabbit told everyone to bring all the boxes they could find to Tigger's old house.

Soon everyone arrived with their boxes. "Wow! Boxes are fun!" cried Roo as he and Tigger bounced in and out of the boxes everyone had brought.

"There'll be time for fun later," grumbled Rabbit.

Tigger packed all his games and his stuffed animals in a box. Rabbit packed Tigger's dishes. Kanga packed Tigger's hats and scarves. Pooh and Piglet packed Tigger's food. Soon Eeyore arrived with his donkey cart. Christopher Robin and Owl hoisted Tigger's bed and table and chairs onto the cart.

After his friends had gone, Tigger put his things just where he wanted them. When he was finished, he sat down to rest.

Hmmm. Seems like an awfully quiet house, he thought.

Just then, Tigger heard a little voice.

"Hallooo!" the voice called.

"Roo!" cried Tigger. "Kanga! Come on in!"

Tigger soon heard all his friends calling outside his new door. They had all brought housewarming presents!

"Our work's all done," said Rabbit at last. "Now it's time for fun!"

Market Day

Abu sat at the window gazing longingly towards the village. "What's wrong, Abu?" asked Aladdin. "Do you want to go to the market?"

Abu nodded happily and the pair set off. They had a wonderful afternoon visiting old friends. Abu played with Salim the goat, joked with Kahlil the ox, and teased Gamal the camel.

Aladdin saw how happy Abu was in the hustle and bustle of the busy marketplace. "You know, Abu," he said, "you can invite your friends from the marketplace to the palace any time you'd like."

The next day, Abu disappeared at sunrise. When he returned, Salim and Kahlil were with him.

"Welcome," said Jasmine. "Please, make yourselves at home." But they already had. The goat was chewing on the curtains and the ox was eating the flowers in the garden.

"We can always buy new curtains or plant new flowers. The important thing is that Abu is happy again," Aladdin said.

The following day, Gamal and several other camels arrived. Jasmine was not pleased when they spat on the new carpet.

"Think of Abu," Aladdin told her.

The day after that, the fruit seller rolled through the palace with his cart. Next came the lady who sold dates and the man who sold pottery.

"Isn't it wonderful that Abu has so many friends?" said Aladdin.

"It is," Jasmine agreed. "But have you noticed that we only see his friends coming and not going?"

"Hmmm… let's find out what's going on," Aladdin said.

The couple followed Abu as he led his guests out to the garden. The entire marketplace was there!

Aladdin burst out laughing. "I guess the next time Abu is feeling homesick, he doesn't need to go any farther than his own backyard!"

Jasmine sighed. "Aladdin, these people can't stay here." But when Jasmine saw the sad look on Aladdin's face, she added, "Well, maybe they could come back next month."

And so began a new tradition – Palace Market Day, which happened once a month. And that made little Abu very happy!

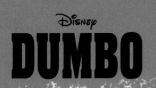

The Best Gift Ever

Other than Dumbo's mother, Mrs Jumbo, all the elephants at the circus made Dumbo feel like a nobody. But Timothy Q. Mouse was different. Since the day he and Dumbo had met, Timothy had encouraged Dumbo. Dumbo was so happy to have a friend like Timothy! He wanted to do something nice for him.

Dumbo decided to give Timothy a gift. At feeding time, he put aside a bale of hay. Then he lugged the hay behind the Big Top and looked around for Timothy. He found him lounging in the shadow of the lion's cage and plopped down the hay bale.

"Hiya, Dumbo!" said Timothy. "What's with the hay?"

Using his trunk, Dumbo nudged the hay bale closer to Timothy.

"For me?" Timothy said. "Wow. Uh… thanks."

Dumbo's heart sank as he realised that mice didn't eat hay.

The next day, Dumbo came upon a patch of flowers. He picked a nice big bouquet and took it behind the Big Top to Timothy.

"Shucks, Dumbo," said Timothy. "You shouldn't have." Tiny Timothy took the bouquet from Dumbo's outstretched trunk and promptly fell over, dropping the flowers everywhere.

Sadly, Dumbo realised the bouquet was too heavy for Timothy to enjoy.

The next day, under the Big Top, Dumbo spotted a bunch of balloons tied to a seat. Those wouldn't be too heavy for Timothy. They stayed up all by themselves. So Dumbo untied them and brought them to Timothy.

But when Timothy took hold of the balloon strings, the helium-filled balloons lifted him right off the ground! Dumbo quickly reached out with his trunk and pulled Timothy back to the ground.

With a disappointed sigh, Dumbo took the balloons back. He wondered if he would ever find a good gift for Timothy.

"Dumbo," Timothy said, "I wanted to thank you for giving me the best gift ever."

Dumbo's eyes widened in surprise. What could Timothy mean? Every gift he had given him had been wrong.

"You're my best friend," Timothy said. "And that's the best gift I could ever ask for."

Dishes, Dishes, Dishes

"Hmmph." Jim Hawkins grabbed another plate from the enormous pile of dishes he was scrubbing and dunked it into the sudsy bucket. "This is not the adventure I had in mind," he said grumpily.

Jim had been dreaming about finding Treasure Planet since he was a kid. And he was finally doing it! But somehow, working in the galley doing dishes for some crazy cyborg had never been a part of his fantasy.

With a sigh, Jim rinsed the plate he was holding and grabbed another one. He wished he was allowed to do something (besides mopping) up on deck. But no. He was stuck in the kitchen, washing dishes. Alone.

Being alone was practically the worst part of it all. It was getting to be that Jim even looked forward to Silver's company. Sure, he was a weird old guy with a creepy cyborg eye. But at least he told some good tales of spacers, and he was better than no company at all.

Yawning, Jim dipped the last dish in the bucket, scrubbed it, rinsed it and wiped it dry. Then he added it to the pile of clean dishes. "There," Jim said with a sigh. But when he looked back, another dish was sitting beside his washtub.

"Hmm. Must've missed one," he said, picking up the plate. "Now that's got to be it," Jim said, drying his hands on a towel. He leaned back on his stool. But what he saw nearly caused him to fall over. Another dirty dish was waiting to be cleaned!

"I know I got the last one!" Jim rubbed his eyes. Maybe he was more tired than he thought. But when he opened his eyes, the dish was still there. "I've been in the kitchen too long," Jim mumbled.

By the time he cleaned it, another had appeared in its place! Jim had to get out of the kitchen. He was starting to go crazy.

Suddenly, the dish he was washing slipped out of his hands. A pink blob burst out of the soapy water, sputtering and giggling.

"Morph!" Jim couldn't help but smile at the little blob of protoplasm and his practical joke. "Thanks for all of your help with the dishes," he said with a laugh.

Bedtime for Gus

Cinderella looked out her bedroom window as the sun was setting. The clock in the tower of the castle struck eight. Cinderella tapped gently on the walls of her attic room.

"Bedtime, everyone!" she called. Jaq, Suzy, Gus and the other mice hurried out of their mouse hole.

"Buh-buh-bedtime?" Gus asked. Gus was Cinderella's newest mouse friend. She had just rescued him from a trap that morning.

"Close your eyes and fall asleep!" Suzy explained.

Gus looked confused. He closed his eyes and started to tip over. Jaq caught him.

"Not fall, Gus-Gus," he said. "Fall asleep. Like this." He put his head on his hands and pretended to snore softly.

Cinderella laughed. "Gus has never lived in a house before. We'll have to teach him about getting ready for bed.

"First, you put on your pyjamas." She went to her dresser and pulled out a tiny pair of striped pyjamas for Gus.

"Now sleep, Cinderella?" Gus asked.

Cinderella smiled. "Not quite yet," she said. "Now you need to wash your face and brush your teeth. Then I'll kiss you goodnight, and Suzy will tuck everyone in."

When the mice were all neat and clean, Cinderella kissed each of them goodnight. "It's time for everyone to go to sleep," she said sweetly.

"Follow me," Jaq told Gus. He ran over to his little bed and hopped in. Then he pointed to the bed next to him. "That's your bed," he said.

Gus grinned and got under the cosy covers.

"Story, Cinderella!" someone cried.

Cinderella smiled. "All right," she said. "Once upon a time, there was a young prince who lived in a castle…" She continued the story for a long time. Each time she tried to stop, the mice begged for more. But after a while, they couldn't keep their eyes open any longer.

When the last mouse had fallen asleep, Cinderella tiptoed to her own bed and climbed in. She snuggled against her pillow and yawned. "If only some of my stories would come true…"

Fairy Medicine

Deep in the forest, in a humble cottage, the three good fairies had been secretly raising Princess Aurora for many years. The king and queen had sent their beloved daughter, now called Briar Rose, into hiding to try to protect her from a curse laid on the princess by the evil fairy Maleficent.

One morning, the girl woke up with a terrible cold.

"We must nurse her back to health," said Flora.

Fauna and Merryweather agreed. While Briar Rose stayed in bed, Flora brought her a bowl of soup, Fauna fetched her a cup of tea and Merryweather gave her a dose of medicine.

"Ooooh!" said Briar Rose, wrinkling her nose. "That tastes awful!"

"Most medicine tastes awful, dear," said Merryweather. "Just drink it down."

"Would you like anything else?" Flora asked.

The princess blew her nose and gazed out her window. "What I really want is to get out of bed," she said.

"Oh, no, dear," said Flora. "You're far too sick."

Then the fairies left Briar Rose and went downstairs.

"I feel bad for the sweet girl," said Fauna. "Staying in bed all day is boring."

"What can we do?" asked Merryweather.

"I know!" cried Flora. "We'll entertain her!"

"Splendid!" said Merryweather. "I'll fetch my wand and conjure up some fireworks, a puppet show, and—"

"No!" Flora cried. "We all agreed to give up our fairy magic until Briar Rose turns sixteen and she's safe from Maleficent's curse. How about if we play card games? That will be fun!"

And so the three fairies went up to Briar Rose's room and played cards with her all afternoon. Briar Rose won almost every game. After a while, Briar Rose yawned and said she was ready to take a nap. So the fairies went back downstairs.

When Flora went outside to do some gardening, Fauna approached Merryweather.

"Tell me the truth," she whispered. "Did you use magic to let the princess win?"

"I just used mortal magic," confessed Merryweather. "No harm in a little sleight of hand. After all, you must admit, if you're feeling down, winning is the best medicine!"

Disney
Peter Pan

A Snappy New Ship

It had not been a good day for Captain Hook. Peter Pan and the Darling children had stolen his ship. Now Hook was stranded on an island with Smee and the other pirates.

"It's a nice island, Captain," offered Smee, trying to cheer up his boss. "And you could use a holiday. Why, look at those dark circles under your eyes."

Captain Hook turned to Smee with a furious look on his face. "Pirates don't take holidays!" Hook boomed. "Pirates seek revenge! Which is precisely what we are going to do as soon as we have a new ship to sail in."

Smee looked around. "Where are we going to find a ship around here, sir?" he asked.

"We aren't going to find one," Captain Hook answered. "You and the rest of this mangy crew are going to build one!"

For weeks, the pirates chopped trees and cut them into planks for the ship. Finally, the ship was done.

"It's ready, Captain!" Smee announced. Even Hook had to admit the ship was magnificent. Shaped like a gigantic crocodile, it was painted a reptilian shade of green. "No one will dare come near this ship. Not even that pesky crocodile. He won't want to tussle with anything this terrifying," Smee assured him.

Captain Hook was delighted. "We set sail tomorrow!" he crowed.

That night, Smee couldn't resist putting one finishing touch on the ship: he painted a row of eyelashes on the crocodile's eyelids.

The next morning, Captain Hook and the crew climbed aboard and pushed off. The ticking crocodile soon appeared.

"Smee!" yelled a terrified Captain Hook. "I thought you said he wouldn't come near us!"

"But look how calm he is," said Smee, puzzled. "He's even smiling!" Smee leaned over the side of the railing. "You know, it might be those eyelashes I painted. Maybe the croc thinks the ship is its mother."

Hook lunged at the first mate. "You made my ship look like a mother crocodile? This vessel is supposed to be terrifying!"

"Mothers can be terrifying, sir," said Smee. "You should have seen mine when I told her I was going to become a pirate!"

Come Out, Come Out

The toys in Andy's room were in a panic. There was something in the wardrobe – and it was alive! Passing by the slightly open door, Rex had seen some red lights blinking in the darkness.

"What do you think it is?" asked Jessie. She picked up Lenny and pointed the binoculars at the wardrobe door, but it was too dark to see.

Woody walked right up to the wardrobe. "Hello in there, and welcome to Andy's room," he called. "Come on out. There's nothing to be afraid of."

But the thing with the blinking red lights stayed right where it was.

"I get it, a shy type," Hamm guessed. The piggy bank jingled the coins in his body. "Show your face and there's a reward in it for you."

Buzz tried next. "In the name of Star Command, I, Buzz Lightyear, space ranger, demand that you show yourself! I have a laser out here, and I'm not afraid to use it," he said in an official-sounding voice.

The stranger in the wardrobe didn't budge. Buzz turned to Rex, who looked like he might faint. "Clearly, the intruder is not threatened by the sheriff or myself. It's up to you as the dominant predator to go in and get him."

"Me?" Rex asked, his knees shaking.

"Yes, you," insisted Buzz. "Just use the techniques I've been teaching you. You can be very intimidating if you set your mind to it."

"Go on, you big lizard!" Hamm yelled. "Make him wish he was extinct!"

"Oh, all right," Rex said. "Here goes." He ventured into the darkness of the wardrobe and gave a spine-chilling roar.

"I got him!" shouted Rex. He emerged from the wardrobe pulling on a shoelace. Everyone stared at him in disbelief.

"It's… a trainer," Buzz said.

"With lights in the heel," added Woody.

Rex burst into tears. "My big moment, wasted on a shoe!"

"Well, look on the bright side," said Hamm.

Rex looked hopeful. "There's a bright side?"

"Yeah," the pig assured him. "At least it didn't stick its tongue out at you!"

Happy Mother's Day

One fine day, Roo hopped over to Winnie the Pooh's house. "I have a problem," Roo told Pooh. "Mother's Day is almost here, and I don't know what to give my mama. Do you have any ideas?"

"Let me think," said Pooh. "Think, think, think. A gift for Mother's Day…" Luckily, Pooh spotted a big pot of honey sitting in his cupboard. "That's it!" he cried. "Mothers like honey!"

"They do?" asked Roo.

"Doesn't everybody?" Pooh asked.

So Pooh gave Roo a pot of honey. Roo bounced over to Rabbit's house next. As usual, Rabbit was working in his garden.

"Hello, Roo," he said. "What's in the pot?"

"It's honey," Roo explained, "to give to my mama on Mother's Day."

Rabbit frowned. "No, no, no," he said. "Mothers don't like honey. If there's one thing a mother wants to get on Mother's Day, it's a big bunch of fresh carrots."

"They do?" Roo said doubtfully.

"Oh, yes," said Rabbit. He reached into his wheelbarrow and pulled out a bunch of freshly picked carrots.

"Thanks, Rabbit," said Roo. Then he hopped to Eeyore's house of sticks.

"What do you have there, Roo?" Eeyore asked.

"Some gifts for my mama for Mother's Day," said Roo.

"I suppose some mothers might like carrots," Eeyore said. "And maybe others might like honey. But in my opinion, you can't go wrong with prickly thistles."

"Prickly thistles?" asked Roo.

"Yes," replied Eeyore. "Here, take these. Then Kanga will be sure to have a happy Mother's Day. If that's what she wants."

"Well, thank you," said Roo, tucking the prickly thistles into his pocket.

The next morning, Roo bounded into the living room. "Happy Mother's Day, Mama!" he shouted.

"Why, thank you, dear," said Kanga.

"I thought and thought about what to give you," Roo explained. "Pooh said honey. Rabbit said carrots. And Eeyore said thistles. But I decided to give you this," he said, throwing his arms round his mummy in a kangaroo-sized hug.

Kanga smiled. "Thank you, Roo. You were right. That's the best Mother's Day gift of all."

A Game of Robin Hood

"Let's play Robin Hood!" Skippy shouted to his friends Tagalong, Toby and Sis.

"All right," agreed Tagalong. "I'll be Robin's best friend, Little John. Toby can be the mean old Sheriff of Nottingham!"

"Well, then, I will be Maid Marian," said Sis.

Robin Hood was loved by the people because he robbed from the rich and gave to the poor. Nowadays many people were needy, for they were taxed heavily by the Sheriff of Nottingham. Everyone knew that the Sheriff was in league with the evil Prince John, and that they used the tax money for their own gain. Prince John's brother, King Richard, was the true king of England. But King Richard was fighting in the Crusades far away. He couldn't protect his people, so someone else had to – and that someone was Robin Hood!

"Hands up, sirrah!" said Skippy gleefully. He and Tagalong pretended to raid Toby's carriage. "We shall lighten your wallet today and give it away to the worthy citizens you have been taxing so heavily."

"Drat! My evil plans have been foiled again!" snarled Toby, handing over his pretend money.

"One day I'm going to get you, Robin Hood!" Toby continued.

Skippy laughed. "You'll never find me, Sheriff!" he cried. "If you come into Sherwood Forest, we will give you such a whipping that you'll wish you'd never heard of Robin Hood!"

Sis giggled, then ran over to a table and climbed up on top of it. "Oh, Robin! Robin!" she cried. "Help me, my darling, my one true love! That mean old Prince John has locked me up in this high tower! He heard that we are in love, and he intends to prevent us from ever being together!"

Suddenly, the children froze. Someone had chuckled from behind the door of a nearby cottage. "Uh-oh," Skippy whispered. "We're toast. It's got to be the Sheriff of Nottingham!"

"He'll lock us up and throw away the key!" Toby said, his voice shaking.

Just then the 'Sheriff' stepped out from behind the door. It was Robin Hood!

"Keep up the good work, kids!" he said with a merry laugh. And then he bounded away into Sherwood Forest.

Dream Tales

One morning, Snow White got up early and prepared a special breakfast for the Dwarfs – fresh cinnamon porridge!

"Good morning!" Snow White greeted the Dwarfs. "Did everyone sleep well?"

"Bike a lady," Doc replied. "Er, I mean, like a baby. What about you, Princess?"

Snow White shook her head. "I had a bad dream," she said. "I dreamed my stepmother, the wicked Queen, was coming to get me."

"Oh, no!" Happy cried. "If she's coming, you'd better hide!"

"And quick!" Grumpy added. "That Queen is trouble, mark my words!"

The other Dwarfs nodded and looked nervous. Dopey even hid under the table.

Snow White laughed. "Why are you hiding?" she exclaimed. "Why, you should know that dreams aren't real!" She smiled at the Dwarfs. "What about all of you? Did you dream about anything last night?"

Happy laughed cheerfully. "I dreamed about the things that make me happy."

"Like what?" Snow White asked.

Happy paused for a moment. "Friends and work and sunny days… well, gosh, I guess all sorts of things," he replied. "Just about everything makes me smile."

Just then, a butterfly flew in the window and landed on Happy's nose. The dwarf smiled widely.

"What about you, Sneezy? Do you remember your dream?" asked Snow White.

"Aaaa-choo!" Sneezy sneezed. "I dreamed I kept sneezing flowers. And every time I sneezed more flowers, they made me sneeze even more," Sneezy said.

"Dopey?" Snow White said. "Did you dream about anything last night?"

Dopey shook his head, looking sheepish.

Grumpy rolled his eyes. "Of course he did," he snapped. "He dreams he's the wisest ruler ever to sit upon a throne."

"That sounds like a marvellous dream, Dopey!" Snow White said, clapping her hands.

"But what about your dream, Princess?" Bashful asked quietly. "Aren't you scared?"

"Not a bit," Snow White replied. "Remember, dreams are just make-believe. They disappear as soon as you wake up!"

"I think it's time to make this breakfast disappear," grumbled Grumpy.

And that's just what they did.

St. Patrick's Day Games!

One morning, Louie had an idea. "Hey," he said to his brothers, "are you two wearing green for St. Patrick's Day?"

"Of course," said Dewey.

"Me too," said Huey.

Louie gestured to the green shirt and hat he wore every day. "I bet we could really confuse Uncle Donald!"

On St. Patrick's Day, the three boys chuckled as they headed towards the kitchen. While Huey and Dewey hid in the hallway, Louie walked in and sat down next to Donald Duck, who was reading the newspaper at the breakfast table.

"Morning, Uncle Donald," said Louie.

"Morning, Louie," Donald replied. "Will you go get your brothers? Breakfast is ready."

"Okay," Louie replied, leaving the room.

Next, Dewey walked into the kitchen. "Morning, Uncle Donald," he said.

Donald looked up only briefly from his paper. "I thought I told you to go get your brothers, Louie," he said.

"No, you didn't," Dewey replied. "And I'm not Louie."

Donald looked up and scrutinised Dewey's face. "Oh," he said. "I'm sorry, Dewey. Would you go get your brothers?"

"Okay," Dewey replied.

A few minutes later, Huey walked into the kitchen and sat down at the table.

Donald glanced up from the newspaper. "Well, where are they?" he asked Huey impatiently.

"Where are who?" said Huey.

"Your brothers," Donald replied. "I asked you to go get them."

"No, you didn't," said Huey.

"Yes, I—" Donald looked up from the paper and stared hard at Huey. "Oh… Huey," he said, realising his mistake. "I thought you were… Hey!" Donald looked at Huey suspiciously. "Are you three trying to confuse me?"

Huey looked up at Donald with a blank stare. "Whatever do you mean, Uncle Donald?"

"It's St. Patrick's Day," said Louie, coming in from the hallway.

"Yeah," said Dewey, following Louie into the kitchen. "That's why we're all wearing green. Happy St. Patrick's Day, Uncle Donald!"

The Spooky Sleepover

It was a quiet morning at Monsters, Inc. and Sulley had arrived early to catch up on paperwork when he got a phone call from dispatch.

"Annual sleepover at Shannon Brown's house. Waxford is out sick. We need a replacement," Sulley told Mike down on the Laugh Floor.

"Piece of cake," Mike said.

Shannon Brown's door slid into his station and Mike walked through the wardrobe into the girl's room. It was empty. "Uh… hello?" Mike called. Just as Mike turned to leave, he heard the sound of laughter.

Suddenly, thunder cracked across the sky. Mike ran to the wardrobe door to return to the factory. He jiggled the doorknob, but it just opened into the wardrobe, not the Laugh Floor! Mike realised that lightning must have struck the door and broken it. He took a deep breath and headed into the hallway.

Meanwhile, back at Monsters, Inc., Sulley was working at his desk when the floor manager came running over.

"Sulley!" he shouted. "Mike hasn't returned from the sleepover. He's never been gone this long on a job!"

Sulley went to check on the door and found that it was broken. He immediately called someone to fix it.

Back at Shannon's, Mike heard laughter down the hall. When he found the right room and went in, it was quiet. Slowly, Mike entered the silent room. All of a sudden, a light went on.

Mike jumped and screamed. Shannon Brown and all her friends roared with laughter! They thought Mike looked funny sneaking into the room.

At that exact moment, the wardrobe door opened and Sulley burst into the room. Sulley was so surprised to find Mike screaming that all he could do was scream, too! Then he and Mike huddled in fright. Shannon and her friends laughed even harder.

"Looks as if our work here is done," Sulley said to Mike as they headed back into the wardrobe.

"I was never scared for a second," said Mike.

"Me neither, buddy," Sulley replied, his fingers crossed behind his back. "Me neither."

Happy Campers

It was a warm, sunny day on Ant Island – the perfect day for Princess Dot and her fellow Blueberries to go on a camp out! Flik volunteered to be their leader.

"This is going to be so much fun, Flik!" said Dot, marching behind him. "Pitching our tents! Making a campfire! Telling ghost stories all night long!"

"Well, we've got to get to our campsite first," Flik reminded her. "The perfect campsite for the perfect camp out!"

"Where's that?" asked Dot.

"I'm not exactly sure," said Flik. "But don't worry! I'll know the perfect spot when I see it."

So on they hiked, until they came to some soft moss beside a quiet stream.

"Is this it?" asked Daisy excitedly.

Flik shook his head. "Definitely not," he said. "Too out in the open."

"We're getting tired," Dot said.

"Chins up, Blueberries," said Flik. "We'll find the perfect campsite soon. I'll bet it's just across that stream."

Flik guided the Blueberries onto a broad leaf. Together they rowed across the water. But the other side of the stream was not quite perfect enough for Flik, either.

"No worries," Flik said. "See that hill over there? I'll betcha the perfect campsite is just beyond it."

The Blueberries followed him up the grassy hill and down the other side.

"We made it!" the Blueberries cheered.

"Not so fast," said Flik, frowning. "The ground is too damp here. We'll have to keep looking."

"But, Flik! We can't go any further," they complained.

"Nonsense!" said Flik, tightening his backpack. "You're Blueberries! C'mon!"

And so, with the Blueberries dragging their poor, tired feet, Flik hiked on. Then, just when the Blueberries thought they couldn't walk another inch, Flik suddenly froze in his tracks.

"The perfect campsite! We've found it! Let's pitch those tents, Blueberries, and get a fire started!"

But instead of cheers, Flik heard only silence. He turned around and saw that those poor Blueberries, still wearing their backpacks, were already fast asleep!

A Good Team

Mulan could hardly believe she was riding through the woods on her way to join the Emperor's army. But what else could she do? If she didn't take his place, her elderly father would be forced to fight against the Huns.

"It will be alright," she told her horse, Khan. "This is the right thing to do."

The horse snorted. For a second, Mulan thought he was answering her. Then he stopped short, almost sending Mulan tumbling.

"Hey," she said. "What are you doing?"

She kicked at his sides. Instead of moving forwards, the mighty warhorse backed up a few steps, his massive body shaking fearfully.

Mulan looked ahead. Just a few yards away, a deep, shadowy ditch crossed the trail.

"Is that what you're afraid of?" Mulan asked the horse. "Don't be silly. It's just a small ditch… step over it, you big chicken."

She kicked again. Still the horse refused to go. He just danced nervously in place.

"Come on!" Mulan shouted impatiently. "You're being ridiculous!"

She nudged him again and again, but Khan wouldn't budge. Mulan tried everything she could think of, but the horse wouldn't take even one step forwards.

Mulan didn't know what else to try. She collapsed onto Khan's neck, feeling hopeless. "Now what?" she said.

She didn't seem to have much choice. Sliding down from the horse's back, she walked towards the ditch. To her surprise, Khan followed her.

Mulan gasped. Could it be? Could the big, bold, strong warhorse really be trusting her to lead him over the scary ditch?

"Come on," she said, reaching for his bridle. The horse allowed her to lead him forwards. A few more steps and he was standing at the edge of the ditch.

"The last step is the big one," Mulan warned.

Holding the reins, she hopped over the ditch. For a moment, she was afraid he wouldn't follow. Then he jumped. Mulan was yanked forwards as Khan landed ten feet past the ditch.

"Good boy." Mulan patted the horse. "I think we might just make a good team after all."

The Dog Show

Every weekend, on the little island of Kauai, Stitch would wait patiently for Lilo by himself whilst she was at dance class. But one day, another pet was waiting outside.

"This is Cashmere," Myrtle explained as the girls left their dance class. "He's a purebred poodle." She scowled at Stitch, who was rolling around in spilt ice cream. "Breeding is so important with dogs."

Lilo felt embarrassed. "Stitch may not be like other dogs, but he's really smart."

"If he's so smart, prove it," Myrtle said as she handed Lilo a flyer for a dog show. "Cashmere and I are planning to win."

When Myrtle had left, Lilo looked longingly at the flyer.

"Myrtle… bully," Stitch said. "Let's show what Stitch made of!"

Lilo nodded and agreed.

The next weekend, Lilo, Stitch and Nani showed up at the dog show. The first round was for each dog to run and leap through hoops. But when it was Stitch's turn, he grabbed the rings and chomped them into pieces.

"No Stitch, you're supposed to jump through the rings!" Lilo said.

"Sorry," Stitch said, his ears drooped.

Soon new rings were up, and Cashmere jumped through effortlessly.

For the next round, the dogs had to run through three tunnels. But Stitch had other ideas. He smashed through the sides of each tunnel. When Stitch looked back and saw no one applauding, he knew he must've gone wrong. He watched sadly as Cashmere navigated the extra tunnels with ease.

The last challenge was to cross a balance beam. Cashmere walked across the beam perfectly. Stitch was far from perfect. He wobbled and fell, having to rely on his alien claws to get to the end. Lilo didn't want to stay for the medals. She knew who'd won. But she hugged Stitch all the same.

"It's okay, Stitch. I should've given better instructions," she said.

That night, Nani gave them some medals made from foil and stone. They said MOST CREATIVE.

"You beat those challenges in your own way," Nani explained.

Stitch hugged Nani and Lilo. He may not have won, but he had something better. A family that loved him no matter what.

A Bouncy Babysitter

Roo was excited. Tigger was babysitting him!

"Now, Tigger, I know you and Roo like to bounce," said Kanga. "But a good babysitter must know when to put the bouncer to bed."

"Don't worry, Kanga!" said Tigger.

For hours, Tigger and Roo had a fine old time bouncing around. Then Tigger looked at the clock and said, "Time to bounce into bed!"

Roo hopped right into his room. *That was easy*, Tigger thought. He followed Roo into his bedroom.

"Now I'll just tuck you in and… hey! I said bounce into bed. Not on it!" cried Tigger.

But Roo wouldn't stop. So Tigger gave up and started bouncing, too!

Then Tigger remembered what Kanga had said. "Wait a minute! I'm the babysitter," said Tigger. "I'm supposed to be tucking you in!"

"I don't want to be tucked in," said Roo.

"What if I read you a story?" asked Tigger.

"No," said Roo. "I'm not even sleepy. I could bounce all the way to Pooh's house!"

"But it's time for bed, not bouncing," said Tigger. "I'll get you some milk. That will make you sleepy."

But when Tigger came back to Roo's bedroom, Roo was gone!

"Uh-oh!" said Tigger. He rushed to Pooh's house.

"I'm sorry, Tigger," said Pooh, "but Roo isn't here."

Tigger returned to Kanga's house. Where could Roo be? Tigger passed Roo's room – and saw Roo in his bed!

"Where were you, Tigger?" asked Roo.

"Where was I?" said Tigger. "Where were you?"

Roo explained that when Tigger had gone to get the milk, Roo had decided he did want to hear a story. But his favourite book was under the bed.

"You were under the bed?" cried Tigger.

"I'm home!" called Kanga at the front door. Tigger sighed with relief.

"How did it go?" she asked Tigger.

"Kanga," said Tigger, "the wonderful thing about tiggers is bouncing – and from now on, I'm sticking with that. Babysitting just has too many ups and downs!"

Hot on the Trail

"Over here!" Simba said, sniffing the trail. "It's going this way!"

"Yup, this way," Nala said with a nod, sniffing a stick.

"I saw that stick first," Simba said. Nala was a good tracker, but Simba had learned from an expert – his mum. She was one of the best hunters in the pride.

"Hmm," Nala said with a sniff. "So what are we following, then, master tracker? Can you tell me that?"

Simba was silent. They had seen some footprints, but they weren't clear enough to read. They had also seen lots of crushed grass and broken sticks.

"Something that isn't very graceful," Simba said.

"Mmm-hmm." Nala nodded impatiently.

"A rhino!" Simba said confidently.

"A rhino?" Nala rolled onto her back, laughing. "Simba, you crack me up!"

"What?" Simba couldn't hide the hurt in his voice. It might be a rhino!

"The footprints aren't big enough," Nala said. "It's Rafiki, the baboon."

Now it was Simba's turn to laugh. "Rafiki likes the trees; he doesn't use trails like a hyena!"

The giggle died in Simba's throat, and he felt the fur on the back of his neck stand up. Hyenas were clumsy and left light tracks…

Nala didn't say anything, but her fur was standing up a little, too.

The two lions walked in silence. Ahead of them they heard noises – thrashing and grunting.

The young lions crept through the grass on their bellies as quietly as they could. The grunting and thrashing grew louder. Something about the smell and the sound was familiar, but Simba couldn't put his paw on it.

As they crept closer, two bodies came into view by the side of a termite mound. Simba pounced!

"Pumbaa! Timon!" he shouted, landing between his friends.

"Simba!" the warthog said, grinning. Termites dripped out of his muddy mouth. "Want some?"

Timon held a handful of wriggling insects towards Nala. "There are plenty to go around."

"Uh, no, thanks," Nala said as she came out of the grass, giggling. She shot a look at Simba. "I think I'll wait for the master tracker to hunt me down some lunch!"

Sillying the Blues Away

"Oh, me, oh, my!" the White Rabbit said as he rushed past Alice.

"Wait! Excuse me!" Alice called to him. But he was gone.

Alice sat down. "I'm never going to get out of here," she said worriedly.

"What's the matter?" a voice asked. "You seem blue."

Alice looked all around but she didn't see anyone. "Where are you?" she asked.

"Is that better?" the Cheshire Cat said as he suddenly appeared out of nowhere.

"Why, yes," Alice replied.

"Would you like some help?" the Cheshire Cat asked.

"You'll help me?" Alice cried.

"Absolutely!" the Cheshire Cat said with a grin. "But you have to do exactly as I say."

"Okay," Alice agreed.

"First," the Cheshire Cat told her, "you have to put on this winter coat."

"But it's spring," Alice protested.

"You promised to do as I say," the Cheshire Cat reminded her.

"Okay." Alice started putting it on.

"Backwards!" the Cheshire Cat ordered.

"But..." Alice began. The Cheshire Cat started to disappear. "Wait, don't go!" she pleaded. "Here, I'm putting it on."

Once the coat was back on, the Cheshire Cat reappeared. "Let's go for a walk," he said, grinning at Alice.

"But I'm feeling a little silly," Alice said.

"Don't worry," the Cheshire Cat told her. "No one's looking."

But the truth was, Alice could have sworn she heard the bread-and-butterflies laughing at her.

"Now, drink this cup of apple sauce," the Cheshire Cat said.

"Don't you mean apple juice?" Alice asked.

"No, I mean apple sauce," the Cheshire Cat said. "Drink it while walking round in a circle three times."

By the time Alice had started her second circle, she was beginning to have doubts. "I think you're playing a trick on me," she said. "You're having me do all these things to make me look silly."

"True," the Cheshire Cat agreed, fading away. "But it's awfully hard to feel blue when you look this silly!"

Alice thought for a moment and realised she had to agree. She was still lost, but now she didn't feel quite so sad about it!

In a Tangle

CRASH! Pinocchio was woken from a sound sleep by a noise downstairs. He jumped up and raced to Geppetto's workshop.

"Is anybody here?" Pinocchio called.

"Meow!" It was Geppetto's kitten, Figaro.

"I hear you, but I can't see you!" called Pinocchio.

Suddenly, the puppets above Geppetto's workbench began to move.

"Yikes!" cried Pinocchio, startled.

"Meow!" cried Figaro. He was tangled in the puppets' strings. The kitten tried to get free, but he only became more tangled.

Jiminy Cricket hopped down from the hearth. He rubbed his tired eyes. "What's going on?" he asked.

Pinocchio pointed to the little kitten and laughed.

"Pinocchio, maybe you should help poor Figaro instead of laughing at him," Jiminy said.

"Maybe I should leave him there," replied Pinocchio. "Then Geppetto can see how naughty he's been."

"That's not very nice," said Jiminy. "How would you feel if you were all tangled up?"

Pinocchio sighed. "I guess I wouldn't like it very much." He was about to free the kitten when, suddenly, he exclaimed, "Hey, Jiminy, look at that!"

Figaro's paws were wrapped around the strings in such a way that when his paws moved, the puppets danced!

"That's a neat trick," said Pinocchio. "Figaro can work the puppets!"

The kitten moved his paws some more, and all the puppets danced.

"I have an idea," said Jiminy Cricket. "Do you want to hear it?"

Pinocchio and Figaro both nodded.

The next morning when Geppetto awoke, he got a surprise.

"Look, Father!" Pinocchio said. "Figaro can make the puppets dance!"

Pinocchio winked at Figaro, and the cat leapt onto the puppet strings again.

"Amazing!" Geppetto cried, watching the show. "We can put on a puppet show for all the children of the town!"

Pinocchio was thrilled to see Geppetto so happy.

"But when did you discover Figaro's talent?" asked Geppetto.

"Last night," said Pinocchio, "when I found him in your workshop… uh, hanging around."

Night-Time of Fires

It was late at night, but Hiro Hamada was wide awake. He was in his lab. As Hiro leaned back in his chair to think, the chair tipped over. "Ouch!" Hiro cried.

Baymax, Hiro's personal health-care companion, stepped forwards. He scanned Hiro. "Your energy levels are low. You need rest. Perhaps a glass of milk would help."

Hiro shook his head. He didn't want to rest. He was trying to create a device that would scan the city for fires and put them out before anyone got hurt.

"If you finish the project, will it help you sleep?" Baymax asked.

"Yes," Hiro said. "But it doesn't work."

Hiro pressed some buttons on his computer. In a special testing chamber, a few pieces of paper inside a rubbish bin began to smoke. His device flew over to the papers. By the time it got there, the smoke had turned into a full-blown fire.

"See," Hiro said. "It's too slow." The device sprayed a green liquid at the bin. The fire sputtered out, but a horrible smell filled the air. The container was melting. "Plus, the spray is so strong, it ruins everything it touches," Hiro added.

Hiro picked up his device to examine it. Just then, the door to Hiro's lab flew open, and his friends came in. They wanted to help. But Hiro did not want help. He nicely showed his friends to the door.

Baymax scanned Hiro again. "Your stress level has increased," he said. "Perhaps now you would like that milk."

Hiro shook his head again. He had to get back to work. Outside his lab, Hiro's friends watched and took notes.

"Studies show that brainstorming with friends is useful when solving problems," Baymax said at last.

Hiro sighed and nodded. "You're right, Baymax. Let them in."

Baymax opened the door to the lab. Hiro's friends had all sorts of ideas. Gogo thought the device would move faster if it was shaped like a disk. Wasabi suggested adding lasers so the device could go straight to the source of the fire. And Honey Lemon knew just how to fix the chemical mixture. "Milk!" she cried.

At last the new device was ready to test. Hiro started a fire. The device flew over to it, sprayed its chemical and instantly put out the fire.

"We did it!" Hiro shouted. "Thanks, guys! Now how about some rest?"

Lady _and the_ TRAMP

Howling at the Moon

Lady had been having a really bad day. First, she'd had a run-in with two nasty cats. Then she'd been put in a horrible muzzle. But because of Tramp, everything had changed.

"It's amazing how a day can start off terribly but end wonderfully," Lady told Tramp as they trotted through the moonlit park. "Thank you for helping me escape that terrible muzzle – and for dinner at Tony's."

"Aw, shucks, don't mention it!" said Tramp. "Hey, you wanna have some real fun?"

"I don't know," Lady said cautiously. While she was very fond of Tramp, she also knew they were very different dogs. Tramp was used to life on the streets, so his idea of fun might be very different from hers.

"Don't worry," Tramp assured her. "This is something I think you'll enjoy."

"What is it?" asked Lady.

"Well, for starters, you have to look up," said Tramp.

Lady did. The sky was filled with stars and a big, bright moon.

"What am I looking for?" she asked.

"The moon, of course!" cried Tramp. "Haven't you ever howled at the moon?"

Lady laughed at Tramp's suggestion.

"What's so funny?" asked Tramp.

"I'm a practical dog," explained Lady. "I bark politely when the situation calls for it, but I don't see any point in howling at the moon."

"Why not?" asked Tramp.

"Well," said Lady, "what's the use of it?"

"You know, Lady," said Tramp, "a thing doesn't have to be useful to be fun."

Lady thought it over. "Okay," she said. "What do I do?"

"First, sit up real straight," said Tramp. "Then look up at the moon, take a deep breath and just let all the troubles of your day disappear in one gigantic howl!" He demonstrated: "Ow-ow-OWWWWWWW!"

Lady joined Tramp and howled as loudly as she could.

"You're right!" she cried. "It does feel good to howl at the moon!"

"Stick with me, kid," said Tramp. "I know what's what."

Lady suspected Tramp did know what was what, but there was an even better reason for her to stick with him. He'd become her best friend!

Disney
POCAHONTAS

A Little Mischief

One day, Pocahontas' father, the chief of the Powhatan, went to visit a nearby tribe. "I'll be back by sundown. I'm putting you in charge, Daughter," the chief said. "Make sure nothing goes wrong in the village."

Pocahontas was determined to make him proud. She spent the morning helping the villagers with any tasks that needed doing, and by the afternoon, the only thing left to do was to check on the fields. On her way, she was stopped by a little girl called Alawa. "A crow took my favourite necklace," she told Pocahontas sadly. "Could you help me get it back?"

The necklace was really high up in a tree. Suddenly, a woman ran over. "Pocahontas, an animal has broken into the corn! Look, this cob is half eaten!"

"Sorry, Alawa," said Pocahontas. "We have to figure out who is stealing our food. I'll help you get your necklace soon, I promise."

By the side of a wigwam was a trail of corn. Pocahontas and Flit followed the trail until it stopped in a small clearing. Pocahontas looked around and noticed a set of claw prints in the soft earth. She soon tracked down the visitor to a small den.

A raccoon suddenly darted out and ran up a very high tree! "Please come down," Pocahontas said to the raccoon. "We aren't angry that you stole our food." She held out the half-eaten cob of corn and slowly the raccoon crept down. He took the corn and started eating.

"I think you need a name. How about Meeko? It means 'little mischief'. Can I call you Meeko?" said Pocahontas. The raccoon nodded happily.

Pocahontas then had an idea. They walked together until they reached the tall tree where Alawa's necklace was. "Do you think you can get the necklace back for us, Meeko?" Meeko nodded… he'd be glad to help!

Meeko quickly ran up the tree and retrieved the necklace. They took it back to Alawa who was so happy! "Thank you!" she cried, giving Meeko a big hug.

As the sun set, Pocahontas' father returned. "How did you fare?" he asked his daughter. "I hope there wasn't any trouble."

"Nothing we couldn't handle," replied Pocahontas, smiling at her new friend.

Flower's Power

It was a warm summer afternoon in the forest, and a shy little skunk named Flower was playing a game of hide-and-seek. He had been looking for his friends for quite a while.

"Come out, come out, wherever you are!" Flower called. "I give up."

"Surprise!" shouted Thumper, bursting out of a thicket. "Here I am! Ugh!" Thumper wrinkled his nose. "What's that smell?"

Flower blushed bright pink. "Sorry," he said miserably. "I sprayed. It happens when I get scared."

"Whew!" Thumper waved his paw in front of his face. "You should warn us before you let out that kind of stink!"

"Well, you should warn me before you jump out like that," Flower said. "Anyway, it'll go away… in a day or two."

But a day or two was too long for his friends to wait. The smell was just too strong!

"Sorry," Bambi told Flower. "I, uh, think my mother's calling me."

"Me, uh, too," Faline gasped. "See you later, Flower… in a day or two."

And the next thing he knew, Flower was all alone.

Poor Flower. No matter what his parents said, being a skunk stunk!

And that's why Flower wouldn't have been very surprised if, two days later, his friends had still stayed away. But to his bashful pleasure, there, bright and early, were Bambi and Faline, with Thumper hopping close behind.

"Want to play?" Bambi asked Flower.

"Anything but hide-and-seek!" said Flower.

"How about tig?" said Thumper. "Ready or not, you're it!"

But before the game could begin, a soft crunch, crunch of leaves made the friends turn.

"Wha-wha-what's that?" Bambi said, staring straight into a hungry-looking red face.

"That's a fox!" said Thumper.

"A fox?" shrieked Flower. "Oh, no!" He spun around and lifted his tail and buried his head in fear.

The next thing the friends knew, the hungry fox was running away, whimpering and rubbing his nose.

"Sorry," Flower said with a sigh, blushing.

"Don't be!" said Bambi and Thumper.

And do you know what? Flower wasn't!

Sebastian's Big Day

It was Sebastian's big day. As composer for the court of King Triton, he had been working very hard on a new piece of music, and that evening he was going to conduct the royal orchestra as they played his song before the kingdom for the first time.

Just before the curtain went up, the musicians began to gather backstage. Music filled the air as the trumpet fish and the conch shell players tuned their instruments. Benny the octopus, the orchestra's drummer, was the last musician to arrive.

"Sebastian!" he exclaimed, rushing over to the conductor. "I… I can't play tonight!"

Sebastian stared at Benny in shock. "What do you mean? You have to play!"

"You don't understand," Benny replied. "I can't. I took a nap this afternoon and fell asleep on my tentacles, and now they're all tingly! I can't hold my drumsticks!"

"What am I going to do?" Sebastian exclaimed, looking around at the musicians. "My composition calls for eight drums. Benny has eight tentacles – one for each drum. Where will I find enough hands to take his place?"

Just then, Ariel and her six sisters swam backstage to wish Sebastian luck.

"Ariel!" Sebastian cried. "Am I glad to see you!" He explained his problem to Ariel and her sisters. "Could each of you help by playing a drum in the concert?" he asked.

"Of course!" the mermaid sisters replied.

Sebastian breathed a sigh of relief. "Okay, we have seven drummers. We just need one more!"

The musicians stared at Sebastian.

"Me?" he said. "But I am the composer and conductor! This is the day my true genius will finally be appreciated! I cannot be hidden in the drum section!"

But there was no other choice. When the curtain went up minutes later, there was Sebastian, drumming away. His day in the spotlight would have to come another time. As he played, he shrugged and smiled.

"Well, you know what they say," he whispered to Ariel.

"The show must go on?" Ariel guessed.

"No," Sebastian replied. "A true genius is never fully appreciated in his own lifetime."

Funny Faces

Hugo, Victor and Laverne were gargoyles at the great cathedral of Notre Dame. Most of the time they were stone, but they came to life in the presence of Quasimodo, the cathedral's bell ringer.

Although they were all good friends, Hugo and Victor were always finding something to bicker over, and today was no exception.

"That's ridiculous!" Hugo snapped.

"No, you're ridiculous!" Victor shot back.

Victor had suggested that Quasimodo tell his master that he wanted to take some time off. Hugo had pointed out that Frollo would sooner become a gypsy than give Quasimodo a holiday.

"Guys, there's no need to argue," said Quasimodo.

"Well, he started it," Hugo said.

"I started it?" Victor asked.

Suddenly, a loud whistle interrupted them. They turned around to find their friend Laverne.

"May I have your attention, please?" Laverne said. "I would like to propose a way for you to settle this dispute like gentlemen."

"What is it?" Quasi asked.

"A face-making contest," Laverne said. "Here are the rules: you two take turns making faces at each other, and the first to make the other laugh wins!"

"I'm going first!" declared Hugo, sticking his tongue out at Victor.

"Child's play," said Victor scornfully. He crossed his eyes at Hugo.

"Ha!" said Hugo. "Try resisting this!" Hugo crossed his eyes, flared his nostrils and stuck his lower jaw out, baring a crooked row of teeth in a hideous grimace.

Victor managed to keep a straight face at this, but Quasimodo couldn't help but laugh out loud.

"Shh!" Laverne said. "Frollo's coming!"

"Frollo?" Hugo and Victor grew pale and quickly turned back to stone.

Frollo marched in. "What's going on up here?" he asked Quasimodo.

"Nothing, sir," Quasi said, trying not to laugh.

"Hmm," said Frollo suspiciously. As he turned to go, Victor and Hugo began making funny faces at Frollo's back. When he was out of sight, all four friends collapsed in laughter.

"You know what?" Quasi said to them. "Being with you is more fun than a holiday any day!"

Lilo & Stitch

The Easter Egg Hunt

The Easter holidays were quickly approaching, which meant one thing: the annual Pelekai Easter egg hunt! Lilo couldn't wait to begin painting eggs.

"This is my favourite part," Lilo said. "I'm going to paint one pink with purple polka dots!"

"I'm going to draw mosquitoes on mine," said Pleakley, grabbing a crayon.

"Blue!" cried Stitch, dunking his egg violently in the cup of blue dye.

Later, while everyone tidied up, Nani went down to the beach to hide the twenty-five eggs. Whoever found the most would win a prize!

The sun shone on the brilliant-white sand as Lilo, Stitch, Jumba and Pleakley searched high and low for the eggs. As the afternoon sun began to sink, everyone gathered to count the eggs. Jumba had six eggs, and so did Pleakley. Stitch had six, too. Then they finished tallying up Lilo's eggs. "… four, five and six!"

But that added up to only twenty-four. That meant one more egg was still hidden on the beach! So they split up and went looking for the last egg.

Finally, Lilo spotted something under a hibiscus bush.

"Everybody, come quick!" she cried. "I think I've found the last egg!"

Nani, Jumba and Pleakley came running.

"Look," said Lilo, "it's a huge foil egg. The biggest chocolate egg I've ever seen!"

"It sure is," said Nani. "This is the prize, Lilo, and since you all found the same number of eggs, it looks like you all get to share it!"

"But where's Stitch?" said Lilo. "He should be here, too!"

Suddenly, the huge chocolate egg began to twitch. It rattled and shook, and then—

Stitch popped out of it, yelling,"Ta-daaa!" Bits of chocolate scattered all over the place.

"Wow!" cried Lilo. "Did you guys plan that?"

"No, Lilo," said Nani, completely confused and a little disturbed. "I have no idea how Stitch got in there without breaking the foil."

"My secret!" said Stitch cheerfully. He began munching on a piece of the chocolate egg.

Nani and Lilo smiled and shrugged, and then they all sat down and ate bits of chocolate egg while they watched the sun set over the water.

Dawson Takes the Case

"My little boy is missing!" a sobbing Mrs Mousington cried to Basil, the great mouse detective. "Can you help me find him?"

"I'm terribly sorry," said Basil. He was examining a brick wall very closely, looking for clues. "But I'm working on an important case for the queen. I don't have time."

"No, wait!" cried Dr Dawson, Basil's partner. "Madam, if the great mouse detective is too busy, then perhaps I can offer you my services."

"A splendid idea!" said Basil.

Before Dawson left with Mrs Mousington, Basil stopped him. "Don't forget this," he said, handing Dawson an umbrella.

"But it's a sunny day," said Dawson, puzzled. "Why would I ever need an umbrella?"

"A sunny day can turn dark quicker than you think," advised Basil.

Dawson shrugged and took the umbrella.

Mrs Mousington took him to a shop with a tall tree in front of it. Dawson searched the area and found a long, white hair. But a closer look told him this was not just any hair. It was a cat's whisker! Calling to a nearby bird, Dawson asked for a lift up.

On the shop's roof, Dawson saw a cat dozing. Beneath its paw was a tiny mouse's tail.

As the bird put Dawson down on the roof, he wondered how he was going to lift the cat's heavy paw. Then he remembered the umbrella! Using one end as a lever, he heaved. Beneath it he found Mrs Mousington's terrified son.

Dawson pulled the little boy free. With relief, he waved at the boy's mother, who was waiting on the street below. But before Dawson could signal another bird for a ride down, the cat woke up.

Dawson opened up his umbrella, scooped the little boy mouse in his arms and jumped. The umbrella filled with air and slowed their fall until they landed gently on the street.

Back at the great mouse detective's house, Basil was delighted to hear how Dawson had saved the little boy.

"It was easy," Dawson told Basil. "Thanks to your umbrella, I'd call it an open-and-shut case!"

DUMBO

Ears a Job for You!

It had been a hard day for little Dumbo. It was bad enough that everyone made fun of his ears. But now they had put his mother in a cage!

What made things even worse was that Dumbo didn't have anything to do. It seemed that he was the only creature in the circus who didn't have a purpose.

Dumbo heaved a sigh and went for a walk through the circus tents. Soon he found himself among the refreshment stands. Everyone there had a job, too. Some were squeezing lemons to make lemonade. Others were popping corn or roasting peanuts. Wonderful smells filled the air.

Finally, Dumbo came to a little candyfloss stall. Dumbo wanted a taste, but there were so many customers he couldn't get close enough.

Suddenly, Dumbo heard a loud buzzing. Then all the customers waved their hands over their heads and ran away from the stall. The smell of sugar had attracted a swarm of nasty flies!

Dumbo reached out his trunk to smell the delicious candyfloss.

"Not you, Dumbo!" the candyfloss seller cried. "It's bad enough chasing away flies. Do I have to chase away elephants, too?"

Poor Dumbo was startled. With a snort, he sucked candyfloss right up his nose.

Aaaachoo! When he sneezed, Dumbo's ears flapped and something amazing happened.

"Remarkable!" the candyfloss seller cried. "All the flies are gone. They think your ears are giant fly swatters!" The candyfloss seller patted Dumbo's head. "How would you like a job?"

Dumbo nodded enthusiastically and started waving his ears. Soon the candyfloss stall was the most popular refreshment stand in the circus – and had the fewest flies. But best of all, Dumbo now had something to do to take his mind off his troubles. He was still sad, but things didn't seem quite so bad. And who knew? Perhaps soon he'd have his mother back.

"I wonder what other amazing things those big ears can do," said the candyfloss seller, giving Dumbo a friendly smile. "I'll bet they carry you far."

Castle Cleaning

It was a particularly warm and sunny April morning, and Belle and Chip the teacup were gazing out of a castle window at the blue sky and the budding trees and plants.

"Well, Chip," Belle said, "it is spring at last. And you know what that means, don't you?"

Chip hopped up and down in excitement. "It means we get to play outside?" he asked.

Belle laughed. "Well, yes, that too," she replied. "But first it's time to do some spring cleaning."

Belle got together a few cleaning supplies. "I think I'll start in the dining room," she said. She pulled the silverware out of the silver cabinet and began polishing a fork.

"Ooh!" exclaimed the enchanted fork. "Careful! Ouch! Not so hard round the tines!"

"Oh dear!" said Belle. "I'm sorry." She gently polished the rest of the utensils.

Next, Belle gathered all the plates and bowls. But when she dipped the first enchanted plate into the soapy water in the sink, it cried out, "Ahh! Too cold! Too cold! Stop!"

Belle gasped, apologised and hurried to add more warm water to the sink.

After finishing the plates and bowls, Belle went to the library to take a break from her cleaning. Chip hopped in behind her. "Oh, Chip," Belle said wearily, "spring cleaning in this castle is a challenge. I'm not used to cleaning enchanted objects!"

Chip giggled. "And I guess we're not used to it either. We always just clean ourselves!"

"Clean yourselves?" said Belle.

That gave her a great idea. If the enchanted objects could clean themselves, they could clean other objects, too!

Belle called the enchanted objects together. "I wonder if I could ask for your help with a little project," Belle began.

Soon Belle had a small army of enchanted objects cleaning everything else in the castle. In a few short hours, the entire castle had been cleaned, and Belle and Chip were relaxing in the library.

"Well," Belle said as she sank into a comfortable chair, "you know what they say: many hands make light work. And a little enchantment never hurt either!"

Bagheera Bears Up

Mowgli danced around the jungle, humming happily to himself.

"What are you doing, Mowgli?" Bagheera asked from his perch in a nearby tree.

"Practising being a bear," Mowgli told him. "You should try it."

"Well, I'm a panther and I happen to like being one," Bagheera replied. "Why on earth would I want to be a bear?"

"Are you kidding?" Mowgli exclaimed. "Bears have the best life! They hang out all day long and they eat ants!"

"Eat ants?" Bagheera asked. "And that's a good thing?"

"Sure!" Mowgli said. "Well, truthfully, they tickle your throat at first. But you get used to it soon enough."

"Have you?" Bagheera asked.

"Not yet," Mowgli confessed. "But I will!"

Mowgli thought for a moment. "And if you were a bear, you would eat fruit and drink coconut juice and you would relax, just like us!"

"If you ask me," Bagheera said, "I don't see anything so bad about being a panther. In fact, I like it very much."

"I think you're scared," Mowgli said.

"Absolutely not!" Bagheera protested.

"What on earth would I have to be scared of?" He gracefully jumped out of the tree and onto the ground.

"Exactly," Mowgli said. "So why not try it?"

"You've got to be kidding me!" Bagheera said.

"You know what your problem is?" said Mowgli.

"I'm afraid to ask," Bagheera replied.

"You're like a beehive," Mowgli told him. "You work too hard. Come on, dance with me!" he cried, grabbing Bagheera's paw and prancing around. After a bit, Bagheera began to dance, too.

"Look at that!" said Baloo, joining his friends.

"You know what?" Bagheera admitted. "This isn't so bad after all."

"Now you're getting it!" Mowgli exclaimed. "Now you see why being a bear is so great!" The Man-cub stopped dancing and threw himself onto a soft patch of moss. "It's not so bad, is it?"

"Actually," Bagheera said, scratching his back against a rock, "it's sort of fun!"

And with that, he and Baloo danced away.

Rise and Shine

"All right, Dwarfs!" Doc called one morning. "Is everyone ready to leave for work? Let's see. We've got Happy, Dopey, Sneezy, Bashful, Grumpy, and—" Doc looked around. "Sleepy?" he called. No answer. Sleepy was nowhere to be seen.

"Oh no, not again," Doc complained, leading the other Dwarfs up the stairs to their bedroom. There, just as Doc expected, they found Sleepy, dozing peacefully in his bed.

"Oh, this is ridiculous!" exclaimed Grumpy. "We go through this every single morning, dragging Sleepy out of bed, and I'm tired of it."

"I have an idea!" said Doc. "We'll have to take the day off from the diamond mine and stay here today to work on my plan, but I think it will solve our problem – once and for all!"

The Dwarfs gathered in a huddle around Doc as he outlined the details. Then they got their tools and set to work. Soon the bedroom was filled with the sounds of hammering, sawing and metalworking. All of the activity centred on Sleepy's bed. But despite the loud racket, Sleepy slept on...

He slept all morning. He slept all afternoon. He slept all evening. He slept through the night.

Then, bright and early the next morning, an alarm clock perched on Sleepy's bedside table sprang to life. Its bell jangled noisily, shaking the clock.

The clock, which had a rope tied round its handle, bounced across the top of the table until it fell off the edge. The falling clock tugged on the rope, yanking a broom at the other end. When the broom moved, the large weight it was propping up dropped to the floor, activating a pulley that pulled up sharply on Sleepy's headboard. The head of Sleepy's bed lifted off the floor, and Sleepy slid down, down, down... right into a wooden tub filled with cold water. Wide awake, Sleepy sat in the tub, blinking and wondering what had just happened.

The other Dwarfs crowded around the bedroom window and peered down at him, grinning cheerfully.

"Good morning, Sleepy!" cried Doc. "Do you like your new alarm clock?"

Disney Cinderella

Dear Sisters

"I had the strangest dream," Cinderella told her mouse friends one morning. "My fairy godmother sprinkled happy dust over Anastasia and Drizella, and they were so nice to me!"

"But that was only a dream," Jaq warned her.

"I know," Cinderella told him, "but it was so nice that I think I'll try to pretend that it really happened. Whenever they are horrid to me, I'll pretend they actually said something sweet and kind."

When Cinderella got downstairs, Drizella threw a pile of clothes at her. "Wash my dresses," she demanded.

"And polish my shoes," said Anastasia, opening her wardrobe door.

"Right away, sisters!" Cinderella sang out, sweetly. "Thank you!"

All day long, Drizella and Anastasia barked orders at Cinderella. But no matter what they asked her to do, Cinderella always sang back, "Right away, sisters!" or "You're too kind!"

Finally, Anastasia pulled Drizella aside. "It makes no sense. No matter what we tell Cinderella to do, she stays happy," Anastasia said.

"Do you think she's gone mad?" Drizella asked.

Anastasia looked worried. "She could be! Who knows just what she's capable of!"

Just then, Cinderella walked in. She stopped, surprised to see her stepsisters looking at her as if she were crazy.

"Why, my dear sisters, whatever can be the matter? I do hope you're not ill," she said.

"D-d-d-dear sisters?" Anastasia stuttered. "You called us your dear sisters?" She and Drizella edged towards the door.

"Of course," said Cinderella. "I adore you both. I'm the luckiest girl in the world to have such kind, caring siblings."

That did it. Convinced that Cinderella had lost her mind, the two stepsisters turned and ran. Cinderella listened as her sisters' doors slammed shut. Then she smiled at Gus and Jaq, who had been watching the whole time.

"They may not actually be caring or good-natured," Cinderella said to the mice, "but they'll be too frightened to come out of their rooms for at least a few hours. Who's up for a game of hide-and-seek while we've got the run of the house?"

Smitten

Robin Hood straightened his hat and smoothed his whiskers. "How do I look, Little John?" he asked.

"You look like you always do," John replied with a wave of his hand. "Like a regular Casanova."

Robin grinned. "Let's hope Maid Marian agrees with you." He put a hand over his heart. "I just hope she still remembers me."

Robin Hood was nervous. Maid Marian was the cleverest and most beautiful maiden in the land. But she had been living in London for the past few years.

What if she didn't remember her childhood sweetheart?

"Get going," Little John said.

Robin nodded and set off through the forest. Soon he was outside the castle gate. He could hear voices – female voices – laughing and talking. Maybe one of them was Marian's!

Robin's heart pounded in his chest. He had to see! He looked around and spotted a large tree with branches that reached inside the castle grounds. Perfect!

Robin leapt gracefully up to the first branch, grabbed hold and began to climb. When he was nice and high, he worked his way out onto another branch. Now he was inside the castle grounds. Robin moved a

branch and leant forwards to see who was talking.

It was Marian! She was playing badminton with Lady Kluck. And she was a good shot!

"Nice one, Maid Marian," Lady Kluck said as Marian won a point.

Robin gazed down at the sight below. Maid Marian was so lovely, and so talented!

"Oops!" Marian said as the shuttlecock sailed off the court completely.

Robin saw it fly towards his hiding place. It landed in the tree just above him! He got to his feet and reached up to retrieve it for Marian. But he lost his balance and fell just as the shuttlecock came loose. The two landed on the ground at the same time.

"Oof!" Robin hadn't meant to make an entrance like that!

"What was that?" Lady Kluck asked as Robin scrambled away, leaping over the fence.

"I do believe it was an outlaw," Maid Marian said with a smile.

Dory's Surprise Party

Dory's birthday was coming up, and Nemo wanted to throw a surprise birthday party for her.

"What kind of food should we have?" Nemo asked his friends.

"Kelp cake and algae ice cream," Sheldon replied.

"How about music?" Nemo asked.

"We could be the band," said Pearl.

"Yeah, I play the clamshell drums," said Sheldon.

"Great!" cried Nemo. "Let's meet here tomorrow after school to practise."

The next day, Nemo and his friends were carrying their musical instruments when they bumped into Dory.

"Hi, Mimo! Hi, kids!" Dory exclaimed. She had trouble remembering Nemo's name. "What are you up to?"

"Music class homework," Tad piped up.

"I didn't know you played instruments," said Dory. "Well, have fun!"

The friends looked at one another. "Phew, that was close!" said Nemo.

The day of the party arrived. Nemo and his friends got up early and started decorating. Then Nemo suggested they practise singing *Happy Birthday*. Just as they finished the line "Happy birthday, dear Dory," Dory appeared!

"How did you know it was my birthday?" she exclaimed.

"You told me," said Nemo.

"Really, Pluto?" asked Dory.

"Now the surprise is ruined," said Nemo.

"What surprise?" said Dory.

It sure was helpful that Dory's memory wasn't very good! "Another close call," said Nemo to his friends.

A few hours later, the guests arrived. They all hid and waited. When Dory and Nemo swam in, everyone shouted, "Surprise!"

"Look, Pluto, it's a party for you!" Dory cried.

"No, Dory, it's for you," Nemo said. "It's your birthday."

"It is? Cool, a party for me!"

Later, she swam over to Marlin and Nemo. "I sure am glad your dad and I found you, Nemo. This is the best birthday I've ever had."

"Hey, Dory!" said Nemo. "You remembered my name."

"What's that, Flipper?" asked Dory.

"Oh, nothing," Nemo said with a sigh. "Happy birthday!"

Piglet's Pink Eggs

Winnie the Pooh had dropped in to visit Piglet, who was busy dyeing Easter eggs. "Easter is coming up, you know," Piglet explained.

On Piglet's kitchen table were six little cups. Pooh peered inside them. Each one held a different coloured dye. Then Pooh noticed a basket filled with some eggs Piglet had already dyed. Every one of them was pink.

"Would you like to dye the last egg, Pooh?" Piglet asked.

"Oh, yes," Pooh replied. "I would like that very much."

Piglet showed him how to place his egg in the wire dipper and how to use the dipper to dip the egg into the cups of dye.

"What colour should I dye my egg?" Pooh asked.

Piglet smiled. "That's the fun of it, Pooh," he said. "You can choose any colour you want!"

Pooh dipped his egg into the cup filled with yellow dye. He let it sit in the dye for a few minutes, then lifted it out again.

"It worked!" cried Pooh. "Piglet, look! What do you think of my yellow egg?"

"Oh Pooh, it's great," Piglet said. "It's b-bright… a-and it's sunny… and, well, it's very, very yellow, don't you think?"

Piglet was quiet for a moment. Then he cleared his throat.

"D-do you think… I don't know for sure, mind you. But do you think it could maybe use a little bit of, say, pink?" Piglet said.

"I think you're right," Pooh said. So he dipped his egg into the cup filled with pink dye. He let it sit there for just a few seconds before lifting it out. The little bit of pink dye on top of the yellow dye made the egg look pinkish-yellow.

"Hmm," said Piglet. "That's very pretty. But – if you don't mind my saying so, Pooh – I think it could use just a little more pink."

"Okay," said Pooh. So he dipped the egg back into the pink dye. This time he let it sit for five whole minutes before lifting it out. More pink dye on top of the yellow-and-pink colour made the egg look as pink as pink could be.

"Well, what do you think?" asked Pooh.

"Perfect!" Piglet exclaimed.

They let Pooh's egg dry. Then Piglet put it in the basket with all the other pink eggs.

"Well, what do you know?" said Piglet. "It fits in so nicely!"

Al's Sky-High Adventure

Al Oft, the Lightyear blimp, was hovering above the big stadium when he witnessed an amazing sight: superstar rookie Lightning McQueen was pushing a broken-down racing car – The King himself! – across the finish line.

Everyone at the racetrack knew who Al was. The fans always cheered when he flew overhead. But he was lonely up in the sky all by himself. Al couldn't help admiring Lightning's pit crew. It was filled with the rookie's close friends. They had come all the way from Radiator Springs to support Lightning at his big race.

When the season ended, Al decided to travel across the countryside. One day, Al saw a town below him that looked like the place Lightning had described. He flew low and spotted Lightning!

"Hey, Lightning!" shouted a rusty old truck. "Lookee there! It's that Lightyear blimp from your big race!"

"Al! How are you doing, buddy? Good to see you. Welcome to Radiator Springs!" the racing car called up.

"My name's Mater!" said the rusty old truck. "Wanna help us round up a stray tractor that busted loose, Mr Blimp?"

"Yeah," said Lightning. "We can't see

where the lost tractor went. But I'll bet you can from up there!"

Sure enough, from high in the sky, Al soon found the lost tractor. He lit up his sign to show Lightning that he had found it.

"Hey, that's great, Al, but we can't get over those big rocks!" Lightning shouted. "Can you see a way for us to get past them?"

Al looked down and all around. He soon found a path the two cars could take to reach the lost tractor. Within minutes, Mater and Lightning were guiding the tractor home.

"Now, this calls for a celebration, Al!" Lightning shouted. "We're having one of our neon cruises tonight. Why don't you join us?"

As the cars in Radiator Springs cruised down the road, Al hovered above them. "That's my friend Al Oft, the Lightyear blimp," Lightning said. "Just look at him. He's got the best neon you've ever seen."

Al smiled. He was having the most fun he'd ever had. And with all his new friends, he knew he'd never be lonely again.

A Major Mess

High in the bell tower of Notre Dame cathedral, the gargoyles Victor, Hugo and Laverne were playing hide-and-seek.

"Ready or not, here I come!" called Victor. "And no one had better be hiding in Quasimodo's underwear drawer!"

And with that, he leapt over a pile of rumpled clothes and began searching among stacks of books and games and other scattered objects.

Quasi had asked them to please look after his things – particularly his carvings and precious bells – while he was away. "And of course," Quasi had told them, "feel free to make yourselves at home." And, boy, had they ever!

They had tried on his clothes and left them scattered all over the floor. They had leafed through his books and played all his games. They had even used his pillows for pillow fights!

So it was with some shock and horror that Victor suddenly stopped their game and shrieked, "Do you know what day it is?"

"Excuse me?" said Hugo, peeking out from behind a pillar.

"It's Friday!" said Victor. "The day that Quasi returns home!"

"Oh!" Hugo gulped, gazing at the mess. "He's not going to be happy with us, is he?"

"Oh, but he is," said Victor. "We're going to clean all this up. If we don't, he'll never trust us to be home alone again."

"Maybe he shouldn't," muttered Hugo.

"Where is Laverne? Laverne!" Victor called. "Come out, come out, wherever you are! We have work to do."

And work they did. They folded the clothes. They made the bed. They put the books back on the shelf. They washed the dishes and scrubbed the floor. They even polished every one of Quasi's bells.

"You missed a spot on Big Marie!" Victor called to Hugo, just as Quasimodo arrived.

"Guys! I'm home!" he shouted.

"Quasi! We missed you. How was your holiday?" the gargoyles asked.

"Great!" said Quasimodo, giving each of the gargoyles a hug. "You should try it sometime."

The gargoyles agreed. After all the work they'd just done, a holiday was exactly what they needed!

Disney·PIXAR

MONSTERS, INC.

Something Different

Sulley groaned and shifted in his reclining chair. "Ate too much again," he said.

"Oh, me too," Mike moaned, reclining beside him in front of the fire. "I feel like all we do is sit around and eat."

"And eat and sit around," Sulley agreed. "Ain't it great?"

"Great if you like the same thing all the time," Mike said glumly. Then his tone changed. "What we need," he decided, "is to get away. We need to go somewhere, do something different. What do you think, buddy?"

"Sit down. Have another chocolate." Sulley waved a box of chocolates at Mike.

But Mike was insistent. "Somewhere with snow!" Mike pounded his fist in his palm. "That's it!"

* * *

"I don't know how you talked me into this," Sulley said a short time later. He and Mike stood at the top of a steep hill with snowboards strapped to their feet. "Can't I use a sledge instead?"

"Come on," Mike said. "Sledges are for old monsters. Are you old? No! So don't worry. You'll be great!"

Mike took off down the hill. He did turns,

he caught air, he went fast and in a spray of snow, he came to a halt. "Your turn," he called up to Sulley.

"Why do I know I will live to regret this?" Sulley asked under his breath, looking down the hill. "Actually, how do I even know I'll live?"

He slid slowly across the top of the mountain. He was moving. This wasn't so bad! But when he tried to turn to go down the hill, things got tricky. His board had a mind of its own... and it had decided to go back to the lodge!

* * *

Sulley groaned and shifted in his chair. He propped his sprained ankle up on a pillow and rubbed his stomach. "Ate too much again," he said. He sighed and rubbed his belly.

"Me too," Mike groaned from his reclining chair beside him. In front of them a glowing fire hissed and popped. "All we do is sit around and eat." He sighed happily.

Sulley smiled sleepily. "Ain't it great?"

"Sure is." Mike sipped his hot chocolate. "I told you we needed to get away and do something different!"

Such a Shame

Mulan nudged Khan into a gallop and kept her eyes straight ahead. She was on her way to town to go to the market for her family. It was a regular trip for her, but the people working on the sides of the road did not seem to think so.

Without even looking at them, Mulan knew that she was causing whispers. But they weren't just talking about her. They were talking about the man riding with her – Captain Li Shang.

Shang swung down from his horse and offered to go inside to buy the rice. Mulan was about to object – she didn't need Shang's help with the shopping. The only reason she'd brought him along was because he wanted to see more of her town. But Shang was already inside the tiny shop.

Mulan sighed. She held the captain in high esteem. She liked him – she really did. But she always found herself disagreeing with him. Even when she didn't need to.

"Shame!" Across the street, an older woman pointed at Mulan, startling her out of her thoughts. "Shame!" the woman said again. "Don't think I have forgotten you."

Mulan blushed, recognising the woman. It was the Matchmaker! Mulan looked at the ground as her cheeks grew even hotter, but they were not as hot as they had been on the day that she first met the Matchmaker – the day she accidentally set the woman on fire!

The Matchmaker continued, pointing and screeching at Mulan as she waddled across the street. "You!" she scolded. "Just because China thinks you are a hero does not mean you can escape your fate. I predict you will bring shame to your family. I feel it."

Mulan did not know what to say to the old woman.

"There is not a matchmaker in the world who could ever find a match for you!" the woman screeched.

"Then it is a good thing she will never need a matchmaker," Shang said. As he walked past the Matchmaker, he accidentally stepped in a puddle, splashing her from head to toe!

The Matchmaker was speechless, her face twisted into a scowl. Mulan could not think of a thing to say, either. But instead of wearing a scowl, her face was set in a wide smile. For once she agreed with Shang!

Escape from the Pixie Dusters

It was Ian Lightfoot's birthday, and as a gift he had received a real wizard's staff, and a Phoenix Gem with a Visitation Spell that would allow his deceased father to come back for one day. Together with his brother Barley, Ian attempted the spell, but it went wrong – only dad's legs appeared and the Phoenix Gem exploded! The only way for the brothers to re-try the spell in time was to find another Phoenix Gem. So, Ian, Barley and Dad set off on a quest!

However, before long, Guinevere, Barley's beloved van, ran out of petrol and spluttered to a stop. To make matters worse, Barley's petrol can was almost empty and there was no petrol station in sight.

Barley suggested the Growth Spell might help. The can would grow bigger and so would the small amount of petrol inside! Casting the spell required intense focus. Ian held up his wizard's staff and recited, "Magnora Gantuan!" The can started to grow! But after Ian became distracted by Barley and the magic, the spell backfired. Now Barley was tiny!

After eventually finding a petrol station, Ian began filling up the petrol can. Just as he finished, he heard Dewdrop – the leader of a motorcycle club of tough-talking sprites called the Pixie Dusters – arguing with Barley. Ian apologised to the sprites and pulled his tiny brother away. Then, Dad accidentally bumped into the Pixie Dusters' motorcycles. One by one, the bikes fell over!

The sprites were furious! Ian, Barley and Dad ran away from Dewdrop and his motorcycle club as fast as they could.

Back in Guinevere, the boys faced a new problem: Barley was too small to drive! Ian had no choice but to get behind the wheel himself if they were to escape the sprites and reach the expressway. However, Ian was terrified about joining the moving traffic.

With his brother's help, Ian overcame his fear and drove Guinevere onto the expressway. But the Pixie Dusters caught up with them! They were getting closer when Ian swerved across several lanes of traffic towards their exit.

They had soon left the expressway, escaped the sprites and were on the way to the next phase of their quest!

Look Sharp, Jiminy

"Gosh." Jiminy Cricket scratched his head between his antennae and yawned a big yawn. Climbing into his tiny matchbox bed, he gazed again at the wooden boy, who was fast asleep.

Jiminy still could not believe his eyes – or his luck. It had been a miraculous night. Not every cricket got to witness a wish granted by the Blue Fairy and see a puppet come to life. And not every cricket was chosen to be somebody's conscience!

Jiminy ran his hands down the new jacket hanging by his bed. He picked up the hat and twirled it. "My, my," he said, shaking his head.

Then he couldn't resist any longer. He put on his new shirt, coat, hat and shoes, and he hopped over to Cleo's fishbowl to see his reflection.

Jiminy whistled low. "Don't you look smart!" he told his reflection. "Smart enough to help that wooden boy. Except for that smudge." Jiminy leant down to inspect a dull spot on his shoe. He breathed on it and rubbed it with his sleeve until it was shining like new.

Suddenly, Geppetto snored loudly. Jiminy jumped and looked up. Outside the sky was starting to lighten.

"Would you look at that?" Jiminy knew he had to get to bed. A good conscience needed to be alert! He hurried out of his new clothes, hung them up carefully and tucked himself back into bed.

"Big day tomorrow." He yawned. "Very big day. Yes, indeed!" A moment later the little cricket was chirping in his sleep.

Jiminy woke to the sound of hundreds of cuckoo clocks. He sat up and rubbed his eyes. He barely remembered where he was. Then the events of the evening before flooded back. Why, he had work to do!

"Get up, Pinoke!" Jiminy called towards the big bed. But Pinocchio was already gone. The bed was made, and Geppetto and Figaro were gone, too! Cleo swished nervously in her bowl and pointed towards the door.

"I must have overslept!" Jiminy said, quickly pulling on his new clothes. "I can't let Pinoke start school without me. You don't have to be a conscience to know that's wrong!"

And, as quick as a flash, Jiminy hopped out the door.

A Tight Squeeze

It was early one morning and Andy had just left for school. The toys were ready to have some fun, so Woody told them all about a game they could play. "It's called Sardines," he explained. "It's like hide-and-seek, except when you find the hider, you hide with them and wait for someone else to find you both. The next toy to find you hides with you, too, and so on, and so on. Get it?"

"So, by the end of the game, we are all hiding together in one spot?" Jessie the cowgirl asked.

Woody nodded. "Right," he said, "except for the last toy, who is still looking for the hiders. In the next game, that toy is the one who hides!"

The toys decided that Hamm the piggy bank would be the one to hide. Woody told the other toys to close their eyes and count to twenty-five. Meanwhile, Hamm hurried off to find a good hiding place. With seconds to spare, he spotted one of Andy's old lunch boxes, hopped inside and closed the lid.

The first toy to open the lunch box lid was Woody. His eyes lit up when he saw Hamm inside. Making sure no one was watching him, he hopped inside and shut the lid. Soon the lid opened again. It was Jessie. She wedged herself between Hamm and Woody and shut the lid again.

Buzz opened the lunch box next and hopped inside. But he couldn't get the lid to close, no matter how hard he tried.

By the time Rex found the hiders, the lunch box was completely full. Soon the rest of the toys were hurrying towards the overstuffed lunch box.

"Oh, well," said Woody with a laugh. "They've found us. I guess this game is over. Everybody out!" One by one, the toys tumbled out of the lunch box and gathered around Hamm.

"Gosh, Hamm, couldn't you have picked a bigger hiding place?" Rex asked.

"Well, yeah," Hamm replied, "but isn't the point of the game to get squished? Like sardines in a can?"

The toys thought it over. They realised he was right. From then on, every time the toys played Sardines, the hider made sure to pick a small hiding place – just to keep things interesting!

Oliver's Sleepover

Oliver couldn't wait. At last, Jenny's limo pulled up to the docks. Even before the chauffeur could open the door, Oliver leapt out the window and began racing towards the barge. Then, remembering Jenny, he stopped, turned round and waved his paw in her direction.

"Goodbye, Oliver!" she called. "Have a fun sleepover!"

Don't worry, thought Oliver. *I will!*

This was the first time, you see, that Oliver had been back to the barge since he'd gone to live in Jenny's mansion. And though he loved Jenny dearly, boy, did he miss his friends!

"Tito! Einstein! Francis! Rita!" Oliver called as he ran in to find his four-footed friends waiting for him.

"Hey! What about me?" barked a voice from the back of the barge.

"Dodger!" yelled Oliver. He leapt up on the shaggy dog and gave him a friendly face rub. "It's so good to see you!"

"So how's life in the mansion?" Dodger asked.

"I can't complain," said Oliver.

He told his friends about his latest cruise on Jenny's yacht. "All those fish!" he said dreamily. Then he told them about her house in the country. "The best part is just lying out in the sun! You've got to come with us some day!"

Just then, Fagin walked in with a great big tray. "Oliver, my good friend! Welcome back! I do hope you're hungry!"

Oliver's eyes grew wide as he took in the piles of hot dogs, chicken fingers and fish sticks (his favourite!) on Fagin's tray. Oliver and the dogs dug in and ate… and ate… until they could not eat another bite. Then it was time for games!

Fagin dealt out some playing cards.

"I'm gonna stay up all night!" Oliver cried.

"Whatever you say, little buddy," Dodger said. "It's your night."

So they played a little Go Fish, then some Duck, Duck, Goose. Then Fagin told them some of Oliver's favourite spooky stories. When he was done, Dodger turned to Oliver.

"So, what's next, little buddy?" he asked.

But Oliver didn't answer. He was fast asleep!

The Chase

Whoopee!" Tod cried as he tumbled head over tail towards the water. He hit the surface with a splash. A second later, his friend Copper landed right next to him.

"It sure is a beautiful day," Copper said.

"Yeah, it sure is," Tod agreed.

Suddenly the friends heard a booming voice.

"Copper!" the voice rumbled. It was Amos Slade, Copper's master. Amos was usually grumpy, but right now he sounded angry. "Where are you, mutt?" he shouted.

Tod silently crawled into a hole between two big boulders by the water. He could tell that Amos had his other dog, Chief, with him. Both the man and the dog wanted to catch Tod.

Copper crept up beside his friend. "I'd better go," he said. "Amos sounds awfully mad."

"Why don't you sneak back so you're there when he gets back?" Tod suggested. "He can't be mad if you're already home when he finds you."

Copper scratched behind his ear. "But he's right in my path, and Chief is with him. Chief will hear me or smell me for sure."

Tod grinned. "You just leave that to me."

He winked at his friend and dashed up the hill, right past Amos and Chief.

"There's that terrible fox!" Amos cried as Chief took off after Tod, barking like mad. Amos gave chase, running as fast as he could on his long, skinny legs.

Tod leapt over branches and darted around trees. More than once, Chief got close, his hot breath on Tod's tail. Finally the fox got away.

"Never mind, Chief," Amos said when he finally caught up. "We'll get him later."

Chief gave a final growl, but Tod had already escaped and was dashing home.

Exhausted, Amos and Chief made their way home, too. By the time they got there, Tod was napping next door in front of Widow Tweed's fireplace. Copper was sitting in his barrel, waiting for his master.

"There you are," Amos grumbled. He shook his head. "And I suppose you've been sitting here almost the whole time. We could have used your help catching that dang fox. It's almost as if you're trying to avoid hunting him!"

A New Reindeer Friend

Spring had finally sprung in Arendelle. Anna, Elsa and Olaf were enjoying the warm weather with a nice walk.

"Hoo-hoo!" called Oaken as the girls entered his trading post. "Big winter blowout sale!"

"Hi, Oaken!" Anna said. "Do you have anything special today?"

Oaken nodded. "These shoes for walking on snow are special. And that sledge for sliding down mountains. Half-price!"

Anna grinned. How could she say no?

Outside, Elsa looked at Anna. "I'm not sure any of that was 'special'," she said.

Anna shrugged. "I'm sure I'll find some use for it," she said.

Olaf was looking over the supplies when a bumblebee buzzed past him. Olaf followed the bee, and Anna and Elsa followed Olaf. Suddenly, the sisters heard a crash. The snowman had chased the bee right off a cliff!

"Hang on," Elsa said. Waving her hands, she caught Olaf and pulled him back onto the cliff.

But Olaf wasn't paying attention to the sisters. He was looking at a young reindeer stranded on the ledge below him.

"You poor thing. How did you get down there?" Anna asked. "And how are we going to get you up?"

Elsa thought for a moment. Then she waved her hands, creating an ice ramp for the reindeer to climb.

The reindeer carefully stepped onto the ramp... but the ice was too slippery, and he fell down!

"Now what?" asked Elsa.

"I know!" Anna said. Grabbing her bag of winter gear, she slid down the ramp. First Anna put the snowshoes on the reindeer's hooves. Then she tied a rope round the reindeer.

"See? I told you I'd find a use for this stuff," she called up to Elsa.

Elsa and Olaf pulled with all their might. Finally, everyone was off the ledge.

Olaf turned to Anna and Elsa. "Can he come home with us?" he asked.

"Of course!" Elsa said with a smile.

Elsa led everyone to the sledge.

"Hold on!" she cried. Then, using her magic, she created a series of snow slides. The group zoomed down the mountain and through the castle gates. Their adventure had been fun, but it was nice to be home.

Friendship Fix-Up

"I've got nothing new to wear, Tia," Charlotte complained. "We need to go shopping."

Tiana groaned. "I hardly have time to sit, let alone shop, Lottie."

Charlotte pouted. "Oh, you're always so busy with your restaurant and Naveen, Tia. I just want to spend time with you."

Tiana knew Charlotte had a point. "All right," she said finally. "Let's go."

To start, Charlotte led Tiana to the Bayou Boutique and tried on a pretty dress. "Isn't this darling?" she said.

"That's swell, Lottie," Tiana replied. "Shall we get it and go?"

But Charlotte wasn't so sure. She wanted to look at everything. Hours later, she finally started to make her choices.

"Almost done?" asked Tiana. "I have to get back to the restaurant."

Charlotte pouted. "All you ever think about is your restaurant. If it's that important, just go!"

Both Tiana and Charlotte felt bad. The next day, they apologised.

"Phew, I'm glad that's over," Charlotte said, "because I have another brilliant idea about how we can spend time together! I'll help you at the restaurant."

Tiana wasn't so sure, but she agreed to give it a try. She showed Charlotte how to make fritters, then left her to make the rest of them.

Charlotte heated up a vat of oil. Soon it was time to fry the fritters! She dropped each one in and – whoosh! "Oh, Lottie! What did you do?" Tiana asked when she saw the burnt fritters.

Charlotte couldn't explain herself. She started to cry.

That night, Charlotte and Tiana met in front of a theatre.

The friends hugged. "I'm so sorry," Charlotte cried.

"Me too," Tiana said. "I want to spend time with you, Lottie, but maybe shopping and cooking aren't the right ways."

"I agree," Charlotte said. "So what can we do?"

Tiana pointed to the theatre. She had an idea.

Tiana knew she and Charlotte wouldn't agree with each other all the time, but they'd always agree on what mattered: being best friends forever!

One Lucky Pup

"Where are we going?" Penny asked. "This will be fun," Perdy said soothingly as she coaxed the puppies into the car. "I promise."

Roger steered the car down a winding country lane. The puppies smelt all kinds of good things. They smelt hay and flowers. Then they smelt something sweet – peaches!

"Here we are!" Anita opened the car door.

"Where's here?" Freckles asked Lucky.

"It looks like an orchard!" Lucky yipped. He loved to eat fruit.

Roger stretched. "You dogs run and play," he said. "We'll call you when it's time for our picnic."

"Don't eat too many peaches," Pongo barked, but the puppies were already running off.

All morning, the puppies romped and played in the green grass until Pongo and Perdy came to call them. "Time for lunch!" Pongo barked.

"I'm not hungry," Rolly said, rolling over in the grass.

"I hope you didn't eat too much," Perdy said.

The big dogs herded their puppies up the hill towards the spot where Roger and Anita were laying out a picnic.

Perdy scanned the group. "Wait a minute," she said to Pongo. "Where's Lucky?"

The black-and-white pack stopped in its tracks. Pongo counted them. Lucky was definitely missing!

"Don't worry, Mother," Pepper said sweetly. "I have an idea." She turned to her brothers and sisters. "Hey, everyone," she barked. "We have to find Lucky!"

All of the puppies yipped excitedly and tumbled over one another to find Lucky's trail. Soon every nose was sniffing the ground. Penny sniffed around a tree and behind a patch of tall grass. She'd caught the scent!

"Here he is!" Penny barked.

The rest of the dogs gathered around to see the puppy asleep in the grass. Lucky's ears covered his eyes, but there was no mistaking the horseshoe of spots on his back, or the pile of peach stones by his nose!

"Lucky is lucky we found him," said Perdy with a relieved sigh.

"And," Pepper joked, "he'll be really lucky if he doesn't wake up with a tummy ache!"

Spring has Sprung!

Spring had come at last to the forest. Sniff, sniff – Bambi could smell the change in the air. The days were growing longer. The nights were getting shorter. Crocuses and daffodils were pushing new green shoots out of the ground. And the forest didn't feel quite as lonely as it had during the cold weather. In just the last few days, Bambi had noticed that there were more animals peeking their heads out of their holes, burrows and dens.

Early one morning on the first day of spring, Bambi decided to take a walk through the forest. He came upon Mrs Possum and her children hanging upside down by their tails from a tree branch.

"Hello, Mrs Possum," Bambi said. "I haven't seen you since autumn. Where have you and your family been all winter long?"

"Oh, we like to spend most of our winter indoors," Mrs Possum replied. "But now that spring is here, it's so nice to be out in the fresh air again."

Then Mrs Possum and the rest of her family closed their eyes and dozed off.

Continuing through the forest, Bambi stopped by a tree filled with twittering birds.

"Hello," Bambi said. "Where have you birds been all winter long? I looked for you, but I could not find you."

"Oh, we fly south for the winter, to warmer places where we can find more food," one bird explained. "But we are so happy it's spring once more. It's lovely to be back in the forest and to see all of our friends."

Then the bird joined her voice with her friends' twittering tunes.

Bambi kept walking, meeting old friends at every turn. He came upon mice moving from their winter quarters back into their spring and summer homes. He noticed the squirrels and chipmunks snacking leisurely on nuts, no longer storing them away for the winter. He heard a woodpecker rapping at a pine tree, and he spotted the ducks out for a swim on the pond.

Yes, thought Bambi, *it had been a long, cold, difficult winter.*

But somehow the arrival of spring made him feel that everything would be all right. Everywhere he looked there was life, there were new beginnings and, most importantly, there was hope.

The Power of Reading

Princess Kida and Milo were helping the fishermen pull their nets to shore after a long day of fishing for tuyeb.

"You actually eat these ugly things?" Milo asked.

"They are very delicious!" the princess insisted. "The meat is sweet, and the tentacles are excellent when fried. We will have some for dinner tonight."

"I think I'll stick to tuna!" said Milo.

Milo and the princess went back to work. It took a long time to drag the nets to shore – so long that most of the tuyeb slipped through the nets and swam away.

"There has to be a better way," Milo sighed, wiping the sweat from his brow.

When they got to shore, Milo yawned. "I'm tired. Let's take a break."

They sat down next to a great big statue of a tuyeb with long, metal tentacles.

"What's this thing for?" Milo asked.

"I do not know," Kida replied. "There are many of these statues along the shore, but no one knows why they are here, because no one can read the words written on the statues."

"I'll bet I can," Milo declared.

He adjusted his glasses and began to read the ancient words. "This is amazing!" Milo cried happily. "This thing is a machine."

"But what does it do?" Kida asked.

"You'll see!" said Milo. "But first you have to power it up with your crystal."

Kida plugged her crystal into a slot in the statue's head.

"Now, watch!" said Milo. He pressed a few buttons and the statue began to hum.

"It's moving!" Kida cried.

"Look out!" Milo warned.

Fishermen on the beach scattered as the mechanical tentacles shot out over their heads, grabbed nets full of squirming tuyeb and dragged them to the beach.

"It is incredible!" Kida cried, clapping her hands. "This machine will make catching tuyeb much easier!"

To Milo's surprise, the princess gave him a big hug. "You have given us a wonderful gift. Thank you," she said.

"It was nothing," Milo replied, blushing. "All I did was read the instructions. That's the power of reading – if you can read, you can learn anything!"

A Feather in His Cap

Peter Pan and Tinker Bell were off on an adventure, and the Lost Boys were bored.

"Never Land is a dull place without Peter Pan," Slightly complained.

Then Rabbit spoke up. "We can play Pirates! That's always fun."

"Can't," said Slightly. "I lost the feather off my pirate hat."

"We could find another feather," Tootles suggested.

"An extraordinary feather," Cubby said. "Like Captain Hook's."

"That's it!" Slightly cried. "I'll steal Captain Hook's feather!"

A short time later, the Lost Boys were sneaking aboard Hook's pirate ship. Luckily for them, the pirates were taking a nap!

There, hanging from a peg on the mast, was Captain Hook's hat.

"There it is," whispered Tootles. "Get it!"

Just then, Smee, Hook's first mate, awoke with a start. He turned and spied the Lost Boys. "Ahoy!" he cried, waking up the other pirates. As quick as a flash, the Lost Boys were caught.

Captain Hook burst out of his cabin. "Lash them to the mast!" he commanded. "We'll catch Peter Pan when he comes to save his friends."

Floating high on a cloud, Peter Pan and Tinker Bell saw their friends being captured. They flew down to Pirates' Cove and landed on the ship's mast. Peter cupped his hands round his mouth and made a most peculiar sound: "Tick-tock, tick-tock!"

Down on deck, Captain Hook became very frightened. "It's that crocodile!" he cried.

"Tick-tock, tick-tock!" Peter could hardly stop himself from laughing.

"Man the cannons!" Hook cried. "Shoot that crocodile!"

The Lost Boys tied to the mast were forgotten. As the pirates ran in circles, Tinker Bell began to flap her wings. Pixie dust sprinkled down onto the Lost Boys. Soon they floated right out of the ropes and up into the clouds. On the way, Slightly snatched the feather from Hook's hat.

Peter Pan, Tinker Bell and the Lost Boys met on a drifting cloud.

"Thanks for saving us!" said Tootles.

"You helped me scare old Hook!" Peter Pan said. "That's a feather in all your caps."

An Uncle Mickey Day

Morty and Ferdie Mouse were very excited. Today was their number-one favourite kind of day – an Uncle Mickey day! That meant their uncle Mickey was going to take them out to do all kinds of special, surprising things.

"Uncle Mickey!" the twins shouted when he came to pick them up. "What are we doing today?"

"What aren't we doing today, you mean," said Mickey. "I thought we'd start with tenpin bowling."

At the bowling alley, Morty and Ferdie discovered that if they rolled the bowling ball together, they could knock down at least four or five pins every time. Then it was off to the park for some hide-and-seek and a game of catch.

"I'm hungry," said Morty when at last they stopped to rest.

"Me too," said Ferdie.

"How about a barbecue?" suggested Mickey.

Mickey led the twins to a grill, where he had set up hot dogs, beefburgers and buns.

"We love barbecues," shouted Morty as he and Ferdie gobbled down their lunches.

"All finished?" asked Mickey. "We'll have to hurry if we're going to go to the carnival."

"All right!" the boys shouted.

After the carnival, where they each won a prize, the boys told Mickey what a fun day it had been.

"Well, it's not over yet," Mickey told them.

"Really?" said Morty.

"What's next?" asked Ferdie.

That's when Mickey held up three tickets – and three mitts. A baseball game! Oh, boy!

There was nothing in the whole wide world that Mickey's nephews liked better than baseball games... and popcorn... and peanuts... and ice cream. And to make things even better, Uncle Mickey caught a foul ball and their favourite team won. They even got to watch fireworks at the end of the game.

"Wow, Uncle Mickey! Thank you so much!" said the twins when they finally returned home, tired and full and very, very happy. "This has been one of the best Uncle Mickey days ever!"

"Oh, this was nothing," said Uncle Mickey. "Just wait until next time!"

A Hair-Raising Experience

Ariel looked at her hair in the mirror and sighed. Ugh! It was so straight… and red… and boring! Ordinarily, it wasn't such a big deal. She'd run a dinglehopper through it and that would be that.

But today, for some reason, she felt like a change. Ariel was still staring at her hair in the mirror when her sisters arrived.

"Hi, Ariel. What are you doing?" the oldest, Aquata, asked.

"Oh, nothing," said Ariel. "Just trying to figure out something new to do with my hair."

"Just parting it on the other side can make a big difference," said Aquata. "Shall I try?"

"Sure!" said Ariel.

But when Aquata had done it, Ariel's sister Andrina shook her head. "Not enough," she declared. "What you need, Ariel, are some curls."

"Okay." Ariel shrugged. She sat patiently as Andrina rolled her hair in curlers and took them out half an hour later.

"Oh, my," said Ariel, gazing into the mirror.

"Still not enough," said another sister, Arista. "Imagine how great your hair would look if we dyed it black with squid ink!" And,

just to prove her point, that's exactly what she did.

"Well, it certainly is different," said Ariel, looking at her new ink-black hair.

"You know what you need?" said her sister Adella, looking at the finished product. "Plaits! Definitely plaits! Girls, come and help me."

And before she knew it, Ariel's hair had been divided into ninety-nine tight, twisty plaits. Ariel looked in the mirror… and then looked away twice as fast!

"What if we just cut it all off?" said her sister Alana.

"Hold it!" said Ariel, suddenly jumping up. "You're not cutting off my hair! I wanted a change, not a total reconstruction!" She reached up and began to take out the plaits.

"Suit yourself," said her sisters. They helped her undo their hard work. Soon Ariel was back to normal, to her great relief. Still, she thought, it had been an interesting experiment. Changing her hair hadn't worked out so well, but what about changing something else?

Barking Up the Right Tree

One day, Lady and Tramp were playing hide-and-seek in the garden. Tramp was the seeker. "Seven… eight… nine… ten!" he called. "Here I come!"

Tramp opened his eyes and spotted two pale brown paws peeping out from beneath the flowers. "Gotcha!" Tramp said playfully, pouncing into the flowers.

"Me-ow!" Suddenly, a blur of soft brown and white fur hurtled past him.

"What was that?" asked Lady, jumping out from her hiding place behind the kennel.

Tramp pointed to the top of an old elm tree, where a fluffy kitten peered down, looking scared. "Tramp was only playing. We're sorry if you're frightened," said Lady. "It's perfectly safe to come back down."

But the kitten didn't move.

"Maybe she's stuck! Oh, Tramp, we have to help her down!" cried Lady.

So, Lady stood on Tramp's back to try and reach the kitten, just as Jock was strolling by. He offered to help, and he stood on Lady's back, creating a dog tower! But he couldn't quite reach. A few minutes later, Trusty wondered over from his front porch. "Miss Lady, what in the world are you and Jock doing up there?" he asked.

Lady explained the situation.

"Unfortunately," she sighed, "we still can't reach the kitten. But maybe if you helped us…"

Before long, the four dogs were standing on top of each other, with Trusty on the bottom. "Can you reach now, Jock?" Lady called.

"Aye!" replied Jock, wagging his tail.

Suddenly, a butterfly landed on Trusty's nose. ACHOO! He sneezed and the tower collapsed into a furry pile. But Jock was dangling by his front paws from the branch!

Quickly, the dogs re-formed their tower. "Here, kitty, kitty," Jock said, gently. Then he stopped. The kitten was not on the branch any more, but sat on the floor by Trusty.

"I just do love happy endings, don't you?" said Lady when everyone was back on the ground. Jock and Trusty agreed.

"Yeah, they're okay, I guess," said Tramp. "But you know what I like even better?"

"What?" Lady asked.

"Playing hide-and-seek! Hey, kitten! You're it!"

THE INCREDIBLES

Disney · PIXAR

Super Annoying

ashiell Robert Parr was bored. It was Saturday afternoon, and he had run out of things to do.

"You know, you could do your maths homework," his mother, Helen, said.

Homework, now? Dash thought. *I'll do that tomorrow. Right now I want to do something fun.*

Brrrng! The telephone rang, and Dash's sister, Violet, raced out of her bedroom to answer it. Dash had spotted his target.

Five minutes later, Violet returned to her bedroom and stopped in her tracks. Things were not as she had left them. The duvet was upside down, and the pictures that normally hung around her mirror had been rearranged.

Only one person could have done it.

"Mum!" Violet yelled. "Dash messed up my room!"

As Helen walked down the hallway, a breeze whipped through Violet's room. Helen looked inside. "It looks fine to me, honey. Dinner's almost ready," she said.

Violet looked at her room again and saw that everything was back in place. Then her eyes fell on the wardrobe door, which was slightly ajar.

"Dash!" Violet exclaimed. "Get out of there, you little insect!"

Dash zoomed around Violet's bedroom

– up onto the bed and down to the floor, all at such super speed that Violet couldn't tell where he was. Dash only came to a halt when he spotted Violet's diary, which had fallen open on her bed.

"Ooooh," Dash said, picking up the diary. "What have we here?"

That was it. Violet had had enough of Dash. "Give that back!" she yelled. Dash tried to race out of the room, but Violet threw a force field in front of the door. Then she turned invisible and lunged at her brother.

Dash and Violet continued to chase each other around Violet's room in a blur of super powers until they heard their mum calling.

Dash froze. Then, in the blink of an eye, he zipped out through the bedroom door and down the hallway to the kitchen table.

"Dash," Helen asked, "did you finish your homework?"

Then Violet appeared at the table. Her hair was all messy.

"Nah," Dash replied with a smile. "I found something much better to do."

Piglet's Night Lights

Winnie the Pooh knocked on Piglet's door. "Ready to go camping, Piglet?" Pooh called. Piglet opened the door and looked around anxiously. "It's getting awfully dark out there," he said.

As Pooh and Piglet walked to meet their friends, Piglet became more and more frightened. "What's that?" he asked suddenly, pointing to a scary-looking shape in the trees.

"Hello!" called a voice from above. Pooh and Piglet both jumped, startled.

"Who's there?" Pooh asked.

"Why, it's me – Owl," the voice answered. "I thought you two might need a little help finding the others. We owls can see quite well at night."

By the time the friends reached the campsite, it was completely dark.

"Have no fear, Tigger's here – with illuminagination!" Tigger said, holding up a lantern.

The friends set up the tent, and Piglet climbed inside and began to unpack. A few minutes later, he poked his head back out. "Oh, no!" he wailed. "I forgot my night light!"

"Don't worry, buddy boy," Tigger said. "You can use my lantern!" But just then, the lantern flickered out.

"Can't go camping without having a camp fire," Eeyore said. The friends went to gather some sticks. Minutes later, a fire was burning.

"Campfires certainly are pleasant," Piglet said. "They make a very good sort of light."

The friends played shadow puppets until bedtime. Piglet wouldn't leave the light of the fire, though, so Pooh kept him company. Soon the fire began to fade. "Maybe we should go to sleep now, Piglet," Pooh said, yawning.

"I can't sleep without a night light, Pooh," Piglet replied.

Looking up at the night sky, Pooh thought of something. "The stars are night lights, Piglet," he said, pointing up at the sparkling stars.

Piglet looked around. "You're right, Pooh!" he cried. Piglet pointed to the moon. "And look how bright the moon is tonight. I feel much better."

"Do you think you might be able to sleep now, Piglet?" Pooh asked with a huge yawn. "Piglet?"

But Piglet was already fast asleep.

The Game

"Hey, guys!" said Woody as he gazed out of Andy's window. "Check this out."

In Andy's back garden, Andy and his friends were playing a game of American football.

"So that's what this thing's for," said Rex, picking up a small, blue, oval-shaped ball.

"I have an idea," said Woody. "Why don't we play our own game in here?"

The toys agreed. Andy's bed would be the field, and Woody and Buzz would each be a captain. Woody chose Rex, Hamm, Slinky Dog and Bo Peep. Buzz ended up with Sarge, Jessie and Bullseye. But who else should he pick? Buzz looked around Andy's room at all the eager toys… and then he saw it! The wobbly headed player that Andy had brought in just the other day. A real player, with a helmet and everything!

"I pick him!" Buzz declared. "C'mon, Number Three. You're gonna win me a game!"

"Okay, team," Buzz said as they gathered in their huddle. He pointed to a play drawn out on Etch-a-Sketch. "Number Three… could you stop nodding for one second? You run straight and watch for me to throw you the ball. Got it?"

The football player nodded eagerly. But no sooner had Buzz fired a pass than he realised Number Three was never going to catch it. His head was wobbling about so much, he couldn't see the ball – never mind the players. Bo Peep snatched the ball out of the air and brought it back for a touchdown.

"Okay, team," Buzz said as they huddled together again. "This time let's really show 'em what we're made of. Sarge, you block Rex and Hamm. Jessie and Bullseye, you block Bo Peep and Slinky Dog. Don't worry about Woody. I'll take care of him. Then, Number Three, I'll hand the ball off to you."

Again, the player nodded like crazy.

But instead of taking the ball when Buzz tried to hand it to him, all the wobbly headed player did was nod, nod and nod. He probably would have kept nodding all day if Slinky Dog hadn't run up and accidentally knocked him over onto his face.

Buzz sighed. "Anybody up for a game of draughts?" he asked.

The Ghost-Light Fish

Nemo loved school. So did his friends Tad, Pearl and Sheldon. Their teacher, Mr Ray, made everything so much fun! He took his students all over the reef.

One day, Mr Ray took his students exploring and gave them an assignment. "Okay, explorers," he said. "Let's see if each of you can find a shell."

Nemo was searching through some seaweed when he heard an odd noise. He looked up and saw his friends bolting out of a nearby cave, screaming loudly.

"What's the matter?" Nemo asked.

"It's a g-g-ghost fish!" Sheldon replied fearfully.

"Yeah, right," Nemo replied.

Just then, Tad realised he had lost the shell he'd found. "I must have dropped it in there. But I'm not going back for it!"

"Don't worry," said Nemo. "I'll find it." Nemo swam bravely into the cave. "See?" he said to himself. "Nothing to be afraid of."

Then Nemo froze. On the cave wall was a huge fish-shaped shadow! He took a deep breath. "Uh, excuse me, Mr Ghost Fish?" he asked.

"A ghost fish?" a tiny voice said nervously. Nemo followed the voice. To his surprise,

the ghost fish was actually a tiny glow-in-the-dark fish!

"Don't be afraid," Nemo said. "My name's Nemo. What's yours?"

"I'm Eddy," replied the little fish. "You mean there's no ghost fish?"

Nemo explained the whole funny story.

"By the way," said Nemo. "How do you glow like that?"

Eddy shrugged. "I just do," he replied.

Nemo thought of someone who would know more about Eddy's glow – Mr Ray! So Nemo invited Eddy to meet everyone.

Outside, Nemo rejoined his friends.

"I didn't find your shell," Nemo said to Tad. "But I did find your ghost fish!"

Everyone wanted to know what made Eddy glow. "Good question," Mr Ray replied. "There are tiny glow-in-the-dark organisms inside these patches on either side of Eddy's jaw."

Everyone oohed and aahed.

Mr Ray smiled at Nemo. "I think you deserve an A in Exploring today, Nemo!" he said.

Surprise!

Basil of Baker Street looked up from his newspaper. He sniffed the air. A mysterious smell was wafting through the room. There had also been some strange noises in the hallway, and the front door had been opened and closed an unusual number of times.

"That doesn't smell like Mrs Judson's usual tea," he muttered grimly. "I sense there's trouble afoot."

Basil hurried to the kitchen. His housekeeper was standing near the oven.

"Er… what is it, Basil?" she asked quickly.

Basil narrowed his eyes. Just then, he noticed a dab of a mysterious blue substance on the worktop. "Nothing," he told Mrs Judson, quickly wiping up the substance. "Nothing at all."

Basil retreated to his study, his mind churning. Could this be a mystery – in his own house? He quickly set up a complicated array of beakers and test tubes, then dropped the blue substance into his new contraption. The little dial at the end spun round. The arrow landed on the words 'unknown substance – edible'.

"Confound it," he muttered. "That doesn't tell me anything!"

Tiptoeing into the hall, Basil heard voices.

"Oh dear, I'll never be ready!" Mrs Judson cried.

"Nonsense, madam. Everything will be fine," someone replied.

Just then, the door opened. Basil's friend Dawson walked through it. Basil was caught! Or so he thought.

"There you are, old chap," Dawson said. "There's something that requires your attention in the drawing room, if you don't mind."

"There is?" Basil asked suspiciously.

Dawson chuckled. "Yes, I need to have a word with you in the drawing room."

Aha! Basil thought. *Perhaps now I will get to the bottom of this mystery!*

Dawson threw open the doors of the drawing room. "Surprise!"

Basil stared in shock. His family and friends all stood there, smiling at him. Mrs Judson was holding a bright-blue cake with candles on it!

Basil laughed out loud. *What kind of detective am I?* he thought. *I didn't even remember my own birthday!*

Ariel's Big Rescue

The news was travelling through the undersea world – a human ship had been spotted not too far away. Ariel was thrilled as she swam to the surface. A captain stood at the bow. On the deck stood a girl who looked like a princess. Suddenly, the ship lurched, causing everyone aboard to stumble and fall. The sailors began scrambling about and shouting. A few minutes later, the captain approached the girl.

"Princess, I'm afraid I have some bad news," Ariel heard him say. "Our ship has hit a reef and sprung a leak. We're close enough to the shore that we can make it, but I'm afraid we will have to toss items overboard to lighten the load."

Ariel and Flounder quickly ducked below the surface. "Maybe we can help," Ariel said. The two friends went under the ship and discovered a large hole. Water was rushing into the ship!

"Quick, Flounder!" Ariel said. "Gather all the seaweed you can! We'll stuff it into the hole. It may give them time to get to the shore!"

Soon Ariel and Flounder had plugged the hole. The two friends swam beside the ship as it started moving towards land.

"Woo-hoo!" cried Flounder when the ship finally reached the shore. "We did it!"

Relieved, Ariel took one last look at the ship and turned for home. As she swam, she saw a suitcase on the ocean floor, overflowing with human clothes.

"Flounder, this must be the princess's bag!" she exclaimed. Ariel pulled out a long blue gown. "I've never seen anything so beautiful!" she exclaimed. Carefully, she held it up and smiled.

"Gee, Ariel, you look almost… human," Flounder said.

"I know," Ariel sighed. "Isn't it wonderful?"

Then she stopped. "I should really return them to the princess," Ariel said.

"Oh no!" Flounder replied. "We're not going anywhere near those humans."

But that night, with Flounder by her side, Ariel took the suitcase close enough to the shore for the tide to wash it up on the beach.

"Maybe some day I'll be able to walk and wear dresses just like hers," Ariel said dreamily. "I'll be a human princess, too."

Disney
DUMBO

Lend Me Your Ears

"I think I can, I think I can, I think I can," chugged Casey Jr the circus train. The train moved slowly round a bend. "I think I can. I think I... Achoo!" he sneezed. Suddenly, Casey Jr came to a halt. "I know I can't," he admitted finally.

The animals and the performers poked their heads out of their train carriages, wondering what was wrong.

"Casey Jr here has a very bad cold," the engineer said. "He's going to need some rest before he can take us any farther."

The Ringmaster frowned. "But we're due at the fairground in a few hours. What will we do? After all, the show must go on!"

The engineer just shrugged and turned his attention back to the sneezing, coughing, spluttering little engine.

The Ringmaster went down the train, swinging open the doors to all the cages and cars. "Come on, everyone," he said. "Might as well stretch your legs."

Dumbo the elephant and his mother, Mrs Jumbo, took a drink from the bucket of water the Ringmaster had put out. Mrs Jumbo gazed around. "Looks like we're in the middle of nowhere," she said. "I do hope poor Casey Jr is feeling better soon."

"Me too," Dumbo's friend Timothy Q. Mouse said hopefully.

Just then there was a clap of thunder. Rain began to fall from the sky. The animals and performers ran for the shelter of the circus waggons. Dumbo held on to his mother's tail.

Suddenly, the wind picked up. The gust caught Dumbo's huge ears and sent him flying backwards!

"That's it!" yelled the Ringmaster over the howling wind. "Dumbo, come with me!"

He led Dumbo over to the train, climbed onto the front waggon and motioned for the little elephant to join him.

"Now spread out those great ears of yours!" the Ringmaster said. Dumbo's ears billowed out, catching the wind like giant sails and pushing Casey Jr along the tracks.

"The show will go on!" the Ringmaster shouted happily.

"I know I can. I know I can. I know I can," chanted Casey Jr, before adding, "thanks to Dumbo!"

THE JUNGLE Book

A Bear-y Tale

It was time for Mowgli, Bagheera and Baloo to go to bed. But Mowgli couldn't sleep. He needed a bedtime story. And so Baloo began:

"Once upon a time, in a house not far from this very jungle, there lived a clan of men. This clan, they cooked their food, and one day, don't you know, they made a mighty tasty stew. Only thing was, when they sat down to eat, it was just too hot. So the mother got an idea. They'd go for a walk in the jungle, and by the time they got back, their stew would be nice and cool. But do you know what happened next?"

"No," Mowgli said.

"Well, that family had barely been gone a minute when an old bear came wandering up and stuck his nose into the Man-house."

"He did?" gasped Mowgli.

"Well, now, can you blame him? That stew just smelt so awfully good. And the next thing you know, he was tastin' it – startin' with the biggest bowl, but that was still too hot. So next he tried the middle bowl, but that was too cold. So he tried the littlest bowl, and, don't you know, it was just right! That old bear ate the whole thing right up!"

"What happened next?" said Mowgli.

"Oh, well, after that, this bear, he started to get tired. And don't you know that right there in that house, looking so soft and comfortable, were three cushy-lookin' pads... I think men call them 'beds'. Anyway, that bear, he had to try them, too. Naturally, he lay down on the biggest one first, but it was too hard. So he tried the middle one, but that was much, much too soft. So he tried the littlest one, and let me tell you, that thing was so comfortable, he fell asleep right then and there! And he would have slept clear through the next full moon... if only that family hadn't returned and—"

"And what?" Mowgli asked. "Don't stop now!"

"And startled that bear so much, he ran back into the jungle... full belly and all."

Mowgli smiled and tried to cover a big yawn. "Is that a true story, Baloo?"

The bear grinned. "Would I ever tell you a tall tale, Little Britches?"

Lessons

In the depths of the forest somewhere in England, Merlin the magician was waiting for a very special visitor. His name was Wart, and he was a clever but reckless young boy.

Wart soon tumbled into the room and landed on a chair in front of Merlin.

"A great destiny awaits you, my boy," Merlin said to Wart. "But first you need to learn a few things. There's no great destiny without a great teacher – and I will be that person! Just let me pack my case and then we'll be off."

First lesson was the world of water. Merlin touched his wand to Wart's head, and the boy transformed into a fish! Merlin transformed himself, too, and the two swam in the moat round the king's castle. Wart waved his fins and made bubbles. He was greatly enjoying this lesson.

Suddenly, a monstrous fish swam straight for them! Quickly, Merlin changed back into human form and saved Wart from the jaws of the pike.

Second lesson was exploring the forest in the form of a squirrel! Wart immediately made a friend – a charming female squirrel who really liked him. But just when a wolf was about to attack him, Wart changed back into a child.

"What's the third lesson?" he then asked his teacher.

"Flying through the air!" answered Merlin, transforming him into a baby bird.

In the company of Archimedes, a grumpy old owl, Wart launched himself into the air. What fun it was to fly! But danger lurked in the air, too: an eagle appeared and threatened the two friends!

Panic-stricken, Wart fled from the eagle and flew into a chimney. He fell into the house – and the clutches – of mad Madam Mim, a wicked sorceress!

Luckily, Merlin appeared in the cottage. To overpower the sorceress, he changed himself into a germ and gave her the measles!

Later, as he walked home, Wart came across a mysterious sword thrust into an anvil. Engraved on the sword were the words: Who so pulleth me out will be King of England.

To everyone's astonishment, the boy effortlessly pulled the sword out of the stone! Wart – or rather, Arthur – was to be King of England. And what better king than one who had learnt his lessons?

Three Cheesy Wishes

Long ago, before there was an Aladdin, a Jasmine or even a sultan, a travelling merchant bought a lamp, along with some other 'junk'. Not knowing its value, he traded the lamp to a cheese seller for some lunch.

Hassan the cheese seller looked at the lamp sceptically. He sighed and began to shine it up. In a puff of smoke, the Genie appeared.

"Hello there! I'm the one and only magical Genie!" the big blue spirit announced.

"Excuse me?" said Hassan.

"Nice to meet you," said the Genie. "And what do you do here in Agrabah?"

"My name is Hassan, and I'm a—"

"Wait!" cried the Genie. "Let me guess!" The Genie put his hand over his brow as he secretly looked around the man's shop. "You sell… cheese! Am I right or am I right?"

"You are right," said Hassan. "But that's an easy guess."

"You're very observant, Hassan," said the Genie. "So I'll give you three wishes."

"Three wishes, eh?" Hassan thought for a few minutes. Then he said, "It's hard to get enough good milk to make the best cheese. I wish I had many, many goats so I would always have enough milk."

POOF! In a flash, thousands of goats filled the streets of Agrabah. Goats were everywhere!

"Goodness!" Hassan cried. "I would have to wish for the biggest cheese shop in the world to sell the cheese from so many goats."

POOF! All of a sudden, Hassan's shop began to grow and grow! His cheese shop was even taller than the highest sand dunes outside the city.

"This is terrible!" Hassan cried. Far below, the people looked like tiny ants. "I can't live and work in such a monstrosity. All I wanted was to make the finest cheese in Agrabah." Hassan turned to the Genie. "I wish I'd never met you!" he cried.

POOF! The Genie disappeared and Hassan found that his shop had returned to normal.

Outside, the marketplace was completely goat-free. Hassan searched high and low for the lamp, but it was gone, too.

"It must have all been a crazy dream," said Hassan. But from that day forwards, everyone said Hassan's cheese was the finest in all of Agrabah!

Robin
hood

Castle Rescue

Robin Hood whistled as he cooked soup for his friends, Maid Marian and Little John, deep in Sherwood Forest. But just as he handed the soup out, Friar Tuck appeared through the bushes. He was out of breath and looked worried.

"Skippy is missing!" Friar Tuck declared. He explained that the young rabbit had gone to Prince John's castle to search for a missing arrow, but never returned.

"He must be lost in the castle," Maid Marian said.

Robin Hood grabbed his bow and arrows. "We have to rescue him, let's go."

Maid Marian led Robin and Little John through a secret entrance to the castle and they began to search the winding hallways. Then, Robin stopped. He could hear voices from the corner up ahead. They turned back, but more voices were coming from behind. They were trapped!

Thinking quickly, Robin tied one end of a rope to a window ledge and the other to an arrow. He fired and created a bridge to another window on the opposite wall. The friends were barely halfway across when the sheriff's voice sounded from behind them.

"Did you hear that?" he asked. He looked out the window, squinting through the darkness.

The friends clung to the rope, desperately trying to keep still. Finally, the sheriff went back inside and they breathed a sigh of relief as they climbed through the opposite window. The first door they found led to a very large courtyard.

"There!" Little John whispered. Skippy was cowering behind a well, clutching his hat.

"Oh no," Maid Marian said, pointing past Skippy. Prince John had entered and was walking right up to Skippy's hiding place!

"Get Skippy. I'll meet you back in the forest," Robin said. He climbed up to the castle's roof and yelled to Prince John.

"Hey! Looking for me?"

Prince John yelled at his guards to seize Robin, but he was too fast, swiftly dodging their arrows. Maid Marian and Little John grabbed Skippy and together they escaped.

Back in the forest, Robin handed Skippy his lost arrow.

"I found this when escaping, try not to lose it again!" he laughed. "Now, who wants soup?"

A Friend in Need

"Whatever could be keeping the Seven Dwarfs?" said Snow White. "They should have been home from work by now!"

Just then, Happy came through the front door looking upset. "Come quickly! A young deer is hurt in the woods."

Snow White followed Happy, and they soon reached a small clearing. Everyone stood in a circle round the deer.

"Thank goodness you're here, Snow White!" said Doc. "This little fella's in trouble!"

"He must be cold," said Snow White, covering him with her long cape.

"Maybe he's just tired," said Sleepy. "A nice long rest should do the trick!"

"Why, you could be right, Sleepy," said Snow White. "But he's not closing his eyes, so I think it might be something else."

"Maybe he has a… aaahhhh… aahhhhhchoooooooo!… a cold," said Sneezy.

"I know!" said Happy. "Maybe he's feeling sad and needs a little cheering up!"

"I, uh, don't know for sure," said Bashful softly, "but perhaps he's too shy to let us know what's the matter."

"We all feel shy sometimes, don't we, Bashful?" said Snow White.

Then Dopey started pacing back and forth and pointing over his shoulder.

"Maybe you're right. He could be lost," said Snow White.

"I'll bet I know what happened," said Grumpy. "The wicked Queen probably cast a spell on him! She's always up to no good!"

Suddenly, Doc approached the deer. "May I lake a took… er, I mean, take a look?" he asked. Doc knelt down beside the deer. "Well, would you look at that!" cried Doc, pointing at the animal's foot. "The poor deer must have stepped on a thorn."

Doc gently removed the sharp thorn from the deer's hoof. The deer jumped up and licked him.

"Oh, how relieved you must be!" cried Snow White.

The deer licked Snow White's hand and ran off into the forest. Then Snow White and the Seven Dwarfs went home to their little cottage.

"I am so proud of each and every one of you," said Snow White, smiling at her friends. "You each did your best to help a friend in need!"

Disney Cinderella

Lucifer's Bath

Cinderella's stepsisters didn't like the idea of Cinderella going to the Prince's ball, so they decided to keep her busy.

"We need to take our baths," Anastasia said.

"You heard my girls, Cinderella," said the Stepmother. "Get their baths ready at once!"

Cinderella already had far too many jobs to do, but she didn't argue. Once Anastasia and Drizella were soaking in their baths, all Cinderella had to do was mend their clothes, clean the house, wash the curtains and give Lucifer his bath – then she could get ready for the ball.

Unfortunately, her stepsisters wouldn't leave her alone. Each time her stepsisters called, Cinderella had to stop whatever she was doing and take care of them.

When Drizella called for tea, Cinderella went down to the kitchen and put the kettle on. Then she let Bruno the dog in for a snack. "Oh, Bruno," she said, tossing him a bone, "if my stepsisters don't get out of their baths soon, I'll never get my chores done in time."

Bruno narrowed his eyes. Those stepsisters were the most selfish, lazy, nasty girls he'd ever known – and their cat was just like them. Bruno wanted to help Cinderella, so when the tea was ready, he followed her up the stairs and down the long hallway.

As Cinderella walked up to Drizella's bathroom door, Bruno noticed Lucifer sleeping nearby.

"Woof, woof!" Bruno barked.

With a screeching yowl, Lucifer ran into Drizella's bathroom. Splash! Bruno chased the cat right into Drizella's bath – and then Bruno jumped in himself!

Drizella screamed and Lucifer jumped out. Then Bruno chased the cat down the hallway and into Anastasia's bathroom.

Splash! Lucifer landed right in Anastasia's bath. Bruno jumped right in after him!

"Get out of your baths this instant!" Cinderella's stepmother cried. "You don't want to smell like that dog, do you?"

Cinderella sighed in relief. Although she still had many jobs to finish before the ball, at least one job was now done. Thanks to Bruno, Lucifer had had his bath!

A Mother's Touch

Work was piling up in the offices of Monsters, Inc.. Celia was off sick with the flu, and there was no one to cover for her. Just then, Mike had an idea.

"I'll call my mum. She'd love to help out," he said.

And so, later that day, in walked Mrs Wazowski. Sulley and Mike went off to discuss some new plans for the laugh factory, while Mrs W made herself at home – very at home. When Sulley and Mike returned at lunchtime, they barely recognised the reception area. Mike's mum had hung ruffled curtains everywhere.

Later that day, Mike rehearsed some new comedy routines. "What do monsters eat for breakfast?" asked Mike. "Anything they want!"

Sulley and Mike laughed until their sides hurt. "I couldn't help but overhear," said Mike's mum. "It might be funnier if you wore a silly hat."

Sulley shot Mike a look.

"Thanks, Mum," said Mike.

A little while later, Sulley and Mike summoned Mrs W over the intercom to come to the Laugh Floor. "Um, Mum, do you know anything about this?" Mike asked nervously.

He pointed to the key cards, which were now filed by colour, making it impossible for anyone to know which card belonged to which door. Sulley turned and spoke to Mike through gritted teeth. "She's *your* mother. Do something!"

Just before the day was over, Mike went to the front desk, sat down and took his mother's hand. He'd never fired his mother before. This wasn't going to be easy!

"Mum, you know I love you. And you make a terrific receptionist, but—"

Just then, Celia walked through the front door.

"Googly Bear!" Celia cried.

"Schmoopsie-Poo! What are you doing here?" Mike asked. "You're supposed to be home in bed."

"I couldn't stand being away from you one day longer," Celia gushed.

Mrs Wazowski beamed. "He is irresistible, isn't he? Well, I guess my work here is done!" she said, gathering up her things.

Suddenly, Mrs W stopped. "Oh, Mikey, what were you about to tell me?"

"Not a thing, Mum," said Mike as he gave her a kiss. "Not a thing!"

Merida's Wild Ride

It was a soggy, stormy afternoon. Merida sat in the stables reading from an old book of Highland tales. "Look," Merida said. "Magical horses. That one is called a kelpie. It's a water horse."

Merida looked up. The sun was coming out. "Come, lad," she said to her horse, Angus. "Let's go for a ride."

As Merida and Angus reached the woods, a flash of grey caught her eye.

Merida guided Angus to a clearing. In it stood a magnificent grey horse. Breathless with excitement, Merida whispered to Angus, "I know that horse is magical."

The horse lowered its head as Merida approached. Patting its nose, Merida swung onto the horse's back. She didn't have a bridle, but she knew she could guide him with her hands wrapped in his mane. The horse bolted but Merida wasn't frightened. She had been around horses all her life.

Merida tried to calm the horse, but he ran on. They were heading towards a large loch – a deep, dangerous lake. Even worse, Merida's hands seemed to be stuck in the horse's mane.

The horse brushed against a tree and trapped rainwater fell down on Merida. One of her hands came free.

Just ahead, Merida spotted a bridle hanging from a tree. Merida stretched to reach, but it was just beyond her fingertips. "Angus, the bridle!" she called.

Merida looked up at the sound of a whinny. Angus galloped up next to them – and he was carrying the bridle!

He tossed it. Merida caught it with her free hand and slipped it over the horse's head. With the reins in her hand, she guided the horse to a path that led away from the cliff's edge.

As they reached the shore of the loch, the horse finally slowed to a stop. Merida was no longer stuck. She jumped off and removed the bridle. The stallion galloped down the shoreline.

Back at the stable, Merida looked at the book she had been reading. She found the legend of the kelpie. "Once a bridle is put on a kelpie, the water horse will do your bidding," she read.

She looked up at Angus. Was it possible? Had she been riding a kelpie?

Island Adventure

Mickey, Minnie, Donald and Daisy were on a holiday by the sea. "I'm going to relax right here!" Minnie declared as she spread out her blanket.

"Me too," said Daisy, opening her umbrella.

"Those waves are just perfect for surfing," said Donald.

"You boys run along," Minnie said.

"We're happy right here," said Daisy.

Mickey and Donald surfed and swam until the sun went down.

The next day was sunny, too. On their way to the beach, Mickey and Donald spied a boat for rent. "Let's go fishing!" cried Donald.

But Daisy and Minnie shook their heads. "We want to relax," they said. So Donald and Mickey went fishing alone.

On the third day, Mickey and Donald wanted to go for a long swim.

"No thanks," said Minnie. "I want to take it easy."

"Me too," said Daisy. "We're going to the cove to relax."

The boys went off to swim. Daisy and Minnie headed for the cove.

While she and Minnie were lounging under the palm trees, Daisy spied a bottle floating in the water. There was a map rolled up inside.

She waded into the water to get it. "It's a treasure map!" she exclaimed.

"The treasure is on an island!" cried Minnie, pointing to a big X on the map.

Minnie and Daisy decided to follow the map. They went up one hill and then down another. They crossed a stream and reached a dock with a boat tied to it.

"That's the island," said Daisy, pointing out to sea. They hopped into the boat and started to row. They rowed and they rowed until they reached the island. Minnie and Daisy were very tired and very hungry.

"Look!" Minnie cried. "I see a fire!"

"Pirates!" exclaimed Daisy.

But there were no pirates. Just Donald and Mickey, waiting for Daisy and Minnie to arrive. A campfire was roaring, and fish sizzled on the grill.

"Looks like they found our map!" Donald exclaimed.

"Your map?" cried Minnie.

"It was the only way to get you two to have an adventure with us!" Mickey replied.

"Now, sit down by the fire," said Donald. "Lunch is served!"

Disney
101
DALMATIANS

The Good Thing About Rain

"Rise and shine!" cried Pongo. One by one, he nudged each of his fifteen Dalmatian puppies with his nose. Most of the puppies yawned and stretched. But Rolly just rolled over and carried on sleeping.

"Aw, come on, Rolly," Pongo whispered in the pup's ear. "It's morning! Don't you want to go out?"

At the mention of the word out, Rolly was instantly wide awake! And he was not alone. As if by magic, the sleepy group had become a pack of jumping, barking puppies. They raced together through the kitchen to the back door, where they jumped up and down, waiting for Nanny to let them out into the garden.

"Okay, here I come," said Nanny as she made her way across the kitchen. Then she flung the door open wide and stepped out of the way to let the puppies race past. But they didn't move. It was raining!

"Oh, go on," said Perdita, trying to nudge the pups out the door. "It's only a little water."

But they wouldn't budge!

The next morning, Patch woke up with a start. With a few sharp barks, he helped Pongo wake the other puppies. Within seconds, all fifteen were crowding round the back door. Nanny again rushed to let them out. And once

again, the puppies were very disappointed to see raindrops falling.

When Nanny opened the door the next morning, the puppies were so surprised to see the sun shining that they didn't know what to do! Then, springing into action, they tumbled over one another in their rush to get out the door. They raced off in different directions, ready to explore.

But then, almost at once, all fifteen puppies froze in their tracks. They looked around at one another, then down at themselves. What was this stuff getting all over their spotted white coats? It was brown. It was wet. It was squishy. It was mud! And it was fun!

From the doorway, Pongo and Perdita looked out at their muddy puppies and laughed.

"You know what this means, don't you?" Pongo asked Perdita.

Perdita nodded. "Baths."

Pongo smiled, watching the frolicking puppies. "Let's not tell them just yet," he said.

Toys in Paradise

Andy ran round his room, throwing clothes into a bag. His best friend's family was going on holiday to Florida and they had invited him along.

When Andy left the room, his toys came to life.

"I'd give anything to go on a tropical holiday," said Bo Peep. "Just think of it. The sandy beaches, the warm sunshine…"

"Hey, I've got an idea," said Jessie. "Why don't we make our own tropical paradise, right here in Andy's room?"

The toys searched the house for the things they needed. Sarge and the Green Army Men found a potted plant. Hamm and Rex raided the kitchen for Buster's water bowl and some sponges. Bo Peep found a doll's umbrella in Molly's room. Soon all of the supplies were gathered in Andy's room.

"Next stop: paradise!" Jessie exclaimed.

The toys got to work. In no time at all, they had created their own tropical paradise. Woody and Buzz stretched out on the sunloungers they had made out of shoe-box tops and sponges.

"Aah. This is the life," Woody said.

But something was missing – an ocean breeze! Jessie climbed onto Andy's dresser and flipped a switch. Within seconds, the wind picked up, blowing Andy's things everywhere. It was a storm! The toys ran for cover as the beach chairs flew across the room.

"It's okay!" Jessie called. She flipped off the switch and the wind stopped. "It was just the fan. I wanted to make our palm tree sway in the breeze. Is everyone okay?"

"Almost everyone," Woody said. He pointed towards the bed, where Rex's tail was poking out from under the duvet. It took a while for the toys to convince Rex to come out of his hiding place. He was still trembling with fear!

"Don't worry, Rex," Woody said. "There won't be any more storms here today."

The toys put the umbrella back in its place, shading the sunloungers from a sun made out of a lamp.

Rex walked back over to the beach. "I hope Andy has a great trip," he said. "Paradise can definitely be fun… as long as you're with good friends!"

What a Crab

Nemo was having trouble at school – and its name was Ruddy. The big crab was mean to Nemo and the other kids whenever he got the chance. The trouble was, he was crafty and never did it when the teachers were looking.

One day, Ruddy shoved Nemo into a rock pool and made him late for their coral lesson. Another time, he taunted Nemo by saying, "My dad's bigger and stronger than your dad!"

"I have tried everything," Nemo complained to his shark friends, Bruce, Chum and Anchor. "But he won't leave me alone. What do you think we should do?"

"Just leave it to us!" said Bruce. "We're experts in behaviour modification."

The next day, three huge shadows fell over Nemo's classmates as they played in the school playground.

"Hello," Bruce said to the crab. "You must be Nemo's new little friend."

While Ruddy trembled, Bruce snarled, "We just wanted you to know that any friend of Nemo's is a friend of ours. You are a friend of Nemo's, aren't you?"

Everyone looked at Ruddy. "Oh, yeah!" he managed to splutter. "Nemo and I are buddies."

"Good!" Anchor said. "Because you don't want to know what happens to anyone who's not nice to our little pal here."

Chum cleaned a piece of seaweed from between his razor-sharp teeth with a spiny urchin. "You should stop by for lunch sometime," he said to Ruddy with a wink, and the sharks swam away.

Ruddy sidled up to Nemo. "You're friends with three sharks?" he said. "Wow! That's pretty cool! I wish I had friends like that. In fact, I wish I had any friends at all."

"How do you expect to have friends when you're so... well, crabby all the time?" Nemo said.

Ruddy admitted that he had decided to pick on everyone else before they had a chance to pick on him.

"If you promise to stop being mean, I promise to be your friend," Nemo said.

"Deal," Ruddy agreed. "Besides, I guess I'd better be your friend if I don't want your shark pals to eat me."

Nemo didn't say a word. Bruce, Chum and Anchor were vegetarians, but Ruddy didn't need to know that!

Laughter is the Best Medicine

"I hope Quasi is okay out there!" Laverne said fretfully.

The other two gargoyles in the bell tower, Hugo and Victor, nodded in agreement. Their friend Quasimodo had just left Notre Dame to help the young soldier Phoebus search for the Court of Miracles. It was sure to be a dangerous mission.

"The only things we can do are stay strong and be hopeful," Victor said solemnly.

Hugo smirked. "How can we not be strong?" he said. "We're made of stone, remember?"

"Good one!" Laverne giggled. "Rock solid."

"You know that's not what I meant." Victor frowned at his friends. "And both of you – don't you have any sense of the seriousness of this situation? Our dear compatriot is out there somewhere, facing grave peril…"

"Grave peril?" Laverne said. "Way to be optimistic, Victor – you've already got poor Quasi in his grave!"

"I see," Victor said sternly. "So you two would rather mock me and crack bad jokes than join me in my concern for poor young Quasimodo."

Laverne stood up and brushed herself off. "Why does it have to be an either-or thing, Victor?" she asked. "Just because we're laughing, it doesn't mean we're not worried, too."

Hugo nodded. "If we spend all our time thinking about how terrible everything is, we'll go nuts."

Waving his arms to help make his point, Hugo accidentally hit a bird's nest that was tucked into one of the eaves. The occupant of the nest squawked and flew upwards. Laverne ducked just in time to avoid having the bird fly straight into her face, but she tripped and fell, ending up on the ground. The bird banked upwards, still squawking as it flew over Hugo.

Hugo leapt backwards – and landed on Laverne's hand! She yelled and yanked her hand out from under him. Hugo lost his footing and landed in a heap on top of Laverne.

Victor stared at his friends, who were trying to untangle themselves. Then he started to laugh. He laughed harder and harder, until he could hardly speak.

"You know," he said finally, "I think you just might be right. I feel much better already!"

Jin's Treasure

After Mulan saved China from the Huns, she returned to her village. She helped out her family the way she always had, and in time, people forgot how brave Fa Zhou's daughter really was.

One day, a group of frightened children came running towards her.

"Help! Help!" they shouted. "Our friend Jin is trapped in a cave!"

"Hurry, take me to him!" exclaimed Mulan. Then she called to her little dragon friend. "Mushu, you've got to come, too!"

The children led Mulan and Mushu to the other side of the mountain.

"A boulder has fallen, blocking the entrance to the cave," explained Wang, the blacksmith. "It will take muscles of steel to move this boulder."

"Yes!" agreed Chung, the carpenter. "If you want to do something useful, go back to the village and fetch us some water."

Mulan returned to the village, but not to fetch water. Instead, she found a shovel and ran back to the cave. Soon, Mulan began to dig at the base of the boulder. Slowly but surely, she formed a tunnel beneath the rock. When the tunnel was finished, Mulan and Mushu climbed under the boulder and into the cave.

"Boy, am I happy to see you!" the boy, Jin, exclaimed.

"We're happy to see you, too!" said Mulan. "But what made you come in here?"

"I saw something shiny and I wanted to know what it was," Jin explained.

Mulan looked round. "You mean that?"

There, in the back of the cave, lit up by Mushu's fire, were many shiny objects. The cave was full of treasure!

"Think of what this fortune could mean for our village!" exclaimed Mulan.

"Come on!" Jin said. "Let's go and show the others." They each grabbed an armful of treasure and headed for the tunnel.

As the pair emerged from the cave, followed by Mushu, the crowd let out a cheer. Then they noticed the gold and jewels.

"What have you found?" asked Wang.

"It's treasure. Now I'll go back to the village and fetch some water," Mulan said, grinning. "I'm pretty thirsty after all that digging."

How Rose Dozed

The moon hung high in the sky, and the stars twinkled around it. It was late at night, and Briar Rose was supposed to be sleeping. But with all those owls hooting and the frogs in a nearby pond croaking, who could sleep? After tossing and turning for hours on end, Briar Rose woke up Flora, Fauna and Merryweather to see if they could help.

"I've got the solution!" Fauna exclaimed. "You need to count sheep."

"Lie down now, dear," Flora joined in, "and picture a fence. Then imagine sheep jumping over it one by one, and don't lose count!"

Briar Rose lay back and did as they said. But when she got to sheep five hundred and forty-four, she knew it wasn't working.

Briar Rose went back to her aunts. "No luck," she said.

"Oh dear," said Flora. "We'll have to think of something else instead."

"Sleep, schmeep!" Merryweather chimed in. "The night has its own brightness, twinkle and shine. It's such a shame to sleep through it all of the time!"

"But if Briar Rose doesn't sleep at night, she'll be tired during the day," Fauna told the other good fairies.

"Good point," Briar Rose agreed.

"Well, then, try reading a book! Reading always puts me to sleep," Merryweather said with a yawn.

"But I like reading," Briar Rose protested. "I'll never fall asleep."

There was a pause as each of Briar Rose's aunts thought and thought about how to help her.

"I know a way to help you sleep!" Fauna said suddenly. "All you have to do is think good thoughts about the day that's passed and hope for the happy things that tomorrow may bring."

"Is that true?" Briar Rose asked.

"Absolutely!" Flora agreed.

"Now, close your eyes, dear," said Merryweather, "and we'll see you in your dreams."

Briar Rose wasn't sure at first, but Flora, Fauna and Merryweather had never let her down before. So she lay back and closed her eyes. She remembered her favourite parts of that day, then thought about the wonders tomorrow would bring.

And wouldn't you know, pretty soon, she was lost in her dreams.

Disney
THE
LION KING

A Prince's Day

It was early morning at Pride Rock. Simba and Nala couldn't wait to go out and play by the river, but then Zazu appeared. "There you are, Simba," said the bird, landing in front of the cubs. "Come along. We have a busy day of training ahead."

Zazu led Simba to the watering hole to teach the young lion about solving disputes between subjects. Then they went to Pride Rock where Mufasa was listening to the animals' concerns. "A king must listen to all the other animals," said Zazu. "You can learn a lot from your father."

Simba tried to pay attention, but the lion cub soon grew bored.

Next, Simba and Zazu were walking past the river where Simba and Nala had planned to play. Simba looked for his friend, but couldn't see her. Then he heard a yell. Simba ran to the river as fast as he could.

It was Nala – she had fallen in the fast-moving river and couldn't get out! "Hurry, go get my father!" Simba ordered Zazu. The bird flew away, but Simba knew there wasn't time to wait. He saw a long branch, which he grabbed and moved over the river. Nala reached out and grabbed onto the branch just in time.

Simba pulled the branch back and dragged Nala out of the river to safety.

When Zazu and Mufasa arrived at the river, Mufasa spoke to his son. "Zazu told me about your day. I know that you want to play with your friend, but Zazu was trying to teach you important lessons about what it means to be king," he said. "But the last lesson you taught yourself."

"I did?" asked Simba.

"Yes, my son. You rescued Nala and showed that a ruler must be brave. I am very proud of you, Simba."

Simba smiled at his father. "Now," Mufasa said. "I think there may just be enough time for you and Nala to play before dinner."

Simba cheered and bounded off to find his friend, as Zazu landed on Mufasa's shoulder. "He'll make a good king someday, sire," said Zazu.

Mufasa smiled. "Yes, he will."

Spaghetti and Meatballs

Tramp had just escaped from the dogcatcher – again. He'd taught that dogcatcher who was boss! Tramp could smell wood burning in fireplaces and dinners cooking. His stomach suddenly rumbled. Escaping from the dogcatcher always worked up quite an appetite!

But where would he go for dinner tonight? He usually stopped by the Schultzes' for some Wiener schnitzel on Mondays, and he had corned beef and cabbage with the O'Briens on Tuesdays… but what he was really craving was some spaghetti and meatballs. So Tramp headed to Tony's Restaurant. He scratched at the back door, as was his custom.

"I'm coming! I'm coming!" Tony shouted. He appeared at the door, wiping his hands on a towel. He pretended not to see Tramp, as he always did.

"Hey, nobody's here!" Tony shouted.

Tramp couldn't take it any more. He was so hungry! He barked.

"Oh, there you are, Butch my friend," said Tony. Tramp – whom Tony called Butch – jumped up and down. "I'll get your dinner," said Tony. "Relax, enjoy yourself."

Tramp sat down and looked around the cluttered alley. This was the life!

Tony reappeared with a plateful of pasta.

He had given Tramp two – no, make that three – meatballs! This was quite a special night.

Tony stood and chatted with Tramp as he ate his meal, telling him about his day: the late delivery of fish, the customer who had complained that the tomato sauce was too garlicky, the trip that he and his wife were planning to take…

Tramp finished eating and gave the plate one last lick. It was sparkling clean.

"That reminds me," said Tony. "There's something I've been meaning to talk to you about. It's time you settled down and got a wife of your own."

Tramp gave Tony a horrified look and began to back out of the alley. Tony laughed so hard his sides shook.

"Goodbye, Butch!" he called. "But mark my words: one of these days, you're going to meet the dog you can't resist. And, when you do, I have a good idea – you bring her to Tony's for a nice romantic dinner!"

Baymax's Journey

One day, Hiro was busy working on a new robot when his microbot started knocking against the edge of its Petri dish. Baymax saw the microbot.

"Your tiny robot is trying to go somewhere," Baymax observed.

"Why don't you find out where?" Hiro said distractedly.

The microbot in the Petri dish worked like a compass. Baymax was correctly following it as long as the microbot was tapping straight ahead. Baymax followed it… right out of the door!

Baymax stared at the microbot. He was so focused on making sure it was pointing straight ahead that he did not bother to look at where he was going. The microbot led him across the street and onto a tram.

From the window, Hiro saw what was happening. He raced to catch up with Baymax, but the tram pulled away.

As the tram rolled down the street, Baymax kept his eyes on the microbot. He was heading in the right direction until the tram turned. It was time for Baymax to get back on course.

Baymax followed the microbot's tapping, even though it meant climbing up to the roof of a tall building.

As Baymax followed the microbot straight ahead, he took a big step… onto elevated railway tracks.

"Oh no," said Baymax. A train was heading full speed right at him!

Luckily, following the microbot led Baymax out of the path of the train and into a large shopping centre.

Baymax followed the tiny robot towards an escalator. He went down… and up. Baymax wondered where the tiny robot wanted to go.

The microbot continued to tap, leading Baymax out of the shopping centre and into an alley.

Finally, Baymax stopped in front of a giant warehouse. Completely out of breath, Hiro arrived behind him.

"I have found where your tiny robot wants to go," Baymax said.

The microbot continued tapping towards a chain-covered door.

"Locked," Hiro said.

"There is a window," Baymax said, pointing up.

Hiro sighed. He wasn't so sure he wanted to know where the microbot was going any more!

The Mysterious Book

"What are you looking at, Belle?" Chip asked.

Belle smiled at the little teacup. "Oh, you caught me daydreaming, Chip," she said. "I was just looking up there." She pointed to the highest shelf in the Beast's library. On the shelf was a single book.

Belle had wondered about that book since the day the Beast had first shown her the library. The trouble was, none of the ladders quite reached the shelf. So the book had remained a mystery.

Belle's curiosity had grown until she could hardly stop thinking about the book. She explained the problem to Chip, who went straight to his mother. Mrs Potts called a meeting of all the enchanted objects. As soon as she told them about the book, they wanted to help Belle.

"What we need is a plan," Cogsworth said.

"Yes!" Lumiere cried. "And I've got one!"

That evening, the enchanted objects gathered in the library. First the Stove stood at the base of the shelves. The Wardrobe climbed on top of him. Soon a whole tower of enchanted objects stretched almost to the top shelf.

Finally Lumiere started to climb. He stretched as far as he could—

"What on earth are you doing?" Belle exclaimed from the doorway.

"Oh, mademoiselle!" Lumiere cried. "You're just in time – voilà!"

With that, he finally managed to reach the book, knocking it off the shelf and into Belle's hands.

A moment later, the tower collapsed in a heap!

After Belle made certain that everyone was all right, she opened the book.

"Oh!" she said when she saw the first page.

"What is it?" Chip asked breathlessly.

Belle smiled sheepishly. "I can't believe it! I've already read this one."

The enchanted objects sighed. Had all their work been for nothing?

"But thank you anyway!" Belle said quickly. "It's one of my favourites – it's full of faraway places, magic spells... well, let me show you!"

Soon all the enchanted objects were gathered round as Belle read the book to them. And wouldn't you know? It became one of their favourite books, too!

Disney
Lilo & Stitch

Laugh, Cobra Bubbles!

Lilo thought she was a pretty lucky girl. She had a bunch of good friends whom she loved to laugh with. Stitch had a funny, scratchy laugh to go with his scratchy voice. Pleakley giggled, and Jumba shouted out big guffaws.

But as for Cobra Bubbles, well, the truth was that Cobra Bubbles just didn't laugh. Ever. And Lilo was dying to find out what his laugh sounded like.

So Lilo tried to get Cobra Bubbles to laugh. She showed him the latest episode of The World's Funniest Lobster Videos, but he didn't crack a smile, even when a lobster ate an entire jar of pickles. She made funny faces at him until her face hurt, but he just looked at her, expressionless.

Clearly, something had to be done. It just wasn't healthy for a person to never laugh.

"Nani, Cobra Bubbles is one of my best friends. He's practically family! But he never laughs. I think I need to help him," Lilo said.

"Well," Nani said thoughtfully, "what have you tried?"

Lilo ticked off the things she had tried.

"Hmm," said Nani, "I think I see the problem. Do you think those things are funny?"

"Well, no," Lilo admitted. "I'm scared of lobsters, and my face still hurts from making funny faces."

"Maybe Cobra Bubbles feels the same way," said Nani. "You know, he might laugh if he's having a good time. Why don't you start out by doing something fun?"

The next day, Lilo enrolled Cobra Bubbles in her hula class. He did his best to follow the complicated steps of the dance, and Lilo did her best to keep a straight face. But it was impossible. Cobra Bubbles in a grass skirt was the funniest thing she'd ever seen. The other kids in the class thought so, too. Soon they were all laughing – even the hula teacher!

To Lilo's surprise, Cobra Bubbles began to smile. And then he chuckled. And soon enough, Cobra Bubbles was actually laughing!

Lilo thought that Cobra Bubbles's laugh was perfect. It was somehow both quiet and big, and very nice. Just like him. What a nice surprise!

A Never Land Story

It was a cold winter night, and John and Michael just couldn't get to sleep. They climbed onto the bed of their older sister, Wendy.

"Oh, tell us a story, Wendy!" said Michael.

"Yes, please. A Peter Pan story!" pleaded John.

"Certainly," said Wendy. "Have I told you about the time that Peter Pan outsmarted the evil Captain Hook?"

"Yes!" said Michael eagerly. "And we want to hear it again!"

Wendy laughed and began her story. "Well, one night, Captain Hook moored his ship in a secret cove close to the island of Never Land. He and his men rowed ashore quietly, for he was intent on discovering the hiding place of Peter and the Lost Boys.

"Fortunately for Peter Pan," Wendy continued, "his dear friend Tinker Bell learnt of Captain Hook's evil plan ahead of time. She flew to Peter and warned him that the pirate was coming.

"'Oh-ho!' laughed Peter. 'We shall be ready for him then!'

"Peter found a clock just like the one the Crocodile who ate Hook's hand had swallowed. He whistled up into the trees, and a group of his monkey friends appeared. 'Here's

a new toy for you!' Peter shouted, tossing the clock up to them.

"When Hook came to the clearing, the first thing he heard was the ticking clock. The sound seemed to be coming at him from all sides! The monkeys were having a grand time, throwing the clock back and forth among the trees and creeping up behind Hook.

"Seized with terror, Hook and his men raced to their boat and rowed madly back to their ship."

Just then, the Darling children's parents came in to check on them. "You're not telling more of those poppycock stories about Peter Pan, are you, Wendy?" their father asked.

"Peter Pan is real, Father!" cried the children. "We know he is!"

As the parents kissed their children goodnight, they didn't see that a boy in green was crouching just outside the nursery window. He had been listening to the story, and he would be back again – soon.

A Royal Sleepover

Pssssst! Elsa?" Anna gently nudged her sister. "Wake up. I can't sleep!" Anna flopped down on Elsa's bed. "Wanna have a sleepover?"

Elsa grinned. That sounded like fun!

Elsa headed to the kitchen to get snacks. When she got back to her room, she found Anna digging through the wardrobe. "Aha!" Anna cried. "I knew it was here!" Anna held up an old book. Her parents had read it to the sisters every night when they were young.

Elsa looked around. It had been a long time since she'd had a sleepover. "Sooo… what should we do first?" she asked.

Anna was ready. "How about we build a fort, like when we were kids?"

Anna stacked pillows and blankets round the room, making lookouts and hidden caves. Meanwhile, Elsa created icy tunnels and snowy turrets.

Suddenly, there was a knock at the door. It was Olaf! The sisters invited the little snowman to join them.

Soon the friends were happily playing. Olaf was a natural at pick-up sticks. And Anna was great at work of art.

"How about a scary story?" Elsa suggested. Anna went first. Using her spookiest, most dramatic voice, she told the story of the Hairy Hooligan.

Suddenly, a sad whine echoed through the room. "OOOOOOOOOHHHHH!" The cry sounded like it was coming from outside the castle.

Elsa, Anna and Olaf ran to the window. There was a shadowy figure walking towards them!

The trio raced outside. It wasn't a monster after all. It was Sven!

"Sven!" Elsa said. "What's wrong?"

"You couldn't sleep, could you?" Anna asked.

"You should come to our sleepover!" Olaf said.

Soon the group was happily settled in Elsa's room. "How about another story?" Elsa suggested. She held up the book Anna had found.

As Anna, Olaf and Sven got comfortable, Elsa began reading. "'Once upon a time…'"

A short time later, Elsa heard the sounds of heavy breathing around her. Everyone had fallen asleep!

Smiling, Elsa climbed into bed. Then, with one last look at Anna and her friends, Elsa, too, drifted off to sleep.

Rabbit's Frightful Garden

R abbit woke up bright and early. He had a lot of work to do in his garden. There was just one problem. Rabbit had lent all his tools to his friends – and they hadn't returned them.

Meanwhile, Pooh and Piglet were enjoying breakfast with Kanga when Roo bounced in with a bunch of wild flowers.

"Thank you, Roo!" Kanga exclaimed, giving him a kiss. "Let me just trim these."

She rummaged round in a kitchen drawer, where she came across Rabbit's gardening shears. "Oh no," Kanga said. "I never returned these to Rabbit after I borrowed them."

"That reminds me," said Piglet, "I still have Rabbit's rake. And, Pooh, I'll bet you still have Rabbit's shovel."

The friends decided the neighbourly thing to do would be to return Rabbit's tools right away. When they arrived at Rabbit's house, though, their friend was not at home. He was on his way to their houses to get his tools back!

"Rabbit's garden could use some work," Kanga said. "Why don't we take care of it for him as a way of saying that we're sorry for keeping his tools for so long?"

Everyone agreed that this was a really splendid plan.

When they had finished working, they spotted some birds hungrily eyeing the harvest.

"This garden needs a scarecrow!" cried Roo.

The work crew sprang into action, and soon a towering scarecrow was planted right in the middle of the garden. "Won't Rabbit be surprised?" Piglet said proudly.

When Rabbit returned home a few minutes later, he couldn't quite believe his eyes. First he looked at the vegetables, all neatly picked. Then he looked at his garden tools, which had mysteriously reappeared. Finally, he looked at the strange scarecrow, which seemed to be looking right back at him!

"D-d-d-did you do this?" he stammered to the straw man. Just then, a gust of wind knocked over the rake resting on the scarecrow's arm.

Convinced his garden was haunted, Rabbit turned and ran for his life.

"Ahhhhhhhhh!" he screamed as he rushed past his friends.

"I told you he'd be surprised," said Piglet.

Blue Ramone

"Dum-da-dee-dum," Ramone sang to himself in his garage.

"Hey there, buddy! Are you painting yourself again?" It was Lightning, and he had Mater with him.

"I'm painting myself blue for Flo's birthday. It's her favourite colour," Ramone replied. "And I plan on staying this colour for an entire week!"

"Gee whiz!" said Mater. "I've never even seen you stay one colour for a whole day!"

That night, the town gathered for a cruise down Main Street for Flo's birthday. Suddenly, the door of Ramone's garage popped open, and a very blue Ramone emerged, driving low and slow.

"Oh, Ramone!" Flo exclaimed. "You painted yourself blue! Now, are you going to take me on a birthday cruise or what?"

Ramone and Flo slowly cruised down Main Street together as the rest of the cars watched.

The next day, Ramone got up early and started cleaning his garage. But after a few hours, he was finished.

Ramone was tempted to paint himself a new colour. Then he remembered his promise, so he went over to Flo's instead.

"Hey, baby, you want some oil?" Flo asked.

"Yeah, thanks," Ramone said. Then he added, "Do you want me to give you a new paint job?"

"Oh, honey, thanks, but no," Flo said. "I have all this work to do."

Ramone stayed blue the next day and the next. He kept asking all the cars in town if they wanted paint jobs, but no one did.

"Ramone! What's wrong with you, baby?" Flo said. "Listen to me. If you want to paint yourself a new colour, just go right ahead and do it."

"But I made a promise," Ramone said, sadly.

"No. A happy, freshly painted Ramone made that promise," Flo said with a sigh. "I miss that Ramone. Just be yourself."

"Yeah," said Mater. "Just be yourself. We like ya that way."

Ramone turned round. It seemed as if the whole town was there to encourage him. So, Ramone happily went to work painting himself every colour he could find!

Bambi

Night-Time Is for Exploring

"Bambi! Oh, Bambi!"

Bambi slowly opened an eye. "Thumper?" he whispered. "Why aren't you asleep?"

"Asleep? Come on!" cried Thumper. "Sleep is for the birds! How can you sleep when there's so much to see and do at night?"

"But everybody knows that night-time is for sleeping," Bambi said.

"Oh brother," Thumper said. "Do you have a lot to learn! Follow me, Bambi. Flower and I will show you how the night is a whole new day!"

At the prospect of a new adventure, Bambi's sleepiness disappeared. He stood up quietly and let his friends lead the way.

Thumper was right – the forest was as busy at night as it was during the day, but with a whole new group of animals. Owls, raccoons and badgers – all those animals that Bambi thought spent most of their lives asleep – were now as lively as could be.

"Wh-wh-what's that?" Bambi exclaimed as a dot of light landed on his nose.

"Don't worry, Bambi, it's just a firefly," Flower said with a giggle.

"Firefly," Bambi said. Suddenly, the little light disappeared. "Hey, where'd it go?" the little deer asked.

"There it is!" cried Thumper.

Happily, the three friends chased the firefly as it flitted behind a tree and all around the forest.

But their game was soon interrupted by a flurry of sound. Thousands of leathery wings were suddenly beating overhead.

"Duck, Bambi!" shouted Thumper just as the whole group of flying animals swooped around their heads.

"Boy, that was close!" said Flower.

"Were those fireflies, too?" Bambi asked.

"Naw." Thumper laughed. "They didn't light up! Those were bats."

"Bats," repeated Bambi. "They're really busy at night."

"You can say that again," agreed Thumper, trying to stifle a yawn. And, since yawns are contagious, Bambi's own yawn was not far behind.

"This was fun," Bambi told his friend. "But what do you say we go home and go to bed?"

But there was no answer. Thumper and Flower were already fast asleep!

Scary Solar Surfing

Things were busy at the Benbow Inn – and B.E.N. wasn't helping much! The clumsy robot had already spilt purp juice on a whole family of Cyclopes, broken a whole set of Mrs Hawkins's Alponian chowder bowls and was now chasing a healthy serving of Zirellian jellyworms across the dining room floor.

"Don't you worry, Mrs H," B.E.N. reassured the innkeeper. "Tell those spacers their lunch will be on the table in just one minute… whoops! Better make that two minutes."

"Jim!" Mrs Hawkins cried, seeing her son. "Going surfing, I see. Wouldn't you love to take B.E.N. out for a ride with you?"

"Oh boy, oh boy! I've always wanted to do this!" said the robot as Jim unfurled the solar sail and they took off. "Where's the steering wheel? Where's the on button?"

"Hang on there, B.E.N.," said Jim. "There is no steering wheel. All you have to do is lean – like this. And there is no on button. In fact, whatever you do, do not touch this button here!"

"Roger that!" said B.E.N. "Stepping on button a no-no. I completely understand and will not, under any circumstances— Aghhhhhh!"

To Jim's dismay, B.E.N. kicked the very button Jim had warned him not to. Instantly, the sail retracted and the solar surfer began to fall.

"Help! Help! Help!" cried B.E.N., leaping onto Jim's back and holding on with all his might.

It was all Jim could do to balance himself as the surfer spiralled out of control! Luckily, there was no better surfer in all the greater galaxy than young Jim Hawkins, and after a few heart-stopping seconds, they were back under control.

"Phew!" sighed B.E.N., wiping his metal brow. "That was a close one, huh?"

"Yeah," muttered Jim.

"But it was pretty cool, too," B.E.N. went on.

Jim started to smile. "Yeah," he said. "It was."

"Wanna do it again?" asked B.E.N.

Jim's smile widened. "Absolutely!" he said.

And off they went.

The Search for the Sultan's Stone

Agrabah was busy preparing for the Day of Unity – the day each year when the city would celebrate its history. This year was Agrabah's five hundredth anniversary! Jasmine and Aladdin were talking about the Sultan's Stone, a precious stone that the palace servants had failed to find.

Aladdin said, "The first Sultan of Agrabah was beloved by all, but the Sultan's brother was jealous, so he stole an important stone that belonged to the Sultan and hid it behind a waterfall in the jungle. No one has ever been able to find it."

Jasmine decided that she and Aladdin were going to find it. As they entered the jungle, Jasmine asked Aladdin what the Sultan's Stone looked like. "Most people believe it's a statue of the first sultan. No one knows what he looked like."

After a few hours of searching, Abu grew hungry. So, he grabbed a bunch of berries from a nearby bush. As he was about to pop them in his mouth, Jasmine cried, "Abu! Those are Nightbloom berries. They're poisonous."

But the berries had got Jasmine thinking. Nightbloom only grew near water. Jasmine rushed ahead and sure enough, there was the waterfall! Jasmine and Aladdin carefully made their way to the back of the waterfall, but there was only a bare cave wall.

She leaned against it to rest, when suddenly the wall moved. "Aladdin, help me push this open!" she exclaimed. They pushed with all their strength, and slowly the wall began to turn. When it was fully open, there was a secret room!

In the centre of the room was an ancient wooden box. Jasmine picked up the box and opened it. Inside was a simple carving of a woman wearing royal robes. There was some writing on the side. "'The Stone of Lilah, the first ruler of Agrabah',"" Jasmine read. "I guess the first Sultan of Agrabah was actually a sultana."

The next day, back in Agrabah, the crowd cheered as Jasmine revealed what she and Aladdin had found in the jungle. The Day of Unity was a huge success, and the people celebrated the return of the Sultan's Stone.

The Game

Koda the cub loved to tell stories. But sometimes he got a little carried away. One day, he was telling a group of cubs about the fishing expedition he and Kenai had been on the day before.

"And then we caught about a hundred fish! I mean, that pile of salmon must have been as tall as a tree. Of course, I caught most of them, but Kenai caught some, too," he said.

"What did you do with all of them?" asked one little grizzly.

"We ate them all. Yep, we were mighty hungry after all that work," Koda declared.

Just then, Kenai lumbered up to the circle of cubs. "Hey, Kenai," asked one, "is it true that you and Koda caught a hundred fish?"

Kenai shot Koda a stern look. "Well, not exactly," he said.

Later that day, Kenai and Koda went walking in the woods. After a while, it became clear that they were lost.

"Kenai," Koda said, "we're goners."

"Koda! Would you please stop exaggerating all the time?" Kenai scolded. "We're not dead, we're just lost!"

"Look… over… there," said Koda, gesturing. A strange male grizzly was approaching, and he did not look friendly.

"You're right," said Kenai. "We're goners."

"Not yet we aren't," Koda answered, suddenly sounding brave. The cub sprang into action. "Look out, you big lug… I'm a ragin' ball of fur!" The cub darted back and forth, throwing kicks and punches at the air. He shrieked and whooped. He jumped up and down and spun around.

The grizzly stood absolutely still, completely confused by the cub's odd behaviour.

Eventually, he turned and walked off.

"Koda, that's the craziest thing I ever saw," said Kenai, shaking his head in disbelief. "Thank you for saving us."

Safely back at the bear camp that night, Koda recounted their hair-raising adventure to the rest of the group.

"Kenai, did it really happen that way?" one of the cubs asked.

"Yes," said Kenai, smiling. "That's exactly how it happened, believe it or not!"

A Talented Mouse

"Look, Dumbo," Timothy Q. Mouse said, pointing to the newspaper. "There's another article about us in here!"

Mrs Jumbo, Dumbo's mother, peered over Timothy's shoulder. "What a nice story," she cooed. "Too bad the picture isn't better. Why, I can hardly see you, Timothy!"

Timothy peered at the paper. "Hey," he said, scanning the story. "This article doesn't mention me at all!"

"It's all right," Mrs Jumbo said soothingly. "Everyone knows how important you are."

But Timothy wasn't so sure. "Am I really that important?" he said. "It's Dumbo who has the talent, not me."

Timothy wandered away sadly. "I have to figure out a way to get famous on my own," he muttered. "But how?" Suddenly, he snapped his fingers. "I've got it!" he cried. "I'll learn to fly, too! That way Dumbo and I can be famous together!"

Timothy climbed to the top of the tallest circus tent. Dumbo had learnt to fly by jumping off things. Timothy just hoped it would work for him, too. He rubbed his hands together.

"Here goes nothing," he muttered.

He leapt off the tent and looked down. The ground seemed very far away.

"Uh-oh!" Timothy gulped. What had he done?

The ground got closer and closer. Timothy squeezed his eyes shut, but suddenly, he felt himself being whisked upwards. Opening his eyes, he saw that he was clutched in Dumbo's trunk.

"Phew!" he gasped. "Thanks, buddy!"

Dumbo smiled at his little friend. He put Timothy in his cap. Timothy settled into the familiar spot. Flying was much more fun when Dumbo's ears did all the work!

Soon they landed beside Mrs Jumbo.

"Oh, Timothy!" she cried. "You're safe! When I saw you fall, I was so worried. Dumbo and I don't know what we'd do without you."

Timothy blinked. "Never thought of it that way," he mused. "Maybe I'm not front-page news, but who cares? I know I'm important, and my friends know it, too. That's what matters!"

Timothy smiled. He had plenty of his own talent, and that was good enough for him!

THE ARISTOCATS

Street Cats

"Oh, Mama!" said Marie. "Paris is so pretty in the morning! May we please go explore just a bit?"

"All right, darlings," their mother replied. "But just for a few minutes. Madame must be missing us terribly. Be sure to stick together!"

The kittens passed a doorway to a jazz hall, where the previous night's party appeared to still be in full swing. "Oh, yeah!" said Toulouse as he danced in the doorway to the swinging beat.

"Come on, Toulouse," said Berlioz crossly. "I'm hungry!"

A few steps down the street, a fishmonger was just putting out his wares in the window of his shop. The fishmonger smiled at the kittens through the window, then came out of his shop and tossed them each a sardine. "Here you are, my pretty cats!" he said to them.

The kittens miaowed a thank-you and gobbled up the tasty treat. "The streets of Paris are the coolest place on Earth!" said Berlioz as they continued walking. "I don't want to go back to Madame's house!"

"Berlioz! You mustn't speak like that!" said Marie. "You know how much Madame needs us—" Suddenly, she stopped talking. Her brothers followed her gaze, which was directed at the window of a fancy pet shop. "Oh, my!"

she cried out delightedly. "Look at those!" In the window of the shop were several jewelled cat collars, all in different shades of the finest leather. Marie thought they were the most beautiful things she'd ever seen – especially the pink one.

"I must say, the streets of Paris are a wonderful place!" Marie said dreamily.

Just then, they heard a deep barking. A moment later, a huge dog came bounding round the corner. The kittens froze. Then all three of them turned and scampered back down the street in the direction of their mother and Mr O'Malley, with the dog hot on their heels.

"Paris is a fine city," said Berlioz, panting, as he raced down an alley. Darting behind some large bins, the kittens were able to lose the snarling dog.

"Yes," replied Marie. "But I'm not sure how I feel about the Parisians – particularly the canine kind!"

A Barrel of Monkeys

Mowgli and his pal Baloo were taking a lazy afternoon stroll through the jungle when they decided they were hungry.

Mowgli knew what to do. He shimmied up a tree, plucked a bunch of bananas and tossed them down to the bear.

"That's my boy!" Baloo cried proudly.

But as he was scrambling back down, Mowgli spotted a flash of orange, black and white.

"Shere Khan!" Mowgli whispered to Baloo. "We've got to get out of here!"

The tiger hated men and wanted Mowgli out of the jungle.

The two friends didn't know which way to turn. Now that Shere Khan had their scent, it would be almost impossible to lose him. Then they heard a lively beat drumming its way through the jungle.

"Oh no," said Mowgli. "King Louie and his crazy band of monkeys. That's all we need!"

Baloo's eyes lit up. "That's exactly what we need, Little Britches!"

Still clutching the bananas, Baloo and Mowgli ran towards King Louie's compound. When they arrived, Baloo disguised himself as an orangutan. The monkeys were so busy dancing and singing that they didn't notice his disguise.

The bear quickly found a huge empty barrel and filled it with the bananas.

"Look!" cried Baloo, peering into the barrel. "Lunch!" The monkeys ran over and jumped right into the barrel! They greedily ate the feast, tossing skins out as they made their way through the bunch.

Baloo signalled to Mowgli, who came out of hiding. "Come and get me, Shere Khan!" the Man-cub taunted.

Within seconds, the tiger appeared in the clearing, a fierce gleam in his eye.

"Hello, Stripes," Baloo greeted him cheerfully. Then the bear picked up the barrel, heaved it and sent King Louie's troop flying at Shere Khan.

The now-angry monkeys landed on the tiger's back, where they frantically jumped up and down, pulling on his tail and ears. Mowgli and Baloo watched as Shere Khan raced back into the jungle, trying to free himself from his shrieking passengers.

"Like I always say," Baloo declared as he grinned at Mowgli, "there's nothing more fun than a crazy barrel of monkeys!"

Disney Cinderella

The Dance Lesson

"Just imagine," said Cinderella excitedly. "There's a ball at the palace tonight in honour of the prince, and every maiden in the land is invited. That means me, too!"

All of Cinderella's animal friends clapped and chirped. They loved their Cinderelly.

"Oh dear," said Cinderella with a sigh. "There is so much to do! And I can only go if I finish my chores."

Suddenly, three loud shrieks came from somewhere downstairs.

"Cinderellllaaaa! Come down here immediately and help us get ready for the ball!" her stepsisters cried together. And so Cinderella set to work helping her stepsisters.

Hours later, Cinderella began her other chores. There was so much to do. How would she ever finish in time for the ball?

Suddenly, Jaq had an idea. "I know!" he said to the other mice. "We help-a Cinderelly!" The mice nodded in agreement. Soon everyone was happily cleaning and singing.

As she worked, Cinderella began to imagine the evening ahead. She would wear her mother's beautiful gown. The ballroom would come alive with music and dancing. The handsome young prince would bow before Cinderella and ask her to dance…

Suddenly, Cinderella looked up, alarmed.

"Oh no!" she cried. "I don't even know how to dance!"

"Don't you worry, Cinderelly!" Jaq smiled reassuringly. "Us show you! Easy as pie!"

With that, Jaq bowed before Perla and extended his hand. "Dance, please, missy?" he asked.

Perla blushed as she took Jaq's hand. Soon the two mice were gliding across the floor.

"See?" said Perla. "Not so scary."

Using her broom as an imaginary partner, Cinderella danced and twirled gracefully around the room. She led everyone across the floor, sweeping and cleaning as they went. Then the mice collapsed on the floor, laughing.

"Good-good, Cinderelly!" said Jaq, beaming. "Lucky prince gets to dance with Cinderelly."

"Thank you all so much," Cinderella told her friends. "With your help, tonight might be the night that all my dreams come true!"

Woodland Washing

Briar Rose sang as she hung the sheets on the washing line. "Don't you just love the sunshine?" she asked a bluebird who was chirping along with her.

The bird chirped a new song in response, and Briar Rose laughed as she pulled her Aunt Flora's red dress out of the basket of clean washing.

Aunt Merryweather's blue dress was next. Briar Rose was just pegging the shoulder to the washing line when suddenly a pair of cheeky chipmunks leapt onto the line from a tree and raced down the length of it, covering the dresses and the sheets with muddy footprints.

"Look what you've done, you naughty chipmunks!" Briar Rose scolded. She shook a finger at the creatures. "It took me two hours to get those dresses and sheets clean! Now I'll have to wash them all over again."

Sighing with frustration, Briar Rose unpegged the sheets from the line and pulled a fresh bucket of water up from the well. Then, taking the washboard and the bar of soap, she began to scrub out the muddy prints. It looked as if she wouldn't have a walk today after all.

Suddenly, a chattering noise caught her attention.

Looking up, she saw the chipmunks hurrying out of the forest with several other forest animals at their heels. There were two rabbits, four chipmunks, three bluebirds, a deer, a skunk and an owl.

Briar Rose laughed. "Why, you've brought all your friends! What a wonderful surprise!"

The chipmunks chattered excitedly and the animals all set to work. The birds lifted the sheet into the air so the edges wouldn't get dirty while Briar Rose scrubbed. The deer, the skunk and the rabbits brought fresh water from the well. And the chipmunks scampered across the bar of soap to get their feet all soapy, then walked across the muddy parts of the sheets until they were clean.

When the washing was done, everyone helped hang the clean dresses and sheets on the line for a second time.

Briar Rose smiled at her animal friends and gave the chipmunks a little pat.

"Finished at last," she said. "Now we can all take a walk in the forest... together!"

Home Is Where the Heart Is

Tod, an orphaned baby fox, was still getting used to his new surroundings in Widow Tweed's house. Why, Tod was so young, he was still getting used to being a fox!

In the kitchen, Tod's attention was caught by the large box with a door that Widow Tweed kept opening and closing. Each time she opened the door, Tod caught a glimpse of the box's brightly lit interior and got a whiff of all kinds of delicious treats inside!

But when Tod hopped inside the box, unseen by Widow Tweed as she was closing the door, he got a surprise. It was cold inside! And as soon as the door closed, Tod found himself sitting in complete darkness.

Luckily, Widow Tweed heard Tod's whimpers and opened the fridge door.

"Why, Tod, how did you get in there?" she said.

Tod hopped out and darted away. Outside, Tod could see his friends Big Mama the owl and Dinky the sparrow chatting on a tree branch. Tod leant forwards to hop outside and join them, but his nose hit something smooth, hard and solid. But it was clear; he could see right through it.

Widow Tweed chuckled as she watched from the living room doorway.

"Discovered glass, have you, Tod?" she asked with a kind smile.

Whatever 'glass' was, Tod supposed he'd have to stay indoors. He hopped onto a table and studied a small square object with some knobs on it. He batted one of the knobs. The knob turned all the way round, and a loud noise blared out of the object. Startled, Tod bolted under the sofa.

Widow Tweed rushed over and turned the knob. The noise stopped. Then she coaxed Tod out from under the sofa. "There, there, Tod," she cooed, cradling him in her arms and petting his head. "That's just the radio. You're having a hard time getting used to everything in this strange new place, aren't you? Here, let's have a snack."

It had been a tricky morning for the baby fox. But there, in Widow Tweed's arms, Tod felt a comforting, familiar feeling at last. It was the feeling of being warm and cared for.

At that moment, Tod's new home didn't feel so strange after all.

The Riley and Bing Bong Band

Riley and her imaginary friend Bing Bong loved making music together. "We should go on tour!" Riley told Bing Bong one day. "To Australia! We can play for the kangaroos!"

"But how will we get there?" asked Bing Bong.

"We can take our rocket!" said Riley.

So, Riley told her mum and dad about her plan to go to Australia.

"Be back for dinner," said Mum. "I'm making my famous mashed potatoes."

Riley and Bing Bong packed up everything they needed. Then they climbed into the rocket and prepared for lift-off.

"Activating rocket booster," said Riley. "Mission Control, all systems are go!"

Riley and Bing Bong began the countdown. "Ten, nine, eight, seven, six, five, four, three, two, one… BLAST-OFF!"

But nothing happened.

"Of course!" said Riley. "The rocket can't fly without fuel!"

Riley and Bing Bong smiled at each other. Once again, they prepared for take-off. But this time, they were really ready.

Riley and Bing Bong began to sing their special song. "Who's your friend who likes to play?"

The rocket answered back, binging and bonging. Then it rumbled and roared as it flew out of the window!

As they soared over the ocean, Riley and Bing Bong saw a shark, a sea turtle, a walrus and penguins. So far, this was the best trip ever!

Soon they could see land. "Australia!" shouted Riley.

The creatures down under welcomed Riley and Bing Bong with big smiles. "Play us a tune, mates," said a koala.

Riley and Bing Bong played all of their songs, and the crowd went wild.

Suddenly, a familiar smell drifted through the air. "Mom's famous mashed potatoes," Riley whispered to Bing Bong. "It's time to go home."

The two played one last song. Then they said goodbye to their new friends and rocketed back to Minnesota.

"So, how was Australia?" asked Dad.

"It was great!" said Riley. "Tomorrow we're going on another trip – to play for the penguins in Antarctica!"

Miss Bianca's First Rescue

The headquarters of the Rescue Aid Society was buzzing with activity. Mice from all over the world had gathered together for an emergency meeting. The chairman of the society had to shout to be heard over the hubbub.

"Attention, delegates!" he cried. "I have called this meeting because a canine urgently needs our help." He clapped his hands. "Mice scouts, bring in the distressed doggy!"

Two mouse workers hurried into the room, leading a small dog with a long body and short little legs. His head was stuck inside a dog food tin.

Suddenly, the door to the meeting room flew open and a pretty little mouse walked in. She wore a fashionable coat and expensive perfume.

"Oh, excuse me," she said. "I seem to be in the wrong place. I'm looking for Micey's Department Store?" Then she noticed one of the mice holding the tin opener. "Dear me, what are you doing to that poor dog?"

"The dog is quite stuck, I'm afraid," the chairman told her. "But don't you worry, miss. We have this situation under control."

The glamorous mouse rolled up her sleeves and marched over to the dog. She kicked the top of the dog food tin three times. Then she gave it a swift twist to the left. The tin popped off!

"Hooray!" the mice all cheered happily.

The little mouse smiled. "That's how I open jars of pickle at home," she explained. "Well, I'd best be on my way."

"Ah, Mr Chairman?" a voice piped up from the corner of the room. It was the Zambian delegate.

"Yes?" said the chairman.

"I'd like to nominate Miss… uh, Miss…" The delegate looked at the pretty mouse.

"Miss Bianca," she told him.

"I'd like to nominate Miss Bianca for membership in the Rescue Aid Society," he said.

The chairman turned to the rest of the mouse delegates. "All in favour, say aye!"

"Aye!" all the mice cried.

"Aroof!" the dog barked happily.

Miss Bianca smiled. "Well," she said, "I suppose Micey's can wait for another day."

A Fine Feathered Friend

One afternoon, Woody was watching his favourite TV show – *Woody's Roundup*. On the show, Sheriff Woody was repainting the old jailhouse. His horse, Bullseye, whinnied and stomped the ground.

"Not today, partner," Woody said. "I've got to finish painting and then I'm helping Miss Tilley with her errands."

Bullseye snorted and wandered off to find Jessie. She was feeding peanuts to a squirrel. Bullseye bent his front legs so she could climb on his back.

"Oh, sorry, Bullseye," she said. "I promised to help this little guy gather some nuts for his friends. Some other time."

Bullseye sadly lowered his head to munch some grass. He felt very lonely. Suddenly, he saw something sitting among the weeds. It was a brown, speckled egg. Bullseye looked around for a mother hen, but there wasn't one in sight. So Bullseye found an old basket nearby and used it to carry the egg back to town.

Bullseye cared for the egg just like a mother hen. He tucked hay round it to keep it warm and checked on it every hour. Finally, one afternoon, Bullseye heard a tapping sound. Tap-tap-tap. It was the egg! He watched it closely. A little beak poked through, then the egg cracked open! A tiny yellow chick with spots on its back appeared. Bullseye named him Horsefeathers.

One day, Bullseye and Horsefeathers met Woody and Jessie at the stables. Horsefeathers was trotting around outside. "Neigh!" he said.

Jessie looked worried. "Horsefeathers should be learning how to be a chicken, not a horse," she said quietly.

"You've done a fine job, partner," Woody told his horse. "But Horsefeathers needs to be with his real family."

Just then, a mother hen and her chicks went past. Woody heard the strangest sound. "Peep! Peep! Peep!" It was Horsefeathers, chirping like a chick for the first time!

Horsefeathers ran over to his real mother and she tucked him under her wing.

"He is one unique bird," Woody said, shaking his head.

"And Bullseye is one unique horse," Jessie added. She gave Bullseye a hug. "Good job, partner!"

Disney
Winnie the Pooh

Eeyore Beats the Heat

Eyore sighed.
"Something the matter, Eeyore?" asked Roo.

"Oh, it's just that it's so terribly hot," replied Eeyore. "If I weren't stuffed with sawdust, I think I would melt."

"Well, come with me!" squeaked Roo. "I'm going to the stream to cool off."

But Eeyore shook his head. "Can't do, Roo," he said. "Not with my sawdust and all, I'd probably just sink. And that's if I'm lucky."

So Roo, who felt sorry for Eeyore, but who was also eager to swim, continued on his way.

Soon another friend came along. And this friend was Winnie the Pooh.

"You're looking a little warmish, Eeyore," Pooh said.

"Same to you," said Eeyore with a sigh. "Same to you."

"Ah," said Pooh, "but I am off to catch a breeze – and pay a call on some bees – with my trusty balloon here. Care to join me?"

"No, thanks, Pooh," said Eeyore. "I never did like feeling as if the ground was missing. And I expect that with my luck, the balloon would probably pop just as soon as I'm high up in the air."

"I understand completely, Eeyore. Wish me luck, then, won't you?" Pooh replied.

"Good luck, Pooh," said Eeyore. "As if anything I ever wish comes true."

The next friend to come upon Eeyore was little Piglet.

"Hello, there, Eeyore," said Piglet. "Whoo! Are you as uncomfortably hot as I am?"

"Oh no," said Eeyore. "I'm sweltering."

"Poor Eeyore," said Piglet. "Why don't you come play in the cool mud with me?"

But once again, Eeyore shook his head. "Afraid mud is not an option, Piglet," he said. "Once I get dirty, I'll never get clean. No. Go enjoy yourself on this hot day like everyone else. All except me. As usual. I'll just suffer."

And suffer poor Eeyore did… until not too terribly much later when his friends all returned with something sure to cool off even Eeyore on this sultry day.

"Guess what we've brought you, Eeyore!" Roo squealed with delight.

"It's ice cream," whispered Pooh.

"Ice cream, huh?" Eeyore sighed. "I suppose I'll have to eat it all before it melts."

And do you know what? He did!

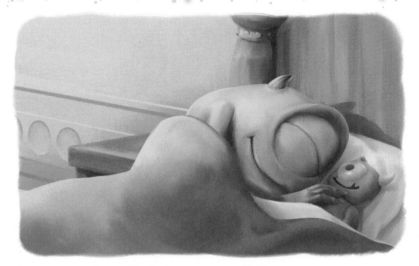

Mike's Worst Nightmare

"AAAAAAIEEEE-AHHHH!"
Sulley sat bolt upright in bed. The anguished yell was coming from his room-mate Mike's bedroom. Sulley raced out of his bedroom and threw open Mike's door.

"Hi," said Mike in a shaky voice. "I guess I must have had a bad dream."

Sulley nodded.

"Uh, Sulley, do you want to hear about it?" Mike asked with a hopeful grin.

Sulley came over and sat down on the edge of his friend's bed. "Okay," he said.

"I dreamt…" Mike began. "This is going to sound really, really crazy, I know, but… I dreamt that there was a kid, a human kid, in my wardrobe over there!"

"Now, now," said Sulley, smiling at Mike. "Maybe it was the movie you watched tonight."

"Kidzilla?" Mike scoffed. "Nah. I've seen it a dozen times and it's never bothered me before."

"Well, why don't you try to go back to sleep?" said Sulley, suppressing a yawn.

Mike cleared his throat shyly. "When I was little, my mum would bring me a sludge lolly when I had a bad dream," he said.

Sulley sighed patiently, then went and brought Mike a sludge lolly from the kitchen.

"She would sing me a little lullaby, too," said Mike.

In his low, scratchy voice, Sulley began to sing: "Rock-a-bye, Mikey, Googly-Bear, with sharp little fangs and shiny green hair! Morning will come when the sun starts to rise, and you'll wake up and open those googly eyes!"

"'That googly eye,'" Mike corrected him, snuggling under his blanket. "Uh, my mum also always checked the wardrobe."

With another patient sigh, Sulley opened Mike's wardrobe door and stepped inside. "Nope. Nothing in here!" he called. Suddenly, there was a loud clatter and a landslide of junk spilt out of the wardrobe door. A yellow mop fell out. It looked just like blonde hair!

"AHHHH!" shrieked Mike, leaping out from under the covers. Then he relaxed. "Oh, sorry, pal. In this dim light, I thought that mop was, you know, a human child!"

Sulley chuckled at the idea. "Don't be silly, Mike," he said. "A kid will never get loose in Monstropolis – what a disaster that would be!"

Disney
Robin hood

The Wrong Shortcut

It was summertime in Sherwood Forest. Birds were singing, bees were buzzing and wildflowers covered the fields. The day was so beautiful that Robin Hood and Little John went into the woods to pick berries. Maid Marian came along, too.

"The sweetest berries can be found on the other side of the creek," Little John declared. "And I know how to get there."

A little while later, the three friends reached the creek. It was wide and deep. A rickety bridge went over the water.

Little John stepped onto the bridge. The wood groaned under his weight. Little John took each step carefully, but in the end, it didn't matter. Halfway across the bridge, a board broke under his feet. Little John landed in the creek with a big splash! Sputtering, he swam to the other side.

"I made it across!" he called.

"But you weren't supposed to get wet!" called Robin, laughing. "Luckily, I'm more clever than you. I can cross the bridge and stay dry, too."

"Oh Robin, let me do it," said Marian. "I'm sure I can cross without falling in the water!"

But Robin just shook his head. "It's too dangerous," he said. "Don't worry, I'm too clever to fall into the creek."

Very carefully, Robin stepped onto the bridge. He tested each plank before he put his foot on it. But before he reached the other side, there was a loud crack. Robin broke through the bridge and plunged into the cold water. Shivering, he swam to the other side. "The bridge is far too dangerous!" Robin called to Marian. "Don't cross. You'll only fall into the water."

But Marian just smiled. Cautiously, she tiptoed her way onto the bridge. Since she was lighter than Robin and Little John, she made it all the way to the other side – without getting a drop of water on her dress!

"How did you do that?" Robin asked later as they danced.

Maid Marian smiled. "Bigger and stronger doesn't always work better," she said. "Sometimes you need a Marian to do a Merry Man's job!"

A Prizewinning Pair

Max and his dad, Goofy, were sitting at the breakfast table. Max looked at the funny pages, while Goofy leafed through the other sections of the newspaper.

"Listen to this!" said Goofy. "Channel Ten is sponsoring the Father and Son of the Year Contest. The father and son who can prove that they have achieved something truly incredible together will appear on national TV."

"Too bad Bigfoot ruined that video we took of him last summer," said Max. "Hey, I know! Why don't we go back and find him again?"

"Okay, Maxie. Count me in!" said Goofy.

Goofy and Max reached the campsite that night, pitched their tent and went to sleep. Soon they were awakened by a loud crash.

"It's him!" cried Max. "Get the camera!"

But when they poked their heads out, they saw it wasn't Bigfoot at all, but Pete and P. J..

"I'm sorry," said P. J.. "I told my dad about your trip, and now he wants us to win that prize. We're out here looking for Bigfoot, just like you two are."

The next day, Pete set up a barbecue with several juicy steaks.

"This will lure him out for sure," he told P. J..

The trick worked. In a matter of minutes, Bigfoot crashed through the trees and made a beeline for the meat. "Tackle him, P. J.!" yelled Pete.

Though he was scared, P. J. did as he was told. Bigfoot threw him around while Pete turned on the camera. "The judges are going to love this!" cried Pete.

"Help!" P. J. begged.

Goofy and Max heard P. J.'s cries and came running from the lake. Without saying a word, Goofy jabbed the monster in the backside with a fishing rod while Max threw a fishing net over the monster's head. "You were awesome," Max told Goofy.

"Right back at you, son," Goofy replied.

Back at home, Pete handed in the video. The judges had decided Goofy and Max deserved the award! But on the day they were to appear on TV, Goofy and Max decided to go to the beach together instead. They realised they didn't need anybody to tell them what an incredible father-and-son team they were.

They knew it already!

16
June

Sarge's Boot Camp

"First gear!" Sarge shouted. Guido and Luigi started moving slowly. "Second gear! Third gear! Fourth gear!"

Luigi raced down Main Street with Guido close behind. Sarge had decided to start a training camp for all the four-by-fours that he was sure would soon be arriving in Radiator Springs.

"Hey!" Sheriff yelled. "Slow down, fellas!"

Just then a big, brand-new four-by-four rolled into town. "Hi," said the four-by-four. "I'm T. J.."

"Welcome to Radiator Springs, T. J.!" Sarge shouted to the newcomer. "You've reached the home of my boot camp!"

"Car camp!" Luigi shouted happily. "It will be tough! But don't worry. Guido and I are fully prepared to change your tyres at any time."

"You mean I might get a flat tyre?" T. J. said.

"You will if you don't change that attitude!" exclaimed Sarge. "Now, let's get going!"

Sarge led the group out of town to a rocky dirt road. "Oh no!" T. J. complained. "I've already got dirt in my grille!"

"No talking!" shouted Sarge. "Now… first gear! Second gear! Third gear!"

"Come on, T. J.," said Luigi. "If Guido can do it, so can you!"

"Okay, team!" said Sarge. "We're going down that slope and across that big, muddy puddle."

T. J. gasped. He could lose control going too fast down the hill! But down, down, down they went. "I'm gonna flip over!" T. J. cried.

"Hit the brakes!" Sarge called out. "Show a bit of courage, soldier!"

Soon they were at the bottom of the hill, crossing the muddy puddle. T. J. hesitated.

"Come on!" Luigi called to T. J. "You're a four-by-four! This should be no problem."

T. J. thought about it and began to laugh. "I'm dirty, my paint is scratched and I'm tired. But I can do it! Thanks, Guido. Thanks, Luigi."

"Now hit the showers!" Sarge shouted. "We've got a big day tomorrow!"

"Sir! Yes, sir!" T. J. yelled.

Luigi and Guido looked up the steep hill in front of them. "Come on, guys! Hop onto my roof rack! I'll give you a ride," T. J. offered.

Together the cars raced up the hill and back to town – excited about the next day of Sarge's boot camp!

A Special Song

King Triton's birthday was in a couple of days, and Sebastian was planning a very special performance. Triton's daughter, Ariel, would sing while the orchestra played a brand-new tune. But they still had a lot of work to do. During rehearsals, a young mermaid named Coral kept accidentally dropping her cymbals.

Sebastian threw down his baton. "Rehearsal is over!" he yelled.

Ariel comforted Coral and invited her to see all the treasures in her grotto. Ariel told Coral the grotto could be her secret place, too.

A few days later, as Ariel swam towards the grotto, she heard someone singing. The voice was strong and sweet. When Ariel arrived, she saw her new friend.

"Coral! You have such a lovely voice! You should be singing in the concert, not playing the cymbals."

The little mermaid shrugged. "I just like singing to myself," she explained. "I've never actually performed for anyone."

The next day at rehearsal, Sebastian made Ariel and the orchestra practise over and over.

"The big day is tomorrow!" the crab said, fretting. "Let's try it again."

By the end of the afternoon, Ariel had lost her voice! Luckily, she knew who could take her place.

"Me?" Coral said when the princess asked her. "But I can't!"

"You must!" Sebastian insisted. "Or King Triton's birthday celebration will be completely ruined!"

Coral knew her new friend was counting on her. "All right," she said. "I'll do it."

That night, Coral took a deep breath, swam onstage and started to sing. Before she knew it, the concert was over and the audience began to cheer!

"Coral," said Sebastian, smiling, "from now on, you're going to be a court singer!"

After the show, Ariel found Coral with her family.

"I didn't know you could sing!" one of Coral's sisters exclaimed.

"No one ever would have known if it weren't for Ariel," replied Coral. "She believed in me."

Ariel still couldn't speak, but she gave Coral a big hug. It had been a wonderful evening!

Knock, Knock! Who's There?

Standing in her brand-new bedroom, Lilo grinned. She wasn't quite sure that the wardrobe was in exactly the right place, but she loved everything else.

Lilo walked out into the living room to join Nani, her sister. Nani was worried. Cobra Bubbles, their social worker, was coming today to see how they were doing.

"Lilo, I want you to stay out of the workers' way," Nani said. "And keep an eye on Stitch! He keeps licking our nice new windows!"

"We'll stay out of trouble." Lilo smiled angelically.

Stitch wasn't exactly staying out of trouble. He had a tool belt round his waist, and his mouth was full of nails. With amazing force, Stitch spit the nails into the floor, accidentally fastening the end of his own belt to the ground.

Lilo shrugged. "That'll keep you out of trouble." Then there was a knock at the door. Lilo opened the new front door. Cobra Bubbles filled the door frame.

"Hey, come on in and see our new digs!" Lilo cried, happy to see her friend.

Cobra Bubbles stepped over a power cable and walked round a pile of flooring.

"You don't actually live here yet, do you?"

he asked slowly.

"Not yet," Lilo chirped. "It's supposed to be finished next month."

"And where is… Stitch?" Cobra Bubbles peered around the room.

Lilo frowned. Stitch was no longer nailed to the floor.

Suddenly, they heard a knock. Lilo and Nani looked at each other. It wasn't coming from the front door – in fact, it sounded like it was coming from Lilo's room!

"Who is it?" Lilo asked quietly.

With a monumental crash, Stitch burst through one of the new walls in Lilo's bedroom.

"Here he is!" Lilo shouted.

"Yes," said Nani nervously. "Stitch sure is, uh, helping out with the DIY. Why, here he's decided on a new spot for Lilo's wardrobe. We didn't really want it where it was, anyway."

Nani gave Cobra Bubbles a weak smile, then turned to look at Stitch's handiwork.

"Actually," Nani said with a real smile, "this is a much better spot for the wardrobe. Thanks, Stitch!"

Doctor Doppler, Daredevil

Dr Delbert Doppler didn't know how he had got himself into this mess. There he was, standing atop a cliff on a solar surfer with fifteen-year-old Jim Hawkins, who was about to launch them into the Etherium on a narrow plank of metal powered by energy-panel sails.

"Hold on, Doctor," said Jim. "Here we go!"

Jim launched the surfer off the cliff. In a flash, they were sailing through the Etherium.

Ever since they had both returned from their amazing adventure on Treasure Planet, the two had become quite close. Doppler had thought solar surfing would be a fun bonding experience. But now he wasn't so sure it was a good idea.

Jim, an expert solar surfer, was in complete control. In fact, he was going easy on Dr Doppler. If Jim had been surfing on his own, he would have been free-falling, rolling and twirling through the air. But he didn't want to scare his passenger.

Dr Doppler tried to put on a brave face. "Wow, Jim," he said through clenched teeth. "This is awful... er... awesome!"

"Really? You like it?" Jim replied. "Well, then, maybe we should try some more advanced moves. Like maybe a barrel roll?"

"No, no, no, no!" Dr Doppler cried out anxiously. "I mean... m-maybe not today. Perhaps never... er... next time."

"Okay," Jim said with a shrug.

Five minutes later, Jim landed the surfer smoothly on a level patch of ground behind the inn.

For Dr Doppler it was not a moment too soon. He leapt off the surfer and knelt down to kiss the solid ground. Then, realising that Jim was looking at him funnily, he stood up and cleared his throat.

"Thank you, Jim," he said, a slight quiver creeping into his voice. "That was really intimidating... I mean, exhilarating!"

Jim smiled. "So maybe I'll take you solar surfing again sometime?"

Dr Doppler flushed, unprepared for the question. "Uh... er... that sounds terrifying... er... terrible... I mean, terrific!"

Just Like Dad

"Dad, when I grow up, I want to be just like you," Simba said to his father.

Mufasa nuzzled his son's head. "All in good time, son," he said.

Simba's friend Nala bounded up to them. "Come on, Simba!" she called. "Let's go play by the river!"

On their way, Simba stopped abruptly. "Listen to this," he said. He threw back his head and roared as loudly as he could. Then he looked at her expectantly. "Do I sound like my dad?"

Nala tried to suppress a giggle. "Not quite," she said.

Simba was eyeing a tree branch that extended over the raging river. "I may not be as big as my dad yet, but at least I'm as brave as he is!" he shouted, and he raced up to the tree. Climbing its gnarled trunk, he began walking along the branch over the water.

Nala hurried over. "Simba!" she yelled. "Come back here! The branch is going to break!"

But Simba couldn't hear her over the loud waters. As Nala bounded away to get help, Simba felt the branch begin to sag.

"Uh-oh," Simba said to himself.

Suddenly, the whole thing broke off and Simba tumbled into the water! The current was strong, and he struggled to swim to the riverbank. He was running out of strength, and he realised he might not make it.

Then he felt himself being lifted out of the water and tossed to safety. Dripping and coughing, he looked up – right into the angry eyes of his father.

"Simba!" thundered Mufasa. "There's a big difference between being brave and being foolish! The sooner you learn that, the better chance you will have of growing old!"

Simba hung his head. Out of the corner of his eye, he saw Nala. She was pretending not to overhear. "I'm… sorry, Dad," he said softly. "I just wanted to be brave, like you."

His father's gaze softened. "Well," he said. "As long as we're soaking wet, why don't we go to a quieter part of the river and do some swimming?" He looked over to where Nala was sitting. "Come along, Nala!" he called.

"Yippee!" cried the cubs, and they all went off together.

A Real Boy

It was morning in the village, and Pinocchio leapt out of bed and rushed to his mirror. He laughed when he saw his reflection. It wasn't a dream; the Blue Fairy had made him a real boy! He stared at his new face, until he smelt a lovely scent coming from the kitchen. As he sniffed, he felt a strange feeling in his stomach.

Is this hunger? he wondered.

Downstairs, his father had prepared a breakfast with lots of different foods. Geppetto grinned when he saw Pinocchio.

"I wanted to cook you something special for your first breakfast, but I couldn't decide. So I made everything!"

Pinocchio tried a bite of each food and savoured the different tastes. After they were both full, Geppetto packed up the remaining food and he and Pinocchio left to explore the village.

The first thing Pinocchio noticed as he stepped out of the dark cottage was the heat of the sun on his skin. He and Geppetto played a game, running from cool shadows, into the warm sun, then back again. But then, Pinocchio's stomach felt strange. It was different to hunger. It was…

Hic.

"What–hic–is going–hic–on?" Pinocchio stammered. He was starting to get scared.

"It's only hiccups," Geppetto explained. "Just hold your breath for a moment."

Pinocchio did just that, and the sensation went away. He wasn't sure he liked this. He was so caught up in the fun side of being real that he hadn't considered the bad things.

They continued their journey until they finally reached a picnic spot. Although Pinocchio was hot and his feet hurt, he had a wonderful time with his father. They splashed in the river and ate more delicious food. The water was cool on his skin and he didn't even mind when he scraped his knee on a willow tree.

Finally, it was time to go home. Geppetto lifted Pinocchio onto his shoulders.

"That was fun, Father," Pinocchio said. "But it was hard, too."

Geppetto nodded. "That's what being alive is. It's fun things and it's also bad things. But I promise, no matter what, I'll be there with you."

The Missing Vegetables

Of all the things Belle loved about the Beast's castle, one of her favourites was the garden in the back. She had read every one of the Beast's books about gardening, and every season she experimented with something new. This summer, she'd decided to try growing vegetables. And now they were ready to be picked. She was planning to use them to make the Beast a salad for lunch.

Belle slipped on her gardening gloves and her sun hat, grabbed her biggest basket and happily skipped out into the garden.

"First," she said out loud, to no one in particular, "let's get some lettuce!"

But when she bent down to where the lettuce should have been, she found a bed of empty soil.

"My lettuce!" she cried. "Where did it go?"

Bewildered, Belle moved on to where her sweet, tender carrots had been growing.

"Oh dear!" she cried. "There's nothing here, either!"

And there wasn't a single pea to be found. "I don't understand," she said.

But facts were facts. The garden was empty, and there was nothing she could do but go back to the castle and look for a book about building fences for next summer's garden!

As she walked inside, empty-handed and disappointed, Belle passed Mrs Potts and Chip.

"What's the matter, dear?" asked Mrs Potts.

"Oh, everything!" Belle sighed. "My whole garden has been robbed." Then she shrugged. "So much for my salad idea."

"Don't feel sad, Belle," Chip said. "Come and have some lunch."

"I'm not hungry," Belle replied with a sad smile.

"Oh, I don't know," said Mrs Potts, steering her into the dining room. "You might be—"

"SURPRISE!" called the Beast.

"What?" Belle gasped. There, laid out on the table, was what looked like every possible vegetable from her garden, washed and sliced and arranged just so on fancy plates.

"You've been working so hard in the garden," the Beast explained. "I thought it would be nice if I did something for you. I hope you like it."

Belle smiled. What a treat!

First Impressions

Bambi was just discovering the wonders of the forest. His mother had brought him to a little clearing in the woods. While his mother grazed nearby, Bambi began to explore. He found a patch of green grass and clover, and he bent down to eat. When his nose was just a few centimetres from the tips of the grass, he suddenly leapt backwards in alarm. A leaf had just sprung up from the patch of grass and landed a few metres away.

Bambi looked round to where his mother stood, still grazing. She seemed to think they were in no great danger. So he followed the leaf all the way to the edge of the clearing, where a wide brook babbled over craggy rocks.

Bambi's fascination with the hopping leaf faded as he approached the brook. Water cascaded smoothly over the rocks, bubbling and frothing in shallow pools. He took a step closer and felt his foot touch a rock at the edge of the water.

Suddenly, the rock moved! It shuffled towards the water and then – plop! – jumped right in and swam away.

Bambi was dumbfounded as he watched it dive beneath the surface and vanish. He stared at the spot where the rock had been for a moment, then bent forwards to have a drink.

Bambi jumped in surprise. There in the water, staring right back up at him, was another little deer! Cautiously, he approached the water again. Yes, there it was!

Bambi turned and bounded back across the clearing to his mother.

"Mama! Mama!" he cried. "You will never guess what I have seen today!"

His mother lifted her head and gazed at him with her clear, bright eyes.

"First," he said, "I saw a jumping leaf. Then I saw a rock with legs that walked right into the water and swam away! And then," he continued in amazement, "I saw a little deer who lives in the water! He's right over there, Mama!"

His mother nuzzled her son's face, thinking over what he had said. Then she laughed gently.

"Darling," she said, "I think you have just seen your first grasshopper, your first turtle and your very own reflection!"

Woody's Hat

It was Saturday morning, and the toys in Andy's room were waking up. Jessie yawned and stretched. "It's time for *Woody's Roundup!*"

On the show, Woody's hat flew off and Bullseye trampled it! Jessie picked up the hat. It looked pretty ragged.

"I have lots of hats," Jessie told Woody. "Maybe you can find a new one."

Jessie brought Woody all the hats she could carry. There were so many, they tumbled out of her arms.

Woody picked up one of the hats and put it on his head. "What do you think?" he asked.

Jessie smiled. "It looks mighty fine."

"I don't know," Woody said. "Do you think it's too brown?"

"How about that one?" Jessie said, gesturing towards a hat with buttons on the band. "It's a lighter brown."

"That one's not brown enough," Woody said.

"Hmm," Jessie sighed. She piled more and more hats onto Woody's lap. "There must be a hat here that you like. Keep trying. How about this one?"

"That one is pink!" Woody said. "I'm sorry, Jessie, but none of those are right for me."

Jessie couldn't believe that Woody couldn't find one hat he liked in the huge pile she had brought.

"What we really need is a plan," she told Woody. "Why don't you tell me just what kind of hat you're looking for, then we can try to find it in the pile."

Woody leant against the fence and thought. "I'd definitely like a brown hat," he said. "Not too dark or too light, but brown is best. It would be nice if it had a wide brim. And it should have stitching round the edge. But I don't think we'll find anything like that."

Woody looked hopeless. Then Bullseye pulled Woody's old hat from the pile!

Jessie laughed when Bullseye held up the hat.

"Woody, I think Bullseye found just the right hat!" Jessie called out.

Woody grinned. "This is exactly the kind of hat I wanted! How does it look?" he asked.

"It's the best hat in the West!" Jessie replied.

Superhero for a Day

Lucky sat glued to the television set. He was watching his favourite show, *The Thunderbolt Adventure Hour*. "I'm going to be just like Thunderbolt when I grow up," Lucky announced.

Patch laughed at his brother. "Thunderbolt can jump across a river," he said. "You can barely climb up the stairs!"

"Just wait!" Lucky said.

While the other puppies went outside to play, Lucky practised his leaping. He leapt from the arm of the sofa onto the chair. Then he leapt from the chair… right into a lamp. CRASH!

Nanny came running.

"Lucky!" she scolded. "Go outside while I clean this up!"

When Lucky got outside, he found Rolly with his head stuck in the bushes. "Don't worry!" shouted Lucky. "I'll save you!" He ran up to Rolly, grabbed him by the leg and pulled.

"Ow!" yelled Rolly as he and Lucky collided. "What did you do that for?"

"You were stuck!" answered Lucky. "I was trying to save you."

"I didn't need saving!" complained Rolly. "We were playing hide-and-seek!"

Lucky's brothers and sisters came over to see what all the fuss was about. "Come on," said Patch. "Let's go inside before Thunderbolt Jr. tries to save anybody else!"

Lucky stayed behind. He'd show Patch! He climbed to the top of the kennel to practise leaping some more.

Below him, Penny had returned to fetch her bone. But she found it had already been snatched by Bruno, the neighbourhood bully. Lucky watched from above as the bulldog growled and bared his teeth.

Suddenly, Lucky lost his balance and tumbled off the roof.

"Ahhhhhh!" Bruno howled when Lucky landed on his back. The bulldog dropped the bone in terror, turned and ran off.

By then the other puppies had come running from the house.

"What happened?" asked Rolly.

"Lucky saved me!" Penny said. "You should have seen him! He flew right through the air and scared Bruno away – just like Thunderbolt!"

Lucky puffed out his chest with pride.

"Wow!" said Patch. "Can I have your autograph?"

Pooh's Neighbourhood

"I say, it's a splendid day in the neighbourhood!" cried Owl.

"Which neighbour wood are we talking about?" asked Pooh.

"Neighbourhood," said Owl. "The place where we live and where all our neighbours live and are neighbourly."

"Oh," said Pooh. "It is a splendid day in it, isn't it?"

"Now I'm off for an owl's-eye view!" Owl said as he flew away.

As Owl flew off, Pooh began to think about what it meant to live in a neighbourhood. He thought perhaps he would bring a neighbourly present to his closest neighbour, Piglet. Pooh went inside his house and took a honeypot out of his cupboard.

When he reached his Thoughtful Spot, Pooh suddenly had a thought: I could take the path straight to Piglet's house. Or I could go up the path and around the whole neighbourhood. And sooner or later the path would take me to Piglet's house, anyway. So that's what he did.

As he walked the long way to Piglet's house, Pooh came across each of his neighbours in turn. He joined Kanga and Roo for a snack at the picnic spot and collected some carrots from Rabbit. After lunch and a longish snooze at Christopher Robin's house, he soon reached Eeyore's Gloomy Place.

Eeyore was feeling sad, so Pooh offered him a nice lick of honey. But the honeypot was empty! Pooh had eaten all the honey on his journey through the neighbourhood.

Pooh walked away from Eeyore's house glumly. Before long, Owl flew over.

"I've seen our whole neighbourhood today," Pooh told him. "But now I have no neighbourly present left for Piglet."

"The bees have been quite busy at the old bee tree lately," said Owl. "Perhaps you can get a fill-up there."

So they walked together until they came to the old bee tree. Up, up, up Pooh climbed. Owl had a thought, and he told Pooh to go to the very top of the tree and look around.

"Our neighbourhood!" cried Pooh. "Our beautiful home!" The Hundred-Acre Wood was spread out below him.

"That's the owl's-eye view," said Owl grandly.

Then Pooh filled the honeypot once more, and he and Owl went to Piglet's house for supper.

Anna in Charge

It was a beautiful morning in Arendelle. Elsa was away and had left Anna in charge. Anna was nervous. All she had to guide her was a letter from Elsa.

As Anna sat down to read the letter, there was a knock on her door.

"Excuse me, Your Highness," a guard said. "You are needed in the throne room."

Anna followed the guard to the throne room, where two farmers were shouting at each other. "Thank you," Anna said to the guard. "Now what seems to be the problem, gentlemen?" Anna asked.

"His chickens are eating all of my corn," one farmer shouted.

"Well, his cows keep eating all the grass in my field," the other farmer yelled back.

Anna listened to the farmers. How was she supposed to solve their problem? Then she remembered Elsa's note.

Anna quickly read the first few lines. *Problems can be hard to solve*, Elsa had written. *You have a good heart. Do what you think is right.*

Anna bit her lip. What did her heart tell her was the right thing to do? Finally, she jumped up. "I have an idea," she said. "Let the chickens eat the corn. The cows can eat the grass. And you both can share the milk and

eggs!"

The farmers looked at each other. Then they nodded. They both liked that idea!

Anna smiled. She had solved her first problem of the day! But she was not done. The Royal Regatta was about to start, and the Arendelle rowing team was one person short.

Anna opened Elsa's note and read the next line: *Don't be afraid to mix it up!*

That gave Anna an idea. Racing down to the water, she jumped into the boat and began to row! The rest of Anna's day flew by. Before she knew it, the sun was setting. Suddenly, Anna realised that she hadn't finished reading Elsa's note. She opened the scroll. *After a busy day, it is nice to see the stars. The best view is from the roof.*

Anna climbed up to the roof. To her surprise, there was a picnic dinner laid out. Next to the food was another note.

Excited, Anna began to read. *Good job today,* Elsa had written. *You can be me anytime!* Anna gasped. She didn't know if she was ready for that!

Looking back down at the note, Anna read the last few lines: *But don't worry. I'll be back tomorrow.*

Rapunzel Finds a Friend

Long before Rapunzel knew she was a princess, she was a lonely little girl. Mother Gothel often left Rapunzel for days, and the only creatures that crossed her path were butterflies, bees and the occasional bird. Bees do not like hugs. Butterflies are notoriously skittish. And no matter how many seeds Rapunzel gave them, the birds never stuck around for long.

Since friends were scarce, Rapunzel did the next best thing: she filled each day with a new activity. She tried painting, but her finished artwork didn't look as good as what she had imagined. Next she tried baking, but her cake came out burnt and black. Finally, Rapunzel tried gardening, but her seeds didn't sprout.

"Worst day ever," said Rapunzel. "I can't paint, I can't bake and I can't grow even one strawberry."

Suddenly, Rapunzel noticed a strange pattern in the dirt. Looking closer, she realised it was footprints. "Let's see where else they show up," she said.

A few hours later, she found the same prints in her paint! When the prints appeared in her flour, Rapunzel knew something was up.

"This is a mystery," she said.

From then on, whenever Rapunzel created art, she spilt a little paint. Whenever she baked, she scattered a little flour. Whenever she gardened, she sprinkled a little dirt. She wanted to see if the prints would reappear... and they always did!

Though Rapunzel still didn't know who was making the prints, she spent a lot of time practising her hobbies. That's how she became very good at painting, baking and gardening.

One day, as she was picking berries, Rapunzel noticed an odd-shaped berry among the others. As she reached for the berry, it changed colour!

Before her was a small, green chameleon.

"So you're the one who's been leaving the little prints!" said Rapunzel.

The chameleon seemed to nod.

"My name is Rapunzel," said the little girl. "I'll call you Pascal. Would you like some cake?"

Rapunzel learnt that Pascal never said no to cake. And Pascal learnt that Rapunzel was the best friend a chameleon could ever ask for.

Sleeping Out

"Good morning, Tramp," said Lady, yawning and stretching. She rolled over on her silk cushion. "Wasn't that just the most wonderful night's sleep?"

But Tramp just groaned. His sleep had been far from wonderful. In fact, he hadn't had much sleep at all. The night before had been Tramp's first night sleeping in Lady's house — or in any house, come to think of it.

"How do you do it?" he grumbled. "That bed is so soft, I feel like I'm sinking in a pool of feathers. And between Jim Dear's snoring and the baby's crying, I could barely hear the crickets chirping."

"Oh, dear," Lady said, feeling truly sorry for her mate. "I know!" she exclaimed. "Jim Dear and Darling love you so, I'm sure they'd let you sleep up on their bed tonight. There's nothing in the world better than that!"

But Tramp shook his head. "I'm afraid it's the outdoors I need," he explained. "I mean, I know you grew up this way and all, but it's just so much fun to sleep under the stars. And the moon, too. There's nothing to howl at in this bedroom."

That night, as soon as the sun set and the moon began to rise, Lady and Tramp went out to the garden. Happy at last, Tramp turned three times and then plopped down. "Oh, how I love the feel of cool dirt on my belly!" he said with a dreamy smile.

Meanwhile, Lady gingerly peeked into the dark and slightly damp kennel. Already she missed the comforts of Jim Dear and Darling's room.

Tramp watched as Lady stretched out on the kennel floor, then got up and moved outside, then back in once again. It was plain to see that, try as she might, Lady just could not relax on the cold, hard ground.

"Don't worry," Tramp announced, "I have an idea."

And with that, he ran into the house. Seconds later, he reappeared with Lady's silk cushion in his teeth. Carefully, he swept the kennel floor with his tail and laid the cushion down just the way Lady liked it.

Lady smiled and laid down. And do you know what? That night, they both had the sweetest dreams either one had ever had.

Good Housekeeping

Snow White and the prince were going to be married. Her dear friends, the Seven Dwarfs, were filled with joy to see Snow White so happy. But they knew they were going to miss her – not to mention her wonderful cooking and how she kept their cottage so clean and tidy!

Snow White was also worried about how the little men were going to get along without her. She decided it was time they learnt how to cook and clean for themselves.

"First, let's see you sweep out the cottage," she said. "Remember to push the dirt out the door and not just move it around the floor."

The Dwarfs all grabbed brooms and set to work.

"Don't forget to open the door first," Snow White added. Then she moved on to the next task. "Now we'll do the washing! First you heat the water over the fire, then you scrub the clothes with a bar of soap, rinse them and finally hang them on the line to dry."

Dopey was first in line. He jumped into the bath and rubbed the bar of soap all over the clothes he was wearing.

"Dopey," said Snow White, "it's easier if you wash the clothes after you've taken them off."

A bit later, the Dwarfs trooped into the kitchen for a cooking lesson.

"Now we're going to make stew," said Snow White. "You take a little of everything you have to hand, throw it into a pot and let it simmer for a long time."

As Snow White was leaving, Doc said, "Don't worry, Snow White. We're going to be fust jine – I mean, just fine."

The next night, the Dwarfs made dinner and invited Snow White and the prince to join them. When the guests arrived, Dopey led them over to the large pot simmering over the fire and grandly lifted the lid. An old boot, some socks, a bunch of flowers and a cake of soap were floating on the top.

"We made it with a little bit of everything we had to hand, just like you said," Sleepy said.

"Perhaps we should go over that recipe again," Snow White said with a laugh.

Happy to Help

Dumbo was walking towards his train carriage, looking forward to a long nap, when suddenly he heard someone shout, "Oh no! My beautiful balloons!"

Dumbo looked up. A bunch of colourful balloons were drifting away from a balloon seller. The elephant quickly sprang into action. He flew after the balloons, grabbed the strings with his trunk and flew back to the ground.

"You're the best!" the balloon seller said.

Happy to have helped, Dumbo continued to make his way towards his train carriage to have his overdue nap. As he walked, he saw a crowd gathering. Using his trunk, he politely nudged his way in to see what was going on. A little girl stood crying in the middle of the crowd.

"I think the poor kid is lost," said a magician. "We must help her. But how?"

Dumbo walked over and tapped the girl on the shoulder with his trunk.

"Great idea, Dumbo!" said the juggler. "You could spot the little girl's mum from above!"

The juggler picked up the girl and put her on the elephant's back. Dumbo and the little girl flew up above the circus tents. They looked down at the crowds of people.

"Mummy! There's my mummy!" the girl shouted.

Dumbo landed gently. The girl climbed off his back and ran into her mother's arms.

"Thank you, Dumbo! Thank you!" said the girl's mother.

Dumbo was glad to have been able to help.

Suddenly, a pie went whizzing by!

Dumbo turned to see some circus clowns throwing pink cream pies at one another. They were covered from head to toe!

"What a mess!" said one of the clowns.

"I think it's time for a shower," said another.

Dumbo had an idea! He flew over to the water tank and filled his trunk. Then he sprayed water all over the clowns! The clowns laughed as Dumbo rinsed away the gooey pink pie. Then, smiling, Dumbo went off to finally take his long-awaited nap!

Disney
Winnie the Pooh

Roo's New Babysitter

"I don't want a babysitter!" cried Roo. Roo's mummy, Kanga, was going shopping, and Pooh was going to babysit. "I want to go shopping!" cried Roo. He had a large bag and was filling it with cans of food when Pooh arrived.

"Hello, Pooh," said Roo. "I'm shopping!" He put more cans in his bag.

Roo and Pooh said goodbye to Kanga. Then Pooh gave Roo a hug.

"How about a nice smackerel of honey?" Pooh said, rubbing his tummy.

"I want to go shopping," squeaked Roo. "I don't want to eat."

"Hmm," said Pooh. "Now what do I do?"

"You don't know how to babysit?" asked Roo. "I'm good at babysitting. I'll tell you how. The first thing a babysitter does is climb!"

Pooh, who was starting to think there was not much sitting involved in babysitting, said, "Okay, let's find a good climbing tree."

They climbed the old apple tree in Roo's back garden. Roo hopped from branch to branch, and Pooh climbed up behind him. "Babysitters always pick apples for dinner," said Roo.

And so Pooh picked some apples.

Next Roo showed Pooh how babysitters poured a whole bottle of bubble bath into the bathwater. Roo disappeared under the bubbles. Pooh blew on the bubbles, but he couldn't see Roo!

"Look at me jumping!" squeaked a little voice. Roo was jumping on his bed, all wet! Pooh dried Roo off, then helped put on his pyjamas.

"Time for your Strengthening Medicine," said Pooh, a little more sternly than when poohs usually say such things. But Roo didn't want it. He folded his arms across his chest.

"Oh well," said Pooh, slumping into a chair. "Why don't you give me a spoonful? I think I could do with it!"

"Now, Pooh, dear, here's your medicine," said Roo in a cheerful, grown-up sort of voice.

"Ah!" said Pooh. "Thank you, Roo. You are a good babysitter."

Just then, Kanga opened the door and saw Roo and Pooh snuggled together in the chair.

"Mama!" cried Roo. "I'm babysitting Pooh!"

"Of course you are, dear," said Kanga.

A Super Summer Barbecue

One hot, summer afternoon, Helen Parr was stood in the kitchen icing a cake. It was almost time to leave for the neighbourhood barbecue.

"Hey, Mom," said Helen's elder son, Dash, running into the room at Super speed. "Why do we have to go to some silly barbecue?"

"Dashiell Robert Parr," said Helen. "We're lucky to have been invited. You know we're doing our best to fit in here. And remember: no Super powers outside the house."

A little while later, the Parrs walked down the street to their first neighbourhood party. Dash watched some children compete in a sack race, but he couldn't join in because it might reveal his super speed.

"Are you too chicken to play?" a boy teased.

Dash scowled. When the mean boy hopped by the young Super, he mysteriously tripped and fell over. Dash smiled to himself and brushed off his trainer. His speed had come in handy after all!

Meanwhile, out of the corner of her eye, Helen saw Jack-Jack atop a high brick wall. He was about to topple off! In a flash, she shot her arm all the way across the garden and caught him. She sighed with relief and cuddled Jack-Jack. The other women just rubbed their eyes and mumbled something about not sleeping much the night before.

As the day wore on, Helen saw the neighbours enjoying her cake. She looked around the garden and spotted Dash telling a story to some other kids. Violet was eating an ice cream with a girl her age. *Wow, it looks like we really fit in here*, Helen thought. But then she overheard the neighbours.

"There's something strange about those Parrs," one of the neighbours said.

Had someone discovered them? Were their Super powers about to be revealed?

"That may be true," someone else added, "but that Helen sure makes a terrific cake!" Everyone agreed, and the conversation ended.

Helen Parr chuckled to herself. Their cover wasn't blown after all! Maybe they were a little strange compared to the average family, but they were doing their best to act normally.

The Fireworks Show

Andy hadn't been home all day. He was out with his family, celebrating the Fourth of July.

"The Fourth of July is the United States of America's birthday," Woody told Buzz. "People celebrate by going on picnics in the afternoon and watching fireworks at night. That must be where Andy and his family have gone."

"It's too bad he didn't take us with him," said Buzz. "I'd like to see fireworks myself. I'm told they look something like Space Ranger Rockets!"

"Well," Woody said thoughtfully, "last year we were able to see the fireworks from the roof. Maybe we could climb up there again tonight."

Sure enough, the toys were able to use Woody's lasso to pull themselves up onto the roof. As the sun sank, the toys settled into their seats for the fireworks show.

"Wow," said Buzz, "there sure is a lot of stuff up on this roof." He looked around and saw a ball, a frisbee, a hula hoop, an old sweatshirt and a shiny red balloon.

"That's because Andy's not allowed on the roof," Woody explained.

"Every time he throws something up and it gets stuck, it stays here."

Suddenly, there was a flicker and a boom. The toys looked up as the fireworks began. Lights exploded across the sky, colours flashed and there was a deep rumbling sound.

"Why don't Andy and his mum set off their own fireworks in the back garden?" asked Buzz. "That way the fireworks wouldn't have to be so far away!"

"Fireworks are very dangerous," said one of the Green Army Men. "If one goes off near you, it makes a huge explosion and a tremendous banging noise, and you could really get hurt."

Just then, there was a tremendous banging noise – right on the roof! The toys jumped. But there was no explosion – just Rex, looking embarrassed, with a deflated balloon hanging from the end of his tail.

"Sorry," he said, "I accidentally sat on the balloon. Did I scare everyone?"

The toys laughed. They agreed that, for once, Rex the dinosaur had actually scared them. They also all agreed that they were glad the real fireworks were far, far away.

The Great Garden Mystery

For the first time in many years, the Sultan of Agrabah had spare time. With Jasmine and Aladdin helping him run the kingdom, the Sultan could spend his afternoons in his vegetable garden. He grew aubergines, chickpeas, parsley, cucumbers, tomatoes and lettuce.

One day, the Sultan came out to his garden and found that there was not one vegetable left in it! The chickpea plants were bare, the lettuce was gone and the tomatoes had vanished. There wasn't even one lonely sprig of parsley!

The Sultan, Jasmine, Aladdin and Rajah searched high and low for clues. Finally, they found one: a set of muddy claw prints. The prints could only belong to one creature – Iago!

The group followed the claw prints over the garden wall and into the city. Finally, Aladdin recognised his old neighbourhood.

"I wonder why Iago would bring those vegetables here?" he said. As they turned the corner, they saw a poor family having a picnic. And in the middle of it all was Iago.

"Iago!" cried Jasmine. "You gave my father's vegetables away?"

The father of the family stood up. "My apologies, Your Highness," he said. "We did not know that the vegetables belonged to the Sultan. This parrot saw how hungry we were and said he would give us something to eat. We would give them back, but we have already made falafel out of the chickpeas and parsley, and baba ganoush out of the aubergines. However, there is plenty to go around, if you would like to join us."

Jasmine thought she had never received such a nice invitation. So they all sat down and dug in.

The baba ganoush was rich, and the falafel was tasty and went very well with the Sultan's tomatoes and lettuce.

"I am delighted," said the Sultan, "that my garden is such a success. I think, however, that it would be even better if the garden was in the city and belonged to everyone. Perhaps I will move the garden to this very courtyard."

Everyone thought that was a wonderful idea, except for Iago.

"Vegetables, yuck!" he said.

Badge Building

Russell *loved* collecting badges. There was just one tiny problem: there weren't enough! But that was about to change.

"Okay," Campmaster Strauch began. "This is your chance to go down in Wilderness Explorer history. Each troop has been asked to submit a new Wilderness Explorer badge idea, and we'll hold a contest in two weeks. To enter, provide a description of your badge and proof that you have completed the work required to earn that badge."

Russell's face lit up. A chance to earn a badge that he invented himself? He *had* to win this contest!

Russell couldn't wait to get started, but he also wasn't sure what kind of badge to design. Russell came up with idea after idea, but nothing seemed right.

Astronomy was interesting, but he didn't have time to properly track the starts.

He thought about farming or agriculture, but he couldn't raise livestock in the city. And besides, Dug had eaten all his seeds!

Russell considered building a robot, but all the robotics books were on loan from the library.

And detective work sounded exciting, but try as they might, Russell and Dug couldn't find anything to investigate.

"You know," Carl said, "maybe none of these are working because they don't mean anything to you. It there anything you *really* want to learn more about?"

"Mr Fredrickson, you're a genius!" Russell cheered. "I love chocolate more than anything in the world!"

The next day, they made their way to a local bakery. Roger, the chocolatier, handed Russell and Carl their very own aprons and chef's hats. "I hope you don't mind getting a little messy!" said Roger.

All morning, Roger taught Russell about making chocolate. Even better, Russell got to taste everything as they baked.

The next day was the contest. Russell looked around at his competition. Everyone had come up with great ideas! Just then, there was a cheer from across the room. The Roller Coaster badge had won!

"You know it's funny," Russell said. "All I wanted was to win, but I got to learn all about something I love with you, and that's worth way more than winning a contest."

Bedtime for Billy

Mike and Sulley were excited about their evening. They were monster-sitting for Mike's nephew, Billy.

"Everything will be fine, sis," said Mike. "Sulley and I will take good care of the little guy. You don't have to worry about a thing."

Billy's parents kissed him goodbye and hopped in the car. Then the three monsters went inside and ate pizza and popcorn while they watched classic films like *Gross Encounters of the Kid Kind*.

After the films were over, Sulley, Mike and Billy listened to music, sang and danced. Soon it was bedtime.

But putting Billy to bed wasn't going to be easy. There was one very important detail that Billy's mother had forgotten to tell her monster-sitters. Billy was scared of the dark!

"Aaaaaaahhhhh!" screamed Billy when Mike turned off the light.

"Wh-wh-what is it?" shouted Mike as he and Sulley ran back into the bedroom.

"There's a kid hiding in the w-wardrobe," stammered Billy. "It wants to g-get me!"

Mike and Sulley searched Billy's room for human children.

"There aren't any kids in the wardrobe," said Mike.

"All clear under the bed," announced Sulley.

"See, there's nothing to worry about," Mike said. "You can go to sleep now."

But Billy was still frightened. Mike and Sulley quickly realised they had to come up with another plan to help him get over his fear. How could they show Billy that children weren't scary?

"I've got it!" exclaimed Mike. "The scrapbook!"

Mike brought out the scrapbook, and the three monsters looked through it. It was filled with photographs of monsters with children, newspaper clippings of them together and laugh reports.

"See, Billy?" said Mike. "Human kids aren't dangerous, and they love to have fun, just like you."

"You know, Billy, sometimes human kids get scared of us," said Mike. "But once they see that we're funny and friendly, they realise there's no reason to be scared of monsters."

Billy soon fell fast asleep as Mike and Sulley watched from the doorway.

"Another job well done, Mike," said Sulley.

How to Unpack for a Holiday

One morning, Donald Duck heard a knock at his door. When he opened it, he found his friend Mickey Mouse standing there. "Today is the day!" exclaimed Mickey.

"Today is what day?" asked Donald with a yawn.

"Don't you remember?" said Mickey. "You're driving me, Minnie and Daisy to the beach for a week's holiday."

"Oh no!" cried Donald. He hadn't packed yet.

"Calm down," said Mickey. "You have time to get ready. Just pack your things now."

While Mickey relaxed on the porch in a rocking chair, Donald went back inside. "What do I pack?" Donald muttered to himself as he raced through his house. "I'll need books and toys, of course, in case I get bored."

Donald ran to his playroom and placed all his books and toys in boxes.

"What else should I pack?" Donald asked himself. "Clothes!" He ran to his bedroom and took out every suitcase he owned. Then he emptied all his drawers and filled his suitcases.

Finally, Donald calmed down.

"That should do it," he said, looking at his pile of boxes and suitcases.

Mickey couldn't believe his eyes when Donald began packing up his car. When Minnie Mouse and Daisy Duck arrived, they were each carrying one small suitcase. They took one look at Donald's car and gasped. Boxes and baskets were crammed into the back and front seats. Daisy opened the boot and found it overflowing with Donald's suitcases.

"There's no room left for our suitcases!" cried Daisy.

"Forget our suitcases!" exclaimed Minnie. "There's no room for us!"

Mickey put his arm round Donald. "It's okay, Donald," he said. "It's hard to pack for a holiday. You have to leave some things behind – even some of your favourite things."

"And besides," added Daisy, "don't you want to leave room in your car to bring back souvenirs, like seashells and T-shirts and sticks of rock?"

Donald brightened. "Seashells and T-shirts and sticks of rock!" he cried excitedly. "Oh, you bet!"

"Good," said Mickey. Then he pointed to Donald's overflowing car. "Now let's all help Donald unpack for this holiday!"

Kida's Surprise

Although it was Kida's 8,500th birthday, she honestly didn't want anyone to make a big deal about it. There were much more important things to think about. Rebuilding the city, for one thing! And yet, as the day wore on and Milo still had not even said "happy birthday" to her, Kida began to feel a little down. If Kida didn't know better, she'd think Milo had completely forgotten.

Just then Kida realised, she did know Milo! And come to think of it, he probably had forgotten. And not just him. For the first time in her life, Kida sadly realised, no one in Atlantis had remembered her birthday.

Kida tried the best she could not to feel sorry for herself. Instead, she concentrated on tuning up her Ketak speeder.

It was hard, though, when Milo finally came up to her later that afternoon and asked if she'd like to help him take his slug-like ugobe for a walk.

"Oh, I don't know," Kida said with a sigh. "I'm a little tired."

"Ah, come on, Kida," Milo said. "I thought it would be such a fun thing to do on this special day."

"Special?" said Kida, suddenly perking up. Had Milo remembered her birthday after all?

"Of course." Milo grinned. "It's exactly eight-and-a-half months since we met!"

"Oh," Kida replied.

"So are you coming?" Milo asked her.

Finally, Kida agreed. Milo put a lead on his ugobe and took Kida by the hand. He led them through the palace courtyard, out onto the street. But instead of turning right, Milo went straight, heading towards the city centre.

"Where are you going?" Kida asked. "There's no place for an ugobe to run this way."

"No?" said Milo. "Are you sure?"

"Positive," said Kida. "There's only—"

"SURPRISE!"

Kida's mouth fell open as thousands of smiling Atlanteans greeted her with a thunderous cheer and a cake the size of a Ketak. The entire kingdom had gathered beneath the great crystal Heart of Atlantis to surprise her!

"Happy birthday, Kida," said Milo. "You didn't really think we'd forget it, now, did you?"

Disney · PIXAR

FINDING
NEMO

Who's in Charge?

Now, Dory," said Marlin, "you have to promise you'll keep a close eye on Nemo while I'm gone. Can you do that?"

"I can do that!" Dory said confidently.

But Marlin was a little worried. Everyone knew that Dory usually forgot things.

"Remember," Marlin instructed, "Nemo needs to do his—"

"Science homework, practise playing the conch shell and clean the anemone," interrupted Nemo. "I got it, Dad."

Finally, Marlin waved goodbye and swam off to do his errands. As soon as he was gone, Dory began swimming in circles around the anemone. "Nemo, betcha can't catch me!"

"Dory, come on," Nemo called to her. "I have to do my science homework."

Nemo explained his assignment to Dory: he had to find an abandoned hermit crab shell to bring in to class the next day. So Nemo and Dory swam around the reef. Before long, Nemo spotted one.

"That's great!" replied Dory. "Now we can play!"

"No, Dory," Nemo said. "Now I need to practise playing my conch shell."

Dory and Nemo swam back to the anemone, where Nemo put his hermit crab shell away and got out his conch shell. Dory kept time while he played the songs that he needed to memorise for band practice.

"Thanks, Dory!" Nemo said at last. "We're done."

"Yippee!" Dory cried, swimming around Nemo. "Now it's playtime!"

But Nemo remembered their work wasn't finished yet. "Not quite, Dory," he said. "I have to clean the anemone before I can play."

"Clean?" Dory said with a frustrated sigh.

Nemo shrugged. "Dad said I should do it before he got home," he replied.

Together, Dory and Nemo cleaned up the zooplankton crumbs. When they were finished, the place was spotless.

"Thanks for helping me, Dory," said Nemo. "That went quickly with the two of us working together!"

"You're welcome," Dory replied. "So, what do you want to do now?"

Nemo laughed. "What do I want to do now?" he echoed. "I want to play!"

"Play, huh?" Dory said, weighing up the idea. "Now that's a crazy idea. I like it!"

Chore de Force

Cinderella watched as a blue-and-pink-tinted bubble floated up from her bucket. "Isn't that pretty?" she said. Gus, Jaq and the rest of Cinderella's mouse friends nodded in agreement.

"I bet it would be fun to float around in a bubble all day! I could see whole cities at a time, bounce on clouds and soar with the birds," Cinderella said dreamily.

Suddenly, Cinderella laughed. "What am I doing?" she said. "I should stay focused on my chores."

Cinderella finished cleaning the windows and prepared to mop the floor. She plunged the mop into a bucket of soapy water, then dragged it across the floor. As the mop slid across the slippery floor, she suddenly realised...

"This is like dancing! How I love to dance!" Gus and Jaq copied Cinderella as she twirled around the room with the mop. "What fun!" she cried happily.

Then Cinderella caught herself. "Oh, my. Did I say that aloud?"

Maybe I just need to get away from all these bubbles, she thought. *Ironing should do the trick!*

She was ironing away and humming merrily to herself when she realised how dark the sky had grown. "Look at the time!" Cinderella exclaimed. "I've been daydreaming the day away and haven't even started dinner."

Cinderella hurried to the kitchen, where she chopped and minced and grated and stirred. "I don't know where this day has gone," she fretted as she added ingredients to her stepsisters' favourite soup. "I've got absolutely nothing done!"

Cinderella's stepsisters, Anastasia and Drizella, barged into the kitchen.

"Where are my piles of washing?" barked Anastasia.

"Done," Cinderella said.

"And my ironing?" Drizella added.

"Done," Cinderella replied again.

"Did you mop the floors?"

"Wash the windows?"

"Make our dinner?"

"Done, done, done!" Cinderella said gaily.

The sisters marched out of the kitchen, muttering with displeasure.

And there Cinderella stood, all alone in the kitchen once more. As she stirred the pot of soup, she thought, *I guess I did get a lot done after all!*

Berry Picking

Briar Rose lived in the forest with her three aunts, Flora, Fauna and Merryweather.

One morning, Flora called everyone together to suggest they go out to search the forest for berries.

"What a wonderful idea," said Briar Rose.

"Yes, indeed," said Merryweather. "If we pick enough, we can make a berry pie."

"If we pick enough," declared Fauna, "we can make enough jam to last us through the whole year."

"Well, we'll never have enough if we don't get started now," said Flora. And so they gathered their berry baskets and set out.

The four berry-pickers followed a shady path through the forest until they came upon a thicket bursting with berry bushes. Without delay, they set to work. But just because they set to work didn't mean their baskets actually got full.

Merryweather, for one, had a terrible time keeping her basket upright. Every time she bent down to pick another berry, her basket tipped and out spilt all but two or three berries. Fauna, on the other hand, had an entirely different problem keeping her berries in her basket – somehow they kept finding their way into her mouth!

As for Briar Rose, her heart and her mind were miles away from her berry basket… dancing in the arms of a handsome stranger.

"All right, dearies," Flora called as the sun began to sink. "It's time to go back to the cottage. Let's see what you've got."

"Um, well," said Merryweather. "I don't seem to have many berries in my basket."

Flora rolled her eyes and moved on to Fauna. "Let me guess…" she said as she looked from Fauna's empty basket to her purple mouth.

"Ah, yes," Fauna said as she guiltily dabbed at a drop of juice on her lips.

Flora sighed. "And you, Briar Rose?" she asked hopefully.

But Briar Rose just looked down sheepishly at the empty basket in her hands. "I'm sorry, Aunt Flora," she said. "I guess I got a little bit distracted."

"Well," said Flora, shaking her head, "no berry pie for us this week, I guess." Then she shrugged. "But we can always have chocolate cake instead!"

The Race

"Good morning, young prince," Thumper greeted Bambi one bright and sunny day.

"Good morning, Thumper," Bambi said.

"I have a great idea, Bambi. Let's have a race," Thumper said. "Whoever makes it to that big pine tree over there first wins the race."

"But it would be silly for us to race," Bambi told his friend.

"Why's that?" Thumper asked, confused.

"Because I'll win," Bambi said.

"What makes you so sure?" Thumper challenged, puffing up his chest.

"Because I'm bigger and faster than you are," Bambi explained.

"If you're so sure you'll win," Thumper said, "why are you afraid to race me?"

Bambi paused. He didn't want to hurt the little rabbit's feelings. "Fine," he said at last. "Let's race."

Flower, who had just joined the friends, agreed to be the judge.

"On your marks, get set… go!" cried Flower. They both took off as fast as they could.

Bambi, with his long legs and big, wide stride, immediately took the lead. But Thumper's small size helped him to dart through bushes and slip round trees. When Bambi looked back, he saw that Thumper was right on his heels. Bambi paused to jump over a tree that had been knocked down, blocking the path. Thumper was able to wiggle under it. He popped up in front of Bambi and took the lead.

Bambi took longer and longer strides, running faster and faster. Soon he had passed Thumper. But in his hurry to go as fast as he could, he got tangled up in a bush. As Bambi struggled to free himself, Thumper hopped past him again.

They were quickly approaching the big pine tree. Bambi was running as fast as he could, jumping over logs and bushes. Thumper, too, hopped as quickly as his bunny legs would carry him, ducking and weaving through whatever obstacles were in his way. And as they crossed the finish line, they were in a neck-and-neck tie.

"See?" Thumper said, panting. "Little guys can keep up!"

"You are absolutely right!" Bambi said, also panting.

And the two friends, both winners, sat down together to catch their breath.

Disney
THE
LION KING

All Wet

Timon pounded his tiny chest and gave a mighty yell as he swung out over the lagoon. He let go of the vine and threw his arms out wide, hitting the water with a small but very satisfying smack. He popped to the surface, shouting, "Ta-da!"

Pumbaa was next. "Look out below!" he called. He backed up on the rock ledge, then charged. The warthog's splash sent water flying high into the air.

"Not bad," Simba said. "But I bet Nala could do better."

"Ha!" Nala laughed. "You know I don't like getting wet."

"Oh, come on, Nala. Give it a try. The water's fine!" Simba said.

"The water is fine," Nala replied slowly, rolling over and licking her paw. "For drinking."

Simba frowned. Nala was making him look silly in front of his friends. Was he king of the Pride Lands or not?

Using his most commanding voice, Simba gave Nala an order. "You will come swimming with us right now, or else!"

Nala didn't even lift her head. She closed her eyes. "Or else what, Your Mightiness?"

Simba couldn't come up with anything, so the argument was over. Nala, as usual, had

won. Accepting his defeat, Simba ran to the edge of the rocky ledge, sprang high in the air and tucked his paws in for a royal dive-bomb.

Pumbaa and Timon were drenched. Slinking slowly out of the water, Simba signalled to them. He pointed at his dripping mane and then up at Nala's rock.

Timon winked, and he and Pumbaa began a pretend water fight to distract Nala. Simba walked quickly but silently. Drawing closer, he crouched, his legs coiled to pounce.

With a triumphant roar, Simba jumped onto Nala's rock and gave his sopping mane a mighty shake. Nala was completely drenched.

Nala leapt to her feet with a snarl. Simba rolled onto his back, laughing.

"What happened, Nala? You're all wet!" Timon laughed.

Pumbaa was laughing so hard, he could barely breathe.

Nala tried to glare fiercely at Simba, but she couldn't. She had to laugh, too. "King of the practical jokers," she said.

Anna's Birthday

Anna was excited. Today was her fifth birthday.

Anna ate a quick breakfast, and then Gerda helped her into her party dress.

Soon it was time for Anna's royal birthday party. She knew that perfect manners were a must at a fancy party. Anna walked into the hall with her head held high. She nodded politely at each guest seated at the table. And when she sat down, she made sure to sweep her skirt under her so it wouldn't crease.

Anna behaved perfectly all the way through dinner. Having perfect manners wasn't exactly fun, but Anna knew her parents would be proud of her. It was all going great… until she let out a loud burp!

"Excuse me!" Anna said, clapping both hands over her mouth.

Her cheeks turned red. Burping was definitely not good birthday manners.

Anna's father smiled. "Don't worry," he reassured Anna. "Sometimes a burp is a compliment to the chef!"

And then the king burped! "There," he said. "Now the chef knows we both enjoyed the meal."

Anna laughed. Her father always knew how to make her feel better.

That night as she got ready for bed, Anna sighed. She had really been looking forward to her birthday. But she'd been focused so much on acting perfectly that she hadn't had a chance to have any fun!

Suddenly, Anna heard a voice: "Psst!" It was Elsa! "Are you ready for your real party?" Elsa asked.

"My real party?" Anna responded. "Isn't that what I just had?"

With a grin, Elsa waved her hand. "Those royal parties are too proper to be any fun."

Anna and Elsa sneaked through the castle as quietly as they could. First they raided the kitchen for leftover birthday cake. Then they built the biggest pillow fort Anna had ever seen! Finally, Elsa gave Anna a painting she had made of the two of them. Anna loved it!

Much, much later, Anna and Elsa finally climbed into bed for the night.

"Did you have a good birthday?" Elsa asked.

"Thanks to you," Anna told her sister, "it was perfect."

Potion Commotion

Emperor Kuzco's royal adviser, Yzma, was down in her secret laboratory, mixing potions. She had enlisted her enthusiastic but dim-witted right-hand man, Kronk, to help her in her work.

"Kronk, I need spider legs, one eye of newt and elderberry juice... and quickly!" Yzma directed.

Kronk hurried across the laboratory to the cupboard that contained all of Yzma's potion ingredients.

"Let's see," Kronk said to himself as he pored over the containers. "Legs, eye, juice. Legs, eye, juice." He found the Legs section. "Newt legs! Check!" Kronk said to himself, confusing Yzma's instructions.

Then he found the Eyes section. "Spider eyes! Got it!" he said, grabbing the jar.

"Kronk!" shouted Yzma. "I said spider legs and eye of newt! Not newt legs and eye of spider! And where's the elderberry juice? Hurry, hurry!"

Kronk hurried back to the cupboard. "Spider legs... eye of newt... spider legs... eye of newt," he recited as he went. This time, he managed to get it right and took down the correct containers from the cupboard. But what was that third ingredient?

"Juice!" Kronk remembered. "Berry juice."

He found a small vial of blueberry juice and brought everything to Yzma.

"Not blueberry juice, you numbskull!" Yzma screamed. "ELDERBERRY!"

"Right," Kronk said. He hurried back across the laboratory and quickly located the Juice section. "Boysenberry... cranberry..." he read, moving alphabetically through the containers.

"ELDERBERRY!" Yzma shouted at him. "Get it over here! And step on it!"

Kronk finally located the right bottle. "Got it!" He rushed it across the laboratory.

Yzma reached out to take the bottle from him. But Kronk didn't hand it to her. Instead, he gently placed the bottle on the floor. Then he lifted his right foot and stomped on it – hard – shattering the bottle and splattering juice everywhere.

"KRONK!" Yzma screamed in surprise. "What are you doing?"

Kronk was confused. "I did just what you said," he explained. "I got the elderberry juice, and I stepped on it."

Tramp's Tale

It was a warm evening, just about the time that the first star comes out to shine, and long past the time for Lady and Tramp's puppies to go to sleep.

"Just one more story, Dad," begged Scamp.

Tramp rolled his eyes. "Well," he said, "okay, but just one."

Happily, the puppies snuggled down onto their cushion. Tramp stretched out beside them.

"Did I ever tell you kids about the time I stole my very first sausage?" he asked.

"Tramp!" Lady warned him from her seat across the parlour. "That hardly sounds like a proper story for the children."

"Oh, tell it, Dad!" Scamp urged him.

"Well, maybe 'stole' isn't exactly the right word," Tramp reassured his wife. "And besides, it's got a great moral!"

And with that, he began his tale:

"Now, this all happened way back when I was just a little pup, already living on my own in the big city.

"Well, one day I was especially hungry, and my nose was picking up all sorts of savoury scents. So you can imagine the interest I developed in a certain spicy smell coming from the butcher shop. Well, I followed my trusty nose, which has still never let me down, and sure enough, there was a heaping tray of steaming sausages. Can you believe it?"

"So you jumped up and gobbled them all up! Right?" Scamp interrupted.

"That's my boy!" Tramp laughed. "But no. Don't forget, I was just a little guy. Couldn't reach the tray. All I could do was think about how to get that sausage. After a few minutes, up walked a lady with a kid in a pushchair. Well, at first I was irate. Competition! But then I noticed the crumbs all over the kid in the pushchair. 'Hey!' I thought to myself. 'This might be the ticket – this kid obviously can't hang on to anything.' Sure enough, when the lady handed the kid a piece of sausage, the kid dropped it, and down it fell into my waiting mouth! Delicious!

"See, Lady?" Tramp added with a grin. "No stealing!"

"And what exactly is the moral of that story?" Lady asked.

Tramp laughed. "Why, good things come to those who wait, of course!"

The Search for Hamm

Woody the cowboy doll opened his eyes. The sun was up and Andy had left for school. The house was quiet. Too quiet. Woody realised that something was wrong. Hamm was nowhere in sight!

Woody asked the other toys, but no one had seen the piggy bank since the night before. The toys decided to form a search party.

The Aliens found the first sign of Hamm on Andy's desk – a pile of coins. *Had Hamm lost his coins?* Woody wondered. *What if Andy had decided that he didn't need a piggy bank any more?*

The toys set off to search the rest of the house. Suddenly, Rex cried out from the hallway. Buzz and Woody rushed out. There was another pile of coins on the floor, and they were wet!

"Do you think it's dog slobber?" Buzz asked.

"What?" Rex cried. "You mean Buster took Hamm? Oh no! I always knew that dog was out to get one of us!"

Woody, Buzz and Rex walked into the living room. Sarge was on the sofa.

"The troops have found a trace of the missing-in-action toy up here," Sarge said. On the cushion was a cluster of coins.

Just then, one of the Green Army Men sounded the alarm. Andy and his mum had arrived on the driveway! The toys raced back to Andy's room.

Seconds later, Andy dashed into the room. He threw his backpack on the floor, and then ran back out of the room.

Suddenly, the toys heard a noise. Clink, clink, clank, clink.

"What was that?" Rex asked. The noise was coming from Andy's backpack. It sounded like... coins!

Woody rushed over and unzipped the backpack. Out tumbled Hamm!

"Hamm!" Woody said. "What were you doing in there?"

"Andy took me to school to collect money," Hamm said.

"We thought you were in trouble," Buzz said. "There were piles of coins all over the house."

"Oh, that was just Andy playing," Hamm replied. "He was tossing me in the air like a baseball when we left this morning. And Buster was following us, drooling everywhere."

"Well, it's sure good to have you back," Woody said, and he gave Hamm a big hug!

Albatross Taxi Service

Orville sighed and leant against a lamp post at the busy intersection of Forty-Fifth and Broadway. He liked to watch the cars zoom back and forth. Just then there was a tap on his wing. He looked down to see an elderly mouse couple.

"Excuse me, sonny," said the grandpa mouse. "Would it be possible for you to help us cross this busy street?"

Orville looked confused. "You want me to go in the middle of the street and stop traffic?"

"Perhaps you could give us a lift over the traffic," the grandma mouse suggested. "We'll buy you a hot dog as payment."

Mmm! Orville couldn't say no to the promise of a tasty hot dog with mustard and sauerkraut, so he readily agreed.

Just then, the grandma mouse whistled to a group of mice standing nearby. "Harvey, Mildred, Polly, Carl – let's go. We have a ride!"

"Wait!" Orville said. "I can't give all of you a ride. Just how strong do you think I am?"

"Think about it this way," said the grandpa mouse. "The more mice, the more hot dogs."

Well, that certainly made sense. With that in mind, Orville agreed to help all the mice across the street. Orville's landings left something to be desired, that was for sure, but soon everyone was across the street, safe and sound.

"Here are your hot dogs!" the mice said.

Orville was disappointed to see that they were offering him hot dogs from the mouse vendor, which were considerably smaller than the human kind. Still, a deal was a deal, and Orville was not one to look a gift horse – er, make that a gift mouse – in the mouth.

Not long after, Orville found a discarded sardine tin to use for seats and began the Albatross Taxi Service for Mice. Word spread, and soon Orville couldn't keep up with the demand! He was quite a successful businessbird.

One day it hit him – he was selling himself short! Forget about Albatross Taxi Service – it was time to think bigger. He'd get himself a scarf and goggles and start Albatross Airlines! He sold his city taxi business to an entrepreneurial pigeon and set up shop at the airport.

Now, if he could only learn how to land, everything would be perfect!

THE LITTLE MERMAID

Ariel Changes the Tune

Sebastian rapped his claw on a piece of coral and cleared his throat. The mermaid princesses kept talking as if the little crustacean was not even there. With a heavy sigh, Sebastian grabbed a huge conch shell. After a lot of effort, he managed to hoist it to his mouth and blow.

The shell sounded like a giant horn! The princesses looked startled and, to Sebastian's relief, they stopped talking.

"Shall we begin?" the small crab asked calmly.

Sebastian raised his claw and was about to bring it down to start the vocal warm-up when Aquata interrupted him.

"Ariel's not here," she said.

"Oh, Ariel!" Sebastian cried. Ariel was constantly swimming off on her own and holding things up.

"Do you want us to find her?" Arista asked.

"No." Sebastian sighed. "Then you will all be lost, and I don't know what I would tell your father."

"We wouldn't get lost," Attina protested.

"We always show up on time," Adella added. The other sisters nodded their heads in agreement.

"Girls, girls!" Sebastian said, trying to calm them. He wished they could go ahead without

Ariel, but her voice was by far the most beautiful.

Suddenly, Ariel swam up with Flounder. "I hope you weren't waiting for me," she said sweetly.

"Where have you been?" Aquata put her hands on her scaly hips.

"You're late, and we still don't have a song for Father!" Attina added.

"We do now!" Ariel said cheerfully. Ariel couldn't tell her sisters, but she had been to the surface. It was forbidden. Her seagull friend Scuttle had given her something very special: a new song!

Ariel began singing the human tune. A moment later, Ariel's sisters began to sing along.

Sebastian closed his eyes and listened as the music washed over him. The song was perfect!

"Where did you learn it?" he asked when they were done.

Ariel looked at Flounder. "A little bird told me," she said with a wink and a smile.

Patch and the Panther

One dark night, fifteen Dalmatian puppies sat huddled around a black-and-white television set. They watched as Thunderbolt, the canine hero of the show, crept through a deep, dark jungle. Suddenly, Thunderbolt pricked up his ears. The puppies held their breath. Two yellow eyes peered out of the bushes. It was a panther!

"How will Thunderbolt escape the hungry panther?" the TV announcer asked. "Don't miss next week's exciting episode!"

"Aww!" the puppies groaned, disappointed that their favourite show was over.

"All right, kids. Time for bed," Pongo said, turning off the television with his nose. He watched as the puppies padded upstairs and settled down in their baskets. Then he switched off the light. Moments later, the sound of soft snores filled the room. The puppies were fast asleep.

All except for one. Patch was wide awake. He was still thinking about Thunderbolt and the panther.

"I wish some ol' panther would come round here," Patch said to himself. "I'd teach him a thing or two."

Outside his room, a floorboard creaked. Patch pricked up his ears. Then he crawled out of his basket to investigate.

The floorboard creaked again. *What if it's a panther?* Patch thought with a shiver. *But I'm not scared of any ol' panther*, he reminded himself.

A shadow flickered across the doorway. The shadow had a long tail. *Panthers have long tails*, thought Patch. Then two yellow eyes peered out of the darkness.

"Aroooo!" Patch yelped. He turned to run, but he tripped on the rug. In a flash, the panther was on top of him. Patch could feel its hot breath on his neck. He shut his eyes—

"Patch, what are you doing out of bed?" the panther asked.

Patch opened his eyes. It was his dad!

"I-I was just keeping an eye out for panthers," Patch explained.

Pongo smiled. "Why don't you get some sleep now?" he suggested. "I can keep an eye out for panthers for a while."

"Okay, Dad," Patch said with a yawn.

Pongo carried Patch back to his basket. In no time at all, the puppy was fast asleep.

Disney
MULAN

The Good Luck Charm

In ancient China, crickets were believed to be good luck. But on one particular night, long, long ago, Mulan's Grandmother Fa was having trouble remembering that. There was a cricket loose somewhere in her bedroom, and every time she was about to drop off to sleep— Cri-cket! Cri-cket! The cricket chirped loudly.

"This cricket will bring good fortune to our home," Grandmother Fa said, looking on the bright side.

All was quiet for a few minutes. Then— Cri-cket! Cri-cket!

"Ugh!" exclaimed Grandmother Fa, throwing off the covers and getting out of bed.

She lit a candle and began her search. She looked everywhere. But there was no sign of the cricket.

She blew out the candle. She got back into bed and tried to sleep.

Cri-cket! Cri-cket!

Grandmother Fa got out of bed again and relit her candle. She searched in her wardrobe. She looked inside her slippers. She checked under her pillow. But she couldn't find the cricket.

One more time, she climbed into bed.

Cri-cket! Cri-cket!

Grandmother Fa sighed and dragged herself out of bed. She relit the candle.

Was there any place she hadn't yet looked for the cricket?

Just then, a slight movement on the windowsill caught Grandmother Fa's eye. There, sitting on the window sill, was a tiny cricket. She scooped it up gently and cradled it in her hand.

That's when Grandmother Fa noticed that the window was open. And it looked like a rainstorm was brewing outside.

"Well, little cricket," Grandmother Fa said, "is that why you were trying to get my attention?" Had the cricket been trying to save Grandmother Fa from waking up to a puddle beneath her open window?

"Maybe you're good luck after all," she said.

She decided she would hold on to the cricket to see if it brought her more luck. So Grandmother Fa pulled out a bamboo cricket cage, gently placed the cricket inside and put the cage on her bedside table. At last, she'd be able to get some sleep.

Cri-cket! Cri-cket!

Or would she?

A Big Buzz

Flit let out a big sigh. Pocahontas was spending so much time with John Smith that she never had time for him any more!

Buzzz, buzzz. Flit was grateful that his speedy wings made a noise when he flew. At least Pocahontas could hear him – even if she pretended she couldn't.

"Look at this, John," Pocahontas said, crouching down towards the path. "Fresh deer tracks."

John leant over to inspect the prints left behind in the mud. Flit buzzed down, too. There were two sizes of prints: large and small.

"A mother and her fawn," John said. He leant forwards for a closer look, accidentally knocking Flit out of the way.

"They're probably looking for food before the snows come, so they'll be fat enough to make it through the winter," Pocahontas explained.

Pocahontas smiled at him and stood up. Flit buzzed up a second later, just as John lifted his hand to push a lock of hair off Pocahontas's face. Once again, Flit was shoved away.

That was it! Flit had had enough of being ignored! He flapped his buzzing wings faster and faster. Then he began to fly in a circle around John and Pocahontas. Zzzzzzzzzzz!

"Do you think he's trying to tell us something?" John asked, leaning towards Pocahontas.

"I don't know," she replied. She leant in closer to John, too. Soon they were nose to nose, looking into each other's eyes.

Flit gave up. He quit buzzing and flopped to the ground, landing in one of the deer tracks. He was exhausted.

"What was that about, Flit?" asked Pocahontas, scooping him up with a laugh.

Flit was still panting. He wasn't even sure he could fly any more. He gazed up at Pocahontas, his eyes wide and his shoulders slumped.

"That is one exhausted hummingbird," John said.

Pocahontas stroked Flit's blue feathers, then leant forwards and kissed him on the end of his long, pointed beak. Then she put him gently on her shoulder.

"You just ride here for a while," she told him.

Flit grinned happily as John and Pocahontas continued on through the forest. Mission accomplished!

Aurora's Royal Wedding

Princess Aurora and Prince Phillip were to be married. But there were so many things to plan!

"Everything seems well in hand, Your Majesty," said Flora to the queen.

The Queen smiled. "Yes, it does, and I couldn't be more delighted. I'll leave you now, Aurora, to enjoy the fun of choosing a cake."

"Thank you, Mother," said Aurora, but she was feeling nervous. She had yet to make any royal decisions on her own.

The royal cooks burst into her room with huge, lavish cakes to choose from. Aurora looked worried.

"What is it, dear?" asked Fauna.

Aurora sighed. "I don't know how to be a princess. What if I'm not a very good one?"

"Nonsense," said Merryweather. "You'll be the finest princess this kingdom has ever seen."

When Prince Phillip came by later, he invited Aurora to join him for a walk.

On their walk, Aurora confided in Phillip. "I'm not sure I know how to act like a princess. I can't even choose a cake!"

Phillip looked at her with love. "My dear, you will be a wonderful princess. But if you're worried, I think I may know someone who can help."

Back at the palace, Phillip spoke to the queen. "Your Majesty," he said, "I think Aurora would like some help – from her mother."

The queen went to find her daughter. "Dear Aurora, I understand that you are worried about being a princess, but being a princess isn't about what you do. Rather, it's about who you are. A princess is honest, thoughtful, clever and kind. And there is no doubt that you are all of these things."

"Oh, thank you, Mother!" Aurora said. "Now, will you help me figure out what kind of wedding cake we should have? There are so many choices."

The queen smiled. "Your father and I had a very simple cake. I think the same thing would be perfect for you."

On her wedding day, Aurora looked and felt every bit a princess. And the cake was delicious!

Stitch Upon a Time

Lilo was telling Stitch a story. But as she started, he scampered away. He wanted a snack.

"You'd better not let Nani hear you," warned Lilo. "She thinks we went to bed."

Stitch crept onto the landing, lifted his big ears and listened. "No Nani," he whispered. Then he dashed downstairs and into the kitchen.

"Juice, pineapple, pickles, coleslaw," recited Stitch, peering into the fridge. "Hmm... pineapple-pickle-coleslaw sandwich!"

Lilo tiptoed up behind him. "You can't put all that in a sandwich," she whispered into his ear.

"Yaaaaaahhhhh!" shouted Stitch, jumping. Lilo had scared him!

"What is going on in here?" demanded Nani, storming into the kitchen.

"Stitch wants a snack," Lilo explained.

"It's not time for snacks," Nani said. She shut the fridge door and marched them both back up the stairs. "It's time for bed."

"Story," said Stitch as he climbed into bed and held up the book. "Time for story."

Nani sighed and said, "Oh, all right. But it had better be a short one."

"Goody!" cried Stitch as Nani climbed into bed, too.

After Nani settled in between Lilo and Stitch, Lilo opened the book and began to read: "'Once upon a time, there was a sad little puppy named—'"

"Stitch!" cried Stitch.

Lilo continued, "'There was a sad little puppy named... Stitch. He was sad because he was lost.'"

Lilo passed the book to Nani and said, "Your turn."

Then Nani began to read, "'But one day, he met a little girl named—'"

"Lilo," whispered Lilo.

Nani smiled. "'He met a little girl named... Lilo.'"

Then Nani continued reading the story, until she reached the very end. "'And they lived happily ever after.'" Nani shut the book.

"Ever after," murmured Stitch, closing his eyes.

"Ever after," echoed Lilo.

Nani waited till they were both sound asleep, then headed downstairs for a snack. Maybe she'd have a pineapple-pickle-coleslaw sandwich!

THE JUNGLE BOOK

Where Mowgli Belongs

Mowgli the Man-cub had lived in the jungle his whole life. Then, one day, everything changed. Shere Khan, the man-eating tiger, heard about Mowgli and came looking for him. The wolves agreed Bagheera should take the boy back to the Man-village, where he would be safe. Mowgli was angry; he didn't want to leave his home in the jungle. But he and Bagheera set off on their long journey.

Along the way, Mowgli encountered a python who wanted to swallow him up, a parade of very noisy elephants and the king of the apes, who wanted to know how to make fire. Mowgli also made a friend, Baloo the bear.

Mowgli still didn't want to go to the Man-village, so he ran away from Baloo and Bagheera. Once he was on his own, it wasn't long before Shere Khan found him. The tiger gave a loud roar. He leapt at Mowgli, taking the Man-cub by surprise! But Baloo arrived and fought with Shere Khan. Baloo was knocked to the ground, and Mowgli was worried that he wasn't going to wake up.

Suddenly, a lightning bolt struck a nearby tree, which burst into flames. Shere Khan was terrified!

Seeing his chance to get back at the tiger,

Mowgli picked up a burning branch. The Man-cub tied the branch to the tiger's tail. Shere Khan screamed as he tried to get it off. Then he fled into the jungle, desperate to get away from the fire. Just then Baloo opened his eyes. Mowgli laughed and threw his arms round the big bear's neck.

Mowgli, Baloo and Bagheera carried on towards the Man-village. Suddenly, they heard someone singing. Mowgli peered through the trees and saw a young girl kneeling by the river.

Mowgli climbed a tree to have a closer look.

The girl turned and smiled. Mowgli shyly smiled back. When she began to walk off towards the Man-village, Mowgli ran to join her.

Baloo and Bagheera were sad that their young friend was leaving. But they knew he would be happy and safe.

"It's where he belongs," said Bagheera. "Come on, Baloo, let's get back to where we belong."

And so, arm in arm, the two friends headed slowly back into the jungle.

Home Sweet Home

As the sun rose above the Seven Dwarfs' cottage, Snow White was already thinking about what to make for supper that evening. She had arrived at the cottage not long before, after her evil stepmother, the Queen, had driven Snow White from the palace.

Luckily, a group of helpful woodland creatures had befriended Snow White and led her to the Dwarfs' little cottage. Now, for the first time in a long time, she felt safe and happy.

"Perhaps we'll have gooseberry pie for supper tonight!" she told her animal friends as they cleaned the cottage. When they had finished, they left the cottage and headed to the forest to pick berries. With all her friends helping, Snow White quickly filled her berry basket.

"How different life has become," she said to her friends. "I don't miss the grand castle at all. I love living in this funny little cottage. A home doesn't need to be grand to be a happy one! Remember that."

The animals exchanged looks with one another. Then they began tugging at her skirt to pull her to her feet.

"What is it, dears?" she asked them. "Oh! Do you want to show me where all of you live?

I would love to see!" she said delightedly.

Two bluebirds were first. Twittering excitedly, they fluttered around their nest, which had been built in a little nook of a nearby tree.

"What a lovely nest!" cried Snow White. The birds looked pleased.

The fawns were next. Pulling at her skirt, they brought Snow White to a sun-dappled clearing in a warm glade.

"How cosy!" exclaimed Snow White. The fawns flicked their tails happily.

Next, the chipmunks and squirrels showed her the hollow in an old tree where they lived.

"You all have such pretty little homes," said Snow White as they made their way back to the Dwarfs' cottage. "Thank you for showing them to me. We are all lucky to live where we do, aren't we?" she said with a smile.

And with that, she skipped the rest of the way back to the cottage to start preparing her pie. She could hardly wait until the Dwarfs got home!

Disney HERCULES

A Growing Boy

Hercules's mortal parents, Amphitryon and Alcmene, had known Hercules was a special child from the moment they had found him, alone and crying in the wilderness, wearing a medal that bore the symbol of the gods. But as the baby grew, they were surprised to see Hercules's superhuman strength grow more powerful with each passing day. He could tie poisonous snakes into knots and lift grown-ups high into the air.

"Ma," said Hercules one day when he was five years old, "I'm bored."

So Alcmene gave Hercules some marbles to play with. She showed him how to use his thumb to shoot one marble at another.

Hercules shot tentatively at first. But soon he grew more confident. Lining up a shot, he flicked his thumb as hard as he could. The marble flew out of his hand, sending the target marble rocketing towards the horizon.

Luckily, the nearest neighbours lived several miles away. But one by one, all of Hercules's marbles were lost this way.

"Amphitryon, I simply don't know what to do with Hercules," Alcmene said to her husband the next day. "He's too strong for ordinary toys. And if he plays with the other children, I worry he may hurt them without meaning to."

"Hmm," Amphitryon replied. "Yes, the boy is stronger than he realises. Why, I do believe he's become as strong as an ox!"

That gave Amphitryon an idea. That afternoon, he walked to the marketplace. When he returned to the farm, he was leading an ox by a rope.

"Hercules," he said, leading the ox over to his son, "come meet your new playmate."

Amphitryon took the rope lead from round the ox's neck. He handed one end of the rope to Hercules. He offered the other end to the ox, who took it between his teeth.

Within seconds, Hercules and the ox had fallen into a friendly game of tug of war.

Hercules laughed. The ox twitched his tail playfully. Hercules's parents looked on and smiled.

"That's our boy," Alcmene said proudly.

A New Chef in Town

Early one evening, Tiana was sitting with her best friend when Charlotte started raving about a new chef in town named Leon Robere. "He just opened up a restaurant in town, and – oh! You just must try his gumbo. It's divine," she squealed.

The next night, Tiana and Naveen went to Leon's new restaurant.

"Now let's see what all the fuss is about," Naveen said when the gumbo was served.

Tiana took a bite. Her brow furrowed. She took another bite. Her eyes widened. She took a third bite.

"Wow, this is almost as good as yours!" Naveen said excitedly.

"Naveen," Tiana said calmly. "This isn't almost as good as mine. It is mine."

Tiana excused herself to speak to the chef. But instead of admitting what he had done, Leon told Tiana her recipe wasn't good enough to steal.

Tiana was shocked. Then she had an idea. "Okay," she began. "If you didn't take my recipe, then prove it. I challenge you to a gumbo cook off tomorrow at noon. No cookbooks or recipes."

The next day, a huge crowd gathered at the restaurant.

When they were finished cooking, the two chefs handed out gumbo to the hungry people. Tiana watched as one person tasted her gumbo and a slow smile spread across his face. Then she noticed something peculiar. People seemed downright disgusted by Leon's gumbo.

Tiana took a bite of Leon's gumbo and nearly gagged. "What is this?" she asked.

Leon let out a heavy sigh. "You were right, Tiana," he confessed. "I did steal your secret gumbo recipe. I stayed up all night trying to memorise it, but I obviously failed." Leon looked at the floor. "I am very sorry."

Looking at Leon, Tiana felt sorry for him. "I have an idea," she said. "I will teach you how to make a basic gumbo. Then you can add some twists to make it your own! In return, you will tell everyone that you borrowed my recipe."

Leon smiled and shook Tiana's hand. "You've got yourself a deal," he replied. "But I have one more favour to ask. Could I have a bowl of your gumbo?"

Tiana laughed. "One bowl of Tiana's Gumbo coming right up!" she said.

Flik Wings It

Flik knew that Hopper and his gang of hungry grasshoppers would soon come to steal all the food from the peaceful ants of Ant Island. So Flik headed off to the big city to find warrior bugs to help fight the grasshoppers.

On his way, Flik saw a shiny dragonfly flitter across the sky.

"Wow, I wish I could fly like that!" he exclaimed.

Suddenly, Flik had an idea. "I wonder if I could invent a flying machine?"

After a lot of hard work, Flik took a step backwards and studied his invention.

"Well, it certainly looks like it could fly," Flik said finally.

Flik decided it was time for a test flight. He put his feet on the little pedals and started to pump.

The green wings began to flap. Flik pushed them faster and faster. Soon, the flier began to rock from side to side; then it leapt into the sky!

"It's working!" Flik cried. He was flying! With the air racing between his antennae, Flik watched the world flash beneath his feet.

"Flying is so much safer than walking," said Flik.

But he spoke too soon, for high in the sky above Flik, a mother bird was teaching her three little hatchlings how to fly.

The bird spied Flik's strange-looking contraption and thought one thing – dinner!

Flik looked up and saw the mother bird and her babies coming down on him like dive-bombers.

"Test flight over!" Flik cried.

Pedalling faster, Flik steered his flier through the limbs of a tall tree. The mother bird and two of her babies were blocked by the branches. But the third baby bird raced between the leaves and caught up with Flik.

Pecking wildly, the little bird ripped a wing from Flik's flier. The machine crashed to the ground.

Luckily for Flik, he had also made a parachute out of a spider's web, and he made a soft landing in the middle of a daisy.

"Another failed invention," Flik said with a sigh. "Maybe some day I'll have a chance to make a flying machine that really works!"

Arlo's Birthday Adventure

Arlo was excited! The next day was the triplet's seventh birthday, and every year, Momma and Poppa planned a special day away from the farm. Arlo shifted from foot to foot. He couldn't wait to find out what his parents had planned.

"Well, Momma," Poppa said when he came in from the field, "would you look at these young 'uns? Why they look like they're just about old enough for an adventure!"

Arlo gulped. An adventure? That sounded scary. Surely his parents wouldn't plan anything too scary. Would they?

Momma smiled. "We're going for a picnic by my favourite waterfall. It's where Poppa and I met."

The next morning, they set off bright and early. Arlo had barely slept. All night he'd been worrying about the hike. What if he got lost? What if he stepped on something and got hurt? There was a lot that could go wrong on a hike.

Momma appeared carrying a basket of Arlo's favourite berries. Maybe the hike wouldn't be so bad after all.

Arlo's eyes darted back and forth as he followed the path. Strange shadows lurked in the trees, and sharp branches poked him as he ran.

"Momma!" he shouted. "Wait up!"

At the top of a hill, Momma pointed at a fallen tree. "This is the path we usually take to the waterfall, but it's blocked. We'll have to go another way."

"It looks like our only choice is across these rocks. That cave might be a dead end," Poppa said.

Arlo gulped. He didn't like the sound of that either.

As Momma started down the path to the rocks, she tripped. The basked of berries went flying into a nearby cave.

"No!" Arlo shouted, running straight into the cave to rescue the berries.

"Hey, guess what!" Arlo called out. "The cave isn't a dead end and leads right to the waterfall!" He turned round and walked back through the tunnel. His family followed.

Poppa smiled at Momma. "It looks like our boy is growing up."

"That he is," Momma said, "Now, I think it's time for that birthday picnic. And the first berries go to Arlo for saving the day!"

Buzz to the Rescue

"There you go, pardners," Andy said as he packed Woody, Jessie and Bullseye into his backpack. He was taking them to Cowboy Camp. Jessie couldn't wait!

Just then, Andy's mum poked her head into his room. "You know the rules. You can only take one toy to camp with you."

Andy sighed. He lifted Jessie and Bullseye out of the bag and placed them on the window sill. Then he left his room. Jessie climbed down from the window and flopped into a box full of books.

Suddenly, a Green Army Man yelled, "Red alert!" Someone was coming. It was Molly's babysitter. She picked up the box of books and took it to the attic. The toys looked at each other in shock. Jessie was still inside the box!

"We've got to do something!" Buzz cried.

In the attic, Jessie looked for a way back to Andy's bedroom. But the attic door wouldn't budge. Suddenly, she had an idea. She found a skipping rope, made a lasso and threw the loop over the window lock. Jessie opened the window a few centimetres and crawled outside.

Just then, she heard someone fiddling with the attic doorknob. *Oh no*, she thought. *The babysitter!* Jessie grabbed the rope and jumped.

But the noise wasn't the babysitter at all. It was the other toys opening the attic door to rescue Jessie. Buzz gasped when he spotted the open window. Then he saw Jessie hanging on to the skipping rope.

"Don't let go, Jessie!" he shouted. "I'm coming for you!"

Buzz spread his wings. Then, taking a deep breath, he dived out the window. Jessie looked up and saw her friend falling towards her. Thinking fast, she swung her legs out and caught Buzz. The two toys swung forwards – right through Andy's open window! The rest of the toys raced down the stairs to Andy's room.

"We saved Jessie!" Buzz announced.

Jessie laughed. "Saved me?" She was the one who had rescued Buzz!

Jessie looked at her friends. They were all smiling. "Thanks, everyone!" she said. "Even though I didn't get to go to Cowboy Camp, this has been the best adventure ever! Yee-haw!"

Wanted: Flynn Rider

Rapunzel and Flynn Rider had a problem! Flynn had been arrested for stealing Rapunzel's crown because witnesses all over town claimed to have seen Flynn running away from the crime scene. Rapunzel knew Flynn hadn't stolen it, but she needed to prove it!

Rapunzel and her friends from the Snuggly Duckling pub questioned the townspeople.

The librarian claimed to have seen Flynn by the paint shop, but a sailor said he'd seen him by the docks. "How did you know it was him?" asked Rapunzel.

"The thief was wearing a green vest, just like the one Flynn wears," replied the sailor.

"But he couldn't have been at the paint shop and the docks! They're on opposite sides of town," said Rapunzel. She was starting to suspect who was really behind all this.

Rapunzel had a plan to catch the real criminals.

That evening, Rapunzel told the King and Queen to tell the town that all the royal jewels had been moved to the throne room for protection, then sent Max to lead all the guards away from the castle in front of all the townspeople.

"They must be going to find the princess' tiara," said one of the townsfolk.

When darkness fell, two shadowy figures lowered a rope from the throne room ceiling and climbed down, looking for the jewels. But the room was empty! It had been a trick!

Rapunzel and her friends burst out from where they were hiding. Once her friends had restrained them, Rapunzel removed their brown wigs to reveal… the Stabbington brothers!

"We knew you'd get to the bottom of this!" said the Queen, giving her daughter a hug.

Rapunzel smiled and went to free Flynn from the dungeons, as the Stabbington brothers were left inside. There was one mystery left to solve. "Where's my tiara?" asked Rapunzel.

"It's here," said one of the brothers, pulling the tiara from beneath his vest.

Rapunzel, Flynn and their friends went to the Snuggly Ducking to celebrate!

Pinocchio

Follow Your Star

Jiminy Cricket was a wanderer. He loved the independence, the excitement and the simplicity of his way of life.

But lately, Jiminy had noticed that there was one thing missing from his vagabond lifestyle: a purpose. Camping one night by the side of the road, he sat on his sleeping bag and gazed into his campfire.

"I wonder what it would feel like to be really helpful to someone," he said.

Jiminy tried to get comfortable on the hard ground as he looked up into the starry night sky. As his eyes scanned the many tiny points of light, one star to the south jumped out at him. It seemed to shine brighter than all the rest.

"Say, is that a Wishing Star?" he wondered aloud. Since he couldn't know for certain, he decided it would be best to make a wish on it, just in case.

"Wishing Star," he said, "I wish to find a place where I can make a difference and do a bit of good."

His wish made, Jiminy suddenly felt a strange impulse: an urge to get up, gather his things and follow that star – the Wishing Star.

Jiminy put out the campfire. Then he gathered his things and he took to the road.

The little cricket followed that star all through the night. In fact, he walked until the sun came up and he could no longer see the star to follow it. Then he pitched camp for the night and slept.

After many nights of walking in this manner, at last Jiminy came to a village.

It was very late as Jiminy Cricket walked into the village and looked around. Every window of every house was dark – except for one window in a shop at the end of a street. So Jiminy hopped over to the window.

Peering inside, he saw that it was a woodcarver's workshop, dimly lit by the embers of a fire dying in the fireplace. It seemed a warm and pleasant place to stop for the night.

Little did Jiminy Cricket know that it was the home of Geppetto, a kind old woodcarver who had just finished work on a puppet he called Pinocchio.

Jiminy did not know it, but he had found a place where he would do more than just a bit of good.

Special Delivery

Roger and Anita had a lot of puppies, and that meant they needed a lot of food. Every Thursday, a van pulled up full of dog food. And every Thursday, Rolly waited by the window for the van.

One Thursday, Rolly and Pepper noticed that the back of the van had been left open. "Are you thinking what I'm thinking?" Pepper asked Rolly.

Rolly nodded. "Snack time!" Rolly and Pepper made a dash for the truck and leapt into the back. Pepper clambered up onto the pile of bags and sniffed around. There had to be some loose food somewhere—

"Bingo!" Pepper cried. "Rolly, up here!"

Rolly was there in an instant. Slurp, slurp, crunch! The two puppies were so busy eating that they didn't see the van driver come out of the house.

Slam! He closed up the back of the van. A second later, it was rumbling down the road.

"Uh-oh," Rolly whispered.

After what seemed like a very long time, the vehicle lurched to a halt. The back door opened, and the driver began unloading bags of food.

Pepper and Rolly jumped out of the van while he wasn't looking. They ran and hid behind the house.

"What do you two think you're doing?" a gruff voice asked.

The puppies spun round. A big bulldog was looking down at them.

"This is my property," the dog said. "It's time for you to scram."

"You don't scare me," Pepper said boldly. "You're not half as bad as Cruella."

The bulldog's mouth fell open. "Do you mean Cruella De Vil?" he asked. "You must be Pongo and Perdita's puppies! I heard about your adventures over the Twilight Bark! Your parents must be worried about you. I'd better get you home!"

Luckily, Pongo and Perdita were out that day and didn't realise what a pickle Rolly and Pepper had got themselves into. But there were ninety-seven puppies waiting as Rolly and Pepper arrived with their escort.

"Wow," said Lucky, after he'd heard their tale. "Were you scared of that big mean bulldog?"

"No way!" Pepper said. "That bulldog was all bark and no bite!"

Scrooge's Nature

"Would you look at that!" Huey pointed to a picture of a Junior Woodchuck relaxing in a hammock while another camper fished in a nearby lake.

"And that!" Dewey's eyes widened. He pointed at a picture of a star-filled sky in the same brochure.

"Camping at Faraway Lake sure looks fun," Louie agreed. "Do you think Uncle Scrooge would pay for us to go?"

"He might," Huey said.

The three boys looked at one another. "Nah!" they said in unison.

"Let's show him anyway," Huey said.

The other boys followed Huey into their uncle's study. Dewey nudged Huey forwards. "Look at this, Uncle Scrooge," Huey said, thrusting the brochure into his uncle's lap.

"Humph." Uncle Scrooge scowled at the glossy photos. "What have we got here, lads?"

"It's a camp, Uncle Scrooge. It's-it's educational," Huey stammered.

"Looks like a waste of my hard-earned money," the old duck said.

"But… but we could camp out under the stars," Dewey said.

"And cook over a fire," Louie chipped in.

"And see nature," Huey added.

Uncle Scrooge's eyes narrowed. He looked from the brochure to his nephews' hopeful faces and back to the brochure. So, they wanted to learn about nature, did they? Scrooge had a plan.

"Here you are, boys," said Uncle Scrooge a short time later. He smiled from the safety of the screened-in back porch. "You have tents," he said, pointing to the three leaky tents set up in the back garden. "And you can see the stars," which was true, although only one or two stars were visible through the branches of the tree the tents were under. "And you're cooking over a fire," Scrooge finished, pointing at the tiny, smoky, little flame.

"This is much better than that Junior Woodchuck nonsense, isn't it, boys?" Uncle Scrooge asked with the smile of a duck who had saved himself some cash.

"Yes, Uncle Scrooge," Huey, Dewey and Louie said.

The boys turned back to the fire.

"I think…" said Huey.

"… next time…" continued Dewey.

"… we ask Uncle Donald!" finished Louie.

Disney·PIXAR
MONSTERS, INC.

JAMES P. SULLIVAN

Monster Moneymaker

Every morning as Mike and Sulley walked through the reception of Monsters, Inc., to the Scare Floor, they passed the Scarer of the Month photos of Sulley hanging on the wall. One day, Mike turned to his big blue friend.

"Sulley," he said, "do you ever think that we deserve a little more?"

"More?" Sulley asked.

"Oh, you know," Mike continued. "You're the top Scarer month after month. All you get is a lousy picture in the hallway, and I get nothin'. We should be famous!"

Then Mike had another idea. "We should set up a gift shop right here in the building featuring 'Sulley the Super Scarer' memorabilia."

"Why would we want to bother with all that?" Sulley asked.

"Money!" Mike exclaimed, rolling his eye.

"I don't know, Mike," Sulley said. "It just doesn't seem right, us making money off these things. But what if we… that's it!" Sulley jumped up, nearly knocking Mike over. "We'll donate the money to charity!"

"Who said anything about donations?" Mike asked.

"That's a great idea!" Sulley said, ignoring Mike.

"How will we bask in any glory if we give the money away?" Mike asked.

"Well, we will, sort of," Sulley explained. "We'll make the donation on behalf of Monsters, Inc.."

"I don't know about that," Mike said.

"This will work, Mike," Sulley said. "It's a wonderful idea. And when we help the company make a generous donation, Mr Waternoose will be very proud of us!"

Mike was suddenly warming to the idea. "And we'll get lots of press!" he added.

"Sure, why not?" Sulley said with a shrug.

"It's a great idea!" Mike cheered.

"I agree!" Sulley said.

"I'm glad I thought of it!" Mike gave his best friend a huge smile.

"You always have such good ideas," Sulley agreed with a grin.

"It's like I always say," Mike added. "Scaring's important, but it's the brains behind the monster that matter most. Right, buddy?"

Disney

Lady and the **TRAMP**

Like Father, Like Son

Tramp had a whole new life. He had gone from being a stray to becoming a member of the Dear household. And now he and Lady were proud parents. But Tramp was finding it difficult to change some of his old ways.

"Tramp," Lady said gently, "you need to set an example for the puppies, especially Scamp."

Scamp had an adventurous side, just like his dad, so it wasn't surprising that father and son often got carried away when they played together. They couldn't resist the urge to roll in a puddle of mud – and then chase each other across the clean kitchen floor.

Aunt Sarah and her two troublesome cats were going to be visiting soon. Lady was worried about how Tramp and Scamp would behave.

"Don't worry. I promise to keep Scamp away from those troublemakers," Tramp said.

"And?" replied Lady.

"And I promise to stay away from them, too," Tramp added.

When the big day came, Lady and Tramp herded their pups into a bedroom and told them to stay put. But Scamp was curious. He slipped out of the room and hid behind the living room sofa. Then he sneaked up behind the cats and swiped at their tails as they flicked back and forth. The cats turned and chased Scamp into a cupboard.

Seconds later, Scamp emerged. When no one was looking, he and his father shared a victory wink.

Father and son were banished to the garden for their antics. When Lady went outside later that evening, she found that they had dug up the entire garden looking for bones. The two saw the look on Lady's face and knew that they were about to get a lecture.

Tramp looked at Lady innocently. "You want him to get exercise, don't you?" he asked.

"What am I going to do with you two?" Lady said, laughing.

Tramp and Scamp dragged a huge bone out from behind the kennel.

"Join us for dinner?" Tramp replied.

"Well, all right," Lady said. "But as soon as we're done, we're cleaning up this garden."

"Yes, ma'am!" chorused Tramp and Scamp, looking very pleased with themselves.

We're the Vultures

"Nothing exciting ever happens around here," Buzzie complained to his vulture singing buddies.

"That's not true," said Flaps. "What about that fight we had with the tiger Shere Khan last week?"

"Blimey, you're right," said Ziggy. "That was pretty exciting."

"But what are we gonna do now?" asked Buzzie.

"Let's sing," suggested Ziggy.

"Only one problem," said Dizzy. "We need a tenor."

"So, what are we gonna do?" asked Buzzie.

"How 'bout we hold an audition?" suggested Ziggy.

"Good thinking," said Flaps.

So the vultures put the word out in the jungle, and a week later there was a line of animals ready to audition for the group. First up was a monkey.

"Name?" Buzzie asked the first applicant.

"Coconut," the monkey replied.

"All right, Coconut, let's hear ya sing," said Flaps.

Coconut shrieked for a few minutes, and the four vultures huddled together.

"He's not very good," said Buzzie.

"And he's a monkey," added Flaps.

"Next!" said Dizzy.

The vultures auditioned a lemur, two sloths, a wolf, a hippo, a toad and an elephant. None seemed like the right fit. Finally, another vulture stepped up.

"Name's Lucky," said the vulture. "Hey, aren't you the four fellows that helped that little Man-cub scare away that tiger, Shere Khan?"

"Yeah," said Buzzie. "We are."

"Then I guess you four might be called 'lucky' yourselves!" cried Lucky.

"Go ahead and sing," said Ziggy, rolling his eyes.

Lucky sang for a few minutes, and then the four vultures huddled together.

"He's not bad," said Dizzy.

"Plus, he's a vulture," said Ziggy.

"And he's the last auditionee left," pointed out Flaps.

That settled it.

"You're hired!" the vultures sang.

"See? Told you I was lucky!" cried the vulture.

"But only with auditions," said Dizzy.

"Yeah," said Buzzie. "When we meet Shere Khan again, we'll see how lucky you really are!"

Fit for a Princess

Cinderella hummed to herself as she slipped the silver needle through the colourful fabric. She had been working hard on her new quilt for weeks, and it was almost finished!

Cinderella knew the quilt would be fit for a princess. The worn fabrics were colourful and soft, and with the cotton stuffing she'd found in the attic, the quilt would be wonderfully cosy. No more shivering under her threadbare blanket!

Gus agreed. He couldn't help but climb between the sewn-together quilt fabric and snuggle into the cotton filling.

Suzy and Perla, who were helping Cinderella with the sewing, giggled. "Go and get us some more thread, sleepyhead," they called. But Gus was already dozing off. The sound of his snores drifted out from between the layers of quilt.

"Gus!" Jaq called. But the snores only got louder. "That mouse hasn't helped with this quilt one bit!" Jaq sighed and went to get the spools of thread himself.

Cinderella was just sewing together the last edge of the quilt when loud footsteps echoed on the attic stairs. It was her stepsister, Anastasia. A moment later, she stormed into the room carrying a fancy blue gown. "My dress was not ironed properly!" she shouted. "Can't you do anything right?"

Then she spotted the quilt. "It's beautiful!" she cried. "And it will look wonderful on my bed!"

Cinderella looked at Anastasia in shock. Would her stepsister really steal her quilt? She knew Anastasia and Drizella could be mean, but that would be downright cruel!

Suddenly, the quilt began to move. A moment later Gus's quivering nose poked out from between the unsewn pieces of fabric.

"A rodent!" Anastasia screamed. She dropped her dress in fright and leapt onto a small wooden chair. "Why, that quilt isn't fit for use in the stable!" she cried.

Cinderella tried not to laugh as her stepsister leapt off the chair and fled down the stairs. Yawning, Gus climbed the rest of the way out of the quilt.

"Well, Gus-Gus," Jaq said, "I guess you did end up helping with the quilt after all!"

How to Win Hide-and-Seek

"Belle!" Mrs Potts called. "Oh, Belle!" Belle was sitting in her bedroom, surrounded by a pile of books.

"There you are!" Mrs Potts cried.

"Hi, Belle," Mrs Potts's son, Chip, chimed in.

"Hello to both of you. Were you looking for me?" Belle asked Mrs Potts.

"As a matter of fact, I was," Mrs Potts told her. "I was just stopping by to enquire as to whether or not you would like some tea."

"Thank you," Belle said. "I would love some."

Mrs Potts poured Belle a piping hot cup of tea. Belle took a sip and thanked her.

Mrs Potts soon headed back to the kitchen, but Chip stayed behind. He wanted to play with Belle.

"How about a game of hide-and-seek?" Belle asked the small teacup.

"How do you play that?" Chip asked.

"It's simple," Belle said. "One person hides and the other person tries to find them."

"I can do that!" Chip said.

"Of course you can," Belle told him. "So, do you want to be the hider or the seeker?"

"I want to be the hider," Chip told her.

"Okay," Belle said. "I'll close my eyes and count to ten. One, two, three…"

Chip took off, darting behind the curtains just as Belle called, "Ten! Ready or not, here I come! Hmm, now where could he be?"

Belle looked under the table. "He isn't there," she said. Then she looked in the corner. "He isn't there either." She looked high and low, but she couldn't seem to find Chip anywhere.

"I give up," Belle said. "Come out, come out, wherever you are!"

Chip silently giggled from behind the curtain, but he was careful not to make too much noise. He was having fun!

"It seems that Chip doesn't want to come out from his hiding place," Belle said. "I guess that means I'll have to eat a slice of Mrs Potts's chocolate cake all by myself."

When he heard that, Chip jumped out from his hiding place and called out to Belle, "Here I am! Wait for me!"

THE **LION KING**

Scaredy Cats

"Nala!" Simba whispered. "Are you awake?"

"Yes," Nala whispered back, stepping out of the dark cave where she slept with her mother. "Why are you here? You're gonna get us in trouble… again."

Earlier, Simba and Nala had gone to explore the forbidden Elephant Graveyard, where they'd almost been eaten by hyenas.

"Come on," Simba hissed. "Follow me."

Soon the two cubs were on the dark savannah near the base of Pride Rock.

"What do you want, anyway?" Nala asked.

"I just wanted to make sure you weren't still scared," Simba said.

Nala scowled at him. "Scared?" she exclaimed. "I'm not the one who was scared!"

"What?" Simba cried. "You're not saying I was scared, are you? Because there's no way I'd be scared of a few stupid hyenas. I wouldn't have been scared even if we ran into a hundred hyenas."

"Well, I wouldn't have been scared even if we saw two hundred hyenas and an angry water buffalo," said Nala.

"Oh yeah?" Simba said. "Well, I wouldn't have been scared of three hundred hyenas, an angry water buffalo and a—"

"FURIOUS HORNBILL?" a new voice squawked from the darkness.

"Ahhhhhh!" Simba and Nala cried, jumping straight up in the air.

A brightly coloured bird stepped out of the shadows. It was Zazu, Simba's father's most trusted adviser.

"Zazu!" Simba cried. "You scared us!"

"I wasn't scared," Nala said with a scowl.

"Me neither!" Simba added quickly.

Zazu glared at both of them over his long beak. "Not scared, were you?" he said drily. "That certainly explains the shrieking."

"You just startled us," Nala mumbled.

Zazu fluffed his feathers. "Listen up, you two," he said. "Everyone gets scared. It's how you respond to it that counts. That's where true bravery lies. Get it?"

"Got it," Simba and Nala said.

"Good." Zazu marched towards Pride Rock. The sun was coming up, and it was time for breakfast. "Now let's get you back home post-haste… or I'll really give you something to be scared of!"

Peter Pan

The Lost Boys Get Lost

The Lost Boys were walking single file through the woods of Never Land, on their way home after an afternoon of adventure seeking, when Slightly, who led the way, stopped in his tracks on the bank of Mermaid Lagoon. The others – Rabbit, the Raccoon Twins, Cubby and Tootles – came to an abrupt halt behind him.

"Wait a minute," said Slightly. "We already passed Mermaid Lagoon. What are we doing here again?"

Behind a bush, Tinker Bell giggled as she watched the Lost Boys looking around in confusion.

Tink had spotted them on their march and had not been able to resist playing a joke. She had flown ahead of them and used her fairy magic to make various landmarks on their route home look different than usual.

Now, here they were, walking past Mermaid Lagoon, when Slightly remembered passing the same spot a good while back.

"I think we're walking in circles!" Slightly proclaimed. "Lost Boys, I think we're... lost!"

Tinker Bell overheard and tried desperately to stifle her laughter. But before she could contain it, one giggle exploded into a fully fledged laugh, and—

"Hey!" said Cubby. "Did you hear that?"

He darted over to a bush growing alongside the path and moved a branch to one side. There was Tinker Bell, hovering in mid-air, holding her stomach and shaking with laughter.

"Tinker Bell!" cried Tootles.

It didn't take them long to work out that Tinker Bell was laughing at them – and that she was the cause of their confusion.

Still laughing, Tinker Bell flitted away, taking her normal route home to the fairy glade: left at the Weeping Willow Tree, right just before Sparrow Bird Grove, right again at Spiky Rock and on towards the Sparkling Stream, which led to Moon Falls and the fairy glade entrance.

But... wait a minute! After turning right at Spiky Rock, Tinker Bell saw no sign of the Sparkling Stream anywhere. Where was she? She had got completely lost.

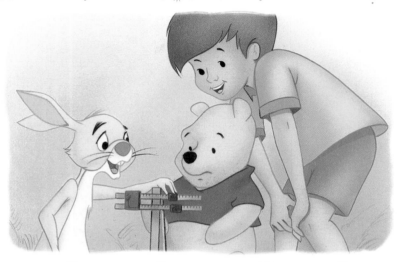

Say Ahhh, Pooh!

"Christopher Robin says it's time for my animal checkout," said Pooh.

"Checkout!" cried Piglet. "Oh p-p-poor P-P-Pooh – you're sick!"

"Sick?" asked Pooh. "No, I'm fine. Though I must say I am feeling a bit rumbly in my tumbly."

"Let's go together," said Piglet. "It's so much more friendly with two."

So Pooh and Piglet climbed the ladder up to Owl's house.

"Christopher Robin, why do I need an animal checkout, anyway?" asked Pooh once they had arrived at Owl's house.

"Silly old bear," said Christopher Robin. "Not an animal checkout – an annual check-up. We need to make sure you are healthy and strong."

Rabbit weighed Pooh and then told him to go into Owl's room. Piglet wished him good luck. Once Pooh and Christopher Robin were inside, Owl entered with a flourish. "Well, if it isn't Winnie the Pooh!" he said. "Splendid day for a check-up, isn't it? I say, how are you feeling?"

"A bit flippy-floppy in my tummy, actually," said Pooh.

Owl felt Pooh's tummy. He felt round Pooh's neck and under his arms and said that everything seemed to be right where it should be. Pooh was glad. Then Owl pulled a small rubber hammer from his bag. "Reflex-checking time!" he said grandly.

"What's a reflex?" asked Pooh. Owl tapped Pooh's knee – and his leg gave a little kick! "Oh do that again," said Pooh. "That was fun." So Owl tapped Pooh's other knee, and that leg gave a little kick, too!

Then Owl said, "Sit right here. It's time for your shot."

"I know it will only hurt for a moment, and it will keep me from getting bumps and weasels," Pooh said bravely.

"That's mumps and measles, Pooh," said Owl.

Piglet came in and sat right next to Pooh while he had his injection. When Owl was done, Rabbit popped back in with a bandage for Pooh's arm.

"Wow," said Piglet. "You didn't even make a sound!"

"An annual check-up is no problem for a brave bear like Pooh," said Christopher Robin.

I'm just that sort of bear, thought Pooh with a smile.

The Flying Blueberries

Everyone in the ant colony was in a good mood. The grasshoppers had been driven off once and for all, and none of the ants had even been hurt! But Flik's amazing fake bird had taken quite a beating, and the Blueberries were determined to fix it.

"Fixing that bird is a big job," said Mr Soil, Dot's teacher, "but I know the Blueberries can do it."

The Blueberries stared at the fake bird. It was one big mess!

"I'll be back in a little while to see how you're doing," said Mr Soil.

With a cheer, the Blueberries went to work. Some picked new leaves to cover the frame. Others glued those leaves into place with sticky honey. After hours of hard work, the bird was fixed.

"Let's sit in it!" Dot said.

Just as the Blueberries crawled inside the bird, the wind began to blow. Suddenly, the breeze caught the fake wings. The bird took off!

It was up to Dot to save the day. She hopped into the pilot seat and took control.

The Blueberries flew round Ant Island once, then twice. Soon they weren't afraid any more.

"Look!" screamed Rose. "Real birds are attacking the worker ants!"

Dot jiggled the controls. The fake bird dived out of the sky and frightened the real birds away.

"Hooray!" yelled the Blueberries. "You did it, Dot!"

"Don't cheer yet!" Dot cried. "This contraption is out of control!"

With a bump and a crash, the bird hit the ground and skidded to a halt.

"It's wrecked again!" said Rose. "And here comes Mr Soil! He's going to be so mad."

But surprisingly, Mr Soil was smiling.

"You're heroes!" he told them. "You saved the worker ants."

"But the bird is wrecked again," said Rose.

"And you can fix it again, too," Mr Soil replied.

"And here is a merit badge for you, princess, in honour of your first flight," Mr Soil continued.

Dot was confused. "I've already made my first flight," she said, fluttering her tiny wings.

"Ah, but this is a special badge," Mr Soil replied. "It's for making your first flight not using your wings, but using your head!"

THE LITTLE MERMAID

A Special Surprise

The underwater kingdom was quiet and peaceful. Every mermaid and merman was in bed fast asleep. Everyone, that is, except for Princess Ariel and her friend Flounder.

Trying not to make a sound, Ariel and Flounder swam away from King Triton's palace and began their journey towards the surface.

Ariel wasn't going to let anything ruin her plans for tonight. Prince Eric, the prince she had saved from a shipwreck, was having a royal ball. Ariel had a very special surprise for him.

"Swim faster, Flounder!" she cried. Flounder raced to keep up. Just as Ariel and Flounder approached the surface, Ariel saw beautiful lights dancing across the water. When they poked their heads out into the air, Ariel and Flounder saw colourful lights exploding in the sky above Prince Eric's castle.

"I've never seen anything so beautiful in all my life," said Ariel breathlessly. "The human world is such a wonderful place!"

"It sure is pretty!" said Flounder.

Off in the distance, Prince Eric stood on the palace balcony. He didn't feel like joining in the royal celebration. He couldn't stop thinking about the mysterious girl with the lovely voice who had saved his life in the shipwreck.

Ariel's heart leapt with joy when she saw Prince Eric. "It's time for my surprise!" she said.

"R-r-ready?" asked Flounder.

With a nod, Ariel closed her eyes, opened her mouth and began to sing. Suddenly, the night was filled with the sweet sound of Ariel's voice.

Hearing her beautiful voice again, Eric's face lit up. "It can't be!" he said.

Eric remained on the balcony, enchanted by the beautiful song filling the night air. When the song was over, Eric looked out across the sea. He hoped to catch a glimpse of the wonderful girl who had saved him. Where could she be?

"Who are you?" he called out into the night. But all he heard was the echo of his own voice.

"I'll be back soon," Ariel whispered as she and Flounder swam towards home. "Just wait and see."

Stuck in the Mud

"Come on, Robin!" Little John called as he stepped over a fallen log.

"Shh," Robin put a finger to his lips. "I think I hear something."

"Let's have a look-see," said Little John. A minute later, they stopped at the edge of the forest and peered out from behind a bush.

There, stuck in a muddy ditch, was a fancy coach.

"I'd know that coach anywhere," Robin whispered. "It belongs to Prince John."

"Get me out of the mud now!" a voice whined from inside the coach. It was Prince John, all right.

The driver's shoulders slumped. "But, sire, the coach is laden with gold. I'll never be able to push it out by myself. Perhaps Your Highness would consider stepping out of the coach so as to lighten the load?"

"Step out of the coach?" Prince John bellowed. "And stand in the rain? I most certainly will not!"

"I believe I have a plan that will help Prince John and his driver," Robin said. "Not to mention the poor."

Little John nodded with a grin. He knew exactly what sort of plan his friend had in mind. Robin reached into his satchel, pulled out a few items and put them on. Little John did the same. Now they looked like two ordinary hunters on a walk.

Little John stepped onto the road. "Need some help there?" he asked the driver loudly. "I'd be more than happy to lend a hand."

Meanwhile, Robin sneaked round to the side of the coach. He was just opening the door when Prince John leant out the window on the other side. "Hurry up, you fools!" he shouted.

Robin saw his chance. While the prince was distracted, he opened the other door and removed several bags of gold.

"Get pushing, then," Prince John snapped.

"I said I'd be glad to," Little John replied. He strolled to the back of the coach and, along with the driver, gave a single push. And while Robin slipped into the woods with the gold, Prince John and his muddy-wheeled coach rolled down the road to Nottingham, the load just a little bit lighter than before.

Bulda's Crystal

Kristoff was on a mission. Bulda's favourite crystal had stopped glowing, and he was determined to fix it for her.

Kristoff found Anna, Elsa and Olaf in the library. He explained that he was looking for a book about the trolls.

Elsa knew which book Kristoff meant. "'Troll crystals can be recharged where lights wake the sky, where sky touches the earth and where waters run long,'" she read.

"Lights that wake the sky could be the northern lights," said Anna.

"A mountaintop could be where the sky touches the earth," said Kristoff.

"And there's a long, narrow fjord by Opplading Mountain," said Anna.

The friends decided to set off at once. After hours of climbing, they finally reached the top of the mountain. To their surprise, there was nothing special on the summit.

"Do you think we went to the wrong mountain?" Anna asked.

The sun was beginning to set, so the group decided to stop for the night. As it got darker, the mountain began to glow.

Everyone got up and gazed at a crack in the overhang behind them.

Sven nudged everyone out of the way and hit the rock with his antlers. CRACK! He created a wedge and a few crystals spilled out. But the crystals stopped glowing as they hit the ground.

Anna was drawn towards the glow. "Perhaps we're going about this the wrong way," she said. "The crystals are glowing inside the mountain. If we put Bulda's crystal inside, maybe it will glow, too."

As Anna held Bulda's crystal up to the crystals inside the wall, a magical spark passed between them.

But when she removed her hand from the rock, Bulda's crystal was still dark.

The next day, the group returned to Troll Valley. "We weren't able to recharge your crystal," Kristoff said, sadly.

"Well," Bulda said, "crystals can be finicky. Let's take a look."

As Anna placed the stone in Bulda's hands, the crystal began to glow brightly!

"You did it!" said Bulda.

"We did?" Kristoff asked.

"Oh, Kristoff. You underestimate your own magic. When you work together and support one another, anything is possible."

The Sky's the Limit

"Captain Amelia and Dr Delbert Doppler were one smart couple. Even at a very young age, their quadruplets – three girls nicknamed Matey, Jib and Tillie (short for "Tiller"), and a boy, Sunny – began to show evidence of having inherited their parents' intelligence. Unbeknownst to their parents, little by little, the Doppler quadruplets were using their talents to make changes to the house where the family lived.

"Jib!" called Amelia, one windy afternoon. "Why are there large sails flying from the roof?"

"I thought they looked pretty up there," answered Jib.

"Tillie, what is that you're building in your room?" wondered Delbert.

"A rocket booster," she answered.

"Well, be careful!" her father warned. "Jet propulsion can be a tricky thing."

Amelia really became suspicious when she found Matey installing a giant steering wheel in front of the attic window. "And this would be?" she asked her daughter.

Matey looked innocently at her mother. "Something that's fun to spin?" she asked.

"Very curious," Amelia said to herself. Then one night, after the children went to bed, the house began to shake. The couple ran to their children's bedroom – and found it empty. A second later, the house began to lift off!

Amelia and Delbert looked at each other in disbelief.

"We did it!" Sunny cried triumphantly. His voice came from the attic.

Amelia and Delbert rushed upstairs.

"What's going on here?" demanded Delbert.

"I'm steering," said Matey, from behind the giant wheel.

"I'm controlling the sails," said Jib as she pulled some levers.

"I blasted us off," Tillie admitted.

"And I designed the whole thing," bragged Sunny.

"What thing?" asked Amelia.

"Mum and Dad, welcome to your new motorhome!" Jib announced.

Amelia and Delbert stared at their children.

"Well, what do you think?" Matey asked eagerly. "Do you like it?"

Her parents both broke out in proud grins. "Aye, aye, Captain!" boomed Amelia.

Disney
HERCULES

Bring a Friend

Hercules was training to be a hero, and boy, was it a lot of work. One day, Phil, his coach, set up a practice course for Hercules. Phil had put a doll somewhere in the course. He said it was a 'damsel in distress' and Hercules was supposed to rescue it.

So the hero-in-training raced into the first section of the course – a darkened cave. Herc plunged into darkness and fell head first into stagnant water.

"Yech!" Hercules spat out the putrid water and scowled.

Feeling his way through the dark water with his feet, Herc noticed something slithery slipping round his ankles. Snakes! He hurried towards the other end of the cave and dived into the daylight, shaking the last snake off his feet. Panting, Herc lay down on the grass to rest for a moment.

"Rest later!" Phil shouted.

Herc slowly rolled over. The doll had to be around there somewhere.

Then Hercules heard stamping hooves behind him and turned round. A huge ox was coming towards him! Herc jumped to his feet and dodged the ox.

At last, he spotted it: the doll was sitting metres above him on the edge of a steep cliff.

At least Phil had left him a rope. In fact, it looked as though Phil had left two. Gripping the first rope in his jaws, Herc moved steadily upwards. He was about halfway up when Phil lit the end of the second rope, which was soaked with oil! The fire raced up the rope towards a stack of dry wood under Herc's damsel.

Hercules threw himself the last few metres. He tackled the damsel, rolling away from the stack of wood, which was now blazing merrily.

Breathing hard, Hercules finally relaxed.

"And another thing…" Phil's gruff voice echoed up to him from the base of the cliff. Hercules held his breath, but not because he was waiting for Phil's next words. Herc was holding his breath because he had spotted a scorpion next to his foot. The insect was poised to sting!

Crunch. Hercules's winged horse, Pegasus, used his hoof to flatten the creature. Hercules smiled at Pegasus as Phil's final words of advice reached his ears. It was the best tip yet:

"Always bring a friend!"

The Storm

One summer afternoon, Jenny invited Dodger and his gang to go on a picnic with her and Oliver in Central Park.

"Go play with your friends," Jenny told the kitten.

As Jenny, Fagin and Winston the butler unpacked the picnic basket, they didn't notice that the animals were romping farther and farther away. Suddenly, thunder boomed and rain poured down. Then lightning struck a tree.

"I must get you home!" Winston insisted, rushing Jenny out of the park.

"Where's Oliver?" she cried.

"Don't worry," said Fagin. "Dodger will take care of him."

In the morning, Dodger woke up under a tree. Oliver had climbed it when the storm had started. The rest of the gang ran to find shelter, but Dodger had stayed with Oliver all night.

"Hey there, kid!" Dodger called. "You ready to go home now?"

"Yes!" said Oliver, climbing down. "And I've made a new friend. He says he's lost. Maybe Jenny will adopt him, too. Wouldn't that be wonderful?"

"Wow," said Dodger. "I didn't know cats could grow so big!"

"I'm a bear cub," the creature said.

"Where did you come from?" Dodger asked.

The bear started to cry. "I don't know!" he wailed. "I was scared of the storm, so I climbed a tree. Then a big wind blew me out of the tree. The next thing I knew I was out here on the lawn. So I climbed this tree and met Oliver. Can you help me find my mama?"

Oliver shook his head sadly. "I'm afraid I don't know where bears live in New York City."

"Wait!" Dodger said. "I think I do." He took Oliver and the cub to a fancy entrance with a big iron gate that read Central Park Zoo. When the zookeeper saw the cub, he rushed over and led him back to his mother.

"Mama!" cried the bear cub. The mother bear hugged her cub close, and Dodger smiled down at Oliver.

"Time to get you home, too."

When Jenny saw that Oliver was safe and sound, she kissed and hugged him – and Dodger, too.

"Thank you, Dodger!" Jenny cried. "You're my hero!"

"Mine, too," said Oliver. "A friend like you makes even the scariest storm bearable!"

Merida and the Missing Gem

"Och!" Merida complained. "I spent all month working on a fancy brooch for Mum. But her birthday's tomorrow and it's still not right!"

Maudie clucked in sympathy, but didn't reply. She was more worried about her latest batch of hot muffins.

"Who are those for?" asked Merida.

"These are for the DunBroch Brownie, the wee elf that lives outside the gate. If the Brownie isn't happy, who knows what mischief he could make?"

Merida sighed again, thinking about her mum's birthday. The brooch had started as a good idea, but when it was all put together, it didn't seem right.

Merida went to her room to take another look at the gem. But it was gone! Then Merida saw her brothers.

"Oh, come now, lads!" said Merida. "Where is it?"

But the boys had lost the gem!

Merida looked more closely at Hubert's shirt. "Is this a thistle?" she asked. "Are those crumbs on your shoes?"

Suddenly, Merida knew where the triplets had been playing that morning.

Merida led the boys outside. "Just as I thought," she said. "You ate the treats that Maudie made for the DunBroch Brownie! Well, now we know where you lost the gem."

Merida and her brothers looked all around the clearing, but they couldn't find the brooch. "What if the Brownie took the brooch because you ate his treats?" Merida said.

Merida told her brothers to get more muffins and thistles. Meanwhile, she tidied up the clearing. When everything was ready, she told everyone to close their eyes.

"DunBroch Brownie," Merida whispered into the air, "we're sorry your treats were taken! But we tried to fix everything. Could you help us, in return?"

Merida opened her eyes. There, in the crook of a tree, was the brooch! Had the Brownie really just returned it? Or had it been there the whole time?

Merida examined the gem more closely. There was something different about it.

The next evening, Merida presented the birthday brooch to her mother.

"My favourite gem, set in a silver thistle!" Elinor exclaimed. "What better luck could I have than to have you as my daughter?"

Mater in Paris

One lazy afternoon, Mater was listening to music. Suddenly, the music stopped and a voice spoke to Mater through the radio. It was British secret agent Holley Shiftwell!

"Hello, Mater!" she said. "Sorry to startle you. I'm contacting you because Finn and I need your help. We're in Paris tracking several Lemons who escaped from the World Grand Prix. Will you help?"

"Sure thing!" Mater said. "Love to!"

Suddenly, Siddeley the spy plane landed in the middle of Main Street! Mater's best friend, Lightning McQueen, drove up.

"Mater, what's going on?" he asked.

"I'm going on a secret mission to Paris," whispered Mater. "You wanna come, too?"

Lightning agreed, and the two set off to meet Holley and Finn.

"We've been tailing these Lemons for a while, but they keep getting away," Finn said.

"Them Lemons are tricky," said Mater. "You just gotta learn how to think like them. If I was a Lemon, I'd make sure I had plenty of spare parts."

"Brilliant," said Finn. "You and Lightning can visit the spare-parts dealer at the marketplace. Holley and I will head to the markets on the west side of Paris."

But Lightning and Mater were too late. The spare-parts dealer had been robbed!

"Them Lemons was here already," said Mater. Then he spotted a trail of spare parts on the ground. The pair followed the trail all the way to a nearby café, where Mater noticed two strange-looking cars. One of them backfired and his grille fell off. It was a disguise!

"Lemons!" cried Mater. "Their old exhausts make 'em backfire!"

The Lemons quickly fled the café. Lightning and Mater followed them through the city. Suddenly, there were not one, not two, but six Lemons surrounding them!

Mater quickly spun his tow hook. He caught one of the Lemons and knocked it out. Soon more Lemons arrived. Mater had an idea...

Lightning and Mater led the Lemons on a chase, all the way to the top of the Eiffel Tower. By the time they stopped, the Lemons were so exhausted, they tipped over. It was another great mission completed by secret agent Mater!

Disney

Lilo & Stitch

Friends Forever

Experiment 626 was a blue creature from a distant planet who was punished for being very naughty and destroying everything around him. One day, he escaped his planet in a police cruiser and headed straight for Earth!

On the tiny island of Kauai was a little girl named Lilo. She found it hard to make friends and was very lonely.

One night, Lilo had a fight with her sister, Nani. Lilo went to her room and slammed the door shut. Out of her window, Lilo saw a falling star and made a wish: "I wish for someone to be my friend," she whispered.

The falling star that Lilo had seen was actually Experiment 626's ship crashing on the island! A lorry driver found him and took him to an animal shelter. All the other animals were scared of 626, but he didn't care. He scrunched two of his four arms in towards his torso so he would look more like a dog. That way, he'd be adopted and have a place to hide from the aliens who were chasing him.

The next day, Nani decided to take Lilo to the shelter to pick a new pet.

"Hi!" Lilo said when she saw 626.

"Hi," the creature replied, and then he gave her a hug. Lilo walked back to the front room and told Nani she'd found the dog she wanted.

"He's good," she said. "I can tell. His name is… Stitch."

They took Stitch home even though Nani thought he looked strange. Nani was glad Lilo finally had a friend.

At home, however, Stitch began to tear things apart and cause trouble for Nani.

"We have to take him back," Nani said.

"We adopted him!" Lilo cried. "What about ohana? Dad said ohana means family! And family means—"

"Nobody gets left behind," Nani finished. "I know."

She remembered how welcoming her parents had been and how important family was to them. She changed her mind. She would give Stitch another chance – for Lilo's sake.

From then on, Lilo and Stitch stuck together through anything that came their way. Lilo helped Stitch learn how to behave, and Stitch became the friend that Lilo had wished for on a falling star.

Late for Supper

Widow Tweed was busy making supper. She filled the large baking tray with meat and vegetables, then rolled out a flaky crust and placed it on top. After crimping the pie's edges, she slid the tray into the oven.

"Chicken pie," she said. "Tod's favourite!" Widow Tweed looked out the window and noticed that the sun was setting.

"I wonder where that clever little devil has got to," she said.

She watched the sun sink behind the rolling forest hills, then sat down and picked up her knitting. She had a project to finish. Besides, the pie would be ready soon, and Tod was never late for supper.

"Knit one, purl two, knit one, purl two," the widow said quietly as she put the finishing touches on a soft blanket she was knitting for Tod's bed.

The smell of chicken pie drifted past her nose, and the widow got up to take it out of the oven. Suddenly, she heard a scratching at the door.

"Right on time, as usual," she said as she opened the door. "Come on, Tod. Dinner's ready."

But Tod wasn't there. The scratching had just been a small twig blown against the door

by the wind.

"Tod?" Widow Tweed called, peering into the darkness. "No playing tricks, now." But the little red fox did not appear.

"Oh, Tod," she said. "Where are you?"

Stepping back into the house, she pulled on her shoes and a jumper. She'd just have to go out to look for him. After lighting an old lantern, she opened the door for a second time – and nearly tripped over the red fox on her front porch. He sat there quietly, a colourful bouquet of wild flowers resting at his feet.

"Oh, Tod!" Widow Tweed cried. She picked up the bouquet and scooped him into her arms. "You sweetie-pie."

Tod nuzzled the widow's neck as she carried him into the house and deposited him on his chair at the kitchen table. Soon, the two were sharing a delicious feast of chicken pie. And after supper, the widow admired her bouquet above the mantel while Tod curled up in his bed with his cosy new blanket.

A Big Surprise

One sunny morning, Snow White visited the Dwarfs' cottage to leave them a surprise. She knew the Dwarfs worked hard, and she wanted to make sure that when they got home that day, they didn't have to do any more work.

After the Dwarfs had left for the mines, Snow White and her animal friends hurried into the cottage and set to work. The birds chirped while they picked up crumbs. The squirrels used their fluffy tails to dust. And the chipmunks washed and dried the plates. With so many helpers, Snow White had the downstairs gleaming in no time. Next, they went upstairs and made the beds. Before long, every inch of the Dwarfs' cottage was neat and tidy.

Back inside the cottage, Snow White and her friends fixed supper. There was soup to be simmered and bread to be made. Before she knew it, the late afternoon sun was casting long shadows across the windowpanes.

Tweet! Chirp! A bluebird was singing outside the window. That was the signal that the Dwarfs were almost home.

Snow White and the animals hurried outside, hid and peeked in through a window. When they got inside, the Dwarfs could not believe their eyes. The floors were swept, the room was tidy and there was even a freshly baked pie cooling on a window sill!

"What is that delicious smell?" Doc wondered.

"Look!" cried Grumpy. He went to the pot of soup.

The Dwarfs were confused. They tried to guess which Dwarf had done this.

Doc noticed that Happy's smile was especially big. Was he keeping a secret? Dopey pointed out that Sneezy seemed extra sneezy. Maybe because he had dusted and swept the cottage?

Snow White giggled as she listened outside the window. "They'll never guess that we did it," she whispered to her animal friends.

After a long workday, their tummies pleasantly full, all Seven Dwarfs were ready to go to sleep. When they climbed the stairs, the Dwarfs found one last treat: seven neatly made beds. As they drifted off to sleep, the Dwarfs decided to tell their good friend Snow White about this wonderful surprise the very next time they saw her.

Watch Dug

Dug bounded over some rocks. The golden retriever was looking for a spot to camp for the night. Following him were his friends, Carl and Russell. Suddenly, Dug saw a good place. It had trees on three sides and a beautiful view across the valley.

Carl put down their picnic basket. Next to it he placed a jug of lemonade. "Okay, Russell," he said. "Let's pitch the tents."

Carl and Russell put up tents and unrolled their sleeping bags. They cooked dinner over a campfire and toasted marshmallows. Soon it was time for bed.

Dug decided that he would keep watch. He was proud to have such an important job. When Carl and Russell went to bed, Dug sat outside the tents, as still as a statue.

Suddenly, he spied something in a tree.

Dug charged towards the tree – and tripped over a rope on Russell's tent. Part of the tent collapsed. Dug hung his head. He had not meant to do that.

Just then, a bat swooped overhead. Dug jumped up in surprise. He accidentally knocked over the jug of lemonade, and it spilt on the ground. Embarrassed, Dug went to stand guard near Carl's tent.

Rustle. Rustle. Rustle.

Dug sneaked across the clearing. He spied an intruder! It was a raccoon, and it was trying to get their food!

"Move away from the basket," Dug said. "That is our breakfast."

The raccoon grabbed a string of sausages in its teeth. Dug took the other end. He tugged. The raccoon tugged. Finally, the raccoon let go. Dug had won!

Dug triumphantly carried the sausages back to the picnic basket. They were a little dirty, and they had some leaves stuck to them. But he was sure Carl and Russell wouldn't mind.

Soon the sky started to lighten and the stars began to fade. Dug was very sleepy. Being a watch Dug was hard work!

Honk-shooo… Honk-shooo. Dug fell asleep.

A minute later, Carl came out of his tent. He looked around the clearing and saw Russell's tent. He saw the dirty sausages and the jug of lemonade.

Carl sat next to Dug. Dug opened one eye. "I found the intruder," he said.

"Yes, I heard you," Carl said. He gave Dug a pat. "Good dog. Good Dug."

And together, the two watched the sun rise over the valley.

A Snack for the Queen

It was a lovely day in Wonderland. Alice was sitting in the gardens, admiring the bread-and-butterflies. As Alice followed them with her gaze, she heard a voice.

"Oh dear, oh dear!"

Alice turned to see the White Rabbit running through the garden.

"Is everything alright?" she asked. The rabbit skidded to a halt.

"The Queen of Hearts is hungry," the White Rabbit said. "If I don't find her a tasty snack soon, she'll have my head!"

"Have you tried the Mad Hatter?" Alice asked. "His tea parties are always filled with treats."

"No way. The Mad Hatter is trouble," the White Rabbit replied. Alice paused, noticing a bush that was growing pink cupcakes.

"Perhaps we don't need to visit him after all…" Alice said. She plucked a cake off the bush and headed to the palace with the White Rabbit.

"There you are!" the Queen of Hearts yelled when she saw the White Rabbit. Then she saw Alice. "Off with your…"

"We brought you a cupcake, Your Majesty," Alice interrupted, handing the cake over.

But then, the cake began to move. Two wings extended and it flew away. It wasn't a cupcake… it was a bird! Alice and the White Rabbit ran.

They tried everything, from Cheshire Cat's blueberries to Tweedledee and Tweedledumb's lollipops, but they all backfired.

"That's it," Alice said at last. "I'm going to see the Mad Hatter."

She found him serving tea to the March Hare at his long table. She took a seat and explained everything that had happened.

"The Queen you say?" the Hatter asked. He handed a cookie to Alice. "This is exactly what she needs."

So, Alice and the White Rabbit brought the cookie to the Queen. She sniffed it.

"Smells good," the Queen said, frowning suspiciously. "And it looks tasty."

But when she bit into it, she started to shrink! She got smaller and smaller until she was no larger than the cookie itself.

"Off with their heads!" the Queen yelled. But she was so small, no one could hear her.

Alice and the White Rabbit hurried away. "The Hatter was right," she said. "That cookie was exactly what she needed!"

Abu's Blues

Abu couldn't believe it. One second he was a monkey. The next – POOF! – he was an elephant! Worst of all, nobody seemed to notice that Abu wasn't thrilled about his new shape. Aladdin was too busy with the Genie and the Magic Carpet.

Abu watched as the Genie waved his arms. POOF! Dozens of exotic white monkeys appeared. Then the Genie conjured up a group of snake charmers.

Abu wandered off, looking for space. He almost tripped over his new trunk a few times as he headed to a quiet spot.

Sighing, Abu sat down. He wished he had a nice juicy melon or a banana. Would he and Aladdin ever wander through the marketplace again, searching for a free meal?

Abu scowled. Princess Jasmine. Talk about trouble – that was where this had all started. Ever since Aladdin had met her, it was as if Abu didn't matter any more.

"Abu! Abu!"

Suddenly, Abu realised that someone was calling him. It was Aladdin!

"There you are, Abu!" Aladdin cried. "We were looking all over for you. Have you really been here all along?"

Abu glared at Aladdin suspiciously. What did he want? Was the Genie going to turn Abu into something else – maybe a big, ugly cobra for Prince Ali's new snake charmers?

"Come on," Aladdin said. "It's almost time!"

Abu had no idea what Aladdin was talking about. He trumpeted at him angrily, complaining about how Aladdin didn't seem to want him around any more.

"Don't be silly, Abu!" Aladdin said. "You're the most important one in this whole parade! Now come over here."

"Ready, monkey boy?" the Genie said. "Er, I mean, elephant dude?" He waved his arms, and a luxurious litter suddenly appeared on Abu's back. The Genie lifted Aladdin into it. Suddenly, Abu understood – he and Aladdin were at the head of the parade! Aladdin wasn't going to forget him just because he'd made other friends!

Lifting his trunk proudly, Abu let out a loud trumpet and led the way towards the Sultan's palace. There was a princess waiting for them!

The Journey Begins

Bernard couldn't believe this was really happening. Even though he was just a caretaker, he had been selected by the Rescue Aid Society to come to the aid of a little girl named Penny, who appeared to be in grave danger. And what's more, he, Bernard, had been selected over all the other mice to be partners with the very beautiful and clever Miss Bianca.

Bernard was very proud to have been chosen. It was Bernard's first rescue mission ever, and even though he was very nervous, he was excited to get started. He packed his bags in minutes, and now he had arrived to pick up Miss Bianca. But she was running late.

"Uh, Miss Bianca?" called Bernard after a while. "We really ought to be going, I think. We don't want to miss our flight!"

"All right, darling!" said Miss Bianca. "Come give me a hand with this suitcase, please!"

Bernard found Miss Bianca trying to close her overstuffed suitcase. She had already packed several boxes as well.

"Are you quite sure you'll be needing all those evening gowns, Miss Bianca?" Bernard panted as he sat on the bag and tried to zip it up. "And that tea set? And…" He paused to count. "Fourteen pairs of shoes?"

"A lady must be prepared for anything, darling," she crooned. "Now, I'll just put on my hat and we'll be off."

After what seemed like hours, Miss Bianca appeared at last in a dizzying cloud of perfume.

"I'll take that!" said Bernard as Miss Bianca reached for the suitcase. It felt as though it were full of bricks, but Bernard managed to manoeuvre it out the door, where he grabbed his much lighter bag in his other hand.

"Darling," Miss Bianca said sweetly as they headed to the airport, "please don't fret. Everyone knows that flights are always delayed!"

Even when the plane is an albatross? Bernard wondered to himself.

Yes, Miss Bianca and Bernard certainly made an unusual team. But Bernard was sure that they would get the rescue job done.

Just as long as he didn't drop her suitcase on his toe!

Tree Trouble

Toulouse and Berlioz scampered out the back door of Madame Bonfamille's house. Behind them, Marie trotted in a more ladylike manner, her long white tail swishing back and forth. But even she couldn't stop herself from launching a surprise attack on Toulouse when his back was turned.

"Here I come!" shouted Berlioz as he pounced on his two siblings. Marie escaped, but Berlioz and Toulouse began to wrestle in the leaves.

"I got you both!" Berlioz exclaimed proudly. "I'm clearly the superior pouncer in the family."

"Oh, yeah?" said Toulouse. "If you're so great, let's see you climb to the top of that oak tree." He raised his chin, gesturing to the towering tree above them.

"Gladly," Berlioz replied. He nimbly leapt onto a low branch and began to climb up, up, up the huge tree.

Soon Berlioz was perched on the highest branch. Toulouse licked his paw. "All right, so you're a good climber," he called up to his brother. "You can come down now."

Berlioz didn't move.

"I said you can come down," Toulouse repeated.

"I-I can't," Berlioz replied. His voice sounded shaky. "I'm stuck." He began to yowl. Soon his brother and sister were yowling, too.

It only took a few minutes for Madame Bonfamille to open an upstairs window. She and Duchess stuck their heads out to see what all the noise was about.

"My goodness!" Duchess cried when she spied Berlioz. "What on earth are you doing up there?"

"Don't you worry; we'll be right out to help you," Madame Bonfamille said reassuringly.

A few minutes later, she and Duchess appeared in the garden, followed by a very grumpy-looking Edgar carrying a long ladder.

"Just climb right up and get him, won't you, Edgar?" Madame Bonfamille asked.

Edgar scowled and mumbled something about foolish felines. But he leant the ladder against the tree trunk and began to climb.

Before long, Berlioz was safely on the ground once again.

Berlioz snuggled against Duchess. He had learnt his lesson. He wouldn't give in to any more of Toulouse's challenges... at least not ones involving trees!

A Yummy Dream

Winnie the Pooh stepped into his house and sat down with a sigh. He and Piglet had been out on a long walk through the woods. Now Pooh was tired. And, more importantly, he was hungry.

"My tummy feels very rumbly," Pooh said aloud. He got to his feet and went over to his honey cupboard. There was only one pot of honey inside.

"Oh dear," Pooh said. One pot of honey was not very much. He sat down and began to eat. He ate every last sticky drop. But when he was finished, his tummy was still feeling a tiny bit rumbly.

"Well, I suppose there's nothing left to do but go to bed," Pooh said sadly. He put on his nightshirt and his nightcap and climbed into his cosy bed. A minute later, Pooh's snores filled the air. And dreams began to fill his head – dreams of honey, of course.

Pooh stood before the honey tree. It was so full of honey, it was oozing out of the trunk! Then, suddenly, a purple heffalump appeared behind him.

"Mmm," the heffalump said, licking his lips. The creature stuck his long trunk into one of the honeypots and gobbled up all the honey inside.

"Those are my honeypots!" Pooh cried. He tried to sound brave, even though he was just a little bit scared. The heffalump looked very big and very hungry.

The heffalump just stared at Pooh. Pooh looked at the honeypots. There were a lot of them. Some were full, but most were still empty. Pooh looked at the honey tree. It was still overflowing with honey.

"I have an idea," Pooh said. "Let's fill the honeypots together, then share a nice snack."

The heffalump nodded excitedly. He picked up a honeypot with his trunk and carried it over to the tree. Pooh did the same, and the sweet, sticky honey dripped into the pots.

When all the pots had been filled, Pooh and the heffalump sat down together. They ate and ate until all the pots were empty and their tummies were full.

When Pooh woke up the next morning, to his surprise, his tummy wasn't even the slightest bit rumbly. Just then, he remembered his strange dream. It had been a dream – hadn't it?

Autumn Cleaning

Mickey Mouse hummed as he tidied up his messy house. He swept up some leaves that had blown in through the front door. Then he shook the mud off his doormat. He was picking up some old magazines when one of them caught his eye.

"'Make a Fresh Start with Spring Cleaning,'" Mickey read aloud. "Hmm. Spring cleaning, eh?" He looked out the window. It wasn't spring – it was autumn! What was he doing cleaning his house?

"Phew!" he exclaimed as he dropped his broom and flopped onto the sofa. "Looks like I have a whole day free now. I think I'll see if Minnie wants to come over!"

A short while later, Minnie Mouse rang the doorbell. "Hi, Mickey!" she said cheerfully. "What do you want to do to—"

She gasped. Mickey's house was a mess!

"What's wrong?" Mickey asked.

"Mickey," Minnie said, "um, when was the last time you cleaned your house?"

Mickey laughed. "Don't be silly, Minnie!" he said. "I don't need to clean this place for months."

"M-m-months?" Minnie gasped.

"Sure!" Mickey shrugged. "Haven't you ever heard of spring cleaning?"

Minnie wasn't sure what to do. She didn't want to be rude, but she had to convince Mickey to clean his house – and that it couldn't wait until spring!

"You know, Mickey," she said casually, "I just read something in a magazine about a fun new trend."

"Really?" Mickey smiled. "What's that, Minnie? Maybe it's something we could do today, since we have the whole day free!"

"Oh!" Minnie pretended to be surprised at the idea. "Why, I suppose we could! I hadn't thought of that."

"So, what's the trend?" Mickey asked eagerly. "Waterskiing? Rock climbing? Fondue parties?"

"No," Minnie said cheerfully. "Autumn cleaning! It's all the rage."

"Autumn cleaning?" Mickey said doubtfully. He blinked, then smiled. "You know, that's so crazy, it sounds like fun! Come on, let's try it!"

Minnie smiled and picked up the magazine with the spring cleaning article in it. "Good," she said. She stuffed the magazine in the recycling bin. "I'll start right here!"

Invincible Mushu

After helping Mulan defeat the Huns and restore the Fa family honour, Mushu had been given back his old job as family guardian. He helped guard the temple of the Fa ancestors.

One day, Mushu was sunning himself on the temple roof when a big cricket waddled up. He seemed to be staring right at Mushu.

Mushu frowned. "Who you lookin' at?" he said to the cricket.

The cricket flicked out his tongue. Mushu was offended.

"Oh yeah?" he said. "Stick your tongue out at me, will you? Well, get a load of this!" Puffing out his tiny chest, Mushu spat out a miniature burst of fire, no bigger than the flame of a match.

The cricket just blinked.

"Not good enough for you, eh?" Mushu said. "All right, tough guy. Try this on for size!"

Mushu cleared his throat dramatically. Taking a deep breath, he opened his mouth and spat a bigger flame at the cricket.

The cricket crouched, lowering his chest to the ground. Then he straightened his legs. Then he crouched again. The cricket was doing press-ups, as crickets often do.

"Oh-ho!" Mushu shouted. "Think you're tough, do you? Well, Mr Scales for Brains, I didn't spend time in the Imperial Army for nothing!"

And with that, Mushu crouched down and began to do press-ups, too.

"… ninety-eight… ninety-nine… one hundred!" Mushu counted, panting.

He leapt to his feet and began to run in circles round the cricket. "Just ask anyone; I'm the dragon that defeated hundreds of Huns. I could eat you for lunch, small fry."

The cricket just sat there. Then – snap! The cricket snatched up a fly that landed on Mushu's nose.

"Ahhhh!" Mushu screamed. He was so startled, he leapt backwards… and fell off the roof. He landed on the ground in a puff of dust.

"Ha-ha-ha-ha-ha-ha-ha!" The air filled with the sound of roaring laughter. The ancestors had seen everything.

"Cheer up, Mushu," one ancestor said. "It looks like you have a new friend."

Sure enough, the cricket had followed Mushu down from the roof. "Well," Mushu said, "I always did want a pet."

Bonnie Makes a Friend

One day, it was Bonnie's induction at preschool. She was feeling nervous and didn't want to go. Woody was worried, so he jumped into her backpack to keep an eye on her.

At preschool, Bonnie picked up a spork and glued a pair of eyes onto it. Then she added arms and legs and wrote her name on her project's stick feet. She decided to name him Forky.

At the end of the induction, Bonnie put Forky into her backpack, right next to Woody. Suddenly, Forky came to life!

Later, back at home, Woody introduced Forky to the rest of Bonnie's toys. Woody explained that Forky was important to Bonnie. They had to make sure nothing happened to him.

But Woody soon discovered that it wasn't easy taking care of Forky. The spork would constantly jump into the bin because he thought he was a piece of rubbish.

A few days later, Bonnie's family went on a road trip. Woody and all the toys went along, too, but Forky was a terrible passenger. At every stop he ran to the nearest bin. Woody had to keep bringing him back before Bonnie noticed.

Later that night, Forky climbed to an open window of the family's campervan. "I am not a toy," he declared. "I am a spork! Freedom!" Then, he jumped out of the moving vehicle.

Woody gasped. He knew he would have to go after Forky, and that Bonnie's family would be stopping soon. "I'll meet you at the campsite," Woody told the other toys, before jumping out the campervan, too!

Eventually, Woody found Forky by the side of the road and began dragging him towards the campsite. Forky didn't understand why he needed to return to Bonnie. "Like it or not, you are a toy," said Woody. "And you have to be there for Bonnie." Woody explained that Bonnie loved Forky the same way Forky loved trash.

"I'm Bonnie's trash!" Forky exclaimed. "We got to get going. She needs me!"

Woody smiled to himself as they set off towards the campsite. He knew that Forky and Bonnie would have many exciting adventures together.

Boy's Best Friend

Like most little boys, Pinocchio wanted a puppy. And, like most little boys, he promised to feed it and walk it and do everything and anything required to care for it.

"Puppies are a lot of work," Geppetto told his son. "And puppies like to chew things, like slippers – and wood." The woodcarver glanced over at the rows and rows of wooden toys on his workbench. "No, I don't think a dog is a good idea," he said finally.

That afternoon, when Pinocchio returned from school, Geppetto had a present waiting. The boy wasted no time in opening the box. Inside was a wooden dog.

Not wanting to hurt Geppetto's feelings, Pinocchio thanked his father and placed the toy on his bed.

A few days later, as Pinocchio was walking home from school, he heard a puppy whimpering in an alley. "Why, you look just like the wooden dog my father carved for me," Pinocchio said. He wondered what he should do with the puppy. "Well, I can't leave you here all by yourself," he decided.

The boy went home and tied the dog to a tree a few doors up the street. Then he sneaked the puppy a bowl of food and went back inside before Geppetto wondered where he was.

After Geppetto had fallen asleep, Pinocchio slipped outside and scooped up the dog. "Now, you're going to have to be very quiet," he warned.

But once inside, the puppy sprang from Pinocchio's arms and made a dash for Figaro!

"Look out!" cried Pinocchio.

Suddenly, Geppetto appeared in his nightclothes. "What's going on here?" he asked.

"Well—" Pinocchio began. Just then, the puppy sprang onto Pinocchio's bed, knocking the wooden dog beneath it. Geppetto blinked. The puppy looked just like the toy he had made for his son!

"Could it be?" the toy maker asked. "Pinocchio! You wanted a puppy so much that the Blue Fairy must have turned your toy dog into a real one!"

Pinocchio was thrilled. But he knew he had to tell his father the truth.

"Well," Geppetto said as he watched the pup carrying the wooden dog round the house, "I suppose we have room for two dogs here – especially if one of them walks the other!"

Mowgli's Nap

Baloo stretched, leant against a tree trunk and scratched his back as he slid to the ground. "Am I ever sleepy," he said. "I think it must be time for an afternoon snooze."

"Good thinking, my friend." High above them, stretched out on a branch, Bagheera the panther dangled a paw. His golden eyes were half closed in the heat of the day.

"A nap? Not for me!" Mowgli shook his mop of dark hair. "I'm not tired."

"Now, hold on a second there," Baloo said. "Don't you want to go hunting with us after it cools off? You're going to need energy."

"I have plenty of energy," Mowgli insisted. "I have energy right now!"

"You may have energy, but if you use it now, you will not have it to use later," Bagheera said wisely.

"Listen to the cat." Baloo yawned. "He knows what he's talking about." And with that, Baloo pulled Mowgli onto a pile of leaves and held him down with one great paw.

"I have energy for now and later," Mowgli grumbled.

"Good nap, Man-cub," Bagheera purred at the scowling Mowgli.

A moment later, the panther and the bear were sleeping soundly. As soon as Mowgli heard their snores, he hoisted up the arm that was pinning him down.

"Good nap, yourself," Mowgli whispered. He tiptoed off to swing in the trees and drop sticks on the animals below.

Baloo's snores shook the jungle for an hour, perhaps two, before Mowgli returned to the shady napping spot again. He'd had a grand time in the treetops, but the sun and the swinging had tired him. The great grey bear looked so soft and peaceful lying against the tree that Mowgli couldn't help himself. He curled up against his friend and closed his eyes.

Not two minutes later, Bagheera woke up and stretched his inky paws. The panther flicked his tail under Baloo's nose.

"I'm up. I'm up and ready to go!" Baloo sat upright. Then, spying Mowgli, the bear gave the boy a good shake. "How about you, Man-cub? You awake?"

But the only sound that came from Mowgli's mouth was a loud snore.

A Visit to the Castle

"All right, men," Doc said. "Here we are. Now, all we have to do is go up and dock on the floor – that is, knock on the door!"

The Seven Dwarfs had just reached the castle where Snow White lived. They had been so busy in the mines that this was the first time they'd had a chance to visit Snow White since she had married the prince.

"Time's a wastin'," Grumpy said. He knocked firmly on the tall wooden door.

A moment later, a guard opened it. "Er, good day," the castle guard said. "New servants round the back, please."

"Oh, we're not flu nervants," Doc spoke up. "Er, we're not new servants. We're here to see the princess!"

"Yes! The princess!" the other Dwarfs agreed. Dopey nodded eagerly.

The guard looked doubtful. "You're here to see the princess?"

He looked them over. The Dwarfs stood up straight, glad that they'd remembered to have a wash that morning.

Finally the guard shook his head. "I'm sorry," he said. "You don't look like the sort of visitors that would interest the princess."

And with that, he began to shut the door.

But Grumpy held the door open. "Mark my words," he growled. "If you don't tell the princess we're here, there'll be trouble for sure."

"Who is it?" a sweet voice called from inside the castle. "Who's at the door?"

"Never mind, Princess!" the guard called. "It's just some strange little men who claim they know you."

"Little men?" Snow White cried, rushing forwards. She peered round the door past the guard, and her lovely face lit up with joy. "Why, Doc, Grumpy, Sleepy, Dopey, Happy, Sneezy, even dear Bashful!"

Bashful blushed deeply. "Gosh," he said. "Hello, Princess."

The guard looked surprised. "You mean you know these fellows?" he asked Snow White. "I thought they were just riff-raff."

"Riff-raff?" Snow White cried. "Why, no – they may look a little different, but they're just like royalty to me! They're my very best friends."

The guard apologised to the Dwarfs. Then Snow White invited her friends into the castle for a nice, long visit.

Tig!

Early one morning, Simba woke up ready to find Nala and continue their game of tig. The night before, when their mothers had made them stop, Simba had been 'it' – which was a terrible way to go to bed! – and he was eager to tig Nala and make her 'it' as soon as possible. But when he arrived at the pride's meeting place, it seemed everyone was there except for Nala.

"Where's Nala?" he asked his mother.

"I heard her mother say she wasn't feeling well," Sarabi replied. "They're staying in the cave and resting until she's better."

"But she has to come out," protested Simba. "I'm 'it' and I have to tig her!"

Sarabi smiled. "I'm afraid you'll just have to wait, little Simba," she said.

"But that's so boring!" Simba groaned.

"You can play by yourself for a little while," she reminded him.

"Aw, all right," Simba sighed.

First, Simba tried hunting grasshoppers. Then he tried scaring giraffes. Next he went to check out the watering hole. But it wasn't as busy as usual. Finally, he tried just lying down and finding pictures in the clouds.

But that was Nala's favourite game, and it made him miss her.

Simba rolled over and swatted a bright wild flower with his paw. "Tig, you're 'it'," he said half-heartedly. Suddenly, an idea popped into his head.

With renewed energy, Simba picked as many flowers as he could carry in his mouth and made his way back to the pride's cave.

"Dees ah fur Nana," he mumbled through his mouthful of stems. Simba dropped the flowers at Nala's mother's feet. "These are for Nala," he repeated. "I hope she feels better really soon."

"Oh thank you, Simba," the lioness said. "But why don't you give them to her yourself? She seems to be feeling much better. Nala!" she called.

Out came Simba's friend, smiling and looking very pleased to see him. She sniffed at the pretty flowers. "Are these for me? Gee, thanks, Simba." Then she turned to her mother. "Can I go out to play with Simba now, Mama?"

"I can't see why not," said her mother.

"Grrreat!" said Nala.

"Yeah, grrreat!" said Simba. Then he reached out and gently tapped her with his paw. "Tig! You're 'it'!"

Flik's Big Date

Flik loved Queen Atta very, very much. So he decided to plan the most romantic evening for the two of them an ant could possibly imagine.

"I'll pick you up at eight tonight," Flik told Atta when he met her in the anthill early that morning. Then he hurried off to get ready for their big date.

First, there was the dinner to plan: sprouted wheat with sunflower seeds, wild truffles and free-range millet on a bed of dandelion greens.

Then Flik went down to the creek to find the perfect leaf for a romantic, moonlit cruise.

"This elm leaf should do," Flik said as he tied the leaf to a root near the shore. "And I'll use this twig as my oar."

"How's it coming?" he asked the circus bugs, who were back for a visit and busy practising their instruments just up the hill from the creek.

"Brilliant!" Slim replied. "Just brilliant. Don't worry about a thing. It's all under control. We'll have Atta's favourite song memorised by tomorrow night, no problem!"

"But our date is tonight!" said Flik.

"Told you so," said Francis.

"Don't worry," said Slim. "Remember, we're professional entertainers. You want an orchestra to dance to, you'll have an orchestra to dance to."

"Are you sure you wouldn't like some magic instead?" Manny the magician asked. "I have found that nothing inspires romance in a lady quite like cutting her in half."

"Um, I think I'll stick with the dancing," said Flik.

Speaking about inspiring romance had reminded Flik of something. He needed to get the fireflies set up.

"Come on, guys!" he called to the glowing insects he'd hired for the evening. "I want some of you in the trees, some of you along the water and the rest of you over there by the picnic blanket… perfect!" he said as their abdomens lit up the darkening night sky. "Everything is ready!"

Suddenly, Flik looked down at his watch, and his heart skipped a beat. "Oh no! It's eight o'clock!" he yelled. "I've really got to go!"

Can you believe it? Flik was so busy getting everything ready, he'd almost forgotten to pick Atta up for their date!

A Roaring Field Trip

Andy was excited. He was going on a field trip to the science museum! His mother was even going to give him some money to spend at the gift shop.

Andy's toys were worried that Andy might find some new toys at the gift shop, so Woody, Buzz and Rex decided they should go along.

The next morning, the toys climbed inside Andy's backpack for their big trip. When Andy's class arrived at the museum, they excitedly followed their teacher inside.

Much to the toys' dismay, Andy left his backpack in the cloakroom!

"I didn't come all this way to sit in here," Buzz said. "Let's go!"

And so the toys set off to explore on their own. They found a map and hid beneath it as they made their way across the museum floor. Rex led them to the dinosaur exhibit and had fun mimicking the other dinosaurs. Then Buzz spotted an outer-space exhibit!

"Buzz, we don't have time for this!" scolded Woody.

Suddenly, the ceiling lit up. Planets, moons and stars moved in the sky above them.

"That, my friends, is our solar system," said Buzz. "The planet closest to the sun is Mercury. Then comes Venus, Earth, Mars,

Jupiter, Saturn, Uranus and Neptune."

"All this is extremely informative," said Woody. "But isn't anyone else worried that Andy might get back to the cloakroom before we do?"

Suddenly, the toys heard an announcement, "Your attention, please. The museum will be closing in five minutes."

"We'll never make it back there in time!" cried Woody. "Andy's going to leave without us!"

"No, he's not," replied Buzz. He pointed to a spaceship hanging from the ceiling.

"Everybody, lean forwards!" Buzz commanded as they climbed aboard. Below them, Andy walked out of the cloakroom. The spaceship picked up speed, zipping along the cable that connected it to the ceiling. When the toys were above Andy's bag, they jumped!

Inside Andy's backpack, Woody found a bag from the gift shop. Andy had bought a roll of stickers.

"Now that's a good choice!" Rex said.

"It's out of this world!" Buzz replied.

Schooldays

obin Hood was looking forward to a jolly day of giving to the poor (and maybe stealing from the rich) when he ran into a troop of happy children.

"Cheerio, kids!" he called.

"Come play with us!" shouted Skippy, Sis and their friends.

"Ah, I wish I could," said Robin. "But, alas, my work is never done. Enjoy yourselves, though. That's what childhood is all— hey, now! Just a minute. Shouldn't you scallywags be in school?"

"School!" exclaimed Skippy. "We haven't been to school for ages!"

"And why not?" asked Robin.

"No teacher will come to Sherwood Forest. They fear Prince John will put them in prison for not paying taxes!" said Sis.

"Will you teach us?" asked Skippy.

"Ah… well… I think not," said Robin. For while Robin Hood knew his sums and spellings backwards and forwards, his sciences and histories had grown a little rusty.

"Then who will?" asked Sis.

"Never fear," said Robin. "A teacher I will find."

But where? he silently wondered.

Robin went back to the forest to seek out his Merry Men. "Little John!" he called. "The children need a teacher, and I think you're just the man!"

"Why, thank you, Robin," said Little John. "But I don't think I can do it. I've already promised my help to the baker and the blacksmith."

In fact, not one of his Merry Men could help Robin Hood. They were all too busy.

Robin sighed. "Is there no one with time to help the children?"

He walked round a bend, and there was Friar Tuck, dozing, as usual, in a mossy glade.

"Wake up, Friar!" said Robin, giving him a shake. "Do I have a job for you!"

Robin explained the situation, and Friar Tuck accepted happily. Then Robin headed off the other way. There was one more thing he had to do.

Later that day, just as Friar Tuck was finishing up his alphabet lesson, Robin Hood appeared, toting a heavy sack.

"What's that?" enquired the children.

"Books!" Robin replied. "Courtesy of Prince John's library! Although," he said with a wink, "he doesn't know it yet."

First Day of School

It was the first day of a brand-new school year for Nemo and his friends.

"Hey, Tad! Hey, Pearl!" called Nemo as he swam into the playground. "Isn't it great to be back at school?"

"Well," said Tad, "I wouldn't go that far."

"What do you mean?" asked Nemo. "It's gonna be awesome! I heard this year we get to learn how to subtract and speak Prawn."

"Sure," said Tad, "but did you also hear who's gonna be teaching us all of that?"

"No," said Nemo. "Who?"

Just then, up swam Sheldon, Jimmy and Jib.

"Hey, Sheldon," Tad called out. "Why don't you tell Nemo here about our new teacher, Mrs Lobster?"

"Mrs Lobster?" said Nemo.

"Yeah," said Sheldon. "Oh, they say she's the worst!"

"Who says she's the worst?" asked Nemo.

"Well, Sandy Plankton, for one. He says his cousin Krill had her last year – and that she was so mean, he'll never go to school again!"

"And you know what I heard from Sandy?" said Tad. "I heard she has these great big claws, and that she uses them to grab children really hard when they say the wrong answer!"

Nemo shuddered. All summer long he'd been looking forward to this day. And now school hadn't even started yet and already he wished it would end!

"Don't look now," Sheldon whispered, "but I think she's coming!"

"I'm gonna ink!" whimpered Pearl.

Nemo shut his eyes and wished with all his might for his dad to come and take him back home—

"Hello there," said a warm voice. "You must be my new pupils!"

Huh? thought Nemo. *Surely this wasn't the Mrs Lobster the kids had been talking about?*

And yet, when he opened his eyes, there she was, taking the register.

"Jib, Jimmy, Nemo, Pearl, Sheldon, Tad… my what a smart-looking class. I do hope you kids are ready to have fun."

Nemo sighed. That silly Sandy Plankton! They should know by now not to believe anything he said. Nemo was pretty sure this was going to be a great year after all!

Disney
THE EMPEROR'S
New Groove

The Hottest Thrill Ride Ever

Scout Leader Kronk wanted to reward his pupils for learning to speak Squirrel. He decided to fix the roller coaster hidden inside Kuzco's castle. Kronk headed into the entrance chamber.

He jumped when a small shadow slid across the floor in front of him. It was Yzma, who had been turned into a cat by one of her own potions.

"Do you know where you are standing?" Yzma asked with a smug purr.

"Over the trapdoor that leads to the roller coaster," replied Kronk.

"Isn't that dangerous?" said Yzma, curling her tail round his leg.

"It's safe as long as no one pulls the lever," Kronk replied.

"What lever?" Yzma asked slyly. She was planning to pull the lever and drop Kronk through the trapdoor!

"This one," said Kronk. He put his hand on the lever to show her, but— "Oops!" He pulled it by mistake!

Down they went, right through the trapdoor.

"Ouch!" Kronk cried when he landed in the roller-coaster car. To Yzma's surprise, she landed right next to him. She hadn't planned on falling down there, too! The out-of-control roller-coaster car headed into a dark tunnel.

"Hold on. It's going to be a bumpy ride," said Kronk.

"You don't know the half of it, you dolt!" Yzma cried. "The brakes don't work and the tracks are broken!"

Kronk grabbed Yzma, and down they plunged.

"Aaaahhh!" screamed Kronk.

"Miaooowww!" howled Yzma.

"In Squirrel that's pronounced 'chit-chit-chitter-chit,'" said Kronk.

"Who cares?" yelled Yzma.

"Yikes!" yelled Kronk, as they raced round a corner. Then they saw the broken track. Kronk jumped out of his seat and landed in front of the roller-coaster car. Bracing himself against the car, he used his feet as brakes. The car slowed and finally stopped, just centimetres away from a giant hole in the track.

"Ouch, ouch, ouch!" Kronk cried, dancing up and down on his smoking feet.

"Serves you right for pulling that lever," said Yzma.

"Yeah," said Kronk with a goofy smile. "But when I fix the brakes and the track, this'll be the hottest thrill ride ever!"

Rolly's Midnight Snack

"I'm hungry," Rolly complained as the puppies settled down for the night.

"You're always hungry," said Patch.

"And you always want to stay awake and have adventures," said Rolly.

Patch sighed. "Too bad we never get what we want."

Hours later, Rolly felt a tap on his shoulder. "Is it morning?" he asked with a yawn.

"No," said Patch. "It's midnight. Wanna explore? I'll get you a snack."

Rolly followed Patch to the kitchen. Patch nodded towards the table. "After dinner, I saw Nanny put some juicy bones up there. She's saving them for tomorrow's soup."

"Soup!" cried Rolly. "What a waste! Bones are for chewing on."

So Patch and Rolly came up with a plan. First, Patch climbed onto Rolly's shoulders to reach the table. Everything went fine until Patch threw down the first bone and it landed in the bin. Rolly chased after it and leapt inside the bin!

"Uh, Patch?" Rolly called. "I think I'm stuck in here." He tried to climb the sides of the bin, but it was too slippery.

Patch tried hard not to panic. He thought and thought until he came up with another plan – a rescue Rolly plan!

Patch raced upstairs and woke Lucky and Pepper. The two puppies followed Patch into the kitchen. Then Patch found his father's long lead and threw one end into the bin.

"Grab hold of the lead!" Patch told Rolly.

"Okay," said Rolly.

Patch turned to the other puppies and said, "Now, let's all pull on this end of the lead on the count of three."

The three puppies pulled. The bin fell over, and Rolly tumbled out onto the kitchen floor.

"Thanks!" said Rolly as the four puppies ran back up to bed.

Before Rolly drifted off to sleep, he whispered to Patch, "Guess you finally got your adventure."

"Yeah," said Patch. "But I'm sorry you didn't get your snack."

"Sure I did," said Rolly. "While I was waiting for you to rescue me, what do you think I was doing? I was eating that juicy bone. And, boy, was it good!"

DISNEP
Winnie the Pooh

A Blustery Day

"Oh, dear," said Pooh, as the wind whipped around him. "It's very windy. Are you sure this is a good idea, Tigger?" He and Tigger were carrying Pooh's kite out into a clearing in the middle of the Hundred-Acre Wood.

"Don't be silly, Pooh Boy," Tigger responded. "Today is the perfect day to fly your kite. After all, what else is wind for?"

"Yes," Pooh replied. "I suppose you're right."

At last, struggling against the wind, Pooh and Tigger reached the middle of the clearing and got ready to launch the kite. Pooh unrolled some kite string while Tigger held the kite.

"Okay, Pooh," said Tigger. "Get ready! You hold on to the string, and I'll toss the kite up into the wind. One… two… THREE!"

With that, Tigger threw the kite, and it was immediately seized by the strong wind and carried high into the air, where it danced and darted this way and that. Pooh struggled to hold on to the roll of kite string.

"Let out some more string!" Tigger said. "Let's see how high we can fly it!"

Pooh let out some more string. The kite sailed higher into the air and, blown around by stronger and stronger gusts, it tugged harder and harder on Pooh's end of the line.

"Fly it higher, Pooh!" exclaimed Tigger. "Higher, higher!"

Pooh let out more and more string, until he had let it all out. Then, all of a sudden, a tremendous gust of wind blew through the clearing. At the end of the kite string, Pooh felt his feet leave the ground as the wind grabbed hold of the kite and carried it sharply upwards.

"My goodness!" said Pooh, realising that he was being lifted up. Then, before he could be carried too high, he let go of the kite string and tumbled gently to the ground.

But the kite sailed on – up and away, dancing on the breeze for what seemed like forever, until it came to rest at last in the high branches of a very tall tree at the edge of the clearing.

"Oh, well," said Tigger, patting his friend sympathetically on the back. "Guess you flew it just a little too high there, Pooh Boy."

Dinglehoppers and Jibbermutts

Ariel sat on a rock, talking with her friends, Scuttle the seagull and Flounder the fish. She loved visiting the surface, although she knew it was dangerous for mermaids to venture there. Her father would definitely not approve, but then, these days, he seemed to disapprove of so much of what she liked to do.

"What's it like on land, Scuttle?" she asked.

"Land?" echoed Scuttle. "Oh! Land! Yeah, well, it's great on land. I know all about humans."

"Like what?" Ariel asked eagerly.

"Well! For instance… you know all about the dinglehoppers they use to comb their hair, right? And the snarfblatts that they make music with?"

"Yes," said Ariel.

"Well, did you know that they also have these strange rectangular objects with sheets of paper inside? They're called jibbermutts. Humans like to throw them to one another," Scuttle explained.

"Oh, Scuttle," said Ariel breathlessly. "Would you fly up to Eric's window and come back and tell me what you've seen?"

Scuttle flew off. While he was gone, Ariel lay back on the rock in the warm sunshine, dreaming of what life must be like on land.

Soon, Scuttle returned. "Did you see him?" asked Ariel eagerly. "What was he doing?"

"Yep, I saw him!" Scuttle replied importantly. "He was trying to eat with a dinglehopper! And he had a jibbermutt, but it almost looked like he was trying to read it instead of throwing it like he's supposed to. Ariel, I don't think your prince is too bright."

Ariel sighed dreamily, imagining her handsome love. She did wonder why he would try to use a dinglehopper to eat, though.

"Don't suppose you'd want his dinglehopper for your treasure chest, would you?" asked Scuttle with a mischievous glint in his eye.

"Oh, Scuttle! You didn't!" shouted Ariel.

"Yep. Just as soon as he put it down, I flew in through the window and grabbed it. Boy, was he surprised!"

Ariel clutched the dinglehopper to her chest. "I'll probably never know what it's like to live on land, but no matter what happens, Scuttle, I will treasure this forever!"

Disney
Lady and the
TRAMP

Lost and Found

Lady stretched and rolled over. It was so cosy up on the window seat. Sunlight shone through the glass and glinted on her diamond-shaped name tag.

Lady sighed contentedly. The tag was her most prized possession. Besides her owners, of course. Jim Dear and Darling were very good to her. Just last night, they had given her and Tramp steak bones to munch on.

The bones! Lady had almost forgotten them. Leaping off the window seat, she hurried to the kitchen. Luckily, the bones were right where she'd left them – next to her food bowl.

Lady began to carry the bones into the garden. It took three trips, but soon the bones were lying in a heap on the grass. Then she set to work.

Dig, dig, dig. The soil piled up behind her as Lady dug yet another hole. She carefully nosed the last bone into its hole and covered it with soil. After prancing delicately on top to pat down the earth, she collapsed in an exhausted heap. Burying bones was hard work!

Suddenly, Lady realised that something was missing. She gingerly felt her neck. Her collar! It was gone!

Panicked, Lady searched the garden for the collar. It was nowhere to be seen.

I must have buried it with one of the bones!

Lady realised with a jolt. She looked at all the freshly filled-in holes.

Tramp will help, Lady thought. She ran inside to get him. He was playing with the puppies, but he ran outside as soon as he heard what was wrong.

Soon the two dogs were busy undoing all of Lady's hard work.

"I see something shiny!" Tramp called.

Lady was by his side in an instant, but it wasn't the collar. It was just an old bottle top. Lady dropped her head sadly.

Lady and Tramp got back to digging. Finally, just as dusk was falling, Tramp found a thick blue band with a golden tag – Lady's collar!

Lady let out a happy bark. Then she carried the collar into the house and sat down at Jim Dear's feet.

"Your collar came off, Lady?" Jim asked as he fastened it round Lady's neck. "It's a good thing you didn't accidentally bury it with your bones!"

Homeward Bound

"Welcome back to our humble abode," Dodger told Oliver. He and his pals had 'rescued' the little kitten from the townhouse he had been living in with his new owner, Jenny, and brought him to the barge where they lived.

"But I want to go back to Jenny's," Oliver said.

"Jenny? So, all of a sudden you have a thing against dogs?" Dodger said. "And after all we've done for you!"

"No, no, I don't have a thing against dogs," Oliver explained.

"Then why in the world would you pick Jenny over New York's coolest canine?" Dodger asked.

"It's not you—" Oliver started to say.

"Oh, I get it," Dodger interrupted, circling round Oliver. "You're all about money now. Got a taste of the finer things in life, and now you wouldn't want to be seen slumming with the likes of us dogs."

"That's not true—" Oliver began.

"Well, I'll tell you one thing money can't buy," Dodger barked. "Freedom!"

"Freedom?" Oliver asked.

"Yeah, on the street you can do what you want, when you want to. Then, if you want to just kick back with the gang at Fagin's, that's cool, too. See what I mean? The freedom to choose instead of being locked up in that big house, doing whatever Jenny wants when she wants it," Dodger said.

"It's not like that!" Oliver protested.

"You could have all the freedom in the world, but instead, you're leaving us for a better cut of prime rib," Dodger said accusingly.

"No, that's not it at all," Oliver explained to his friend. "I like it at Jenny's. It's comfortable, and I get lots of love. Jenny needs me, and I need her too!"

Dodger thought about this for a moment. "You know what, kid? I can't argue with that. Stay with Jenny if you want."

"Okay." Oliver suddenly felt kind of sad. "We can still be friends, though, right? Even though we see things differently?"

"Sure," Dodger agreed.

"And, you'll come visit?" Oliver asked.

"Visit?" Dodger considered this for a moment. "Absatively posolutely!"

Oliver grinned. It was the best of both worlds. What more could a kitten ask for?

Together is Better

The Beast paced up and down his castle's long hallway. Click, click, click went his claws against the marble floor.

"It's been hours," he grumbled. "What do you suppose she's doing in there?" the Beast asked Lumiere.

"Reading," Lumiere replied. "After all, monsieur, it is the library."

"I know it's the library!" bellowed the Beast. "I know my own castle!"

Suddenly, the library doors burst open. Belle stormed out. She looked around the hallway.

"What is going on?" she asked.

"It's the servants," lied the Beast. "They make too much noise."

"Don't blame them," said Belle. "You're the one who's been clicking your claws for hours."

"I have not," said the Beast. "You were hearing things."

"And then you started bellowing," said Belle.

"So what if I did?" roared the Beast. "It's my castle!"

A door opened, and Mrs Potts rolled up on a serving trolley. "Anyone care for tea?"

"Not me," huffed Belle.

"Me neither," huffed the Beast.

"Oh, come now. Just a spot?" asked Mrs Potts, rolling her trolley into the library.

Belle and the Beast followed her in and sat down.

"Why were you so angry?" asked Belle, sipping her tea.

"I was bored," said the Beast. "I guess I… missed you."

"Why didn't you just say so?" Belle asked.

"Because… I didn't think you missed me," said the Beast.

"I just love to read," Belle said.

"I know," said the Beast.

Belle thought for a moment. "I have an idea," she said. "How about we read together?"

Belle picked out a book about a beautiful princess and a brave dragon. First Belle read aloud to the Beast, and then the Beast read aloud to Belle.

"That was fun," said the Beast.

"Yes," said Belle. "Let's do it again tomorrow night."

In the hallway, Lumiere sighed with relief.

"Maybe now we'll get some peace!" he said to himself.

Tiger Lily

It was a warm night in Never Land – so warm, in fact, that the poor Lost Boys couldn't sleep. And so it was decided that instead of trying to stay in their hideout in Hangman's Tree, Peter Pan and the Lost Boys would camp out for the night in the wilderness.

"It's dark out here," said Cubby.

"And awfully quiet," said Tootles.

"Won't you tell us a story, please, Peter?" asked Slightly, who was shivering in his fox suit despite the sticky heat.

"Very well," agreed Peter. "If it will make you all be quiet! I will tell you the story of the very first time I ever camped out in the wilderness – which, by the way, was the first time I met Tiger Lily.

"I had made myself a fire, a great big one, 'cause it was autumn and the nights were getting colder. I'd just laid my head down on a patch of nice, soft moss, when all of a sudden I heard a rustling in the shadows."

The Lost Boys gasped. "Indians?"

But Peter shook his head. "Not Indians," he told them. "That's what I thought at first, too. No, this was something bigger. It was a bear! It jumped out of the trees, growling and waving its big paws in the air like Captain Hook swattin' blue flies. I've never seen such a mean,

angry beast, before or since!"

"So wha-wha-what did you do?" asked Slightly.

"Told him to get lost, of course. To scram! But he just kept charging.

"Well, I'm not going to lie to you; I started to get nervous. And then, there she was – Tiger Lily, as quiet as a mouse. Without a 'hi' or 'how do you do', she grabbed a stick from my fire and waved it at the bear. The next thing I knew, the bear had turned round and was running off crying! I suppose Tiger Lily saved my life that night," said Peter.

"Um, Peter?" said Cubby, peering out into the darkness. "Do you know what ever happened to that bear?"

Peter thought for a moment.

"Nope," he said and shrugged. "Probably still out there, wandering around, I guess."

Peter Pan yawned a big, mischievous yawn.

"Now stop yer yammerin' and close your eyes and go to sleep already!"

Two Tigers

Princess Jasmine and her pet tiger, Rajah, were riding through the busy streets of Agrabah when they came upon a big, colourful circus tent. The tiger's eyes opened wide as he stared at the circus poster.

"That looks like fun," Jasmine said to Rajah. "But we really should be going. It's almost time for lunch."

Back at the palace, the tiger hardly touched his food.

"What do you think is wrong with Rajah?" Jasmine asked.

Aladdin shrugged. "Maybe a nice long carriage ride would make him feel better," he suggested.

Soon Jasmine, Aladdin, Abu and Rajah were riding through Agrabah in the royal carriage. As they rolled past the circus poster, the tiger suddenly perked up.

"Hmm," Aladdin said. "Maybe we should take Rajah to the circus."

Inside the circus tent, the announcer said, "I now present Mallika – the star of our show!" Out walked a beautiful tigress. Jasmine saw Rajah's face light up. He was in love!

When the show was over, Jasmine and Aladdin took Rajah to meet Mallika. The two tigers were very happy to be together – and

clearly did not want to be apart.

"Can Mallika please come and live at my palace?" Jasmine asked the circus owner. "She would be very happy there."

"I'm sorry, Mallika is our star," the owner replied. "Without her, we wouldn't have a circus."

That night, there was a knock at the palace door. It was the circus owner – and a very sad-looking tigress.

"Ever since Rajah left the circus, Mallika won't eat," the circus owner said. "Even though she's the star of my show, I want her to be happy. So I've come to give her to you."

The two tigers ran to each other and gently touched noses. Jasmine and Aladdin were very happy for Rajah and Mallika, but they felt bad for the circus owner. Without his star tigress, the circus would surely close.

Suddenly, Jasmine had an idea.

The very next morning, the circus tent was moved right next to Jasmine's palace! Mallika could perform at the royal circus every day and come home to Rajah every evening.

It was perfect!

Listen with Your Heart

It was a clear, crisp day. Pocahontas had just finished visiting Grandmother Willow. Now she was climbing to the top of a high mountain with her friends Meeko the raccoon and Flit the hummingbird.

Soon the friends came to a fork in the path.

"Which direction should we take, Meeko?" asked Pocahontas.

The raccoon pointed to the wider, flatter path, which made Pocahontas laugh.

"Let's try this one!" she said, pointing to the narrower, steeper route. They climbed and climbed, and the path grew narrower and steeper.

As Pocahontas sat down on a large tree stump to catch her breath, the winds suddenly picked up. Then the clouds moved in and rain poured down on them.

"Uh-oh," said Pocahontas, jumping to her feet. "We can't stay here, and it's too slippery to climb back down. We need to keep moving!"

Pocahontas paused. Where should they go? "I need to listen," Pocahontas said to herself. "I must listen with my heart to the spirits all around us, and they will keep us safe."

Pocahontas tried to listen, but it was hard to hear anything over the pouring rain and rushing winds.

Suddenly, she heard them. The spirits spoke to her! They told her to climb a little higher, just a bit, and there she would find shelter.

"Come on, Meeko! Come on, Flit!" she called over the wind and rain. "We'll find shelter just a little way up!"

Sure enough, the friends found an opening in the rocks just a bit higher up the path. Between the rocks was a small cave, and inside it was warm and dry.

The storm soon passed, and the sun came out. "Come on!" Pocahontas cried to Meeko and Flit. "Let's go see what it looks like at the top!" They hurried the rest of the way up the trail until they came out on a wide, flat ledge. Far below, they could see the forest and, beyond it, the sparkling blue sea.

"You see, Meeko? See, Flit?" said Pocahontas. "We're seeing the world in a different way. Isn't it beautiful?

"And just think," she said, more to herself than to the other two, "if I hadn't chosen that unexplored path, I would never have heard the spirits talk to me!"

Wherever You Go, There You Are

"Oh, dear! Oh, dear!" said Amelia Gabble. The goose and her twin sister, Abigail, had been waddling along the road to Paris when Amelia suddenly stopped.

"What's wrong?" asked Abigail.

"Just look and you'll see," said Amelia. Stretching out one big white wing, she pointed to a fork in the road ahead.

Behind the geese, O'Malley, Duchess and her three kittens gathered together.

"I wonder what's wrong," said Duchess.

"Guess I'd better find out," said O'Malley. He sauntered forwards. "Ladies, ladies, what's going on?" he asked.

"We know this is the road to Paris," Amelia explained. "But we don't know which way to turn. I think we should go right," said Amelia.

"And I think we should go left," said Abigail.

"Mr O'Malley, are we lost?" asked Marie in a small, frightened voice.

O'Malley smiled down at the little white kitten. "Lost? What's lost? I don't know the meaning of the word."

"I do," said Berlioz. "If you're lost, then you don't know where you are."

"But you know exactly where you are," said O'Malley. "You're right here – with your mother and me and the Gabbles. So how could you be lost?"

Duchess shook her head. "Mr O'Malley," she said, "if we want to get to Paris and we don't know the way, then I do believe that we are lost."

"But Paris is just a place," said O'Malley. "And places are easy to find."

"Look, Mama, look!" Toulouse shouted. "I see something over that hill. It's the top of the Eiffel Tower!"

"Why, you're right, Toulouse," Duchess said.

"Nice going, little tiger," said O'Malley. Then he turned to the Gabble sisters. "Well, ladies, looks like Paris is thataway!"

Pretty soon the whole group arrived in Paris. Marie sighed with relief. "I'm glad we're not lost any more."

"Aw, honey," said O'Malley, "some day you'll understand. Places may come and places may go, but when you're a free spirit, you can never be lost."

"Never?" asked Marie.

"Never," said O'Malley. "'Cause wherever you go, there you are!"

Marie nodded. She liked the sound of that!

A Stitched-Up Date

Nani was going to the cinema with David and had asked Old Lady Kingsley to look after Lilo.

"How is she going to look after us when she can barely see?" Lilo asked Stitch. "And," she continued, "do you know what film Nani and David went to see? *Invasion of the Bug-Eyed Aliens, Part Six: The Sliming* – without us!"

Lilo stood up and said, "Come on, Stitch. Let's go and see the film ourselves."

Lilo and Stitch sneaked past the snoring Mrs Kingsley. Lilo opened and shut the front door as loudly as she could. Then, doing her best impression of Nani, she shouted, "We're back, Mrs Kingsley! Thanks!"

Mrs Kingsley woke up, tottered to the door, and peered blindly at Lilo. "Is that you, Nani? Well, I hope you had a lovely time."

And with that, the two made a break for the cinema.

Once they got there, though, they had two problems – money and…

"Sorry, kid, no dogs allowed in the cinema," the ticket man said.

Lilo had to think quickly. "He isn't a dog. He's my teddy bear."

"He doesn't look like a stuffed animal," the ticket man said.

"They make them very lifelike these days," Lilo fibbed. "My mother is looking for us, and if we don't find her soon, I think I may start to cry."

"Okay, okay," the ticket man said.

By the time the two had got into the cinema, the bug-eyed aliens had begun the sliming, and everyone was screaming. Lilo and Stitch joined in – perhaps a little too loudly, because Nani and David noticed them right away!

"Excuse me," Nani said as she made her way out of her row and down the aisle, cola spilling and popcorn flying. Nani grabbed hold of Lilo's arm and dragged her out of the cinema. David and Stitch were right behind them.

"I'm so angry with you, I'm going to… I'm going to…" Nani stuttered.

David finished her sentence. "Take you out for ice cream."

"Out for ice cream?" Nani said.

"It's a beautiful night, and I can't think of anything more wonderful than two sisters having ice cream together." David turned to Lilo and Stitch. "Don't you think?"

Buzz's Backpack Adventure

It was space day at school. Andy couldn't wait! He put Buzz in his backpack and set off for school.

In class, the teacher taught Andy and the other children about the solar system. Just then, the lunch bell rang. Andy and his friends went to eat lunch, leaving their bags behind.

With the kids gone, Buzz stepped out of Andy's backpack. All around him were models of the stars and planets. Buzz was thrilled! He loved anything about space.

Just then, Buzz spotted a large cage. Inside was a hamster. Buzz had never seen one before. "Greetings, strange creature," he said. When the hamster didn't reply, Buzz lifted the lid off the cage so he could go inside.

Startled, the hamster jumped out of the cage! It ran into Buzz and sent him flying.

Andy and his friends still weren't back, so Buzz looked inside some of their desks. He found old chewing gum, broken yo-yos and mouldy sandwiches, but no sign of the hamster. He put down a desktop and made his way over to a table.

There he spotted some creatures from space! Or at least, he thought they were from space.

They were actually toy aliens that Andy and his friends had made from clay.

"Greetings," Buzz said. "Have you seen a strange, furry creature?"

When the clay aliens didn't answer, Buzz tried to shake hands with one of them to show that he was friendly. But as he moved the alien's arm, it fell off.

"Sorry about that!" Buzz cried.

Buzz looked around. The room was a mess. Buzz knew he had to clean up – and fast!

The bell rang just as Buzz finished cleaning. The space ranger quickly hopped back into Andy's backpack.

Buzz looked at the cleaned-up classroom. *No one will ever know what happened,* he thought.

Suddenly, Andy's classmates pointed at the blackboard ledge. The hamster was sitting on it.

"How did you get out?" the teacher asked, bringing it back to its cage.

The hamster smiled at Buzz. The space ranger smiled back. He couldn't wait to tell Woody and the others about his exciting day.

Dumbo's Parade Pals

When Dumbo's circus came to town, the animals and circus folk marched in a big parade. The crowd loved seeing all the circus animals marching down the street in a big line.

Suddenly, Dumbo noticed a peanut on the ground. He picked up the peanut with his trunk and ate it. Then Dumbo saw another peanut, and another.

Leaving the parade, Dumbo followed the trail of peanuts all the way to a park round the corner.

"See, the peanuts worked!" exclaimed a little girl with pigtails. "Now we have our own elephant to play with."

"Let's have our own circus," said a boy.

"I'll be the ringmaster!" cried the little girl. "Ladies and gentlemen! Presenting our star attraction – the Little Elephant!"

Dumbo knew just what to do. He stood up on his two back legs. Then he juggled some balls with his trunk. The children cheered.

Soon Timothy Q. Mouse appeared. "Here you are!" he said to Dumbo. "We have to get back to the circus camp to get ready for the show!"

Dumbo nodded and waved goodbye to his new friends.

"I wish I could go and see him in the circus tonight," one of the children said. "But I don't have enough money for a ticket."

Dumbo was sorry that the nice children he had met would not be able to go to the circus.

That night, he felt very sad as he put on his stage make-up and warmed up his ears. Dumbo tucked Timothy into the brim of his hat and sadly climbed onto a tall platform.

"Ladies and gentlemen!" the Ringmaster cried. "I give you Dumbo, the Flying Elephant!"

Dumbo leapt off the platform, and his giant ears unfurled. The crowd cheered as Dumbo flew round the tent.

Far below in the crowd, Dumbo spotted his new friends sitting in the first row! He swept by them, patting each child on the head with his trunk. The girl with pigtails waved at Dumbo. "Your mouse friend gave us free tickets!" she cried.

Dumbo smiled and reached his trunk up to the brim of his hat, where Timothy was riding. He was the luckiest elephant in the world to have such wonderful friends!

Disney Bambi

The Secret Adventure

Early one morning, Thumper hopped over to a thicket and woke up Bambi. "Come on! It's time for an adventure. But where we're going is a secret," he said.

On the way, Bambi and Thumper spotted their skunk friend, Flower.

"We're going on a secret adventure," Bambi said. "Do you want to come?"

"Oh gosh! I do," Flower said shyly.

Above them, a bird named Red sat unnoticed. *They are heading out all by themselves,* Red thought. *I'd better tell their mothers.*

Meanwhile, Bambi, Thumper and Flower reached a meadow.

"Shh!" Thumper whispered. "We are close to where all the bunnies graze – including my mama."

But Thumper's sisters had seen them. They wanted to know what their big brother was up to, so they followed him.

Soon the three friends came to a stream. A beaver walked up to them.

"My name is Slap," the beaver said. "Where are you going?"

"I wanted to show my friends what you build in the river," Thumper explained.

"We call it a dam," said Slap.

Carefully, Slap and the three friends stepped out onto the logs. There were other beavers there working on the dam.

"Why do they call you Slap?" Flower asked their new friend.

Slap slapped the logs with his flat tail. The dam shook so much that a log broke loose and started drifting downriver.

"Help, Thumper!" four little voices cried. It was Thumper's younger sisters! The log they were sitting on was floating away!

The beavers jumped into the water and quickly swam towards the log. High above, Red saw the whole thing and went to get help.

Thumper's sisters held on, but they were getting close to a waterfall! The beavers eventually reached the log. They slapped their tails with all their might and got the log to the riverbank. Thumper pulled his sisters to safety and thanked the beavers.

Just then, Bambi's, Thumper's and Flower's mothers arrived!

"Oh, I'm so glad you are safe!" cried Bambi's mother. "Luckily, Red was keeping an eye on you."

"I'm very happy to see you, too, Mother," Bambi said, glad that the adventure was over.

A Refreshing Cup of Tea

"Twinkle, twinkle, little bat!
     How I wonder what you're at!
     Up above the world you fly,
Like a tea tray in the sky."

The song came from behind the tall tree with the mitten-shaped leaves. Alice knew it could only have been sung by one person: the Mad Hatter!

"Oh, bother!" Alice sighed. Truly, the hatter and his friends were among the last creatures she wished to see.

"And yet," Alice went on to no one but herself, "a nice cup of tea would be quite refreshing."

In the clearing, the hatter, the March Hare and the Dormouse were sitting, much as they had been upon Alice's last visit, round their ample tea table.

"Ahem," Alice made her presence known to them by clearing her thirsty throat.

"Well!" exclaimed the hatter. "If it isn't our dear, dear old friend! I say, what was your name again, dear old friend?"

"Alice," Alice patiently replied.

"Well, have a seat, Alice, dear!"

"Thank you," said Alice. "I could use a cup of tea."

"And how would you use it?" the hatter asked. "Carefully, I hope."

"Very carefully," Alice assured him.

"Ah, well, that's good. And that's also bad."

"Bad?" Alice asked.

"You heard him!" said the March Hare. "Can't you see? We have no tea!"

"No tea?" asked Alice, gazing about at the table.

"No tea?" sobbed the Dormouse, stirring from his sleep. "No tea!"

"There you go upsetting him again!" shouted the hare.

"I didn't…" Alice began. Then she remembered how pointless it was to argue with a hare who was mad. Instead, she left the March Hare to his shouting, and the Dormouse to his crying, and the hatter to his… whatever it was he was doing, and walked over to the stove.

Finding a tin of fragrant tea leaves, she dropped some in an empty teapot and filled it with hot water. Then she reached for the cleanest cup she could find and filled it up.

She was tempted to offer her hosts a cup as well. But on second thoughts, she decided, perhaps it was better to just… go.

Disney
THE
HUNCHBACK
OF
NOTRE DAME

The Four-Legged Festival

Quasimodo was a kind young man who was always quick to offer help to anyone in need. It wasn't surprising, then, that Quasimodo had a growing collection of orphaned animals. First he had taken in a stray kitten, and then an abandoned puppy. Next he adopted a lamb, an old donkey, a baby bird and an ox.

Esmeralda and Phoebus helped him build a pen. But they weren't sure how he could afford to continue feeding so many pets.

"I'll find a way – somehow," Quasimodo told the couple. "They're counting on me!"

The Festival of Fools was coming up, and Quasimodo was a little worried about how his pets would react to all the noise and excitement.

"While you're helping with the puppet show at the festival," said Esmeralda, "why don't we have Djali keep an eye on the animals?" Djali was Esmeralda's clever little goat. He was used to crowds and often danced with Esmeralda in the village square.

"Why, thank you, Esmeralda!" replied Quasimodo. "That's a wonderful idea."

Soon the day of the festival arrived. Esmeralda brought Djali and put him inside the pen with the other animals.

When Djali heard the tinkling of Esmeralda's tambourine on the far side of the square, he nibbled at the latch of the pen. The gate flew open and Djali ran out. The other animals followed – even as the goat crashed through a stall full of masks for sale!

Everyone turned to see the animals, which were now disguised as jesters and kings, songbirds and queens. The masked animals danced right past the puppet waggon and onto Esmeralda's stage.

Quasimodo watched in amazement as Djali and the others joined in the gypsy's merry dance. The crowds cheered and showered the performers with coins.

When the show ended, Esmeralda climbed down from the stage and delivered the money to Quasimodo. "This should take care of whatever food you need to buy for your pets," she said happily.

Quasimodo felt like dancing for joy – but he decided to leave that to the animals!

Monster Nursery

Mike always arrived at Monsters, Inc. at half past eight, put his lunch box in his locker and promptly reported to his station on the Laugh Floor. But one morning, as he came out of the locker room, Celia was waiting for him.

"We have a little problem, Mike," she said. "The nursery teacher is sick today, so we need a replacement. And seeing as how you've already met your laugh quota for the month, I thought maybe you—"

"Nursery!" cried Mike. "Wait just a—"

Just then, Sulley stepped in. "Happy to do it, Celia," he interrupted. "Nursery, here we come."

"Are you crazy?" Mike grumbled.

"What's the big deal?" Sulley shrugged. "We took care of Boo, didn't we? What's a few more kids? We'll eat a few snacks. Watch a few films. Play a little peekaboo. It's like having a paid holiday, Mike, my man!"

But the minute they opened the nursery room door, they both knew Sulley had been wrong.

There were monster children everywhere! Swinging from the ceiling. Slithering up the walls. Bouncing from corner to corner. Mike's and Sulley's jaws dropped open. What were they going to do?

Sulley took a deep breath. "We just have to let them know who's in charge, that's all," he told Mike.

"I think they know who's in charge," Mike said as an oversized, six-handed monster kid scooped him up and threw him to his twin. "Help!"

Sulley quickly intercepted Mike and put him back down on his feet.

"All we need to do," said Sulley, calmly, "is get their attention. Let's see… a film?" But the TV was too covered with monster slime and finger paint for anyone to watch it. A snack? Nope. Every breadstick and banana had been gobbled up already.

"How about a song?" said Mike finally, out of desperation.

"Great idea!" said Sulley.

And do you know what? It was! They sang 'The Huge Gigantic Spider' and 'The Wheels on the Monster Bus'.

"What did I say, Sulley? I said it'd be like a paid holiday, and it is! I don't understand why you were so reluctant," Mike said.

Sulley rolled his eyes. "Whatever you say, Mike."

Berry Blunder

Madame Medusa thrust a pail into Penny's hand. "I only want the plumpest, juiciest berries!" she screeched. "And don't come back until the pail is full!"

"Yes, Medusa," Penny replied.

Carrying Teddy in one hand and the pail in the other, the little girl set off into the swamp.

Penny looked around. It wasn't easy to find her way through the swamp because everything sort of grew together. Luckily she knew where to go.

A few minutes later, Penny stood before a bush heavy with plump berries. She put Teddy down in a tangle of branches. "You'll be comfy here while I pick," she explained.

She was plucking the first berry off the bush when Brutus, one of Medusa's crocodiles, lumbered forwards and opened his massive jaws. He grabbed Teddy and threw him into the murky water.

"Teddy!" Penny cried. She snatched her friend up, hugged him to her chest and glared at Brutus, who was munching on the berries.

"You creep!" she said. "You could have hurt Teddy. And those berries are for Medusa!"

Brutus responded by snatching another dozen berries off the bush. Then Nero,

Medusa's other crocodile, joined him, chomping away. Soon, half of the branches were empty.

Scowling and holding her dripping Teddy, Penny looked around. When she spied a patch of bright-red fruit growing several feet away, she smiled to herself.

"Nero, Brutus!" she called cheerfully. "There's another berry patch over there! Take a look!"

Lifting their massive heads, the two crocs looked where Penny was pointing.

A second later, they had crossed the swamp and were scoffing down the plump red fruit.

Penny began to giggle. With their eyes wide and their nostrils flaring, Nero and Brutus began to desperately gulp down swamp water. The nearby 'berries' looked like berries, but they were actually hot peppers!

"You shouldn't eat so fast, boys," she said sweetly as they squirmed in the water.

Penny picked until her pail was full. Then, taking Teddy by the arm, she headed back to the ship. *How berry sorry I am!* she thought.

To the Rescue

Snow White and her prince spent nearly every day together. But one morning, the prince told Snow White that he had an errand to take care of. He saddled his trusty steed, Astor, and bid Snow White farewell.

That afternoon, Snow White spotted a cloud of dust on the road. Astor was returning. But where was the Prince?

Snow White's tender heart filled with dread. *Surely the prince is in trouble*, she thought.

Astor stamped her hoof on the ground and nodded towards her empty saddle.

"Do you want me to get on?" Snow White asked. Again, Astor nodded.

The princess barely had time to sit down before Astor was racing down the road towards the forest.

Astor ran deeper into the woods, with Snow White tugging uselessly at the reins. If only she knew that the Prince was safe!

Then, suddenly, Snow White spotted a piece of red cloth caught on a sharp thorn. Could it be? It was! A scrap torn from the Prince's very own riding cloak! And that wasn't all. As they continued through the forest, Snow White found his hat dangling from a tree!

The princess gripped the reins with one hand. She clutched the prince's hat and tried to think positively. Finally, they emerged into a sunny clearing, and Astor slowed to a stop. Snow White spotted the Prince lying on the ground. She slipped out of the saddle and raced across the clearing. Breathless, Snow White reached the Prince just as he sat up and stretched.

"What a nice nap!" he said. "I hope you're hungry!"

Snow White was bewildered. Next to the Prince lay a lavish picnic spread out on a soft blanket, and he was as happy and as healthy as ever!

"I knew Astor would get you here quickly," the Prince said, beaming. "Tell me, are you surprised?"

Snow White paused for a moment to catch her breath. "Oh, yes, very surprised," she said at last, smiling. She picked up an apple and offered it to Astor. "And," she added, "I'm very glad you have such a dear and clever horse!"

Show-and-Tell

"Please?" pleaded Lilo. "He'll be good. I promise!"

"Oh, all right!" Nani said crossly. Lilo had been pestering her big sister all morning to let her take their pet, Stitch, to dance class for show-and-tell. Nani was worried it would cause a lot of trouble.

The girls her age were not kind to Lilo, who had trouble fitting in. As a result, Lilo tended to lash out at them and get herself into trouble. And her strange pet, Stitch, was the same way. Nani was convinced that the strange creature they picked up at the pound wasn't even a real dog.

When they arrived at dance class, Nani gave her little sister a quick hug. "You behave yourselves!" she said.

"You'll behave yourself," Lilo said to Stitch. "I know you will."

"All right," said the dance teacher. "What have you brought today, Lilo?"

Lilo stood up. "This is my dog. His name is Stitch. I got him at the pound."

"He sure is ugly!" said Myrtle.

"Now, Myrtle, be nice," the teacher said.

"Can he play fetch?" Myrtle asked. She threw a water balloon that she had brought for show-and-tell right at Stitch!

Stitch caught the balloon and threw it back at Myrtle.

"No!" yelled Lilo, throwing herself in front of Myrtle, accidentally knocking the other girl over. The water balloon hit Lilo and broke, sending water flying everywhere!

"Oh, Lilo," said the teacher, "I think it's time for your pet to go home."

Lilo picked up Stitch and ran outside. "You got us in trouble today," Lilo said to him. "Why did you throw that water balloon at Myrtle?"

Stitch growled.

"Oh, that's right," said Lilo, "you don't play fetch. How could I have forgotten?" She looked thoughtful. "How about we play catch instead? That's almost the same thing as fetch, but there's an important difference. Fetch is something you play with a pet, and catch is something you play with a friend. I think you're more my friend than my pet, Stitch."

Stitch nodded eagerly and held up a ball.

Lilo smiled, and the two friends spent a lovely afternoon together playing catch.

Chief Mischief Maker

Like all raccoons, Meeko was curious – and that often got him into trouble. And though Pocahontas had a lot of patience when it came to her small furry friend, other members of the tribe were not as understanding.

"Pocahontas, you must teach that animal how to behave!" Chief Powhatan exclaimed when he caught Meeko playing with the tribe's peace pipe.

"Don't worry," Pocahontas told Meeko. "They can't stay angry with you for long. Tomorrow is your birthday after all!"

Meeko chattered excitedly. He loved his birthday – especially opening presents!

Meeko slipped into Pocahontas's tent and spied his wrapped present. He wasted no time unwrapping it and discovered… a headdress just his size, filled with beautiful feathers!

Meeko couldn't wait to try it on. He didn't want to be discovered, so he grabbed his gift and scampered off towards the river. There, he put on the headdress. The raccoon gazed happily at his reflection.

But as he was admiring himself, the headdress fell into the water! The raccoon fished it out and headed back to the village.

On the way, the headdress got caught on some bushes, and some feathers fell out.

Then Meeko tripped over a log and landed on his gift, and even more feathers were lost! By the time he reached the village, only one feather remained in his once-beautiful headdress.

Meeko knew what he had to do. He found Pocahontas and showed her what was left of the present.

"Meeko, I am proud of you. You had the courage to admit what you have done," she said. "But you must try to do better."

On his birthday, Meeko behaved perfectly all day. That night, Pocahontas presented him with a gift. It was the headdress, but now it had two feathers instead of one. "For every day that you are able to stay out of other people's belongings, we will add another feather," she said.

Meeko was grateful to Pocahontas for being so understanding, and he was determined to make her proud. He would do his best to fill the headdress – but he knew it would probably take him until his next birthday!

Disney
DUMBO

Death-Defying Dale

One morning, Chip and Dale woke up to find a giant red-and-white-striped tent just outside their tree. The chipmunks were curious, so they went over to the tent and peeked through the door.

Inside, a man was shouting through a megaphone.

"Ladies and gentlemen!" he cried. "Welcome to the World's Greatest Circus!"

The chipmunks tiptoed inside. They watched a silly clown with orange hair and a big red nose perform somersaults. Nearby, a lion tamer cracked his whip at a lion. And high overhead, trapeze artists tumbled though the air.

Dale smelt something delicious. There on the ground, right by the centre ring, was a bag full of peanuts! Dale's tummy rumbled. He needed a snack. Chip and Dale hurried over to the peanuts.

Chip was about to take a bite when he realised someone – or something – was standing behind him. He turned round and his eyes opened wide.

It was a huge elephant!

Chip squeaked in surprise and ran away, but Dale was face first in the sack of peanuts and didn't hear him. Just then, the elephant reached into the sack with its trunk, looking for a peanut. But it didn't grab a peanut – it grabbed Dale!

"Paaawooo!" the elephant trumpeted. With a flick of her trunk, she flung Dale away.

"Eek!" Dale squeaked as he sailed through the air. He was heading straight for the lion's open mouth!

Dale closed his eyes.

Whoosh! Suddenly, something scooped Dale out of the air. He opened his eyes. One of the trapeze artists had accidentally grabbed Dale as he flipped through the air.

Dale sighed with relief.

But a second later, the trapeze artist let go. "Eek!" Dale cried as he fell right into a bucket of popcorn.

Dale popped out of the popcorn. Suddenly, a spotlight shone down on him.

"Ladies and gentlemen," the ringmaster announced. "Please give a round of applause to our surprise guest, the Death-Defying Chipmunk!"

Dot Rules

Atta was exhausted! Ever since she had taken over as queen, she had not had a moment's peace. There were so many decisions to make and disagreements to settle.

Princess Dot didn't like her big sister being so tired and cranky all the time.

"Why don't you just take a day off?" Dot asked.

"But who will run the colony?" Atta said irritably.

"I will. I am a princess, you know," Dot said.

The next day, Dot began her reign. The first problem arose when their mother's pet, Aphie, ate some leaves that were going to be used to build a rain shelter.

"You need a time-out!" scolded Dot. She put Aphie in a pen for ten minutes. When he came back out, he was a model aphid.

Later, she found Cornelius and Thorny disagreeing over the best way to transport seeds.

"I want you to cooperate and come up with a solution," Dot said. A short time later, Thorny and Cornelius reached a compromise. It turned out they were both right!

Flik was the next ant to receive Dot's help. "I can't seem to get this new ant mover to work," he complained.

"How long have you been working on it?" Dot asked.

Flik thought for a moment. "Since I woke up," he answered. "I worked right through breakfast and lunch."

"Flik," Dot said, "you can't think properly if your body doesn't have fuel. You need to stop and eat something. And why don't you take a nap while you're at it?"

Dot had a lot of advice to share with her subjects that day. She reminded Mr Soil's conservation class that everyone should have a turn to speak. She insisted that the ant boys pick their toys up off the ground. And she firmly told her mother that there was no whining allowed – even if she was upset about Aphie getting a time-out.

By the end of the day, both Atta and her mother had to admit that the colony had run smoothly with Dot in charge.

"What's your secret?" asked Atta.

"It was easy," Dot explained. "Time-outs, cooperating, taking naps and taking turns – I learnt it all in my Blueberry troop!"

Dance, Daddy-o!

Deep in the jungle at the temple ruins, the monkeys and their ruler, King Louie, were always looking to have a swingin' time.

"Let's have a dance-off!" King Louie suggested to the monkeys one evening.

"Hooray!" the monkeys cheered.

"What's a dance-off?" one monkey asked.

"You know, a contest," said King Louie. "An opportunity for everyone to get down, strut their stuff, throw some shapes! And whoever lays down the smoothest moves is the winner!"

"Hooray!" cheered the monkeys, again.

King Louie rubbed his chin. "The first thing we need is some music," he said, pointing at the monkey musicians. "Hit it, fellas!"

The musicians blasted out a jazzy tune, blowing through their hands like horns, knocking out a beat on some coconuts and drumming on a hollow log. Soon, all the monkeys were gathered round the musicians, tapping their toes and shaking their tails.

King Louie moved his hips from side to side. He waved his arms in the air. He closed his eyes so he could really feel the beat.

"Dance, daddy-o!" one monkey cried.

King Louie boogied and bopped like he had never boogied and bopped before. Then, when the song was over, he stopped dancing and scrambled back onto his throne. "Now it's time to choose the winner!" he said.

"But King Louie..." one monkey began to object.

All the other monkeys were thinking the same thing: didn't you need more than one dancer to have a dance-off?

"Oh, silly me," said King Louie with a chuckle. The monkeys looked at one another and smiled, expecting that the king had realised his mistake. But King Louie said, "Of course, we need a judge! Who will judge?"

Everyone raised their hands. King Louie looked around, then said, "I choose... me!"

"Hooray!" the monkeys cheered.

"And as the judge, I will now choose the winner of the dance-off," King Louie continued. He looked around at all the monkeys. "Now, let's see. I choose... me! Let's hear it for the winner!"

"Hooray!" the monkeys cheered, because, after all, King Louie was their king – and a pretty swingin' dancer, too!

Looks Can Be Deceiving

Yao, Ling and Chien-Po missed Mulan. They had become friends in the army – although when they had first met her, Mulan had been disguised as a young man.

Now Mulan's three friends decided they would go to her village and follow Mulan in whatever adventure she might embark on next.

"But what if Shan-Yu is seeking revenge?" Ling said. "He might be looking for us. After all, we did help Mulan defeat him."

Yao thought they should disguise themselves. So the friends donned kimonos, wigs and make-up and left for Mulan's village, looking like a trio of women.

When they arrived, the Matchmaker instantly approached them. "And who would you lovely ladies be?" she asked. The Matchmaker was desperate. There weren't many single women in the village, and she had a list of bachelors a mile long to marry off!

"Visitors from far away," said Chien-Po, speaking in a high voice.

"And are you unmarried, ladies?" the Matchmaker asked.

Ling looked at his friends. "We're unmarried, all right!" he said.

"Well, let me be the first to welcome you to our village," the Matchmaker said, ushering them into her house. "Would you like some tea? Perhaps you would like to pour?" she asked Yao. He tried to remember the way his mother served tea at home. Yao set out the cups and poured as daintily as he could.

"Cookie?" the pleased Matchmaker asked Chien-Po, holding out a plate. Chien-Po resisted the urge to grab a fistful of cookies. Instead, he chose one, stuck out his little finger and ate it in small bites.

Next the Matchmaker asked Ling what his favourite pastime was.

"Wrestling," he answered. Then, seeing the shocked look on the Matchmaker's face, he added quickly, "Yes, I find that resting keeps my complexion lovely." He batted his eyelashes.

The Matchmaker led the three back outside, just as Mulan was riding into the village. "Stop! You can't marry them off!" Mulan cried, seeing her friends with the woman.

"I certainly can," said the Matchmaker. "Unlike you, Mulan, these three are real ladies!"

Catching Gold

One rainy autumn day, Woody the cowboy sat in front of the TV with his horse, Bullseye. They were watching *Woody's Roundup*.

On the shore, the Prospector grabbed his gold-mining pan and went down to the water's edge. "I've got a hunch there's some gold in this river!" he exclaimed.

Jessie went for a walk to look for some wild flowers, while Woody stayed in his favourite fishing spot. He hadn't had a single bite yet, but he was hopeful.

Meanwhile, the Prospector came to a shallow pool. He held out his gold-mining pan and began to sift through the sand from the riverbed. When the water had all sloshed out, he looked at the empty pan. There was no gold. He headed back up the river to where Woody was fishing.

"Any fish yet?" the Prospector asked.

"Nope," replied Woody. "What about you? Any gold?"

Just as the Prospector was about to answer, he saw something shiny in the water. He stepped closer to take another look.

"Eureka!" he cried. "I see gold!" He jumped into the river. Splash! He tried catching the gold with his pan, but it kept sliding back into the water.

"Come help me, Sheriff," the Prospector shouted. "This is the slip-slidin'est gold I ever saw!"

Woody put down his pole and leapt into the water. Together they dived after the gold. But each time, they came up empty-handed. Then, Woody had an idea. "We can use our hats!"

"Good thinking," said the Prospector.

The two used their hats to try to scoop up the swirling bits of gold. Just then, Jessie appeared. "What are you two doing?" she asked.

"Catching gold!" said Woody.

Jessie took a closer look inside their hats and began to laugh.

"What's so funny?" the Prospector asked.

Jessie smiled. "Take a look at your catch!"

Woody and the Prospector looked at their hats. They were surprised to see goldfish swimming around!

"I can't believe it!" Woody laughed. "The Prospector was looking for gold, and I was looking for fish."

Jessie giggled. "I guess you both found what you were looking for!"

How Does Your Garden Grow?

Alice had just eaten a mushroom that made her shrink. Now, everything around her was gigantic!

"The Caterpillar said one side of this mushroom will make me bigger and the other will make me smaller," Alice told a nearby dandelion.

"Which do you want?" asked the dandelion. "To grow bigger or smaller?"

"Bigger!" cried Alice.

"Put your roots in the ground and turn your leaves to the sun," said the dandelion. "You'll grow bigger in no time!"

"But I'm not a flower," said Alice.

"Of course she's not," said a daffodil. "She's a bug!"

Suddenly, Alice heard another voice. "Little buuuug…" it sang.

Alice placed the mushroom pieces in her pocket and approached the plant. Its flower buds looked very strange – like split green peas with fine hairs round the edges.

"Get in," said the plant eagerly.

Alice climbed inside one of the strange buds. Immediately, she felt the bud begin to close up tight, trapping her inside!

"What kind of plant are you?" cried Alice.

"A Venus flytrap," said the plant.

"But I'm not a fly," Alice protested.

"Doesn't matter," said the flytrap. "I eat other bugs."

"I'm not any kind of bug!" cried Alice, banging on the springy green walls.

The flytrap just laughed. "I can tell you're going to be a tasty treat, little bug," it mumbled.

"You know," said Alice angrily, "it's not polite to talk with your mouth full! Why, if I were my normal size, I'd—"

Normal size? she thought. Suddenly, she remembered the pieces of mushroom in her pocket. She pulled out the two pieces. Taking a chance, she bit into one.

All at once, Alice began to grow. She got bigger and bigger and burst out of the flytrap.

Still angry, she peered down at the flytrap. It looked completely harmless now, no higher than her ankle. She gave it a glare, and then went on her way.

The flowers watched her go. "That was the biggest bug I ever saw," said the daffodil, in a quaking voice.

"I can't believe I let it go," the Venus flytrap said wistfully. "That bug would have been breakfast, lunch and dinner for the next fifty years!"

Playing Schools

Now, it just so happened that when the wind changed ever so slightly and the leaves began to turn scarlet or golden, Christopher Robin returned to school. Not so surprisingly, his friends in the wood felt as if they should really do the same.

But playing schools, as you might suspect, is not as similar to real school as perhaps it should be. And, after sitting at their desks for what seemed like a good three-and-a-quarter hours (but was really just five minutes or so), Winnie the Pooh and his friends came to the conclusion that something rather important in their game of schools was missing.

"Perhaps it's time we had a snack," suggested Pooh.

"I don't think that's the problem, Pooh," said Piglet.

"Our problem," announced Owl, "is that we do not have a teacher. Of course, I am quite happy to offer my considerable expertise."

"Just a minute, Owl," Rabbit interrupted. "Why is it, exactly, that we should let you be the teacher? Some might say – myself included – that I'm better suited to the job."

Owl scowled. "You?"

"Perhaps we should have a vote," said Piglet. "I'd like to nominate Pooh."

"Me?" Pooh said. "Why thank you, Piglet. I gladly accept. Now… what's a teacher again?"

"Really!" said Owl, with no small amount of scorn. "A teacher, my dear Pooh, is the someone who stands before the class."

"To give out snacks?" asked Pooh.

"No, Pooh," said Owl. "To give out knowledge."

"Oh," said Pooh. "I don't think I'd enjoy that nearly as much."

"Well, if it's all the same to you, and if anyone cares, I'll be the teacher," Eeyore said glumly. "I probably wouldn't have made a good student, anyway."

"Hi-ho!" said Christopher Robin, returning from a thoroughly enjoyable, and very well-taught, day at school. "Whatever are you up to?"

"Playing school… I think," said Pooh.

"Only we don't have a teacher," Piglet explained.

"I could teach you. I learnt ever so many things today," said Christopher Robin.

"Hooray!" cheered Roo. "Let's start right away!"

Stackblackbadminton

Ariel was a guest at Prince Eric's castle. After dinner, she went into the drawing room with Eric and Grimsby to relax.

"My dear, do you play?" Grimsby asked Ariel. He pointed to a table. On it sat a red-and-black-chequered board. Ariel couldn't answer because she had exchanged her voice for legs, but she nodded eagerly.

"I'll make the first move," Eric said, and he slid a black disc from one square to another.

That seems simple enough, thought Ariel. The game seemed similar to a merpeople game called Conch. She reached over and pushed the same black disc to a third square.

Eric laughed. "No, no. I'm black. And you're red. You move the red pieces."

"Perhaps I should show the young lady?" suggested Grimsby.

He took Ariel's seat, and the two men moved the discs all over the chequered board. Suddenly, Ariel heard a flapping sound at the window. It was Scuttle!

Ariel pointed at the men and shrugged.

"They're playing Stackblackbadminton, a popular human game," said Scuttle.

Ariel's eyes widened. That sounded like something she had better learn if she wanted to fit in to Eric's world.

"You see those discs?" asked Scuttle. "Those are chips. At the end of the game, players stack their chips. Then the dealer – the person not playing—"

Ariel pointed to herself.

Scuttle nodded. "Yes. It's up to you to end the game by collecting all the chips off the board."

Ariel smiled. She would show Eric she did know how to play.

She walked right over to the two men. They seemed to have finished playing. They were staring hard at the board, and there weren't many chips left on it. So she bent down and swept all the pieces off the board.

Eric and Grimsby yelped. The little mermaid grinned. Eric didn't think she knew how to play his game, but from the stunned look on his face, she'd given him quite a surprise!

Ariel smiled and began to lay the chips out as if they were shells in a game of Conch. This Stackblackbadminton game was all right, but she couldn't wait to teach Eric and Grimsby how to play a really good game!

Disney
Cinderella

The Masquerade Ball

"Where could she be?" Cinderella asked.

Cinderella and her new husband, the prince, were holding a masquerade ball. Cinderella had sent a special invitation to her fairy godmother, who had promised to come. But the ball had started almost an hour ago, and Cinderella still hadn't seen any sign of the cheerful little woman.

"Don't worry, my love," the prince said. "I'm sure she'll— what's this?"

A messenger handed Cinderella a note.

Never fear – I'm here, my dear. Just seek and you will find which mask I am behind!

Her fairy godmother was playing a trick on her!

"I'll find you," Cinderella whispered.

Was her fairy godmother wearing that beautiful unicorn costume? Was she the milkmaid standing by the fountain? The dancing harlequin clown? The fuzzy brown bear? Cinderella felt a little dizzy as she turned round and round. How would she ever find her fairy godmother in the crowd?

Cinderella looked around thoughtfully. When she turned back to the fountain, the milkmaid was gone! Instead, someone in a butterfly mask was standing there.

"Looking for someone, Princess?" the butterfly asked in a deep voice.

"No, never mind," Cinderella said.

She wandered away, still searching. But she kept thinking about the twinkling eyes behind the butterfly mask. Then she remembered something – the milkmaid had the same twinkling eyes! Could it be?

Cinderella hurried back to the fountain. But there was no sign of the milkmaid or the butterfly. The only person standing nearby was wearing a beautiful pink princess costume.

Cinderella stared at the princess. Mischievous eyes twinkled behind the gold-and-pink mask. Suddenly, Cinderella laughed out loud.

"Aha!" she cried. "I caught you!"

She pulled off the mask. Her fairy godmother smiled back at her.

"You win!" she exclaimed. "How did you find me?"

"I almost didn't, the way you kept magically changing costumes," Cinderella said. "Then I remembered how you magically changed my outfit not too long ago – and I figured it out!"

Bedtime for Duchess

"Come, my precious ones!" Duchess called to her kittens. "It's time to go to sleep."

"Oh, Mother!" Toulouse complained.

"But I'm not tired!" Marie joined in.

"I'm not going to sleep," Berlioz added. "Night-time is when things start happening for us alley cats." Berlioz crouched down low and pounced on an imaginary opponent.

"Now, now, it's been a long day," Duchess said. "I don't want to hear any more protests."

"We need a bedtime story!" Marie insisted.

"A story? I'm sorry, darlings, but it's way past your bedtime, and I'm just too tired tonight," replied Duchess.

"Then why don't we tell you a story?" Toulouse offered.

"Once upon a time," Marie began.

"There was a big, mean, ferocious alley cat," Berlioz continued.

"Berlioz!" Marie protested. "It's not supposed to be scary. She'll have nightmares!"

"Sorry, Mama," Berlioz said.

"That's quite all right," Duchess said.

"Now, where were we?" Toulouse asked.

"Once upon a time," Marie began again.

"Yeah, once upon a time there was this kitten," Toulouse said.

"He could paint like no other kitten."

"And that's because the model for his paintings was the most beautiful kitten you've ever laid eyes on," Marie added.

"Give me a break!" Berlioz said, grumbling under his breath. He and Toulouse sniggered.

Marie was not amused. "Can we please get back to the story?"

"Okay, okay," Berlioz continued. "This kitten was a painter by day and a smooth-talking, alley-hanging hepcat by night. He was—"

Suddenly, Toulouse tapped Berlioz with his paw. Berlioz couldn't believe Toulouse was interrupting him. He was trying to tell a story! Then he saw why Toulouse had stopped him. Duchess had fallen asleep!

Berlioz, Toulouse and Marie each gave their mother a kiss goodnight.

"Goodnight, Mama," said Marie.

"Goodnight, Mama," said Toulouse.

"Goodnight, Mama," said Berlioz.

Then all three curled up beside Duchess and promptly fell asleep, too.

Jasmine's Jewel Thief

"This is so much fun!" Jasmine cried. She and Aladdin were flying over the desert on their favourite flying carpet. Jasmine leant against Aladdin and reached up to smooth back her windblown hair. But as her fingers brushed past her ears, she noticed that one of her earrings was gone!

"What is it?" Aladdin asked when he saw Jasmine searching the carpet.

"It's nothing. Just an earring," Jasmine said. She tried to stay calm, but her eyes gave her away.

"Just an earring?" Aladdin said. "Didn't your father give them to you?"

"Yes," Jasmine confessed. "They're my favourites. At least, they were."

"Are," Aladdin said firmly. "We'll find the other one."

Back at the palace, Aladdin and Jasmine looked everywhere. They searched their chambers, the gardens, even the fountains. They were about to search the kitchen when Aladdin saw Abu scamper by.

Aladdin looked at the monkey suspiciously. "You haven't seen a shiny gold earring, have you?"

Abu shrugged, but he wouldn't look Aladdin in the eye. Aladdin knew the monkey was up to something.

"Are you sure?" Aladdin asked sternly.

Slowly, Abu motioned Aladdin to follow him. When he saw the monkey's bed, Aladdin almost started to laugh. Why hadn't he noticed before how lumpy it was?

Abu pulled back the covers and Aladdin laughed out loud. Abu's bed was covered with shiny objects! There were spoons, goblets and coins. And from beneath his small pillow, Abu pulled out Jasmine's earring.

Aladdin shook his head and smiled at Abu. "You don't have to scavenge any more. We live in the palace!"

Aladdin and Abu brought the earring to Jasmine. "You found it!" she cried, leaning down to give Abu a kiss. The little monkey blushed.

"Here, Abu, take this ring as a reward for finding my earring," Jasmine said. She removed a gold ring from her finger and gave it to the monkey, who did a happy jump and tucked it into his hat.

"Actually, Abu didn't really—" Aladdin began. Then he saw Abu glaring at him. "Well," he continued, amused. "Yes. Um, good job, Abu."

The Late Shift

The shift on the Scare Floor at Monsters, Inc. had just ended when Sulley pulled Mike aside.

"Mike, our paperwork is always late," he said. "I'm worried about us getting a bad reputation."

"You're right, Sulley," Mike said earnestly. "From now on, I'm a new monster. You and Celia will be so proud of me— uh-oh…"

"What is it, Mike?" Sulley asked.

"Oh, nothing!" Mike grinned. "Sulley, I'll see you later. I've got lots of catching up to do. Paperwork, here I come!"

As soon as Sulley was gone, Mike's smile faded. "What do I do?" he cried. "I have a date with Celia, and I'm already late!" Finally, Mike came to a decision. "I'll catch up tomorrow," he said to himself.

Mike headed to the locker room, whistling a jaunty tune. He had just entered the quiet, empty room when he heard a noise.

"Who's there?" he asked nervously.

"Gagoooo," said the voice.

That was definitely a kid! Mike turned to run, but he tripped over a can of odourant someone had left on the floor and went flying across the room. Footsteps sounded behind him. Mike looked up, expecting to see a human kid. But instead he saw Sulley!

"What gives?" he asked Sulley.

Sulley was laughing so hard, he couldn't even talk. Finally, he said, "I just couldn't resist! After you shooed me out I ran into Celia, who told me about your date. I knew you would rather skip the paperwork than disappoint Celia."

Mike nodded, embarrassed.

"But I told her that you were really behind on your work," Sulley continued, "and I asked if it would be okay for you two to have your date tomorrow night instead."

Mike looked up, surprised. That hadn't even occurred to him. "Did she say yes?" he asked.

"She sure did," Sulley said. "And she also said that since I'm your partner and all, I should really stay here to help you catch up. So, here I am! Now, let's grab some sludge lollies and get to work."

"Okay, Sulley," said Mike. And the two monsters went off to show that paperwork what they were made of.

The Best Fisherman of All

Simba and his friends Timon and Pumbaa were hungry. They wandered through the forest until they came to an old, rotten tree. Timon knocked on the trunk.

"What's it sound like, Timon?" Pumbaa asked.

"Like our breakfast!" Timon replied.

He yanked at the bark, and hundreds of grubs slithered out. Timon threw Simba a grub.

"No thanks." Simba sighed. "I'm tired of grubs."

"Well, the ants are tasty," said Timon. "They come in two flavours: red and black."

Simba shook his head. "Don't you eat anything but bugs?"

"Fish!" Pumbaa declared.

"I love fish!" Simba exclaimed.

"Why didn't you say so?" said Timon. "There's a pond at the end of this trail." The three friends headed for the water.

"What now?" asked Simba when they arrived at the pond.

"That's the problem!" said Timon. "We're not the best fishermen in the world."

"I'll teach you!" Simba said.

The lion climbed up a tree and crawled onto a branch that hung over the water. Then he snatched a fish out of the water with his sharp claws. "See?" Simba said, jumping to the ground nimbly. "Not a problem. Fishing's easy."

"Not for me!" Timon cried. He dangled from the branch, but his arms weren't long enough to reach the fish.

Simba laughed. "Better let Pumbaa try."

"What a joke!" cried Timon. "Pumbaa can't even climb this tree."

"Want to bet?" asked Pumbaa.

"Stay there," Timon warned. "I don't think this branch is strong enough for both of us."

With a hop, Pumbaa landed on the branch next to Timon.

"Yikes!" Timon cried as he leapt to another tree.

Crack! The branch broke under Pumbaa. With a squeal, he landed in the pond.

Simba started to laugh. So did Timon. Pumbaa was sitting in a pool of mud where the pond had been. He'd splashed so much of the water out that dozens of fish squirmed on the ground, just waiting to be gobbled up.

"Wow!" Timon cried. "I think Pumbaa is the very best fisherman of all!"

A Bright Idea

One day, Geppetto told Pinocchio, "I am off to deliver these puppets. I will be gone for a few hours. Stay out of trouble!"

Geppetto had not been gone for fifteen minutes before Pinocchio became bored. "I have nothing to do," he said.

"You could clean the shop," said Jiminy Cricket.

"That's no fun," said Pinocchio. "I'll paint a picture instead."

"Where will you get the paint?" Jiminy asked.

"From the workbench," said Pinocchio.

"You know you're not supposed to go near Geppetto's workbench," warned Jiminy.

But the cricket's warning came too late. "Oops!" Pinocchio cried. He'd spilt red paint all over the workbench. Hurriedly, he grabbed a rag and tried to clean up the mess, but the paint just smeared. He'd made the mess even bigger!

Pinocchio looked around desperately. When he noticed Geppetto's kitten, Figaro, sleeping by the hearth, he had an idea.

"I'll say Figaro did it," Pinocchio said.

Jiminy shook his head. "That would be wrong," he told the puppet. "Why don't you paint it?"

"That's a very good idea!" said Pinocchio.

So he set to work. First, he painted the bench's top bright red. Then he painted the drawers green and yellow. Figaro woke up and investigated, getting paint all over his whiskers.

Soon, the job was done.

"It's a work of art!" Geppetto cried when he got home. "It's so colourful, it makes the whole shop more cheerful."

Then Geppetto saw the paint on Figaro's whiskers. "Did Figaro knock over the paint again?" he asked. "Is that why you painted the workbench?"

"No," Pinocchio said. "I spilt the paint. I couldn't clean it up, so I painted the whole workbench. I'm sorry."

Geppetto was quiet for a moment, and then he said, "I'm proud of you, Pinocchio. You told the truth and apologised instead of telling a lie. That takes courage. Now, every day when I see my workbench, I'll remember you did the right thing, and that will make the colours seem even brighter!"

Anna, Elsa and the Secret River

One night, Elsa and Anna's mother sang them a lullaby about a secret white river flowing with answers to the past.

Later, Elsa had just closed her eyes and drifted off when Anna shook her awake. "Let's go find the white river!" she exclaimed.

"Let it go," said Elsa. "It's time to sleep."

"But I have a million questions," replied Anna. "And the white river could have all the answers."

Elsa turned over and pulled the duvet over her head, but Anna wouldn't give up. "And don't you wonder why you have magic?"

At that, Elsa sat up and said, "Let's go!"

It didn't take the young sisters long to slip out of the castle and into the forest. "How will we find the white river?" asked Anna.

"We've got to use our eyes," said Elsa.

Suddenly, Anna spotted a gleaming reflection and they ran towards it… but it was only a stream. "Now what?" sighed Anna, disappointedly.

"Maybe if we listen we'll find the white river," suggested Elsa. Just then, Anna heard the sound of rushing water and they ran to meet the water!

But all they found was a boulder with wind rushing through it. "If only we could smell the white river," said Anna.

"What would it smell like?" asked Elsa.

"Answers," said Anna. Then she noticed a herd of reindeer stood near them. "And… reindeer."

"This is ridiculous," said Elsa.

The sisters had used their eyes, their ears and their noses, and still hadn't found the white river!

The sisters were about to give up, when Elsa found an old shield glinting in the moonlight.

Suddenly, the wind lifted Anna into the air. Its power took the girls by surprise and something caught Anna's eye!

The wind gently returned Anna to the ground, and the sisters raced towards the white river… but it was only an ice mountain glittering in the breaking dawn.

"It's almost morning," said Elsa.

"What do we do now?" asked Anna, sadly.

"Sleep!" said Elsa. Suddenly, they were both snuggled up back in their bed.

In the morning, Anna shook Elsa awake. "Let's go find the white river!"

"It's only a lullaby," said Elsa. But then, she wondered if their adventure had all been a dream.

A Rainy Night Out

"Yip!" Scamp barked at the squirrel nibbling on an acorn in the grass.

"Yip!" Scamp barked again, and the squirrel darted across the lawn. Scamp chased the squirrel, which zipped over the fence and leapt onto a nearby tree branch. That was the problem with squirrels. They always got away too easily.

Disappointed, Scamp trotted along the pavement, stopping when he got to an open field. The grass there was tall, and butterflies flitted from wild flower to wild flower.

"Yip! Yip!" Scamp raced through the tall grass. He chased the butterflies to the end of the open field and back again.

It was getting dark. Scamp decided it was time to head home. He hadn't caught a single butterfly, but he'd had fun trying. He couldn't wait to tell his sisters about the new game he'd invented. They'd be so impressed!

Scamp trotted up to the front porch and tried to get through the dog flap. Thunk! His nose hit the wood, but it didn't move. The door was locked!

Scamp sat there for several minutes, barking. Nobody came to the door. Suddenly – boom! – thunder echoed overhead. Lightning flashed and rain began to fall.

Scamp bolted over to the big oak tree, sat down and covered his eyes with his paws. Thunderstorms were scary!

"I'm not going to cry," he told himself as his eyes started to mist over. He shivered in the dark. He'd probably catch a cold by morning!

Scamp let out a little whimper and moved even closer to the tree trunk. He buried his wet nose in his wet paws and closed his eyes. He was just falling asleep when a sound made him jump. Somebody was coming up the drive!

By the time Jim Dear and Darling were out of the taxi, Scamp was dashing across the lawn as fast as he could go. He bolted through the door just as it opened.

"Scamp, you're soaking wet!" Darling declared as the puppy found his sisters napping in front of the fire. As he lay down among them, Jim Dear came over with a warm towel to dry him off.

Home sweet home, Scamp thought happily as he drifted off to sleep.

Kronk's Feast

"One more time!" Kronk cried. The Junior Chipmunks looked at their leader, took deep breaths and launched into 'We're Not Woodchucks' for the fourth time. Next to them, Bucky the squirrel and three of his friends sang along – in Squirrel. "Squeak sq-sq-squeak. Sq-sq-squeak squeak, squeaker, squeak."

While the kids and chipmunks began another verse, Kronk stood at the fire. He mixed, flipped and seasoned in a frenzy. He had been cooking for hours, and the smells drifting towards the tired troop were delicious.

"I'm… almost… ready." Kronk struggled to balance several platters on his arm before spinning round to present them to the kids in the troop. "Voilà!" The big man grinned. "Bon appétit!"

The kids leant forwards and smiled. The food looked as good as it smelt! They began to help themselves.

Everyone was pleased. Everyone, that is, except for Bucky and the squirrels. Where was their food? This was an outrage! The squirrels were Junior Chipmunks, too!

"Squeak! Squeaker, squeaker, squeak," Bucky mumbled behind his paw. He gave a quick nod, and all of them ran off towards Kronk's tent.

Bucky held open the tent flap, and the squirrels ducked inside. "Squeak," Bucky commanded as he pointed at Kronk's sleeping bag. The other squirrels nodded. They knew what they were supposed to do – chew holes in Kronk's bedding!

Just as the squirrels were about to get started, they were interrupted.

"Oh, squeeeaak," Kronk's deep voice crooned from outside. "Squeaker squeeaak!"

The squirrels peeked outside the tent.

There was Kronk, holding a new platter. Balanced upon it were a golden-brown acorn soufflé and a bowl of steaming wild-berry sauce.

Bucky shrugged sheepishly at the leader.

"Thought I forgot you, huh? Would Kronk do that?" The leader put down the tray. "How about a hug?"

The four squirrels grasped the large man's legs and squeezed. All was forgiven. Together, all the Junior Chipmunks enjoyed their meals.

Orator Owl

On their way home from a leaf-collecting excursion on a cold, blustery autumn afternoon, Pooh, Rabbit, Piglet and Eeyore made their way past Owl's house. They could not help but notice the cheerful lights glowing in all the windows – a light so warm and so inviting that the chilly group seemed to thaw out just looking at it. And so it happened that they soon found themselves warm and cosy in Owl's living room.

"Owl, thank you for having us in to warm up," said Pooh. "It's awfully windy and cold outside."

"Well, it is getting on towards winter," Owl replied. "Naturally that means it will only get colder before it gets warmer."

Owl was just beginning to expound upon the particular subject of frostbite when Rabbit interrupted, hoping to give someone else a chance to talk.

"Yes, Owl," he said. "I know that Piglet was very glad to have his scarf on today, weren't you, Piglet?"

"Oh yes," Piglet said. "Kanga knitted it for me."

Owl cleared his throat. "Ah yes, knitting," he said. "An admirable hobby. Did you know that knitting is done with knitting needles?

But they aren't sharp, as one might assume. They are not, for example, as sharp as sewing needles. Or cactus needles, or…"

Owl continued with a comparison of many, many different types of needles. An hour later, when Owl seemed ready to jump into a discussion of pins, Rabbit again tried to change the subject.

"Speaking of pins," Rabbit began, "how is your tail today, Eeyore? I hope it is suitably secure and well-attached?"

"Seems secure," Eeyore replied with a shrug, "but it always falls off when I least expect it."

Rabbit saw Owl sit up in his chair and take a deep breath – a sure sign that he was preparing another speech about tails, or expectations or goodness knows what – so Rabbit decided it was time to go.

Goodbyes and thank-yous were said, and soon the four visitors were outside, making their way home through swirling leaves. And all the way home, Rabbit tried to decide who was windier – the great autumn wind or long-winded Owl!

Marmalade Moon Night

Rapunzel sighed. Mother Gothel was away, leaving Rapunzel alone in the tower. Luckily, Pascal was there to keep her company.

Rapunzel looked out the window. "Look at the moon, Pascal!" Rapunzel exclaimed. "It looks like a giant bowl of marmalade!" Just then, a flock of birds flew across the night sky, making a strange face in the glowing moon. "Ohh, that is scary…" Rapunzel shivered with glee. Suddenly, she had an idea. "I know! Let's make tonight Marmalade Moon Night! We can start our very own spooky tradition."

"What should we do first?" Rapunzel asked. "Oh! Let's play a game!" She glanced at the items in the fruit bowl. "These look just like the Marmalade Moon!" she said, picking up a few peaches.

Rapunzel filled a large bowl with water and added the peaches, which floated to the surface. "Okay, Pascal," she said. "Try to pick one up. But no hands or feet! You can only use your mouth."

Pascal seemed to think about it. Then his long tongue flicked out, lassoed a peach and plucked it out of the water.

Rapunzel laughed. "No fair!" she cried. Then she took a turn. She plunged her head into the water, mouth wide open. She came up coughing and sputtering – without a peach. Rapunzel tried and tried, but she just couldn't seem to catch a peach.

By then, Rapunzel was soaking wet. As she dug through the cupboard for a towel, she had an idea.

"Boo! I am the Marmalade Moon ghost!" she said, whipping a sheet over her head.

Pascal took one look at the figure that suddenly appeared, and hid!

Realising she must have really scared Pascal, Rapunzel said, "I'm sorry. This was supposed to be fun, not scary."

Pascal peeked round cautiously from his hiding spot. He breathed a sigh of relief. When Rapunzel stood up, there was Pascal, right in front of her. "Aaah!" she cried, and fell over backwards, completely startled. "Okay," Rapunzel admitted with a laugh, "that was a little more scary than fun. No more tricks," she said. "I promise. How about some treats instead?"

So it was that the two friends celebrated Marmalade Moon Night with some cupcakes… and it was very sweet indeed.

Tricky Treats

It was almost Halloween. Ralph was visiting Vanellope in Sugar Rush.

"C'mon. Let's go for a ride!" Vanellope said.

"Whooo!" she whooped a minute later as they tore round a turn.

"Gah!" Ralph yelled. "Pumpkin!"

"Pumpkin?" Vanellope said. "What are you talking about?" Then she looked around her. "Where are we?"

The go-kart track was gone. Ralph and Vanellope had been taken somewhere else.

Ralph shrugged. "It happened when my head hit that floating pumpkin."

"This must be the Halloween bonus level where Boo Bratley lives!" Vanellope said.

Suddenly, a marshmallow ghost appeared out of nowhere!

"Soooooo haaaaaappy you've heeeeard of me," Boo Bratley taunted. "Tooooo bad that won't help you goooooo hooooome."

"Hey, wait a minute!" Ralph leapt off the kart. "We need to go back."

"You neeeed to caaaaaaaatch meeeeeeee first," the ghost moaned. Then he floated into his castle and out of sight.

"Come on!" Vanellope yelled. She stomped on the accelerator, and they sped into the castle. Soon they reached a big wall made out of solid chocolate.

Ralph raised his fists and started smashing at the chocolate wall. Vanellope waited for just the right moment. Then, closing her eyes, she glitched over to the other side of the wall.

"Ha!" Vanellope said. She tapped Boo on the shoulder. "Got you!"

Fireworks went off and sirens blared. Vanellope and Ralph had beaten the Halloween bonus level!

A candy-cane doorway suddenly appeared. "Ready to go back to Sugar Rush?" Vanellope asked. Ralph nodded.

"Wait!" Boo Bratley floated up to Vanellope and Ralph. "Please don't go," he said. "Won't you stay for a little while?"

Suddenly, Boo didn't look naughty any more. Now he just looked… lonely.

"You should come with us, Boo," Vanellope suggested.

"Oh, no," Boo replied. "That's very kind of you. But I couldn't possibly leave."

"Wait, I have an idea!" Vanellope said.

A few hours later, the Halloween party was in full swing at Boo Bratley's castle.

"Thank you, Ralph and Vanellope!" Boo said. "This has been the best party ever."

INCREDIBLES 2

Babysitting Mode

Fashion designer Edna Mode wasn't thrilled when Bob Parr, better known as Mr Incredible, asked her to babysit his son Jack-Jack. Edna simply wasn't good with babies. But Jack-Jack was no ordinary baby. As soon as his dad left, Jack-Jack began to float! Edna was delighted and she wondered what else he could do.

Edna caught up with the Super baby near her lab. Jack-Jack smiled and pointed at his new discovery. He had found the security system for Edna's testing room and the alarm began to beep. In the blink of an eye, Jack-Jack morphed into a pint-sized Edna and the alarm stopped!

Edna marvelled at the miniature version of herself; she had never seen anything so extraordinary. Inside the lab, Jack-Jack discovered some of the Supersuits Edna had designed. He tried on bits and pieces of many different costumes – he even fashioned a cape for himself. "No capes!" Edna said, reminding the baby of her one and only design rule.

However, Jack-Jack loved the cape and didn't want to take it off. He got so angry that he turned into a little monster!

Edna didn't panic, she was used to working with Supers of all kinds. She wondered if music would help Jack-Jack change back into a baby. Edna played Beethoven for the little monster and it worked! Jack-Jack transformed back into an adorable baby.

But suddenly, one Jack-Jack multiplied into two… three… four… five Jack-Jacks!

Edna changed the music to Mozart. Success! All the Jack-Jacks merged back into one baby. He began to giggle as he watched his bottle heat up on the stove… WHOOSH! Jack-Jack burst into flames! Edna remained calm, she had seen it all before.

When she'd put out the flames, Edna told Jack-Jack a story about the adventures of his family, the Incredibles, and their heroic little baby who used his amazing powers to save the day! Before long, Jack-Jack drifted off to sleep.

When Bob arrived the next morning to pick up his son, he asked Edna, "How much do I owe you?"

"Babysitting this one," replied Edna. "I do for free, dahling."

Sweeter Than Clover

"Hi, Bambi," said a soft voice. Bambi looked up from the grass he was eating. Standing there was the pretty young fawn he had met that spring.

"Hi, Faline," Bambi said. "It's nice to see you!"

"It's nice to see you, too," Faline said shyly.

"Faline!" a young male deer called across the meadow. "Come over and play with me!"

Bambi's eyes narrowed. He didn't like the idea of Faline going off to play with someone else.

"No, don't go," he said. *But what can I say to make her stay?* he wondered. Suddenly, Bambi had an idea.

"I want to show you something special," he told her.

"Something special?" asked Faline.

"I know where to find the sweetest clover you'll ever taste," Bambi said. Thumper had shown him exactly where to find it.

"Where?" asked Faline.

"Just follow me!" exclaimed Bambi.

He led her across the meadow to the babbling brook. Then he followed the brook all the way up a steep, grassy hill. Finally, they came to a big waterfall.

"The sweet clover is right here by this weeping willow tree," said Bambi. He couldn't wait to share it with Faline.

But when they got to the tree, there wasn't one single clover blossom left.

"Oh, that Thumper!" complained Bambi. He shook his head. He felt very silly. He'd brought Faline all this way, and now he had nothing special to share with her! Bambi looked up at Faline, but something else caught his eye.

"Look," he whispered. "Up in the sky!"

Faline looked up and gasped.

Shimmering bands of colour had formed an arch over the waterfall.

"It's so beautiful," whispered Faline. "I've never seen anything like it."

"Neither have I," said Bambi. "But I remember hearing my mother talking about it. I think it's called a rain… bow."

"It's wonderful!" cried Faline.

"I'm glad you think so," said Bambi, a little relieved. "But I'm sorry you came all this way for no clover."

"Oh Bambi," said Faline. "I came because I wanted to be with you. And besides, a rainbow is a much sweeter surprise than some silly old clover, anyway!"

We're Going on a Picnic

"Cap'n?" Mr Smee knocked softly on Captain Hook's door. There was no answer. The chubby first mate pushed his way inside, carrying a breakfast tray. "I've got breakfast, Cap'n."

"I'm not hungry!" Captain Hook replied. "Go away!"

"But, Cap'n, you have to eat." Smee was getting worried. The captain hadn't eaten in days. In fact, he hadn't even got out of bed! "I know you feel bad about Pe—" Smee stopped himself from saying the dreaded name just in time. "That flying boy. And the Croc— I mean, that ticking reptile, too."

Captain Hook was really angry about being beaten by Peter again. Even worse, Peter had helped put the crocodile right back on Captain Hook's trail. "But we haven't seen hide or scale of either of them for a week. I think the coast is clear."

There was no reply from Captain Hook.

Smee thought for a minute. "I know how to cheer you up!" he cried. "We'll have a nice old-fashioned picnic! Won't that be lovely?"

Again, silence from Captain Hook.

"Ah-ah-ah! No arguments!" Smee left the breakfast tray and hurried down to the galley. A picnic on Mermaid Island was just what the doctor ordered!

When the picnic basket was packed, Smee called down to Hook, "It's time to go, Cap'n!"

After a while, Captain Hook finally appeared on deck, blinking in the sunlight. "Fine," he said grumpily. "But I know I'm not going to have fun!"

Smee let the rowing boat down into the water, and Hook began to climb down the rope ladder. Once he was safely inside the boat, Smee picked up the picnic basket.

Tick-tock, tick-tock, tick-tock!

"Smee!" cried Hook. "Help me!"

Smee peeked over the side of the ship. The Crocodile was about to take a bite out of the rowing boat! In a panic, he threw the only thing he had to hand – the picnic basket. It landed right in the Crocodile's open mouth. The Crocodile stared at Smee in surprise. Then, without a sound, it slipped back under the water.

"Next time you have any smart ideas about cheering me up," said the captain, glaring at his first mate, "keep them to yourself!"

Riley's Haunted Halloween

It was autumn in San Francisco and everyone was looking forward to Halloween. Everyone, that was, except for Riley. She was finding it hard to get into the Halloween spirit.

One morning at breakfast, Riley told her parents that she would be giving Halloween a miss that year. "I'm getting a little old for trick-or-treating, anyway," she said.

"Whatever you think is best, Riley," Riley's dad said. "But I bet there are some other new girls who feel the same way."

"Isn't there another new girl in class? Faye? I bet she'd like to go trick-or-treating, too," Riley's mum added.

That week at hockey practice, Faye bounded over to Riley. "Hey!" she said. "Do you wanna hang out on Friday? You know, for Halloween?"

Riley smiled. "Well, I'm not sure if I'm up for trick-or-treating, but would you want to check out the haunted house?"

Faye nodded. "That sounds like fun!"

The days flew by, and soon it was Halloween. When Riley arrived at the haunted house, she found Faye waiting for her. "Ready to go inside?" Faye asked.

Riley nodded. At the door, a vampire greeted the girls. "Velcome to my lair! Please,

von't you enjoy a nice treat?"

The woman held out a dark box. Inside were what felt like eyeballs!

The girls giggled and squealed. Suddenly, a man in a furry werewolf costume jumped out at them. Riley and Faye laughed and ran from the room.

The next room was a giant mirror maze! Faye and Riley practised their most ferocious pirate faces.

"Hey, thanks for inviting me out tonight," Riley said. "I almost skipped Halloween this year."

"No way! Me too," Faye said. "But then my parents kinda hinted that I should invite you out for Halloween."

"Wait! My parents told me to invite you out for Halloween," Riley said.

"Hmm. I think we've been tricked!" Faye said. Then she smiled. "Maybe parents do know best after all. But don't tell my mum I said that!"

Riley grinned at her new friend. "Hey, as long as we're dressed up anyway, want to do a little trick-or-treating?"

"That sounds great!" Faye said. Then, linking arms, the two set out to get sweets!

For Old Time's Sake

Prince John had taken advantage of the people of the kingdom while his brother, King Richard, was away at war. He had taxed them until no one had any money – and he had it all! But at last, good King Richard had returned to Nottingham and sentenced greedy Prince John and his cronies, the Sheriff of Nottingham and Sir Hiss, to hard time in the rock mines.

The king summoned Robin to the castle one day soon after his return. "Brave Robin Hood," he said, "in recognition of all you have done to defend and protect them while I was gone, I ask if you would do the honour of returning this money to the citizens of Nottingham, to whom it rightfully belongs."

Robin Hood beamed. "Your Majesty," he replied, "it would be my honour."

The next day, at the appointed time, Robin Hood arrived at the castle, ready to perform his duty. He found King Richard waiting for them just inside the main gate. Next to the king was a waggon overloaded with bags of gold coins.

Robin Hood smiled and looked at the waggon. He looked at Little John. He looked at the king. He looked back at the waggon. Then his smile faded.

"Something doesn't feel right," Robin Hood said, turning to face Little John. "Something is… missing."

"Missing?" Little John said, surprised.

"Of course!" Robin Hood cried. For all those years under Prince John's rule, he had robbed from the rich to give to the poor. That was his thing. Giving to the poor without the robbing from the rich part felt somehow… incomplete. Now that generous King Richard was back, there would be no need to rob from the rich.

Naturally, thought Robin, *that was a good thing. And yet… it was the end of an era.*

"Your Majesty," Robin Hood said to the king, "I don't suppose you could make this handing over of the money a bit more… oh, I don't know… challenging?"

King Richard wrinkled his brow. "Challenging?" he replied, puzzled.

Robin Hood turned to Little John, who also looked confused. "What do you say? One last heist… for old times' sake?"

Show Time

Andy's toys had just moved into their new home in Bonnie's room. Dolly had a plan to help everyone get to know one another better. "Let's have a talent show!" she said.

All the toys were excited. But as they started practising, Buzz stood by himself. His friends all seemed to know what to do, but he wasn't sure. He wanted to do something truly spectacular – something that would impress Jessie.

Buzz noticed Hamm and Buttercup working on their comedy routine. Buzz knew Jessie loved a good joke. Grabbing Woody's hat, he shouted, "Howdy partners, I'm Sheriff Woody. Did you know there's a snake in my boot?"

"I don't know about sounding like Woody," said Hamm with a smirk, "but you definitely sound wooden."

Buzz wasn't listening, though. He'd noticed that Mr Pricklepants and the Aliens were doing a play. *Jessie loves to watch plays*, Buzz thought. The Aliens were very excited about their show. Mr Pricklepants was the director.

"There are plenty of parts for all," Mr Pricklepants said. "We're doing Romeo and Juliet!"

Buzz wanted to change the play so it was set in space! But Mr Pricklepants didn't think that was such a good idea.

"Hey, guys! Time to start the talent show!" shouted Dolly.

Up on the stage, Bullseye turned on the music. A lively tune filled the room. Suddenly, Buzz's whole body shook. It was as if the music was taking over his body! Unable to control himself, Buzz started dancing. He couldn't stop! He danced straight to Jessie. Jessie grinned.

She knew exactly what had happened – the music had switched Buzz into his Spanish mode! "It's okay, Buzz," she whispered. "Just go with it!"

Buzz smiled shyly back at Jessie. "Um, well then," he said. "May I have this dance?"

Jessie nodded and the two danced across the stage and smiled at each other. All their friends cheered. When the music ended, Buzz and Jessie took a bow together. Buzz was beaming. He'd finally impressed Jessie, and discovered a talent he never knew he had!

Puppy Trouble

Nanny was watching all fifteen Dalmatian puppies.

"Let's get Nanny to take us for a walk!" Lucky said.

Nanny turned and saw fifteen puppies holding their leads in their mouths.

"Oh, all right, little ones," she said with a laugh.

When they reached the park, Nanny unhooked their leads and breathed a sigh of relief as the puppies scampered off to play. They were so busy playing that they didn't see Lucky chase a butterfly over the top of a wall and disappear.

Lucky landed in the back of a fire engine as it started speeding down the road!

"Woof! Woof!" Lucky barked. "I'm a fire dog!"

Lucky enjoyed his ride, but he was glad when the fire engine stopped. He knew that he had to get back to the park, so he jumped down to the ground.

"A puppy!" someone squealed.

Lucky looked up and saw a little girl pushing a doll pram. She stroked him.

"You can be my new dolly," the little girl said as she picked him up and put him in the pram.

Suddenly, the little girl spotted something on the ground. As she bent down to pick it up, Lucky jumped out and ran away as fast as he could.

When he got back to the park, Nanny and his siblings were just leaving. Nanny looked up at him as he approached her.

"Why, hello, little pup," she said to Lucky. "Too bad you can't come home with us – you're not a Dalmatian."

Lucky was confused, but then he spotted his reflection in a puddle. He was covered with dirt. Nanny didn't recognise him!

Lucky looked around the park and had an idea. He ran over to some children who were playing in a fountain. The children giggled as the little Dalmatian splashed about with them, washing off all the dirt.

Then Lucky ran home. He grinned as he spotted Nanny in front of the house, unhooking his brothers' and sisters' leads. He joined them just in time!

Later, when Pongo and Perdita came home, they saw all of the puppies were fast asleep.

"You see?" Pongo whispered to Perdita. "I told you nothing would go wrong."

Happy Halloween

"Boo?" Sulley whispered, poking his head through the door. "Hey, Boo, are you here? I came to wish you a happy Halloween. Boo?"

There was no answer. The big, furry blue monster took one step into the quiet bedroom, then another.

Sulley sighed, his shoulders slumping. "Oh, well. Guess you're not here right now," he murmured. He couldn't help feeling disappointed. He'd been looking forward all day to visiting his favourite human child that evening.

There was no Halloween in Monstropolis, but Sulley knew that it was the one day of the year when human kids actually liked being scared. It seemed like a good day for a visit from a monster – especially a friendly monster.

Sulley yawned. "Guess I could just sit down here and wait," he murmured, sitting on the edge of Boo's bed. His eyes drooped. He leant back on the bed and yawned again.

"Guess I could just rest my eyes for a little..." Sulley mumbled as he drifted off to sleep. Zzzzz.

The next thing Sulley knew, a cool breeze was tickling his fur. He felt someone poking him in the foot. "Not yet, Mike," he grunted. "It's too early to get up for work, I— ahhh!"

He had just opened his eyes. Instead of Mike's familiar round green body, he saw...

"A GHOST!" he shrieked. He leapt up and started to run out of the room to escape the horrifying, flapping white creature standing at the end of the bed.

The ghost giggled. "Kitty?" it said happily.

Sulley stopped in his tracks. "Er, what did you say?"

"Kitty!" the ghost cried again. It reached up, grabbed its ghostly white hood and pulled it back from its face.

When Sulley saw what was underneath the hood, he broke into a smile.

Suddenly, Sulley felt very foolish. He'd completely forgotten that every Halloween, human children dressed up in costumes to try to scare each other.

"Boo!" he exclaimed joyfully, reaching out to hug her. "It's you! Happy Halloween, you little monster!"

Runaway Hippo

"Mmm, crispy, crunchy bugs," said Timon. He was eating breakfast with Simba and Pumbaa. Suddenly, a sad cry came from the jungle.

"The sound is coming from over here," said Pumbaa.

He led them to a muddy pond full of thick vines. In the middle of the swamp was a baby hippo. He was tangled up in vines and half buried in mud.

"Help!" the hippo cried.

When the little hippo saw Simba, he became very frightened. "Oh no, a lion! He's going to eat me!" he cried.

"Take it easy," Simba replied. "These guys have got me on an all-bug diet."

Timon grabbed a vine and swung over to the hippo. He began digging the little hippo out of the mud. Meanwhile, Simba jumped onto the hippo's back and began tearing at the thick vines with his teeth. That made the hippo even more afraid!

"You are trying to eat me!" he cried.

Finally, Simba and Timon got the hippo out. Free at last, the muddy creature started to cry. "P-p-please don't eat me," he said to Simba.

"I'm not going to eat you, I promise," said Simba. "How did you get stuck in the mud?"

"I was angry at my little brother and I bit his tail and made him cry. I was afraid my parents would be upset, so I ran away from home," said the little hippo.

"I'll bet your parents are upset," said Simba, "because you're gone and they're worried about you."

"They won't care," the hippo said.

"Come on," said Simba. He led the little hippo to the edge of the river. When they got there, they could hear the other hippos calling: "Oyo! Oyo! Oyo!"

"Listen!" said the hippo. "Oyo's my name. They're calling me! They miss me!"

"Sure," said Simba. "You can't just run away without being missed. When you're part of a family, no matter what you do, you'll always belong."

"What about your family, Simba?" Timon asked as they watched the little hippo rejoin his family. "Do you think they miss you?"

"I didn't used to think so," Simba replied thoughtfully, "but now I wonder."

The Rivera Family Band

The Rivera shoe workshop was busy as Miguel and his cousins, Abel and Rosa, prepared for the upcoming celebrations for the Day of the Dead. Miguel then had an exciting idea! "Tomorrow is the talent show in Mariachi Plaza," he said. "What if our family performs together in a band?!"

Meanwhile, in the Land of the Dead, someone else was having the very same idea. "What if," pondered Mama Imelda, "for this year's Dia de los Muertos, all the Riveras perform together in the Land of the Living?"

"I think performing together will be fun," agreed Héctor. "Especially now that music has returned to our family."

Back in Santa Cecilia, Miguel, Abel and Rosa were practising playing their instruments. Suddenly, Abuelita appeared, interrupting the rehearsal. "Miguel, what's going on?" she asked.

"We're starting a music group – the Rivera Family Band!" replied Miguel. "Join us. I want the whole family to perform together at the talent show tomorrow."

"I don't think so, mi hijo," said Abuelita.

But Miguel didn't give up. He knew that if he could convince Abuelita to perform, the rest of the family would, too. Later, Miguel went to find Abuelia, and to his surprise she was singing.

"You've got to be part of our band for the talent show!" cried Miguel. "It's a way of remembering and honouring our family."

Abuelita thought for a moment. "Okay, let's find the rest of our family and get the band ready!"

Later that evening, the Riveras walked into town to perform. When the relatives from the Land of the Dead had made their way over the marigold bridge, they were amazed to find the living Riveras singing! They rushed to the stage to join the band. As the living and dead family members performed together, the love and joy could be felt by them all.

"This was a great idea," Héctor whispered to Mama Imelda. She beamed. The feeling of music and love was electric. The moment felt even better than she had imagined.

It was the greatest Dia de los Muertos that any Rivera could remember.

The Wrong Gift

"Wow, Flounder, everyone's here!" cried Ariel. Mermaids and mermen had come from all over the ocean to wish Ariel's sister Aquata a happy birthday. Unfortunately, Ariel still needed to pick out a gift for her sister.

Ariel and Flounder left the party and swam to her secret cave.

"How about this?" asked Flounder, holding a pretty pink flower.

"Too ordinary," said Ariel.

"Or this?" suggested Flounder, nudging a single gold earring.

"Too small," said Ariel. Suddenly, Ariel noticed a music box. "This is it!" she cried. "The perfect gift! I've listened to this one again and again, and it plays a really beautiful song."

Ariel swam back to the celebration. Beside King Triton, Aquata sat on a clamshell. One by one, the guests presented her with their birthday gifts.

While Ariel waited in the queue, Sebastian the crab swam by. "Hello, Ariel," he said. "What gift do you have for Aquata?"

When Ariel proudly told Sebastian, his jaw nearly dropped to the ocean floor.

"Are you out of your mind?" he cried.

Ariel's eyes widened. Sebastian was right! King Triton hated humans. And Ariel was not supposed to have anything from their world. That's exactly why she'd kept her cave a secret!

Suddenly, King Triton's deep voice bellowed, "Ariel, you're next."

Ariel hid the present behind her back.

"What gift do you have for your eldest sister?" asked Triton.

"Uh—" Ariel began.

"A song!" Sebastian announced.

Ariel racked her brain for a song to sing, and then she hit on it! She opened her mouth and sang the melody from the music box.

When she finished, Flounder swam behind her, replacing the gift in her hand with a starfish for Aquata's hair.

"It's beautiful!" said Aquata. "And so was your song!"

King Triton smiled approvingly, and Ariel sighed with relief. How she wished her father would change his mind about humans!

"I'd give almost anything to see what the human world is like," she told Flounder. "Do you think my father will ever understand?"

"Maybe he will," said Flounder.

A Not-So-Relaxing Holiday

No doubt about it: Hercules needed a holiday – badly!

"But what about your training?" argued Phil. "You can't stop now! If you're ever gonna be a god, you've got to train like one!"

"If I don't take a break," said Hercules, "I'm never going to become a god because I'll be so burnt out."

And with that, he put away his dumb-bells and his javelins and rounded up Pegasus.

"We're off to the Greek islands, my friend," he told the winged horse. "Sandcastles, beach blankets, umbrella drinks, here we come!"

And before you could say Mount Olympus, there they were, at the finest resort in the ancient world, soaking up the sun and doing absolutely nothing.

"A hero could get used to this," said Hercules as he bobbed in the water, sipping a smoothie.

Suddenly, a cry rang out from the beach. "Shark! Shark!"

"Shark?" said Hercules. "In the Aegean Sea?"

Sure enough, a big grey dorsal fin was speeding towards the crowded shore!

"Help!" cried the people in the water.

"Help!" cried Hercules… until he realised he was the one who could save them.

He swam up to the shark, grabbed it by the tail and threw it up into the sky, all the way to the Atlantic.

"Phew," said Hercules as the people clapped and cheered.

But not five minutes later, another frightened scream rang out – this time from the hills.

"Volcano!"

Hercules knew what he had to do. He raced around the island until he found the biggest boulder. He rolled it all the way to the top of the mountain and then, with one great push, he tipped it over the edge and into the bubbling mouth of the volcano. The volcano was stopped.

Before any more natural disasters could occur, Hercules decided it was time to pack up and head back home.

"Back so soon, Herc?" asked Phil, pleasantly surprised.

Hercules shrugged. "Let's just say that for a hero, work can sometimes be easier than a holiday!"

Month-O-Grams

"What are you doing, Dot?" Flik asked.

Dot was sitting on the floor surrounded by acorns, leaves, dried flowers, sap and little pots of berry juice.

"I'm making month-o-grams!" she said.

"Oh, right, excellent!" Flik exclaimed. "Month-o-grams, of course!" Then his smile faded. "Uh, Dot? What's a month-o-gram?"

"You've never made a month-o-gram?" Dot asked.

"Apparently not." Flik was beginning to feel sheepish.

"Well, don't worry," Dot told him. "We're in luck! Today's the fifth of the month, and that's exactly when month-o-grams are sent out."

Dot thrust a handful of leaves, some berry ink and a writing splinter at Flik. "Get started!" she said.

"What do I do?" Flik was nervous.

"Just take the leaf." Dot demonstrated. "Then decorate it and write something nice on it."

"Who do you send month-o-grams to?" Flik wanted to know.

"Everybody!" Dot exclaimed. "The Blueberries send them to our family and friends every month to let them know we care about them."

Flik and Dot set to work. Soon they were surrounded by piles of month-o-grams, enough for every ant in the entire colony.

"Flik, it's getting late," Dot said. "We had better start delivering these."

Just then, two worker ants rounded a corner and bumped right into each other. They tumbled down, tangled up in a jumble of legs and antennae.

"Hey, watch where you're going," they growled at each other.

"Let's give them a month-o-gram," Dot whispered.

Dot and Flik walked up to the ants, helped them untangle themselves and handed each of them a month-o-gram of his own.

"Happy November!" Flik and Dot cheered.

The ants smiled broadly. They hugged Dot. They hugged Flik. They hugged each other, and then they strolled off together, leg in leg.

"See!" Dot told Flik. "It works!"

Flik and Dot went to make the rest of their deliveries. They handed a month-o-gram to every ant they saw, spreading happiness and cheer throughout all of Ant Island.

Wild Life

Tod the fox had just arrived at the game reserve, a vast, beautiful forest where wild animals were protected from hunters. His kind owner, Widow Tweed, had brought him there to keep him safe.

At first, Tod didn't understand why Widow Tweed had abandoned him in the middle of this strange forest, alone and afraid. But she had seemed to be as sad about leaving him as he was about being left.

The first night was dreadful. It had poured with rain, and though he tried to find shelter in different hollows and caves, they were always inhabited by other animals. There was no room for the poor, wet little fox.

But the next morning, things started to look up. Tod met a pretty young fox named Vixey. She showed him round the forest, which had many beautiful waterfalls and streams full of fish.

"I think I'm going to like it here, Vixey," said Tod.

Having lived his whole life with Widow Tweed, he had never met another fox before, let alone one as lovely as Vixey. But Vixey had lived the life of a wild fox, and she knew more about the world than Tod.

"You must be very careful, Tod," she warned him. "Remember, we're foxes, and we have many enemies. You must always be on the alert for danger!"

"Come on, Vixey," scoffed Tod. "We're in a game reserve! What could possibly happen to us here?"

Suddenly, a huge shadow fell over the two foxes. A look of great fear crossed Vixey's face.

Turning round slowly, Tod saw why. A huge bear was standing up on its hind legs. And it was staring straight at them!

"Run!" yelled Vixey.

Tod didn't need to be told twice. The two foxes dashed away from the bear, scampering over hills, racing through a hollow tree and jumping over a narrow stream. When they were well away from the bear, they stopped and leant against a rock, panting hard.

"Okay," Tod said when he had caught his breath a bit. "I see what you mean about the dangers, Vixey. I promise to be careful."

"Mmm-hmm," she replied. Then she smiled. "Come on," she said to Tod. "Let's go fishing!"

Lights Out!

Wasabi was hard at work in his lab when, suddenly – BANG! The lights went out.

"I must have blown a fuse," Wasabi told his friends.

Wasabi looked around. "I'll go to the basement and check the fuse box," he said. But he didn't move.

Wasabi wasn't a fan of dark places. And the basement was definitely dark!

Hiro could tell Wasabi was nervous. "We'll all go to the basement," he said.

Wasabi grabbed the laser he'd been working on and he and his friends headed downstairs.

A long row of high windows lined one wall, with the fuse box underneath. Wasabi stepped closer. Then he gasped. There was something outside the windows!

"Wasabi?" came a strange voice from outside. "Is that you? Wasa-a-a-a-bi?"

Just then, a branch crashed through the window. A whoosh of air rushed through the room, slamming the door shut.

Honey Lemon grabbed a chem-ball and threw it at the broken window. In no time at all, the hole was sealed.

Fred tugged at the door handle. "It's locked," he said. "We can't get out."

Wasabi flipped the switch and the lights flickered on. In the corner, he saw a spare optical amplifier. Quickly, he finished his laser. Then he used it to cut a large space out of the closed door.

Together, the gang rushed outside into the wet, windy night. From around the corner, the same eerie voice called out.

"I think the voice is being distorted by the wind," Hiro said. He held up a voice-enhancement device he had been working on. "This should help."

As the voice came again, Hiro paused. "That sounds like—"

"Aunt Cass!" Wasabi said.

Aunt Cass held an umbrella over her head, shielding herself from the rain.

"It was getting late. I figured you guys might be working through dinner, so I brought you something to eat."

Wasabi gave Aunt Cass a hug. "I'm so glad you're not a bad guy!" he cried.

Just then, the rain stopped, the wind died down and the stars came out.

Baymax scanned Wasabi. "You are no longer afraid. I will make a note of this. Friends and food. They are the perfect cure."

Mango Hunting

Once upon a time, long before Mowgli came to the jungle, Bagheera the panther met Baloo the bear for the first time. This is how it happened.

Bagheera was younger then, but no less serious. One day, Bagheera was edging along the branch of a mango tree leaning out over a river. There was one perfectly ripe mango right at the end of the branch, and Bagheera loved mangoes.

The only problem was that the branch was slender, and when Bagheera moved towards the end of it, it began to creak and bend alarmingly.

Bagheera, crouched on the middle of the branch, was just coming up with a clever plan when he heard a noise. He looked down and saw a great big grey bear. "It looks like you could use a hand," said the bear.

"No, thank you," said Bagheera politely. "I prefer to work on my own."

But the bear paid no heed and began climbing up the tree. "I'll tell you what," huffed the bear. "I'll just sit at the base of that branch and grab your tail. You can climb out and grab the mango, and I'll keep a hold of you in case the end of the branch breaks off."

"No, I don't think that's a very good idea," said Bagheera impatiently. "I doubt this branch can hold both of us any—"

Snap!

The bear had, of course, ignored Bagheera and climbed out onto the branch. And the branch had, of course, snapped under their combined weight. And now a very wet, very unhappy panther sat in the river next to a very wet, very amused bear.

"Oh, ha-ha-ha-ha!" hooted Baloo (for it was Baloo, of course).

"Oh, come now," he said, seeing how angry Bagheera was, "it's not a total loss, you know." Baloo held up the broken branch with that perfect mango still hanging from the end of it.

"I'll tell you what," said the bear, "let's go climb onto that rock and dry off in the sun while we eat this mango. I'm Baloo. What's your name?"

"Bagheera," said the panther as they climbed up onto the warm, flat rock. And then, almost despite himself, he smiled. And then, very much despite himself, he laughed.

And Baloo laughed right along with him.

Don't Mock Jock

Aunt Sarah was visiting, and she had brought her Siamese cats, Si and Am, with her. Before long, Si and Am had found the dog flap that led out to the garden.

"What works for doggies works for kitties, too," hissed Si.

They slunk out into the garden and found a small hole in the garden fence. They poked their heads through the hole and spied Jock snoozing by his kennel.

"Time for a wake-up call?" asked Am. Si smiled and nodded. They squirmed through the hole and stole silently across the grass until they were sitting on either side of the sleeping Jock. Then, at the same moment, they let loose a shrill, ear-splitting yowl.

Jock woke up with a jump. By the time he had identified the culprits, Si and Am were halfway across the lawn, heading for the fence. Jock tore after them, but the cats squirmed through the small hole and out of Jock's reach.

The opening was too small for Jock. He had to be content with sticking his head through and barking at the cats as they strolled casually up the back steps of Lady's house and through the dog flap. Then they collapsed in a laughing fit on the kitchen floor.

"Dogs are so dim-witted," Si cackled.

They waited a while, then crept out through the dog flap again, itching to try their trick a second time.

Peeking through the hole in the fence, Am and Si spied Jock sleeping in front of his kennel again.

But this time Jock was ready for them. When the cats got within five feet of him, the feisty Scottie leapt to his feet and growled. The cats jumped in shock, turned round and raced for the fence, only to find the way blocked by Jock's friend, Trusty the bloodhound, who stood, growling, between the cats and the hole.

Jock and Trusty chased Si and Am round Jock's garden until Jock was confident they had learnt their lesson. Then they allowed the cats to retreat through the hole in the fence.

This time, Si and Am didn't stop running until they were through the dog flap and safely inside.

And inside is where they stayed!

Pooh Welcomes Winter

Pooh had heard that Winter was coming soon, and he was very excited about having a visitor. Pooh and Piglet decided to throw a party to welcome Winter to the Hundred-Acre Wood. The two friends set off to tell everyone.

Outside, it was snowing. They met Tigger along the way, and they walked to Kanga and Roo's house together. They all decided to go by sledge to the party. Owl landed on a branch overhead.

"Winter has arrived!" he declared. "I heard Christopher Robin say so."

Pooh told Owl about the party, and then they all jumped on the sledge and slid down the hill towards Christopher Robin's house together.

"There's Winter!" Tigger cried. "Tiggers always know Winter when they see him. That big white face – that carroty nose. Who else could he be?" said Tigger.

"Well," said Pooh, "he looks shy. We should be extra friendly." He walked right up to Winter. "How do you do? We are throwing a party in your honour."

But Winter did not say anything.

"Oh d-d-dear," said Piglet. "He's frozen!"

"Quick!" cried Tigger. "We'd better get him to the party to warm him up."

They hoisted Winter onto the sledge. When they slid up to Pooh's house, the others were already there. Owl had hung a big friendly sign over Pooh's door. It said, *Welcome Winter*. Pooh and Tigger wrestled Winter off the sledge.

Just then, Christopher Robin tramped up to the door in his big boots. "Has anyone seen my snowman?" he asked.

"No," said Pooh glumly, "but we brought Winter here for a special party. He doesn't seem to like it."

Christopher Robin laughed. "Silly old bear!" He explained to Pooh that Winter was not a person, it was a season. A time of year for cold snow, hot chocolate, warm fires and good friends.

Pooh scratched his nose thoughtfully. "Yes, I see now," he said. "Of course, I am a bear of very little brain."

With Christopher Robin's help, Pooh put the snowman back where it belonged. He and his friends decided to have the party anyway to celebrate winter. So everyone sang songs and danced round the snowman until they couldn't dance any more. What a party!

Around the World

"I can't believe it!" the Genie shouted as he sped away from Agrabah. "I'm freeeeeeee!"

Now that the Genie didn't have to hang around in his lamp any more, he couldn't wait to see the world. First he transported himself to the Great Wall of China. "Ah!" he exclaimed as he enjoyed the view of the Chinese countryside. "Now, this is what I call a wall! Eh, Al?"

The Genie looked round, and then laughed at himself. Aladdin couldn't answer. He was back in Agrabah.

"Oh, well." The Genie scratched his head. "Now what? I know!"

A second later, he was in India, staring at a magnificent palace. It was big. It was white. It was an awful lot like the Sultan's palace back in Agrabah.

The Genie shrugged. Not every place could be totally new and different. But for his next destination, he wanted a real change of pace.

The Genie went to the Amazon rainforest, the Sahara Desert and Mount Olympus. But as he leant against a column of the Parthenon at the Acropolis, he couldn't help thinking that his travels weren't quite all he had expected them to be.

"It's like there's something missing, you know?" he commented to a passing eagle.

The eagle soared up into the sky, not seeming to have any answers. The Genie sighed. What was wrong with him? Why wasn't he having more fun?

"Al would probably know," he muttered. "He has a knack for figuring things out. He and that crazy little monkey, Abu. And, of course, Princess Jasmine – now she's a smart cookie—"

The Genie gasped, realising the answer had been right there in front of him all along.

"That's it!" he cried. "That's what's missing – friends!"

Being free and travelling was fun. But all the interesting and exotic sights in the world couldn't offer the one thing that Agrabah had – the Genie's best friends.

He laughed out loud. Now that he was free to do anything he wished, he knew exactly what he wanted to do next. Gathering his suitcase, he sped towards the horizon.

"Next stop, Agrabah!" he cried.

Sunnyside Boot Camp

Early one morning, Buzz and Rex arrived at Sunnyside Daycare. As soon as it was safe, they popped out of Bonnie's backpack. Even though they lived with Bonnie now, Buzz and Rex still liked to come and visit the toys at Sunnyside.

Buzz greeted Sarge and asked how things were going. Sarge told Buzz he wished he had more soldiers.

"There are recruits all around you," Buzz said. "Let's have a boot camp."

"I have lots of boots in my wardrobe!" Ken cried. He ran off to get them before anyone could explain what a boot camp really was!

During the children's nap time, the toys sneaked outside and started training. Sarge ordered everyone onto the bouncy cars in the playground. Rex hopped on one and started rocking it slowly. Big Baby joined Rex and rocked it faster!

"Too fast!" cried Rex. "Stop!"

But when Big Baby stopped rocking, Rex went flying! He landed on top of the climbing frame! Sarge and Buzz had a new mission: to rescue Rex.

"We're going to have to work together if we're going to save him," Buzz said.

All the toys agreed to help – except Ken. "These are vintage," he said, pointing down to his boots.

The other toys made themselves into a tower, but it was too short to reach Rex! They needed Ken's help.

Ken thought for a moment, then nodded. "Fashion has never held me back before!"

He quickly removed his boots and climbed to the top of the tower. But he still couldn't reach Rex!

Then Ken had an idea. "Stretch," he called, "hand me my 1972, cherry-red, striped platform boots!" He put them on and reached out to Rex. "Gotcha!" said Ken.

"We did it!" cheered the toys.

"Good work, troops," said Sarge. "Mission accomplished."

It was time for Buzz and Rex to go. They said goodbye to the other toys, but Buzz couldn't find Ken. Finally, he spotted him. "Thanks for your help today," Buzz said. "You're a great soldier!"

"Thanks, Buzz. But great doesn't cut it," said Ken. "Once I finish designing our new army boots, we'll be fabulous!"

Variety is Best

"What in the world is that?" The Queen of Hearts stopped short. It was a crisp autumn day, and she was taking a stroll in the royal gardens.

"What? What is it, Your Majesty?" several of the queen's servants cried.

The queen pointed to a tree. "Look!" she commanded. "That leaf. It's red!"

"Yes, my dear," the king said calmly. "You see, it's autumn, when many leaves change colour."

The servants quivered, waiting for the queen's usual cry: OFF WITH THEIR HEADS! But instead, the queen… smiled!

"Red," she murmured. She looked down at her own red outfit. "Yes, perhaps this tree is on to something. Red is a fine colour for just about anything." She cleared her throat. "From now on, I want everything to be red!"

The servants nodded and ran off in a tizzy. Soon everyone was busy painting things red.

Later, the Queen of Hearts went for another stroll with the king. "Look, my dear," the king said. "Everything is red, just as you wished."

The queen looked around. The leaves were red. The trunks of the trees were red. The grass was red. Even the castle was red! The queen frowned. Somehow, all the red didn't look quite as wonderful as she'd expected.

"Hmmph," she said. "I don't like it. TOO MUCH RED!" She glared at the servants still holding their red paintbrushes.

"Yellow!" she bellowed. "I want everything yellow instead!

"Wait!" the queen shouted. "I changed my mind. GREEN! No more yellow, GREEN!" Out came the green paint.

"No, PURPLE!" Out came the purple paint.

"No, ORANGE! No, BROWN! No, PUCE! MAGENTA! LAVENDER! NAVY! LIME! PINK! SKY BLUE! TAN! SILVER! CYAN! BLACK! GOLD! CREAM! OLIVE! WHITE! BLUUUUUUUE!"

The queen stopped to catch her breath. She looked around. "Now that's more like it," she said to the king. "Plenty of variety, just as it should be."

The king blinked. He stared at the purple leaves, the yellow tree trunks and the pink grass.

"Of course, my dear," he said. "Just as it should be."

The Last Laugh

"Feeling funny today?" Sulley asked Mike on the Laugh Floor one morning.

Mike smiled. "You bet!"

Just then, laughter filled the floor, catching Mike off guard. A group of employees were standing round another monster.

"Who's the comedian?" Mike asked.

"Stan, our newest recruit," Sulley replied. "I'll introduce you."

"Good morning!" Stan said when he saw Sulley.

"Hey, there's someone I'd like you to meet." Sulley turned to Mike. "Mike Wazowski, this is Stanley Stanford. Mike here is our top Laugh Collector."

Mike and Stan shook hands. "What were you guys laughing about before?" Mike asked.

"I was just telling them about the time I met the Abominable Snowman and his mother. I said to him, 'Hey Mr Snowman, where's your mother from?' And he said, 'Alaska.' And I said, 'Hey, don't bother. I'll ask her myself!'"

Everyone burst out laughing all over again – everyone except Mike, who couldn't help feeling green with envy. Mike felt like his position as best Laugh Collector was being challenged!

"Hey, good one, Stan," Mike said when the laughter had died down. "But have you heard the one about the skeleton who decided not to go to the party?" All eyes turned to Mike. "He had no body to go with!" Mike exclaimed.

Everyone laughed. He was back on top!

Soon Mike and Stan were having an all-out joke war. The employees gathered round the two jokesters. Then, suddenly, Mike's mind went blank! He began to jump up and down, hoping to jump-start his brain. As he jumped, Mike landed on the edge of a wheeled cart.

"Waaaaaaah!" Mike cried as the cart took off, rolling across the room and carrying him with it! The employees watched as Mike rolled wildly across the Laugh Floor. They fell down, laughing their heads off! When Mike landed in a pile of cardboard boxes, the joke-off was over. Mike was the winner.

Lucky's Last Laugh

It was getting quite late at Pongo and Perdita's house, but their darling little puppies were still not asleep. That was because Lucky wouldn't stop talking!

"And then," he was saying, "there was the part at the very beginning, when Thunderbolt jumped across that canyon. Whoosh! Like a rocket!"

"Yes, Lucky, we remember," his sister Penny said. "How could we forget? You've reminded us a hundred times!"

"Yeah! It was so great! And then there was that part when—"

"Lucky!" wailed Rolly. "We all watched the same episode of Thunderbolt tonight. You don't have to tell us about it."

"Yeah, I know, but I just wanted to tell you about that great part when Thunderbolt found the little girl, then ran back to tell the sheriff—"

"Lucky! It's late! We want to go to sleep!" barked Patch.

Lucky laid his head on his paws. "Okay," he said. "I'll be quiet."

All the puppies closed their eyes.

"Oh! But what about the part when the sheriff told Thunderbolt to climb up that cliff, and he got to the top, and he grabbed that rope with his teeth and he pulled up the little girl—"

"Lucky!" yelped Pepper. "We don't care about Thunderbolt. Go to bed!"

"Right." Lucky sighed, lying down once again. Then he suddenly sat up. "Wait a sec! Don't care about Thunderbolt?"

"We mean," said Freckles, "that we want you to be quiet so we can go to sleep!"

"You mean," said Lucky, "you don't want me to tell you about the last part where Thunderbolt ran back to the mountains and into that cave and found that amazing thing?"

"Yes!" Lucky's brothers and sisters shouted together.

"Oh. Okay," said Lucky. "Goodnight."

And with that, Lucky closed his eyes. For a minute, everyone enjoyed the silence. Then Penny sat up.

"Hey, wait a minute," she said. "What thing did he find?"

"Yeah," said Patch. "I missed that."

"Me too," said Rolly. "What was it exactly that he found, Lucky? Tell us."

But there was no answer. Lucky was fast asleep. And now the other Dalmatian puppies were wide awake!

My Side of the Story

Perhaps you know the story of how Pocahontas and John Smith made peace between their people. Well, I've got a much more interesting story for you – mine.

My name is Percival, but my friends call me Percy. Once upon a time, I was the pet pug of a very important man named Governor Ratcliffe. I lived a life of luxury. But life felt... well, pretty boring.

That all changed the day we arrived on the shores of America. Ratcliffe was after one thing and one thing only – gold. And Ratcliffe didn't care about the people who lived in this new land.

John Smith cared, but I didn't care much for John Smith. He was always trying to pat me on the head.

Not long after we had arrived in the new land, I was having a bath when suddenly – splash! – a raccoon landed in the water! Well, if there's one thing my mother taught me, it was to avoid all animals without a pedigree. This wild creature was filthy and uncivilised! The raccoon ate my cherries and then ran off. After that, I had one thing on my mind – revenge!

The next time I saw the raccoon, he was eating bones out of my personal bone collection. So I had to chase him – it was a matter of pride! But wouldn't you know it, the brazen little devil trapped me in a hollow log.

That's when I ran into John Smith and Pocahontas. And guess who was with them? That's right. It was that bone-thieving raccoon! He grabbed a little hummingbird and started waving it at me like a sword. It would have been funny if it weren't so annoying!

And then the weirdest thing of all happened – a tree talked to me! Grandmother Willow said I shouldn't chase Meeko. By chasing him, I had started trouble between us; now it was time to stop the fighting. Of course, I understood immediately.

It took the humans a little longer to get the picture, but it all worked out okay in the end. I decided I didn't need my fancy, highfalutin life, so I became a settler and stayed with my new friends! John, however, had to go back to England.

I knew he would miss me. So when he reached out to pat my head, I actually let him.

For the Love of Racing

Cruz Ramirez and Lightning McQueen sprinted round Willy's Butte. Cruz used to be a top-notch trainer of next-gen race cars, but now she was a racer and Lightning was her crew chief! They were back in Radiator Springs getting ready for her next big event.

Cruz pushed herself, but got frustrated over silly mistakes. Lightning believed in Cruz. He knew she had all the skills to be a great racer, but was having trouble believing in herself.

"Trust you're the best and let your tyres do the rest!" Lightning told her.

Cruz wanted to believe that... but deep down, she still wondered if she could be the best. She knew she could drive better than this!

Lightning could see that she was pushing herself too hard. "I don't know what's wrong," she admitted.

Lightning and Sally led Cruz to the Hudson Hornet Racing Museum, which showcased mementos, posters and film reels about Doc, the legendary racer.

"Doc helped me see that real racing isn't just about winning," Lightning continued. "It's about teamwork, sportsmanship and enjoying the thrill of doing something you love."

"I've been so focused on my mistakes, I almost forgot how much I love to race," Cruz said with a smile.

As Sally led Lightning and Cruz on a beautiful ride through the mountains of Carburetor County, something shifted in Cruz. It was clear her confidence was growing.

The next morning, Cruz woke up and found a note on her alarm clock. Meet at Flo's.

She arrived to find the whole Radiator Springs gang was there to support her. "You're a part of the Radiator Springs family," said Lightning.

Out on the highway, Lightning called out, "Trust you're the best and..."

"Let my tyres do the rest!" shouted Cruz as she whipped through the turn at top speed.

They came to a stop and looked back to see the gang cheering. "You've got what it takes," said Lightning.

"I sure do," said Cruz. "I have the skills, a crew chief who believes in me... and friends who won't let me forget how much I love racing!"

Lightning smiled. "Spoken like a true race car."

Starry Night

Bonnie was camping out. She gathered her toys and brought them to the garden. Then she carefully set up her tent and arranged the toys inside.

Just then, her mum called to her. "Bonnie! Dinner time!"

"I've got to go and eat my dinner. But I'll be back," Bonnie told the toys.

Left alone in the tent, the toys began to explore.

"This is a right comfortable spot," Jessie said, admiring Bonnie's sleeping bag.

"Yes, the accommodations are quite satisfactory," Mr Pricklepants agreed with a nod.

"Well, shine my spurs!" Woody cried, noticing a camping lantern. He turned it on, and a warm glow lit up the tent. "How about a sing-along," Woody suggested.

Soon all the toys were singing. Then they decided to head outside. They all wanted to explore.

"Look!" Buttercup said.

"The stars are coming out!" Buzz smiled.

"That is the Big Plough – seven stars that form a ladle shape," said Dolly.

Jessie hopped on Bullseye. "I'm gonna look around the garden!" she shouted.

"Follow me!" called Buttercup. "I'll show you the rose bed."

Trixie turned to the other toys. "Who wants to play stuck in the mud?" Before anyone could answer, she tapped Rex with her horn. The rest of the toys began running away as Trixie chased after them.

"I'm wiped out," Hamm said a little later.

"How about a shadow-puppet show?" said Mr Pricklepants.

"Good idea," Woody said, leading all the toys inside the tent.

The toys used Bonnie's torch to create shadow puppets on the wall.

"A sleepover wouldn't be complete without a scary story," Mr Potato Head said. He switched off the torch. "Once there was a toy in a forest. The forest was dark. Very dark."

Suddenly, the toys heard the sound of someone running.

"Ahhh! " Rex shrieked as a huge shadow loomed over the tent. The toys all flopped over and went still. The tent flap opened up.

"I'm back!" Bonnie said, smiling at her toys. "Did you miss me?"

The New Neigh-bour

Pegasus grazed peacefully outside his home. Hercules and Meg had gone to greet their new neighbours, and had left Pegasus behind.

Suddenly, Pegasus heard a soft whinnying. He turned to discover a beautiful mare approaching him. His heart soared. But then Pegasus remembered the time he had been kidnapped by bad guys pretending to be a filly. He was determined not to fall for their trick a second time. He spread his wings and charged, shooing the horse down the hill.

The mare raced past Meg and Herc as they returned home. "Pegasus, what are you doing?" asked Meg. "That's no way to make our neighbours' horse feel welcome."

Pegasus gulped. The beautiful horse who had tried to meet him really was a beautiful horse!

"If I were you, I'd get over there and try to make it up to her," said Hercules.

Within minutes, Pegasus pranced across the neighbours' field, stopped in front of the mare and struck a noble pose. But the lovely horse was unimpressed. She turned so that her tail swished right in Pegasus's face! Herc's horse knew he would have to do something amazing to impress this beauty. He flapped his wings and rose into the air. Then he dipped and swooped and somersaulted across the sky. When the filly started to walk away, he flew alongside her – and crashed right into a tree!

Hercules was watching from the hillside. "Pegasus sure does need some help," he said.

Meg had an idea. "The right gift might convince that mare to forgive him," she said.

She piled a basket high with apples and oats and tied a huge red ribbon round it. But when Pegasus went over to deliver the gift, holding the basket handle in his teeth, the female horse kicked it over.

Finally, Pegasus realised what he had to do. He sheepishly walked over to the filly with his head bowed. Then he gently nudged her with his muzzle.

The filly neighed and nuzzled him back. All she had wanted was for Pegasus to say he was sorry. Now she understood that her new friend had a good heart.

A Cool Contest

Today was the annual ice-carving contest. "Good morning!" Elsa greeted the crowd. "Welcome to the contest! The rules are simple. Each team will have until the sun sets to finish their sculpture. Then I will choose the winners. Good luck!"

Anna and Olaf picked up their tools and together they began chipping away at the ice.

Meanwhile, Kristoff and Sven carefully searched their block of ice for lines and cracks. Kristoff put his ear to the ice and closed his eyes. "Okay, Sven. Now I know where the ice will break!" Kristoff said.

Nearby, Anna saw Kristoff and Sven carefully start to carve their ice. She stopped and looked down at her own block of ice. She and Olaf had been having so much fun chipping away that their ice didn't look like anything.

Anna put down her tools and studied the ice. Suddenly, she noticed all the small cracks in the ice. Now she knew where it would break! The friends picked up their tools and started chipping away again.

The pair's laughter caught Kristoff's attention. Their sculpture looked a little funny, but they seemed to be having a good time. Kristoff looked at his block of ice.

"Maybe we don't need to be so careful,"

Kristoff told Sven. Kristoff used his chisel, and Sven used the sharp points of his antlers. Soon they were laughing, too.

All too soon, the sun set. Elsa looked at Kristoff and Sven's sculpture. She smiled. "It looks like Sven!" she said. "It's too bad you weren't able to finish it."

Next Elsa moved to Anna and Olaf's sculpture. "Well, you finished your sculpture," she said. "But what is it?"

"It's an ice man!" Olaf said.

"Oh, of course," Elsa said politely.

Elsa moved from team to team. Finally, she stopped at Olina and Kai's sculpture. They had carved the castle.

Elsa turned to the crowd. "Olina and Kai are the winners!" she announced.

"You know," Kristoff told Anna, "I bet we could make something great if we worked together."

Anna grinned. "You can listen to the ice…"

"And you can make sure Sven and I don't get too serious," Kristoff added.

The two friends shook hands. They couldn't wait until the next contest!

Fish Food

Figaro the cat was scared. He, Geppetto and Cleo the goldfish had just been swallowed by a whale!

"Don't worry, Figaro," Geppetto said, seeing the cat's worried look. "We'll get out of here somehow – and when we do, we'll keep searching for Pinocchio."

Pinocchio! Figaro growled. After all that Geppetto and the Blue Fairy had done for Pinocchio, he had run away from home without a care in the world. That was how they'd ended up inside the whale! They had been searching for Pinocchio when the whale swallowed their whole boat.

Figaro decided then and there that if they ever found Pinocchio, he would use both of the wooden boy's legs as scratching posts. It would serve him right.

Meanwhile, Geppetto was peering into the puddle of water at the bottom of the whale's stomach. Figaro watched curiously.

"Let's see," Geppetto murmured, bending over and poking at the water. "There must be something in here... aha!" he cried happily. He was clutching a small, soggy clump of seaweed.

Seaweed is fish food, Figaro thought with a scowl. Surely Geppetto didn't expect him to eat that for dinner.

But as he watched, Geppetto carefully divided the seaweed into three portions. He placed one portion in Cleo's bowl. He placed one portion in front of Figaro. The third he kept for himself.

"Let's eat!" Geppetto said, smiling bravely.

Figaro sniffed his seaweed. He stirred it round with his paw. But he just couldn't eat the soggy green stuff. With a twitch of his tail, Figaro turned away.

Geppetto watched the little cat with sad eyes. Figaro sighed. He couldn't help but feel ungrateful.

Reluctantly, Figaro turned back to his dinner. He nibbled at the seaweed. It was cold. It was slimy. But it tasted like... fish!

Figaro gobbled down the rest of his meal. With his belly full, the little cat felt better. He decided that if they found Pinocchio, he would only use one of the puppet boy's legs to sharpen his claws on.

Probably.

Breakfast - O'Malley Style!

"Mama, I'm hungry," said little Marie.

"I know, my darlings," Duchess told her kittens.

The day before, they had walked for hours to reach Paris. Now, this morning, their empty stomachs were rumbling.

"I wish we were at the mansion," said Marie.

"Hey, now," said O'Malley, their alley-cat friend. "Don't you like my attic pad?"

"Yes," said Marie, "but at the mansion, Edgar the butler brings us our breakfast every morning."

"On a golden tray," said Toulouse.

"Oh, I get it," said O'Malley. "Well, I can't give you the four-star treatment, but I can get you breakfast – alley-cat style."

Duchess and her three kittens followed O'Malley into the bright Paris morning. They trotted along until they came to a little café.

"I've got a little arrangement here," O'Malley told Duchess. He led her and the kittens to the back of the café. Then he jumped onto the ledge of a window.

A young woman in a white apron came to the window and cooed, "Bonjour, monsieur."

O'Malley jumped back down and went to the back door. When it opened, the young woman put down a saucer of cream and said, "Here is your breakfast, monsieur."

O'Malley called to Duchess and the kittens. "Pssssst. Come on over."

"You've brought some friends!" the woman said.

The woman brought out two more saucers of cream – big ones. The kittens raced to the plates and began sloppily lapping up the cream.

"Children! Children!" cried Duchess. "Where are your manners?"

The kittens looked up sheepishly, thick cream dripping from their furry chins.

"Thank you, Mr O'Malley," they said. Then Marie kissed him on the cheek!

"Aw, don't mention it," said O'Malley, embarrassed.

"I see I've made a mistake, monsieur," said the young woman in the doorway. "These are not your friends. They are your family!"

Wow, thought O'Malley, *she sure got that wrong!* But then he stopped himself. He did love Duchess and her kittens. Maybe that was what made a family after all.

Pink or Blue?

On the day of Prince Phillip and Princess Aurora's wedding, no one was happier for them than the three good fairies.

"Such a happy day!" exclaimed Flora from a balcony overlooking the crowded ballroom. "Fauna, don't you agree?"

When Fauna didn't answer, Flora looked over to find her weeping. "Fauna, why are you crying?" asked Flora.

Dabbing her eyes, Fauna said, "I love weddings even more than happy endings! Both make me cry with joy!"

"It is a joyful day," said Merryweather. "Everyone in the kingdom is here. And look at all the wedding presents!"

"Oh, my!" said Flora. "It will take days for the bride and groom to open them all."

"Point them out again, dear," Fauna asked Merryweather. "I had tears in my eyes."

Without thinking, Merryweather used her magic wand to point. Zzzing! She accidentally turned all of the white packages her favourite colour, blue.

"Merryweather!" snapped Flora. "Change those packages back this instant."

"I don't know," said Merryweather, tapping her chin. "I like them this way."

"Oh, do you?" said Flora. "Well, look again!"

Using her own magic wand, Flora sent a second blast of magic across the room. Zzzing! Now the wedding presents were her favourite colour – pink!

The two fought for some time, changing the colour of the presents back and forth.

"Now, dears," said Fauna, trying to make peace, "can't you two get along? Today is a happy day!"

Fauna had had enough. Taking out her magic wand, she waved it round in a circle and chanted: "Presents changing pink and blue, wed your colours, then stay true!"

With a final zzzing! Fauna sent her magic spell across the room, and the presents changed one last time.

"What did you do?" cried Flora and Merryweather.

Fauna shrugged. "I simply mixed your colours together and locked them in. Pink-and-blue-striped wrapping paper is all the rage this year," she said. "Now let's all go and eat some wedding cake."

"Wedding cake?" said Merryweather. "Hmm… I wonder what colour the icing will be."

A Friend for Philippe

Belle loved life in the castle with her prince, and she loved her faithful horse, Philippe. Lately, however, Philippe had been acting strangely. Belle decided to try to cheer him up. She asked her friends for some help.

First, Lumiere helped Belle brighten up Philippe's stall. They covered the walls with wallpaper and trimmed them with gold.

"Voilà!" Lumiere cried. "What more could a horse ask for?"

But Philippe just stared sadly out of the window.

Next, Belle treated Philippe to a bath fit for a king. "If this doesn't make him smile," Belle told Chip, "I don't know what will!"

But Philippe was just as glum after his bath – and Belle was just as puzzled. She asked the prince if he had any suggestions.

"A good walk always cheers me up," the prince said.

Belle thought that was a wonderful idea. She rode Philippe to a big, open meadow, but he wasn't interested in galloping.

"Oh, Philippe," Belle said in despair. "I just don't know what else to do!"

Suddenly, Philippe's ears pricked up. Belle barely had time to grab the reins before he charged off!

Before long, they emerged into a clearing filled with wild, beautiful horses! Philippe whinnied, and several of the horses answered him. Finally, Belle realised what Philippe had wanted – to be with other horses!

All afternoon, Belle watched Philippe race and play. Soon Philippe had even made a friend. The two horses grazed, chased each other round the clearing and dozed together in the warm sun.

All too quickly, the day was over and the sun began to set. Belle put Philippe's saddle on him and they went back to the castle.

Soon Belle heard the sound of hooves behind them. Philippe's new friend was following them home!

"Welcome to our castle!" Belle told the new horse when they arrived. Then she hurried off to tidy up the stall next to Philippe's.

"There," she said when she was finished. "Now this looks like a stable where a horse – or two! – could really live happily ever after!"

And that is exactly what they did.

Disney
Lilo & Stitch

The Meaning of Thanksgiving

"Here, Stitch," Lilo said. "Hold up this Pilgrim man while I stick up his wife."

Stitch was confused. He was hungry and didn't understand why Lilo was running round hanging up decorations instead of eating.

"It's Thanksgiving," Lilo said. "You're supposed to be very, very hungry before we eat. Just like the Pilgrims, you know."

Now Stitch was even more confused.

"That's where Thanksgiving comes from," Lilo explained. "The Pilgrims were hungry, so the Indians made them a big dinner, and so they were all thankful."

"Pilgrims?" Stitch repeated uncertainly.

"Pilgrims," Lilo said firmly. "The Pilgrims were some people who came across the ocean in these big boats, and—"

Just then, Lilo had an idea. "I know how to explain it!" she cried. "Stitch, the Pilgrims were sort of like you – remember how you came to Earth, far, far away from your old planet, in a spaceship?"

Stitch nodded. He remembered that very well.

"Okay," Lilo said, "and remember how you were lost and all alone, and you weren't sure what to do, and everything seemed strange and unfriendly, and then you joined our family, and it was okay?"

"Family!" Stitch cried happily. He nodded again.

"Well, that's the same thing!" Lilo said. "You're like a Pilgrim. And now you're thankful to be here, right?"

"Right," Stitch agreed.

"That's how the Pilgrims felt, too," Lilo said. "They were thankful. So now we celebrate Thanksgiving to remember that. Get it?"

Stitch nodded. He understood about being thankful. He still wasn't sure why Lilo was hanging up so many decorations, and he still wasn't sure why they had to wait so long to eat the turkey he could smell cooking in the kitchen, but he decided it didn't matter. When Lilo left the room to get more decorations, Stitch took a small bite out of the cardboard Pilgrim. By the time Lilo returned, the whole Pilgrim was gone. She looked around in confusion.

"What happened to the Pilgrim?" she asked Stitch.

Stitch grinned at her. There was a tiny piece of the Pilgrim's hat stuck in his teeth. Lilo stared at it suspiciously.

"Happy Thanksgiving!" Stitch cried.

Donald Goes Camping

Uncle Donald was taking Huey, Dewey and Louie camping! When they arrived in the woods and found a camping spot, Huey and Louie helped their uncle put up the tent while Dewey read from a camping guidebook.

"The guidebook says to keep the lid on the cool box when we're not using it," said Dewey.

"I know everything there is to know about camping," Donald said. "The food will be all right on the picnic table."

Just then, two squirrels scampered down from a tree and snatched a bag of peanuts. "Hey!" Donald shouted. "Come back here!"

"The guidebook says it's good to share with little animals," said Louie.

"I don't care what the book says. Those are my peanuts!" replied Donald.

The two squirrels ran along the tree branches and chattered at Donald again. This time, they seemed to be laughing at him. "I'll get even with you!" Donald yelled. He climbed up the tree towards the squirrels. Just as he was about to grab them, they leapt onto a thin branch.

"The book says to stay off small branches!" Dewey called out to his uncle.

CRRRACK! Suddenly, the branch broke and Donald fell into the river.

"Help!" Donald cried. "Pull me out!" He tried to swim towards land, but the current was too strong. He spotted a rock and grabbed on to it. "Do something!" he called to his nephews. "Look in the guidebook!"

Huey, Dewey and Louie started flipping through the book. They only looked up when the squirrels returned – with a beaver! The beaver waddled to a tree that stood beside the river and began to gnaw at it.

"He's trying to help!" Dewey said. "If the tree falls into the river, it might be long enough to reach Uncle Donald."

A few minutes later, the tree fell over with a crash. Donald climbed along the tree trunk towards dry land. Once safely ashore, Donald ran towards his car.

"Where are you going?" his nephews called.

An hour later, Donald returned. His car was filled with presents for the beaver that had helped him, and for all the other animals, too. They were delighted and munched on their treats!

Disney
Peter Pan

Where's Tink?

Peter Pan was in a hurry to meet Tinker Bell. They had a date for a game of tig. "Tink!" he called as he arrived at his hideout. He took off his hat and placed it on the table. "I'm home!"

But there was no reply.

How strange, thought Peter. Tinker Bell was never late.

Peter called her name again as loudly as he could. But still there was no answer.

"Wake up! Wake up!" he shouted to the Lost Boys, who were napping in hammocks. "Tinker Bell is missing!"

"Where would she go?" asked Tootles.

Peter thought for a moment. He knew that Tinker Bell liked to fly around Never Land. And she really liked paying visits to other fairies. But not when she had a game of tig to play with Peter.

"The question," Peter Pan finally declared, "is not where would she go, but who could have taken her!"

"Oooh," the Lost Boys shuddered.

"Do you mean…" the Raccoon Twins began.

"Indians?" finished Peter. "I certainly do. I can see it right now: while you were sleeping, a whole band crept into our hideaway and stole our Tinker Bell away."

Then Slightly spoke up. "Or what if it was—"

"Pirates!" cried Peter. "Of course! Those dirty, rotten scoundrels! It would be just like them to lure Tinker Bell outside, ambush her, kidnap her and hold her for ransom!

"Men!" Peter cried. "We can't just stand here while Tinker Bell suffers in the grimy hands of bloodthirsty pirates. Why, she could be in mortal danger! I hereby declare that a rescue mission be formed at once. What do you say? Are you with me?"

"Hoorah! Hoorah!" the boys cheered.

Suddenly, Peter heard a sound.

Ring-a-ling! Ring! Ring! Rrrring!

"Tink!" Peter exclaimed as his missing – and furious! – friend shot up into the air.

"Where have you been? You had me worried sick!"

Tinker Bell just jingled angrily at Peter. She hadn't been kidnapped. She'd been trapped underneath Peter's hat the whole time!

Hanukkah Fun

"Happy Hanukkah, Pooh Bear!" Roo exclaimed as he opened the door for his first guest. It was the first night of Hanukkah, and Roo and Kanga were having all of their friends over to join in some Hanukkah fun.

"Happy Hanukkah, Roo!" Pooh replied. Just then a delicious smell wafted under his nose.

"Something smells yummy!" Pooh cried.

Kanga was making little potato pancakes called latkes, a special Hanukkah treat. "Try to be patient, Pooh," Kanga said with a smile. "We'll have these latkes a little bit later."

Before long, Piglet, Eeyore, Rabbit, Tigger and Owl had also arrived, and it was time to light the menorah.

"First," Kanga explained, "we light this centre candle, called the shamash. Then we use the shamash to light one other candle for the first night of Hanukkah."

Tigger noticed that there weren't any candles in the other seven candleholders of the menorah. "When do we light the other candles?" he asked Kanga.

"Well, Tigger," Kanga said, "Hanukkah lasts for eight nights. So tomorrow, on the second night, we will light two candles with the shamash. On the third night, we will light three

candles, and so on… until, on the eighth night, we will light all the candles!"

Just then Pooh said, "Um, Kanga? Is it a little bit later now?"

Kanga understood: Pooh was hungry for a latke! Kanga brought the potato pancakes to the table, and everyone enjoyed the delicious treats.

When they were all eaten, Roo said, "Now let's spin the dreidel!" He got out a four-sided clay top. Roo explained the rules, then each player took turns spinning the dreidel. Depending on what side the dreidel landed on, the player might win or lose treats.

"This is fun!" Piglet exclaimed. "And to think, there are seven more nights of Hanukkah!"

"Hey, Mama," said Roo, "there are eight of us and eight nights of Hanukkah. Can our friends come over every night of Hanukkah and take turns lighting the menorah?"

Everyone, including Kanga, thought that was a wonderful idea. So that was exactly what they did.

Winter Nap

Bambi nosed under the crunchy leaves, looking for fresh grass. There was none. He looked up at the trees, but there were no green leaves there either.

"Don't worry, Bambi," Thumper said when he saw the confused look in Bambi's eyes. "We find what we can when we can, and we always make it until spring."

Bambi sighed and nodded.

"Besides, it's better to be awake than napping all winter. Yuck!" Thumper hated going to bed, even at bedtime.

"Napping?" Bambi didn't know that some animals slept through the winter months.

"Sure. You know, like Flower and the squirrels and the bears. Haven't you noticed the chipmunks putting their acorns away the past couple of months?"

Bambi nodded.

"That's their food for the winter. As soon as it gets cold enough, they'll just stay inside and sleep," Thumper explained to his friend.

"But how will they know when it's time to wake up?"

Thumper tapped his foot. It was a good question. Since he had never slept through the winter, he wasn't sure of the answer.

"Let's go ask Flower," he said.

And so the two friends headed for the young skunk's den.

"Flower, you sleep all winter, right?" Thumper asked.

"It's called hibernation," Flower said and yawned a big yawn.

"Bambi wants to know who wakes you up in the spring," Thumper said.

"You'll be back, won't you, Flower?" Bambi asked worriedly.

The little skunk giggled. "Oh, we always come back. Just like the grass and the flowers and the leaves," Flower explained. "I never thought about what wakes us up. It must be the sun."

Bambi smiled. He didn't know the grass and leaves would come back in the spring, too! He was feeling much better about the forest's winter nap.

Suddenly, Thumper started laughing. He rolled onto his back and pumped his large hind feet in the air.

"What is it?" Bambi and Flower asked together.

"You really are a flower, Flower!" Thumper giggled. "You even bloom in the spring!"

A Party of Three

Widow Tweed hummed cheerfully as she decorated her cottage. Tod, the little fox she had adopted not long before, watched with excitement. This was his first birthday in his new home!

"Now, Tod," said the widow, "who shall we invite to your party?"

Tod jumped on the window sill and looked over at Amos Slade's farm. Then he jumped on the kind woman's lap and gazed up at her with big, sad eyes.

"Oh, Tod! Stop looking at me like that. Well, all right! You can ask Copper over just this once!"

Later that afternoon, Tod invited Copper to the party. "I'm not supposed to leave the farm," Copper explained. "I'll get in trouble with my master."

"Don't worry," Tod said. "I've got it all figured out."

Then Tod headed over to Amos Slade's chicken yard. He ran among the birds, causing them to flap their wings and cluck in panic. That was Copper's signal to bark as loudly as he could. Slade burst out of the cabin just in time to see Copper chasing Tod into the woods.

Copper followed Tod all the way to Widow Tweed's back door.

"Quick, scram!" she said, shooing the two into the cottage.

While Amos Slade wandered around the woods trying to find Tod and Copper, the party festivities at Widow Tweed's were just beginning. The three played hide-and-seek, pin the tail on the donkey and stuck in the mud. Then it was time to cut the cake.

As everyone had seconds, the widow spied Amos Slade coming out of the woods. She let Copper out the back door, where he stood, barking ferociously.

"Good tracking, Copper!" Slade cried. "Did you chase that no-good fox all the way through the woods?"

Copper wagged his tail.

"Copper," the man said, "what's that on your face?"

The hound turned his head and quickly licked the cake crumbs off his muzzle.

"Hmm," said Slade. "Guess I must be seeing things. Let's go home, then, boy."

Inside the cosy cottage, Tod smiled. It had been a wonderful birthday – and sharing it with his best friend had definitely been the icing on the cake!

Buzz's Space Adventure

Bonnie was away and the Peas-in-a-Pod were bored. Buzz knew just what to do. He decided to tell them a story about space!

"Once upon a time," Buzz began, "the evil Emperor Zurg stole a top secret Space Ranger Turbo Suit. Star Command knew I was the only one who could get it back!"

"Wow," said Woody. "I wonder how it feels to be a space hero."

"Me too," said Rex. "Hey, Buzz! Can I be in your story?"

"Sure, why not?" Buzz said, before continuing his story. "I was heading into dangerous space. I knew I needed backup, so I called on First Lieutenant Woody and Second Lieutenant Rex!

"As we touched down on Planet Zurg, we heard a loud humming sound. Suddenly, we spotted an army. Hundreds of Emperor Zurg's loyal Zurgbots were grouped together, humming. I knew that Woody and Rex could take care of the Zurgbots, so I went off to find Zurg's headquarters… and the Turbo Suit!

"I hadn't gone far when I saw a lone Zurgbot. I knew that something strange was happening. Zurgbots rarely travelled alone. His humming sounded odd, almost like a melody.

"'Hold your fire!' the Zurgbot cried. 'My name is Zenny. I'm not like the others!'

"Apparently this Zurgbot also opposed Zurg! But with the entire galaxy at stake, how could I trust him?

"'I will take you to the Turbo Suit,' Zenny promised.

"True to his word, Zenny led me into the heart of Zurg's lair – and to the Turbo Suit. But as I reached for the suit, a band of Zurgbots captured me. They had my lieutenants, too!

"Suddenly, Zurg appeared. Our doom seemed near.

"'Not so fast, Zurg,' a voice called out. It was Zenny!

"Before Zurg could say a word, Zenny began to sing. As his voice grew louder, stalactites fell from the cave's ceiling. They dropped to the floor, trapping Zurg. Zenny freed us and I climbed into the Turbo Suit. With the help of Zenny and my lieutenants, I defeated the Zurgbot army!

"As we headed home, we could see Zenny below, teaching the other Zurgbots to sing. We knew that Planet Zurg would be a happier place from then on. The end."

Go Fish!

"Okay, small fry," said Baloo the bear. "Today I'm going to teach you how to fish like a real bear!"

Mowgli was delighted. He loved his new friend Baloo.

"Now, watch this, kid," said Baloo as they arrived at the riverbank. "All ya gotta do is wait for a fish to swim by, and then—" Whoosh! As quick as a flash, Baloo held a wriggling silver fish in his paw. "Now you try it!" he said to Mowgli.

Mowgli sat very still, waiting for a fish to swim by. Then – splash! – he toppled head first into the water.

"Hmm," said Baloo after he had fished Mowgli out and put him down, dripping. "Maybe I should show you my second technique."

Baloo and Mowgli walked towards another part of the river. This time, the fish could be seen occasionally leaping out of the water as they swam down a little waterfall. Baloo waded a few steps into the water, waited for a fish to jump, then – whoosh! – he swiped a fish right out of the air. "Now you try, buddy."

Mowgli waded in just as Baloo had done. He waited for the fish to jump and then leapt for it. Splash!

"Okay, plan C," said Baloo after he had fished Mowgli out of the water a second time. "I'll take you to the big waterfall. The fish literally fall into your paws. All ya gotta do is reach out and catch one!"

Mowgli followed Baloo to the big waterfall. Sure enough, silvery fish were jumping all the way down the falls. It would be easy to catch one of these! In the blink of an eye, Baloo held up a fish for Mowgli to admire.

"I'm going to do it this time, you watch me, Baloo!" said Mowgli excitedly.

He scrunched up his face with concentration. For an instant, Mowgli actually had a silvery fish in his hands. But a second later, the fish shot out of his grasp and jumped into the water again. Mowgli looked down at his empty hands with a sigh.

"You know what, kid?" said Baloo. "I think you're working too hard. That's not how life in the jungle should be! It should be fun, happy and carefree. So come on. Let's go shake a banana tree instead!"

Mowgli cheerfully agreed.

Tod's Homecoming

Tod the fox wanted to show his fox friend Vixey where he had grown up. He took her to the top of a hill where they could look down on a beautiful valley.

"I grew up on Widow Tweed's farm," said Tod, pointing with his paw at a farm nestled in the valley. "She took care of me when I was just a cub. And that's my best friend, Copper," Tod said, pointing to a handsome hound on a nearby farm. "Copper lives at Amos Slade's farm. His house is right next door to Widow Tweed's." He sighed. "Let's go visit him."

"Not me!" Vixey declared. "I'm a fox, and I'm not fond of hounds. I'll catch some fish for our dinner. See you later."

Alone, Tod scampered down the hill, excited about seeing his old pal. But when he got there, he spotted a strange man sneaking into Amos Slade's henhouse.

"Wake up, Copper!" yelled Tod. "A chicken thief is raiding the henhouse!"

Copper woke up straight away and leapt into action. But the rope round his neck held him back. "You'll have to stop that chicken thief yourself!" cried Copper.

"But I can't stop him alone!" Tod replied.

"We'll help," someone chirped. Tod looked up and saw Dinky the sparrow and Boomer the woodpecker sitting on the fence.

"Let's go!" said Tod.

Tod burst into the henhouse first. The thief was there, holding squawking chickens in both hands.

Tod bit the man's ankle.

"Ouch!" howled the thief.

Boomer flew through the window and pecked at the chicken snatcher's head. The thief dropped the chickens and covered his head with his arms.

Meanwhile, Dinky had untied the knot that held Copper. Now, Copper was free – and angry, too! Barking, he charged at the burglar.

Eggs flying, the chicken snatcher screamed and ran. As he raced down the road, Dinky and Boomer flitted round his head, pecking him until he was out of sight. The fox and the hound trotted back to the farm.

"Good to see you, Tod," said Copper, wagging his tail. "What brings you here?"

"I just stopped by for a quiet visit," Tod replied.

"It was real quiet, all right!" said Copper.

Jim Hawkins: Space Cadet

On the first day of his second semester at the Interstellar Academy, Jim Hawkins stepped aboard a solar sloop. For a second, he felt like he was back on board the Legacy – the vessel where he had become a real spacer. But the feeling vanished as his classmates pushed past him, eager to begin the fun part of training.

Jim allowed the more confident students to crowd in front of him. Just a few days before, he couldn't wait to get back to the academy and resume studying to be a captain – especially since the second term was when pilot training began. But now he felt as if he'd lost his space legs.

"Tie up." A multi-legged purple kid beside Jim handed him a lifeline. "We're out of here."

As Jim secured his rope, the instructor showed one of the more daring students how to navigate away from the port. Several other students anxiously waited their turn at the helm. One by one, the instructor let them take the wheel.

The instructor looked up, spotted Jim, and waved him over with a cat-like paw. Her almond eyes reminded Jim of Captain Amelia. So did her way of barking orders at the crew.

"You there! Stop skulking. Come take the wheel." Jim shuffled over and flipped his hair out of his eyes. Grasping the wheel, Jim pulled to the right. He wanted to try something tricky. The craft lurched. The awkward ship was not at all what Jim was used to.

"Look out!" an insectoid alien shrieked.

"Turn!" someone else yelled.

Silver's voice echoed in Jim's head. Take the helm and chart your own course. "Trim the sails!" Jim yelled loudly. He must have sounded commanding because three students sprang into action. Jim held the wheel steady. He did not turn, and as the sloop picked up speed, he manoeuvred between two space whales, smoothly emerging on the other side.

"Unconventional," the instructor said sternly, "and well beyond your years, Hawkins. But one thing – never, ever do that again."

Jim smiled. He knew a challenge when he heard one.

The Helpful Dragon

Princess Aurora and Prince Phillip were out for a ride when a small dragon popped out from behind a tree and ran over to them.

"Oh, he's so cute!" Aurora exclaimed. "Let's take him home. I'm going to call him Crackle!"

"He does seem like a harmless little fellow," Phillip agreed.

When Phillip and Aurora rode into the courtyard, the three good fairies were hanging banners for a ball. King Stefan and the queen were coming to the castle.

Flora gasped when she saw Crackle. "Dragons can be dangerous!" she said.

"I think he's sweet," Merryweather spoke up.

Just then, Crackle noticed a kitten in a basket of wool. Crackle listened to it purring. Then he tried to purr.

"Purrgrr, purrgrr!" Clouds of smoke streamed from his nose and mouth! Crackle looked sad.

"Oh, Crackle," Aurora said gently. "You're not a kitten. You're a dragon."

Aurora noticed that Crackle still looked unhappy, so she took him to the castle. But King Hubert heard Crackle and rushed into the room.

"How did a dragon get in here?" he shouted.

Frightened, Crackle ran to the garden.

Aurora found the little dragon sitting beside a fountain, watching a fish.

Splash! Before Aurora could stop him, Crackle jumped into the water.

"Crackle, you're not a fish!" Aurora exclaimed. "You're not a kitten either. Do you think no one will like you because you're a dragon?" she asked. Crackle nodded.

"You can't change what you are," Aurora said kindly. "But you can be a helpful dragon."

Suddenly, thunder boomed. Rain began to pour down.

"I'm afraid King Stefan and the Queen might lose their way," Prince Phillip said.

Aurora looked at Crackle. "Crackle? Would you please fly to the top of the tower and blow the largest, brightest flames you can to guide my parents to the castle?"

Crackle nodded. Soon gold and red flames lit up the sky.

"See?" Aurora told the little dragon later that night. "Never try to be something you're not, because who you are is already wonderful!"

Growing Up

One day, Bambi and Thumper were playing in the meadow when they heard a rumbling noise coming towards them.

"Look, Bambi!" exclaimed Thumper. It was a thundering herd of stags.

"I wish I could be a stag!" Bambi exclaimed.

"Well, you know what my father always says," said Thumper.

"I know," said Bambi. "'Eating greens is a special treat. It makes long ears and great big feet.'"

"No, not that!" said Thumper. "He says, 'If you want to hop well, but your hop is all wrong, then you have to practise all day long!'"

"I have to hop all day long?" asked Bambi.

"No!" cried Thumper. "If you want to become a stag, you have to practise!"

Bambi glanced back at two big deer. They suddenly ran towards each other, locking horns to test their strength.

"Lower your head," Thumper told Bambi.

Bambi lowered his head. "Now what?" he asked, staring at the ground.

"Run straight ahead," said Thumper.

Bambi ran straight ahead – towards the trunk of the old oak tree! But before he got there, a voice cried, "Stop!" Bambi did, skidding to a halt only a few inches from the tree trunk.

Thumper and Bambi looked up. Friend Owl looked down at them with big curious eyes. "Bambi, why were you going to butt my tree trunk with your head?" he asked.

"I'm practising to become a big stag," said Bambi.

Friend Owl laughed and said, "Bambi, the stags have antlers to protect their heads! And becoming a stag is not something you can practise. It's something that will happen to you with the passing of time."

"It will?" said Bambi.

"Of course!" Friend Owl assured him. "Next summer, you'll see. You'll be bigger and stronger. You'll also have antlers – and, I hope, enough sense not to butt heads with an oak tree!

"Now go on, you two," Friend Owl continued. "And don't be in too much of a hurry to grow up. You'll get there soon enough, I promise you!"

"Okay," said Bambi and Thumper.

Then the two friends returned to the meadow to play.

DISNEY

THE ARISTOCATS

The Best Kitty-Sitter

Duchess and O'Malley had planned a lovely dinner at Paris's finest restaurant.

O'Malley had even found a kitty-sitter for Duchess's kittens. His friend Scat Cat had offered to watch them for the night!

Duchess and O'Malley told Toulouse, Marie and Berlioz to behave for Scat Cat.

After they left, Scat Cat turned to the kittens. "Listen up, cool cats," he said. "I'm not the regular kitty-sitter, so this isn't going to be a regular kitty-sitting evening. Got it?"

"Yeah!" they all shouted.

Scat Cat had three instruments with him: a double bass, a trumpet and a small piano.

"Gather 'round, you cool cats. We're making music!" Scat Cat exclaimed.

He showed Toulouse where to put his fingers on the bass. Next he gave Marie the trumpet and put Berlioz on the piano. Together they jammed for over an hour, having a grand old time.

"Okay, let's go," Scat Cat said.

"Go where?" Marie asked.

"We've got a gig and we don't want to be late," Scat Cat said. "You three cats are going to perform, dig it?"

Scat Cat led the three down the street to a club, where he had signed them up for the weekly open-mic jazz show.

"I don't think we can perform tonight," Berlioz said, shaking his head. "We're not very good."

Scat Cat looked at the three kittens. "You have to play from here," he said, pointing to his heart. "You all have soul – you can't teach that. If you miss a note, just keep playing. Feel the vibe."

The kittens smiled. "All right," they said. "Let's jam!"

As they strutted onto the stage, the familiar faces of Duchess and O'Malley greeted them from the crowd. They had been about to return home from their evening when they saw Scat Cat leading the trio into the club.

"One, and a-two, and a-three," Scat Cat counted, and they began to play.

Throughout the club, heads bopped and paws tapped. The crowd was mesmerised.

"This is the best jazz group I've ever seen," O'Malley whispered to Duchess, and the happy couple sat back and let the music take over the night.

Dumbo's Snowy Day

One chilly day, the circus animals were travelling to a new town. Their train, Casey Jr., was struggling to get through the snow. He battled through until his wheels slid, and then decided it was too perilous to continue. Dumbo was so happy that the train had stopped. He'd never played in snow before! At first, it felt awfully strange. But after some encouragement from this mother, Mrs Jumbo, he soon got used to it.

Soon he was making snow elephants and playing hide-and-seek. But all the while, they were getting further and further from the train. Dumbo suddenly leapt down a snow-covered hill, daring Mrs Jumbo to follow. But when she reached the bottom, she realised there was no way back up!

"You have to fly and get help," Mrs Jumbo told Dumbo. So, he flew as fast as his ears would take him.

As he soared towards the train, the wind began to blow. Dumbo struggled against the cold, putting all his strength into flapping his ears. Finally, he reached the rest of the animals. Dumbo explained what had happened and everyone gathered around.

"What are we waiting for?" asked Timothy Mouse. "Let's go!"

Dumbo led the animals back to the cliff, but poor Mrs Jumbo had been pushed by the windstorm and was now close to the edge.

"What do we do?" asked Giraffe.

Timothy snapped his fingers. He had an idea. "Everyone, line up!"

He ordered the animals to grab one another's tails and help Ostrich stretch her neck down to Mrs Jumbo.

"Now pull!" Timothy yelled.

The animals worked together, huffing and puffing, until Mrs Jumbo finally made it safely to the top of the cliff.

"Hooray!" everyone shouted.

That night, when everyone was safely back in the train, Mrs Jumbo gave Dumbo a warm bath.

"Thank you for flying to find help today," Mrs Jumbo said. "I'm so proud of you."

Dumbo smiled and blew water out of his trunk.

"Hey, don't forget about me!" Timothy said from his teacup bath. "I helped, too!"

Mrs Jumbo nodded. "You certainly did. Thank you."

"Aw, gee," said Timothy. "It was nothing. Nothing at all!"

Disney
Cinderella

The Perfect Gifts

The Christmas holidays had always been Cinderella's favourite time of the year. She loved the cheer and good feeling of the season.

Every year she cooked delicious treats and crafted small decorations. And she had always managed to set aside time to make some small presents for her mouse friends.

Now that she lived in a beautiful castle, Cinderella found that she enjoyed Christmas time even more. This year, Cinderella wanted to give especially wonderful gifts to her mouse friends.

First, Cinderella went to the royal kitchen. "My mouse friends like cheese," she told the cook. "Could you make some cheese pudding?"

The cook assured her that the cheese pudding would be the best in the world.

Then Cinderella went to the royal tailor. She told him the mice's favourite colours, and he helped her pick out rich, beautiful fabrics. "I will make mouse outfits the likes of which have never been seen," he said, rubbing his hands together.

Finally, Cinderella went to the royal carpenter. "My mouse friends don't have any nice furniture. Can you help me?" she asked.

The carpenter said he would gladly make tiny beds and chairs and tables for the mice.

The next day, as Cinderella and Prince Charming were having tea, the cook, the carpenter and the tailor arrived to deliver the presents for Cinderella's mouse friends. Cinderella thanked them and sent them each on their way with a kind word.

The pudding was a beautiful colour, the clothes were artfully sewn and the tiny furniture was grand and elegant. But none of it seemed quite right for Cinderella's mouse friends.

"I don't understand," Cinderella said sadly. "The cook and the tailor and the carpenter are the best in all the land. So why don't I like what they made?"

"Well," answered Prince Charming, "you know your mouse friends better than anyone else. Maybe you should make their presents."

"You know, that's a wonderful idea." Cinderella was delighted. "I'm going to make my friends the nicest gifts they have ever received."

Belle to the Rescue

In the kitchen at the Beast's castle, Mrs Potts was telling Belle about a bag of the Beast's clothes she had left in the foyer. "The master has asked me to rid of his clothes. They don't, er, fit him any more."

"Not to mention that none of them have a hole for his tail!" said Lumiere.

"Luckily, the peddler is coming today," replied Mrs Potts. 'He'll be happy to take them off his hands."

Just then, Chip appeared and asked Belle if she would like to play hide-and-seek. "I would love to!" said Belle. "Why don't I count while you hide?"

While Belle was counting, she was interrupted by a knock on the door. A peddler stood at the door, proudly displaying his goods. Belle looked at some shiny ice skates. "You have so many lovely items, but we don't need anything today," she said. "But I do have this bag of clothes for you."

The peddler was so pleased, he gave Belle the ice skates. Once the peddler was gone, Belle remembered she was meant to be looking for Chip. She searched all over the castle, but couldn't find him anywhere.

She asked the other enchanted servants if they had seen him, but they hadn't. "Oh no! He must have been hiding in the bag of clothes," Belle realised. "We need to find him before he's lost forever."

Belle grabbed her new ice skates, just in case, and followed the tracks the peddler's waggon had left in the snow. Belle raced along on Philippe, until she spotted the peddler by the lake.

However, as soon as Philippe stepped on the frozen lake it began to crack. He was too heavy! Belle had an idea, she quickly strapped on the ice skates and stepped onto the ice.

At first she was wobbly, but after a moment she was skating smoothly. Finally, Belle reached the other side. "Monsieur!" she cried. "I think something very dear to me fell in the bag of clothes."

She opened the bag and there was Chip, cosy as could be. "Great hiding spot, huh?" he whispered.

"They very best," said Belle with a grin.

Survival of the Smallest

Dot and the other Blueberries were heading out for the First Annual Blueberry Wilderness Expedition. Their journey would take them to the thicket of tall grass next to the ant colony. It was only a few yards from home, but to a little ant, it seemed like an awfully long way.

As the group prepared to leave, some boy ants arrived to tease them.

"How do you expect to go on an expedition without supplies?" asked Jordy.

Dot put her hands on her hips. "For your information," she said in a superior tone, "the whole point is to survive on our wits. Whatever we need, we'll make when we get there."

When the Blueberries reached the tall grasses, Dot consulted her survival guidebook. "Okay," she said, "the first thing we need to do is build a shelter from the sun."

"I know!" Daisy volunteered. "We could make a hut. All we have to do is stick twigs into the dirt side by side to make the walls, then lay leaves over the top for the roof."

The rest of the Blueberries decided this was a great idea. With a lot of teamwork and determination, they completed a shelter to comfortably hold the troop.

"Now," said Dot, looking at the book again,

"it says here we need to protect our campsite."

So the girls dug a narrow trench in front of the hut, just as the guidebook instructed.

A short while later, they heard a scream. When they went to investigate, they discovered Reed, Grub and Jordy at the bottom of the trench.

It was clear to the Blueberries that the boys had been up to no good.

"Girls," said Dot, pointing to the boys, "observe one of the Blueberries' most common natural enemies – though certainly not one of the smartest."

When it was time for the Blueberries to pack up and hike home, the boys were still stuck in the trench. "Say the magic words and I'll get you out of there," said Dot.

"Okay, okay!" Reed, Grub and Jordy agreed. "Blueberries rock."

Dot lowered a ladder she had expertly made of sticks. "You bet we do!" she said. "'Cause if we can survive you, we can survive anything!"

The Desert Race

The Sultan was angry. The Desert Race was coming up, and he was sure Agrabah would lose to Prince Fayiz of Zagrabah!

"I have an idea!" Jasmine said eagerly. "I could ride Midnight in the Desert Race. He's the fastest horse around!"

"Oh, no!" The Sultan looked shocked at the suggestion. "The Desert Race can be dangerous."

"How about if I ride Midnight in the race?" Aladdin spoke up.

The Sultan's face brightened. "What a splendid idea!" he cried.

The next day, Aladdin and Jasmine went to the stables. But when Aladdin climbed onto Midnight, the horse bucked and threw him off.

Finally, the day of the race arrived. Prince Fayiz rode in on his impressive white stallion, Desert Warrior.

"What an odd-looking horse Aladdin is riding," the Sultan said to Jasmine. But the princess was nowhere to be seen. The Sultan shrugged. "We can't wait any longer," he said, and he started the race.

A black horse with a veiled rider took the lead. As soon as they were out of view, the rider threw off the veil. It was Jasmine! "I just had to prove that you were the fastest," she whispered to Midnight. "Now let's go win!"

Aladdin's horse spotted an oasis of water and jumped in. "Now that's more like it!" exclaimed the horse. Aladdin had a secret. His horse was actually the Genie!

On land, Jasmine and Midnight galloped off without a backwards glance. Prince Fayiz and Desert Warrior stayed on Midnight's heels until the horses had to jump a ditch. Midnight sailed over easily, but Desert Warrior skidded to a stop!

Now there was nothing to keep Jasmine and Midnight from winning. Suddenly, Jasmine heard the sound of hooves close behind her. It was Aladdin! Their two horses crossed the finish line at the same time.

"Congratulations!" Aladdin said.

"Same to you," Jasmine replied. "But where did you find such a fast horse?"

"Er," Aladdin looked at his feet.

"Surprise!" the Genie cried, turning back into himself.

"Sorry, Princess," the Genie said, winking. "We were just horsing around!"

Tinker Bell's Bedtime Story

"Shove over!"

"No. You shove over."

The Raccoon Twins were at it again. Peter Pan knew the bickering wouldn't stop until one of the boys had pushed the other out of the hammock.

"Say, Tink," Peter said, "how'd you like to be the new mother to all of us boys?"

Tink looked at Peter like he was crazy.

"Aw, c'mon," Peter said. "You've seen the guys since Wendy left. They're fighting all the time. They need someone to tuck them in at night and tell them a bedtime story."

Tink was silent for a moment.

"I guess I could ask Wendy to come back," Peter said, looking at Tinker Bell slyly.

That did it. The last thing Tink wanted was for Wendy to return!

"Tink is going to tell us a bedtime story," said Peter. The boys settled down. "Go ahead, Tink." Peter smiled. His plan was working perfectly!

Tink sat down and crossed her arms over her chest. She began to jingle.

"Once upon a time," Peter translated, "there was a beautiful fairy who, against her better judgement, lived with a pack of dirty, unruly, silly boys. And the dirtiest, unruliest, and silliest of them all was Peter Pa— hey!"

Peter interrupted his translation.

Tinker Bell jingled spitefully at him.

"Okay," Peter said with a sigh, "I know it's your story. Go ahead."

Tink continued, and Peter translated: "One day, as the lovely Tinker Bell was minding her own business, the very smelly and unpleasant Peter Pan – Tink! – asked her to tell a bedtime story. Well, Tinker Bell didn't know any bedtime stories, so she went to fetch Captain Hook so that he could tell one."

With that, Tinker Bell flew out the window.

"Tink! Tink, come back!" Peter cried.

Tinker Bell returned and hovered in the window, jingling with laughter.

"That was a dirty trick!" Peter scolded. "And besides, that's no way to tell a bedtime story." He sat down next to the boys' beds. "You have to do it like Wendy did. Like this."

Now it was Tink's turn to smile. While Peter told a bedtime story and the Lost Boys drifted off to sleep, Tink curled up in her own little bed and closed her eyes. Her plan had worked perfectly!

Sledging

Lady stood on the porch as Jim Dear and Darling walked up the front path. Jim pulled a sledge, and Darling held their son. They were all covered in snow, rosy-cheeked and smiling from ear to ear.

"That was fun! Wasn't it, Darling?" Jim asked.

"I don't know the last time I had so much fun," Darling agreed, patting Lady on the head.

"But we should get out of these wet clothes before one of us catches a cold," Jim said, leaning the sledge against the side of the house.

"I agree," Darling said. And the three of them hurried inside.

Just then, Tramp came walking up the front path. "Hey, Pidge," he said to Lady. "What do you say we take this old thing for a spin?"

"What is it, anyway?" Lady wanted to know.

"A sledge!" Tramp told her.

"What do you do with it?" she asked.

"You ride down hills," Tramp said. "Come on. I'll show you. It'll be great! You saw how much fun Jim Dear and Darling had."

Tramp grabbed the rope in his teeth and pulled the sledge across the porch and down the steps.

Lady took off after him. "Wait for me!" she cried anxiously.

"Come on, Pidge!" Tramp encouraged her. "Jump on!"

Lady jumped onto the sledge, and Tramp pulled her down the snowy street and up to the top of a nearby hill. "What a view, huh?" he said.

"What a view indeed," Lady agreed. "What now?"

"Now, we ride," Tramp said. He pushed the sledge forwards and took a running leap onto it, sending them racing down the hill.

"Oh, dear!" Lady yelped as they went down the hill, the wind blowing back her ears.

"Just hold on!" Tramp instructed.

Lady squeezed her eyes shut, and Tramp barked with excitement. But suddenly they hit a patch of ice, the sledge spun and they went flying – right into a pile of snow!

Tramp jumped to his feet. "Pidge, are you okay?" he asked anxiously.

"Okay?" Lady asked. She was already pulling the sledge back up the hill. "Hurry up, Tramp! Let's do it again!"

Disney·PIXAR
MONSTERS, INC.

Monster Laughs

Sulley was worried. As the new head of Monsters, Inc., it was his job to make sure the power levels stayed high. But none of the monsters seemed to be getting enough laughs.

"Mikey, we've got a power problem," Sulley said to his friend. "It's been a year since we switched from scare power to laugh power, and the monsters aren't funny any more. All their routines are old and dull."

Mike thought for a moment. "I got it!" he said, snapping his fingers. "I'll write some new jokes for all the monsters!"

Mike spent the next few nights writing jokes and inventing gags. He made a huge list. Then he gave his jokes to the other monsters.

But things didn't go so well when the monsters took the jokes into the kids' rooms.

A monster called Pauley tried one of Mike's jokes on a little girl.

"Why did the one-eyed monster have to close his school?" he asked. "Because he only had one pupil!"

The girl just gave Pauley and his sixteen eyes a blank stare.

"They're terrible!" said Mike. "I need to round them up for some practise. If they can learn to perform the jokes just like me, Monstropolis's power levels will go through the roof!"

"But, Mike, that's the problem," said Sulley. "The other monsters can't perform the jokes like you, because they're not you."

The next day, the monsters were feeling downhearted.

Suddenly, a very tall monster called Lanky slipped on a banana skin. When he landed, his arms and legs were all tangled up. Lanky started to laugh. Soon all the monsters were laughing. It was great!

Mike thought for a moment. "That's it!" he cried. "Instead of copying me, you just have to be yourselves! That's how to be funny!"

"That's right," said Sulley. "If you've got sixteen eyes – use them! If you have really long limbs – use them! Be proud of who you are!"

A few days later, the Laugh Floor buzzed with activity. Behind wardrobe doors, kids roared with laughter.

"Great job, Mikey," said Sulley. "Power levels are going back up!"

Having a Ball

It was was getting closer and closer to Christmas Day, and the puppies couldn't wait!

"Do you puppies know what comes before Father Christmas and dinner and presents?" Perdita asked.

Patch wasn't sure. He sat down on the hall rug to think.

"We have to decorate and sing carols," Perdita said, wagging her tail.

At that very moment, Roger and Anita threw open the door to the study and invited all the dogs inside. Patch blinked. He couldn't believe his eyes. "What's a tree doing in the house?"

"Just watch." Perdy gave Patch a quick lick.

While the dogs looked on, Roger and Anita began to decorate the tree. They hung lights and angels, snowmen and tinsel. Of all the decorations, Patch liked the glittering glass baubles the best. Baubles were one of his favourite things! He couldn't take his eyes off them.

When the tree was ready, Anita brought in hot chocolate and dog biscuits. Munching on a biscuit in front of the fire, Patch didn't think the evening could get any better. Then Roger sat down at the piano, and everyone began to sing Christmas carols.

Patch howled along with the others, but he could not stop looking at the baubles on the tree. A large red one was hanging near the floor. Patch reached over and gave the bauble a pat with his front paw. It swung merrily above him. Looking at his reflection, Patch started to laugh. His nose looked huge!

Penny stopped singing to see what was so funny. "What are you doing?" Then Freckles joined them, then Lucky. The puppies took turns knocking the bauble and watching it sway, then – crash! – it fell to the floor, shattering.

The singing stopped. Poor Patch was sure the special evening was ruined!

"Oh dear." Anita scooped the puppies out from under the tree. "Careful, now," she said. "Baubles aren't for playing with."

While Roger swept up the glass, Patch cowered. He knew he was in trouble.

"Maybe I should give you all one gift early," Anita said, smiling.

Patch couldn't believe his luck! Instead of a firm talking-to, each puppy got to rip open a small package. Patch tore off the paper. Inside was a brand-new red rubber ball!

Royal Help Wanted

Prince John and Sir Hiss had just finished repaying their debt to society in the rock mines. They discovered that Robin Hood had given back the citizens' hard-earned money. And that meant that Prince John had not a penny to his name and no one to boss around any more – except Sir Hiss, of course!

"Well, it's quite obvious that you will need to get a job," the prince told Hiss.

"Me, sssssire?" hissed the snake.

"Of course!" John replied. "You can't very well expect me to get a job."

And so Hiss set off into the town.

First, he stopped by Friar Tuck's church.

"Everyone deserves a second chance," Friar Tuck told him. "And I just happen to need a bell-ringer." He pointed up to the huge bell that hung in a tower of the church.

And so, every hour, Hiss grabbed hold of the rope and pulled with all his might. The sound of the bell was deafening! It wasn't so bad at one o'clock, when he had to ring the bell once. But around six o'clock, the clanging started to give him a colossal headache. At twelve o'clock, he quit and went looking elsewhere for a job.

Hiss tried the bakery, but they told him he needed hands (or at least paws) to knead dough. Then he went to the blacksmith and asked him for a job putting horseshoes on horses. But the horses were terrified of snakes.

Finally, Hiss gave up and returned home.

Prince John was not pleased. "Now what are we supposed to do for money?" he demanded. "I refuse to beg! Those wretched commoners would give anything to see me humiliated."

"You're absolutely right, sire – they would!" exclaimed Hiss. "That's it! Follow me!"

Before Prince John could protest, Hiss had the lion locked in the stocks in the middle of the village square. "Pay a farthing and pelt the prince with a tomato!" called Sir Hiss. In minutes, a queue of adults and children stretched into the distance. Most of them had a pretty good aim.

"Wah!" cried Prince John, his face dripping with tomato juice.

"But, sire," Sir Hiss said, "look at all these coins!"

Fast Friends

"Here, kitty, kitty," called Penny, peering underneath her bed. "Come on, I won't hurt you." She reached her hand out towards the old orange cat she had seen race into the girls' dormitory room and dart under the bed.

Penny had lived at the Morningside Orphanage for a long time. But in all her years there, she had never known that a cat lived there, too.

"Whatcha doin' under there?" Penny asked.

Surprisingly, the cat answered her. "I'm hiding from the headmistress," he whispered. "Is she coming this way?"

Penny looked up and towards the door of the dormitory. She saw the headmistress poke her head into the girls' room, glance round hurriedly, then head off down the hallway.

"Nope, she's gone," Penny said. "The coast is clear."

Breathing a sigh of relief, the cat came out from under the bed and jumped up onto the window sill.

The cat was wearing a red wool scarf round his neck and a pair of glasses on his nose.

"Thanks," he said. "That was a close one."

"Why was the headmistress after you?" Penny asked him.

"Oh," the cat said with a chuckle, "she got me a while back to keep mice out of the basement." The cat stretched, yawned and jumped down to lie in a patch of sunlight on the floor. "But I don't mouse too well any more. I'm getting too slow to chase anything. I'm not as young and spry as I used to be. Say, my name's Rufus. What's yours?"

"Penny," she replied with a smile. She reached under her pillow and pulled out her teddy bear. "And this is Teddy."

"Well, hello, Penny," said Rufus. "And hello, Teddy.

"Quiet little guy, huh?" Rufus said to Penny. "What's the matter? Cat got his tongue?"

Penny giggled. "Teddy's very good at keeping secrets. And so am I. You can come hide under our bed whenever you need to. We won't tell."

"You won't?" Rufus replied. "Aw, that's mighty good of you." And so, feeling safe and secure with his new friends, Rufus closed his eyes and settled down for a catnap.

Wreck the Halls

Ralph should have been excited. It was his first real Christmas. But he couldn't stop thinking about how lonely the other Bad Guys would be.

"Let's throw the Bad Guys a Christmas party," Vanellope suggested.

Ralph loved that idea, so he called a special meeting of the Bad-Anon support group. "I want everyone to meet here in the support group room on Christmas Eve," Ralph said. "And get ready for the merriest Christmas ever!"

Ralph and Vanellope made gifts for each Bad Guy. Then they found a perfect lollipop tree in Lollistix Forest.

"How are we going to carry all this to the support group room?" Ralph asked.

"In a sleigh, of course," Vanellope said.

Vanellope dragged Ralph across Sugar Rush to the kart bakery. Soon their sleigh was ready!

On Christmas Eve, the two friends met up to bring Christmas to the Bad Guys.

"Okay, let's get this thing moving!" Ralph called out, reaching for the sleigh's left and right rocket switches. He flipped them both, but his powerful grip snapped one of the tiny rocket switches like a toothpick! Only one rocket turned on – and the sleigh spun out of control!

The rocket spiralled lower and lower until – gloop! – it came to a lurching stop in the middle of Great Caramel Lake. The sleigh and all the presents were ruined.

Empty-handed and covered in caramel, Ralph and Vanellope made their way to the support group room. "I've wrecked their Christmas," Ralph said sadly.

For once, Vanellope didn't have a snappy comeback. "Time to face the music, big guy," she said, shaking her head.

But when they opened the door, the friends' jaws dropped. The room was completely decked out! The Bad Guys greeted them with a big cheer.

"Vanellope and I made presents, and trimmed a tree… We even made a sleigh, but I wrecked it. I wrecked everything."

"Don't be silly, Ralph!" said Satine. "You're the reason we're here – spending Christmas together! That's a pretty great gift. Merry Christmas, Ralph!"

Disney
Bambi

First Frost

Bambi blinked sleepily. Something was different. The forest did not look the same. The air was crisp and cold, and everything was frosted and sparkling.

"Jack Frost has been here," Bambi's mother explained. "He's painted the whole forest with ice crystals."

Bambi was about to ask his mother who Jack Frost was and how he painted with ice, when he heard another voice – an impatient one.

"Get up! Get up! Come look at the frost!" It was Thumper. He tapped his foot impatiently. "We haven't got all day!"

Bambi scampered out of the thicket. He looked closely at the colourful leaves on the ground. Each one was covered in an icy-white pattern. He touched his nose to a big orange oak leaf. "Ooh, it's cold!" he cried.

"Of course it is!" Thumper laughed.

"I think it's beautiful," said Faline as she stepped into the clearing.

"Me too," Bambi agreed.

"Well, come look at this!" Thumper hopped away, and the two young deer followed, admiring the way the sun sparkled on the frost-covered trees and grass.

Thumper disappeared under a bush. Then Bambi heard a new noise. Creak, crack.

Faline pushed through the bushes with Bambi right behind her. There was Thumper, cracking the thin ice on a puddle with his feet.

Bambi had never seen ice before. He pushed on the thin ice with his hoof. It seemed to bend. Then it shattered!

Soon the three friends were all stomping on the ice-covered puddles. When all the ice was broken, Faline had an idea. "Let's go to the meadow!"

Bambi thought that was a great idea. The grass would be sparkling! They ran, bounding and racing one another through the forest. But when they got to the meadow's edge, they stopped.

They looked, sniffed and listened quietly. They did not sense danger – no, the trouble was that in the meadow, nothing was different. There was no frost.

"What happened?" Bambi asked.

"Frost never lasts long," Thumper explained. "It melts as soon as the sun hits it. But don't worry. Winter is coming, and soon we'll have something even better than frost. We'll have snow!"

21
December

Mater Saves Christmas

One morning, Mater arrived at Flo's V8 Café with his letter to Father Car-mas! All the townspeople had written one. Just as Mater was dropping his letter in the postbox, Chick Hicks, one of Lightning's rivals, showed up. He began to tease Mater, saying that Santa Car didn't exist.

Just then, Sheriff raced up to them with some bad news. All the fuel from the area had been stolen!

The townspeople were shocked. Without fuel, the post vans couldn't deliver letters to Santa Car! But Mater wouldn't give up. He decided to deliver the letters to the North Pole himself.

Lightning was worried about his friend. He couldn't let him go alone! "Mater, I'm coming with you," he said. Luigi and Guido gave Mater and Lightning new snow tyres and the two set off.

Finally, Lightning and Mater arrived at the North Pole. Lightning stared in wonder. "Santa Car is real!" he said.

But Santa Car had some bad news. His reindeer snowmobiles had been stolen! Just then, Mater remembered how strangely Chick had been acting. He realised that Chick wanted the top-secret flying fuel the reindeer used. "Chick Hicks took your reindeer!" he cried.

Santa Car filled Mater's tank with the top-secret fuel and the three cars set out for Radiator Springs.

Back in town, Luigi and Guido had been cornered by Chick and his gang.

"Ha! You're too late, boys!" Chick shouted. "I'll fly round the track and never lose to Lightning McQueen again! And you know the best part? No more Christmas! If I can't have presents, no one can!"

Suddenly, the air filled with the sound of jingling bells. Mater soared over the hill, towing Lightning and Santa Car. Chick raced away, flying just above the ground. Lightning flew after him. Santa Car had filled his tank with the magic fuel, too!

Chick was no match for Lightning McQueen. The thief soon spun out of control.

"Tow him straight to jail," said Doc.

Later, the Radiator Springs gang celebrated with Santa Car and his reindeer snowmobiles. Everyone cheered. Mater had saved Christmas!

Elsa's Birthday

One bright winter morning, Queen Elsa woke up with the strangest feeling that she was forgetting something important. Suddenly, she gasped. *Today's my birthday*, she realised. *Maybe Anna will forget, too. Then I won't have to go to a party.*

But it was clear when Elsa entered the dining room that her sister had not forgotten. Anna jumped up and gave Elsa a big hug "for no reason." And Kristoff had made special pancakes "just because".

Suddenly, Kai appeared with a note for Anna. "This must be about the flowers," Anna said. "I mean the towers," she continued. "You know… the ones we're adding to the south wing. I'd better go."

A few minutes later, Olina entered the dining room. "The royal baker said he can't manage fifty cake layers," she told Kristoff.

Kristoff shook his head. "Cake? What cake? There's no cake," he said nervously. "Fifty players is what he meant. For the, uh, chess tournament."

Elsa smirked as she watched Kristoff race out of the room. She knew very well that there was no chess tournament.

All day long, Elsa tended to her royal duties. As day turned to dusk, she looked out over Arendelle. Usually she would have a quiet dinner with Anna and Kristoff, then read by the fire or take a walk with Olaf. But that night Elsa knew she would have to be more social. *They're doing this because they love you*, Elsa reminded herself.

At that moment, Anna appeared. "Elsa," she said, "I was just looking for you. I need you to come have a look at the new… uh… towers."

Anna led Elsa through the castle in an awkward silence. Finally, Elsa took pity on her sister. "You don't have to pretend, Anna," she said. "I know you're throwing me a surprise party."

Anna gave her sister a sly smile. "Oh, it's a surprise, all right," she said.

Anna opened the doors to the ballroom.

Elsa looked around in astonishment.

"It's just us," Anna said. "A quiet little party with your family and friends."

Elsa smiled. "I thought for sure you were planning a huge bash."

Anna smiled. "You love quiet evenings with your family and your best friends. And on your birthday, you should get exactly what you want."

A Merry Christmas

"Merry Christmas!" Ebenezer Scrooge crowed as he watched the Cratchit children open all the gifts he'd brought for them.

"A teddy bear!" Tiny Tim exclaimed. His sister had a new doll, and his brother was busy playing with a new train set. And that was just the beginning.

"And there's another present, too," Scrooge said with a twinkle in his eye. "I'll be right back."

Scrooge walked outside. A moment later, he reappeared carrying a big package wrapped in red paper and tied with a giant green bow.

The children ripped off the paper and squealed in delight.

"Father, it's a sledge!" Tiny Tim cheered happily.

"I can see that," Bob Cratchit replied, looking up from the turkey he was carving. Scrooge had brought the turkey over that very morning.

"Can we go sledging? Can we? Can we?" the children chorused.

"Of course," Cratchit replied. "But not until after dinner."

"And dinner is ready right now," Mrs Cratchit said.

"Dinner!" the children shouted as they scrambled to their seats at the table.

Mrs Cratchit sat down. "I can't remember when we've had such a feast, Mr Scrooge," she said happily. "Thank you ever so much for all the gifts you've given us."

Scrooge raised his glass in the air. "That's what Christmas is all about," he said warmly. "Happiness and goodwill. Merry Christmas!"

Everyone clinked glasses, then tucked into their food.

When they were done with the turkey, Mr Cratchit said, "Now, how about that sledging?"

Minutes later, everyone was bundled up and ready to go.

Scrooge pulled the children all through town, singing Christmas carols at the top of his lungs.

"Why is everyone staring at Mr Scrooge?" Tiny Tim whispered to his father.

Mr Cratchit smiled down at his son. "Because they like him," he said.

"I like him, too," said Tiny Tim. "This is the best Christmas ever!"

Under the Tree

Woody and the other toys gathered round the baby monitor. Downstairs, Andy was unwrapping his Christmas presents. Christmas morning was always difficult for Andy's toys. They all lived in fear of being replaced by something bigger and better.

Rex wrung his tiny hands. "Let it be a new video game!" he cried.

"As long as it's not another spaceman," Buzz said.

"It's a…" The toys leant closer. But before Sarge could finish his report, Woody switched off the monitor.

"What are you doing?" Hamm cried.

"Woody, we need to be debriefed in order to face the enemy!" Buzz sounded alarmed.

"Now hold on a minute, guys." Woody put his hand up to silence the toys. "Let's just think a minute. I want each of you to remember what it was like when you were unwrapped. Remember when you first met Andy."

"He chose me from the shelf himself," Rocky Gibraltar boasted.

"And it was a great day, right?" Woody asked, looking around at everyone.

"I was a birthday present," Rex said.

The other toys all chimed in, smiling and laughing as they told each other about their arrival.

"And we're a team, right?" Woody interrupted.

"Sure we are." Buzz nodded. "We can fight the new enemies together."

Woody shook his head. "No, Buzz. That's what I'm talking about. These new toys aren't our new enemies. They're our new friends!"

Slowly, Woody's words began to sink in. "You mean, they come in peace," Buzz said.

"Exactly!" Woody cried. "So instead of sitting around here moping, we should be planning a welcome party!"

"Oh, Woody," Bo Peep said. "I love it when you show your soft side."

Woody blushed. Then he turned the monitor back on. "Sarge, I want you to stand down. I have new orders. I repeat, new orders."

"Yes, sir. What can we do for you, sir?" the sergeant barked.

"Gather your troops and come upstairs. Andy's toys are throwing a hoedown for the new toys. It'll be our first annual Christmas Welcome Party! Let's get started!"

Stocking Surprise

Pooh was sitting at home thinking when there was a knock at the door. When he opened it, he found himself face-to-face with a snowman!

The snowman's voice seemed strangely familiar to Pooh. He invited the creature inside. As it stood in front of the fire and began to melt, Pooh discovered with surprise that the snowman was his friend Piglet! He had been covered in snow on his walk to Pooh's house.

Suddenly, Pooh realised he had forgotten to get Christmas presents for his friends! Piglet seemed a little disappointed, and he went back home to wrap his own Christmas presents. Pooh watched him heading off in the snow. Though Pooh didn't know how to sort out his mistake, he knew someone who would.

Pooh arrived with frozen paws at the house of his friend Christopher Robin.

The little boy happily invited him in.

Pooh saw the stockings hanging on the fireplace and, intrigued, asked him, "Are you drying them?"

"No, Pooh. Father Christmas will leave presents in there," the little boy explained.

"Oh, my! Presents, that's right. That's what I forgot!" exclaimed Pooh. "And I don't have any stockings either!"

Christopher Robin was a good friend, and he gave Pooh a stocking for each of his friends in the Hundred-Acre Wood. Pooh hurried off to put the stockings outside of his friends' homes with a little note saying: *From Pooh.*

When the bear arrived home, he was exhausted. He settled down in his armchair in front of the fire. He was pleased his friends now had stockings, but he still didn't know what he could give them for Christmas. He closed his eyes and fell asleep.

The next morning, Pooh was woken by his friends knocking on his door. Pooh invited his friends inside and was preparing to apologise to them when they all started thanking him!

Each of them had found a special use for the stocking Pooh had left at their house: a vegetable holder for Rabbit, a stone pouch for Gopher, a warm layer for Eeyore and a hat for Piglet.

Pooh was happy – he had realised that Christmas really was magical! Merry Christmas, Pooh!

A Royal Visit

Snow White was very happy. She had married her true love and she lived in a beautiful castle. But she missed her good friends from the forest, the Seven Dwarfs, very much.

"Well, why don't you go for a visit?" the prince said.

"That would be lovely!" Snow White cried.

Snow White wrote a note to tell her friends that she was going to visit, and she asked a bluebird to deliver it.

At the Dwarfs' cottage, Doc read the note and ran downstairs to tell the others.

"Hooray!" Happy cheered. "Snow White is coming!"

But the other six Dwarfs looked around their messy cottage. "We have a lot to do, men!" said Doc.

"She'll want lunch," Grumpy huffed. "Someone's gonna have to cook!"

"Why don't you and Happy fix somethin' suitable for Snow White to eat?" Doc suggested.

The Dwarfs started to work on their chores right away, but it didn't go very well. Sleepy got tired and lay down. Sneezy kept sneezing as he dusted. And Dopey knocked furniture over as he swept. Meanwhile, Happy and Grumpy couldn't agree on what kind of sandwiches

Snow White would like.

All too soon, Snow White arrived. The Dwarfs smiled as Snow White hugged each of them and kissed their foreheads.

"Please forgive the mess, Princess," Bashful whispered to her. "We didn't quite get it cleaned up."

"Oh, please," Snow White said with a laugh. "Forgive me for giving you such short notice! Besides, I've come to see you – not your cottage."

"Would you care for a ham and jam sandwich?" Doc offered, holding up a platter. "Or peanut butter and cheese?"

"Oh, how sweet," Snow White replied. "If I had known you'd go to all this trouble, I wouldn't have brought a picnic with me."

"Picnic!" the Dwarfs exclaimed.

"Well, yes. I remembered how much you liked it when I cooked, so I brought some of your favourites. But let's eat your sandwiches first."

The Dwarfs looked at one another, and Doc cleared his throat.

"We can have ham and jam any time," he said. "Let's enjoy your picnic and have a great afternoon." And that's exactly what they did.

THE JUNGLE Book

Manners, Mowgli

A strange but delicious smell drifted past Mowgli's nose. Turning round, he spied several platters of food. A moment later, people filed in and sat in a circle round the food.

Mowgli had just come to live in the Man-village, and he was about to have his first meal!

Mowgli lunged forwards and grabbed a piece of meat. He shoved it in his mouth and chewed. He had never tasted cooked meat before, and it was delicious! As the juice dribbled down his chin, he grinned at the humans surrounding him.

They did not grin back. In fact, they were looking at him in disgust. Surprised, Mowgli's mouth dropped open. A piece of half-chewed meat fell out.

"Disgusting," said an elderly woman.

"Why, he eats like an animal!" said a girl.

Mowgli didn't understand a single word they said. But it suddenly dawned on him that he didn't live in the jungle any more. Humans did things differently from the jungle creatures. Mowgli sighed. Would he ever fit in there?

Smiling sheepishly, Mowgli finished chewing and wiped his mouth with his arm. Then he sat back and watched the others eat.

Mowgli tried to copy them, with little success. The sharpened stick didn't cut nearly as well as his teeth, and half the food fell off the paddle.

At the next meal, Mowgli watched for a long time before he began to eat. The food was strange to him – warm liquid with soft vegetables. Holding his bowl in one hand, he tried to scoop the broth into his mouth with the paddle. But the soup kept slipping off, leaving him with almost nothing.

Mowgli put his bowl and paddle down with a frustrated sigh. Then, ever so slowly, he picked up the bowl a second time and lifted it right to his lips. Then he took a big gulp of soup, swallowing and smacking his lips.

The others stopped and stared yet again. Then the village elder nodded and lifted his bowl to his mouth, taking a long sip and finishing with a lip-smack of his own.

Soon everyone was gulping the broth, slurping and smacking away. Mowgli grinned. It looked like he might fit in after all!

Lighting the Way

Rapunzel had spent her whole life in Mother Gothel's tower. Now, free for the day, she was taking in the hustle and bustle of the village.

Rapunzel loved the village! Everywhere she looked, there was something exciting happening. A baker was putting out the most delicious-smelling loaves of bread Rapunzel had ever smelt. A florist was selling the pinkest roses Rapunzel had ever seen. Behind her, a band was just starting to tune their instruments.

Laughing, Rapunzel dragged Flynn from one corner to the next. Suddenly, Flynn froze. "Don't look now," he said, "but there are guards heading this way."

Rapunzel looked round nervously. The last thing she wanted was for Flynn to get caught by the royal guards! If she lost her guide, she'd never see the floating lights! Grabbing Rapunzel's hand, Flynn darted through the crowd and into an alley.

"I think we lost 'em," Flynn said, looking back. "They went the other way."

Maximus, the royal horse, snorted. He was not used to running from guards. But Rapunzel barely heard them. She was looking in the window of a small dusty shop.

"Look!" she said, pointing. "Lanterns!"

Rapunzel pushed open the door to the little shop and walked inside. Lanterns of every size and shape covered the walls. Rapunzel looked around in awe. They were all so beautiful!

Suddenly, a small lantern in the corner caught Rapunzel's eye. She picked it up, a smile forming on her face.

"That's a pretty one," Flynn said.

"I used to have a lantern just like this," Rapunzel said softly, "when I was little. In the tower, I would stay up late at night, reading by its light. It reminded me of the lanterns in the sky. It helped me keep alive my dream of seeing the lanterns."

That night, surrounded by floating lanterns, Rapunzel thought back to the shop.

"Thank you for taking me to the lantern shop today," she told Flynn. "It reminded me how important my dream is to me. And now, thanks to you, I'm finally living that dream."

"It's been quite an adventure," Flynn said softly.

Rapunzel smiled. "And there's no one else I'd rather share it with."

DISNEY·PIXAR

MONSTERS, INC.

Relaxopolis

It was another cold, blustery day in Monstropolis. Sulley and Mike were on their way to work. Mike sighed heavily.

"What's wrong, little buddy?" asked Sulley.

"I'm sick and tired of winter!" Mike replied. "It's cold, it's windy and it gets dark early." He thought for a moment. "Sulley, I think I have the winter blues!"

Suddenly, Mike spotted a big advert. On it was a big pink monster sitting in a sunlounger on the beach, wearing sunglasses and sipping what looked like an ice-cold booberry drink. In big letters it said: *Beat Those Winter Blues in Relaxopolis!*

Mike stopped in his tracks and grabbed Sulley's furry arm. He pointed at the sign, too excited to say a word.

"That's a great idea!" Sulley cheered. "A week on a tropical island is just what we need!"

Mike and Sulley arrived in Relaxopolis a few days later. They went right to the beach, where they each ordered an ice-cold booberry drink. As the friends lay down on their sunloungers on the sunniest part of the beach, Mike said, "This is the life, isn't it, buddy?"

"You bet," said Sulley. "Do you think you need some of this Monster Tropic sunscream?

You'd better be careful. You don't want to get too much sun on your first day!"

"I'll just soak up the rays for a little while first," said Mike, happily. "My winter blues are just melting away."

After a while Sulley grew bored of sunbathing and decided to go for a swim. Then he let some little monsters bury him in the sand up to his neck and built a sandcastle with them.

A couple of hours later, he returned to the sunloungers, where Mike was sound asleep. Sulley took a closer look. His little green friend had not changed position since Sulley had left. He hadn't put on any sunscream either. Without meaning to, Mike had burnt himself in the sun!

"Hey, little buddy," said Sulley as Mike woke up. "Guess you chased those winter blues away, huh?"

Mike just looked at Sulley sleepily. "You aren't blue any more," Sulley explained. "Now you're bright red!"

Timon and Pumbaa Tell All

It was a very hot day on the savannah. Simba, Timon and Pumbaa were lying in the shade, barely moving. Pumbaa had just finished telling a story about the biggest insect he had ever eaten. A silence fell over the little group.

"I know," said Simba. "Hey, Timon, why don't you tell me the story of how you and Pumbaa met each other?"

Timon looked at Pumbaa. "Do you think he's ready for it?" he asked his friend.

"Knock him dead," said Pumbaa.

"It all started in a little meerkat village far, far away," began Timon. "In that little meerkat village there was one meerkat who didn't fit in with the rest. All the others were content to dig, dig, dig, all day long," said Timon.

"I was that isolated meerkat. How I hated to dig! I knew I needed to go elsewhere, to find a home of my own, a place where I fit in.

"So I left. Along the way I ran into a wise old baboon who told me what I was seeking – hakuna matata – and pointed me in the direction of Pride Rock. So I boldly set off towards this rock of which he spoke. And on my way there, I—"

"Met me!" Pumbaa interrupted.

Timon gave him a dirty look and continued. "I heard a strange rustling in the bushes. I was scared. What could it be? A hyena? A lion? And then I found myself face-to-face with a big, ugly warthog!"

"Hey!" said Pumbaa, insulted.

"We soon realised we had a lot in common – our love for bugs, our search for a home to call our own. So we set out for Pride Rock together. A lot of bad things happened along the way – hyenas, stampedes, you name it. But before long we managed to find the perfect place to live. And then we met you, Simba!"

"That's a nice story," Simba said with a yawn. "Now I think I'm going to take a nap."

Pumbaa cleared his throat. "It all started near a little warthog watering hole far, far away," he began. "Back then, I—"

"You always have to get the last word, don't you?" said Timon.

"Not always," said Pumbaa. And then he continued telling Simba his side of the story.

An Out-of-This-World Party

Every year, on the 31st December, one of Lilo's classmates had a party. One year, Lilo begged Nani to let her have the party at their house.

Lilo wanted to show off her new friends Jumba and Pleakley to her classmates – and to prove to them that even though Stitch wasn't a very good dog, he was a great alien!

Lilo gave invitations to all her classmates – even Myrtle, but only because Nani said Lilo had to invite her.

Myrtle didn't want to go to the party any more than Lilo wanted to have her there, but she didn't want to be left out either.

On the night of the party, Lilo ushered all the kids over to a stage in the back garden. Then she pulled back the curtains to reveal Stitch in a fancy rock-and-roll costume.

Stitch crooned into a microphone while swivelling his hips and strumming his guitar. All the kids thought he was cool – except Myrtle. When Stitch tried to give her a kiss on the cheek during a love song, she shrieked, "Ooooh! Yuck! Dog germs!" and ran away as fast as she could.

Jumba turned to Lilo and gave her a wink. "Who wants to play Pin the Smile on the Man in the Moon?" he asked.

"I do! I do!" shouted Myrtle.

Jumba hustled Myrtle into a small spaceship with no windows. Then he handed her a large paper smile.

"When you pass by the moon in a few hours," said Jumba, "try to pin the smile in the correct position. Remember that you will be travelling at several thousand miles per hour, so act quickly!" Then he shut the cockpit door.

"But the spaceship is fake," Lilo said to Jumba. "It's not moving or anything."

"Ah, but Myrtle doesn't know that," Jumba replied. "Inside the ship, it looks like she's heading to the moon. This should keep her busy for a few hours while we enjoy ourselves." He smiled. "Now, who's up for cake?"

The kids cheered, and everyone moved over to a picnic table, leaving the spaceship behind. "This is the best party ever!" Lilo heard one of her friends shout happily.